THE
EDGE

THE EDGE

By

Mark Olshaker

CROWN PUBLISHERS, INC.

New York

Published by Crown Publishers, Inc., 201 East 50th Street, New York, New York 10022. Member of the Crown Publishing Group.

Random House, Inc. New York, Toronto, London, Sydney, Auckland

Crown is a trademark of Crown Publishers, Inc.

Manufactured in the United States of America

Library of Congress Cataloging-in-Publication Data

Olshaker, Mark
    The edge / by Mark Olshaker.—1st ed.
        p.   cm.
    1. Serial murders—Washington (D.C.)—Fiction. 2. Police—
Washington (D.C.)—Fiction. I. Title.
PS3565.L823E34   1994
813'.54—dc20   94-8656
                                                                                  CIP

ISBN 0-517-58044-6

10   9   8   7   6   5   4   3   2   1

First Edition

For Marty Bell

AUTHOR'S NOTE

THIS is a work of fiction, and though certain real people and events are mentioned in the narrative, the specific scenes and situations, treatment and dialogue are all fabrications of my imagination.

That said, however, I must also say that, as always, I've had a lot of help from some very special people. *The Edge* began with an idea planted by my brother Robert Olshaker, M.D., who then helped me nurture it and flesh it out and was there for any question or speculative problem I threw at him. As has been so in the past, Robert's remarkably wide-ranging mind is well reflected in this book.

My friend Richard Restak, M.D.—neurologist, psychiatrist, and first-rate author—was also extremely influential, giving of his knowledge and insight both as expert and sounding board and guiding me through that eerie and fascinating netherworld between the brain and the mind. Thanks also to George Udvarhelyi, M.D., professor emeritus of neurosurgery at Johns Hopkins. These three can take credit for what I got right, but not be faulted for any excesses and liberties I have taken in the interests of my story.

I received equally solid support on the law enforcement front and I cannot adequately express my gratitude to Special Agents John Douglas and Jim Wright of the FBI's Investigative Support Unit, National Center for the Analysis of Violent Crime in Quantico, Virginia. Not only did they share the mysteries of mind-hunting and criminal personality profiling with me, they also made themselves available for ongoing consultation and then graciously agreed to lend their personas and appear as characters in the novel. Certainly above and beyond the call.

From her triple perspective as mind hunter, former homicide detective, and woman in a traditionally male field, Special Agent Jana Monroe offered unique insight and guidance on both character and plot which proved invaluable. Bob Chaney, a legendary D.C. homicide detective now with the U.S. Attorney's Office, was equally generous with his guidance and help, as were many men and women of the District of Columbia Metropolitan Police Department Homicide Branch, especially Detective Pamela Reed.

Special thanks to Harriet Bell, Beverly Camhe, Jim Hennigan, Andrew Marin, Ann Merz, Mark Stein, Douglas Steinberg, and my parents, Thelma and Bennett Olshaker, M.D., and brother Jonathan Olshaker, M.D., for their ideas, support, and encouragement.

My editor, Jim Wade, understood from the outset what I wanted to do and then did whatever it took to make sure I did it as well as I possibly could. This book would not be what it is without him. And my agent, Jay Acton, has been there since the beginning as close friend, sensitive critic, and shepherd of my career.

I said in my last book that my wife, Carolyn, was always there to love, sustain, and inspire me; that she was also my first-line editor and critic, as well as the springboard for all of my ideas. It's still true, and always will be.

Finally, there's Marty Bell, who got me into this business and whose friendship, enthusiasm, encouragement, and good ideas have kept me going. For those and many other reasons, this book is dedicated to him.

—Mark Olshaker
Washington, D.C.

Whoever fights monsters should see
to it that in the process he does
not become a monster. And when you
look into an abyss, the abyss also
looks into you.

> Friedrich Wilhelm Nietzsche,
> *Thus Spake Zarathustra*

No one who, like me, conjures up
the most evil of those half-tamed
demons that inhabit the human
breast and seeks to wrestle with
them, can expect to come through
the struggle unscathed.

> Dr. Sigmund Freud,
> *"Dora" Case History*

Flectere si nequeo Superos,
Acheronta movebo.

> Virgil, *The Aeneid*
> quoted by Freud as the epigraph
> to *The Interpretation of Dreams*

It translates:
If I cannot move Heaven,
I can raise Hell.

THE
EDGE

IT was incredible. Almost transcendental. Minds on the same wavelength.

Let's just say he was playing my strings—excitingly aggressive and yet coolly precise—in a way they hadn't been played in far too long. Every particle of my body and soul was tingling with life. We were gathering speed, nearing the crescendo, just about to go into orbit, and through my inhuman ecstasy I could hear a voice that sounded vaguely like my own breathlessly chanting, "Oh! Oh! Oh! Oh! . . ."

That was when my pager went off.

"Oh, shit."

You'd have thought we could carry through on momentum alone, but the unexpected intrusion was all it took for him to lose it. And so without saying a word I got up and padded naked to the phone in the other room. And when I came back less than a minute later and rummaged for my panties, all the while offering my awkward apologies, he was very understanding and, sure, no problem, we'll take a rain check and all that. But in my business you learn to look for what they're really saying, and what he was really saying was that this and what it represented wasn't the kind of thing he—or just about any other person of his sex in the known universe—could handle. And so even if I called him or sent him one of those endearingly cute little notes, I'd been through this drill often enough to know that this was it. A done deal. Just like all the others. We come into this life alone and we go out of this life alone, and if we're not alone in the meantime, we're ahead of the game. But it ain't something to count on.

So I zipped up my dress and gazed down on him, still in bed, propped up on his side. And I knew I was looking at history.

This better be a good one to get me out like this.

———————

It was one of those squat and slightly seedy little red-brick apartment houses on Q Street, on the far eastern fringe of Georgetown. My cab pulled up alongside a convention of scout cars and two Dodge Ram Mobile Crime Labs. The morbidly curious had already assembled.

Vince Robinson came out through the police line and waved to me. He must have known when I'd arrive. We have kind of a sixth sense with each other. As he made his way toward me, the crowd parted around him. In white areas of the city, people tend to keep their distance from large black men.

He took my elbow and escorted me through the crowd into the building. He pointed to the stairwell. "Top floor, no elevator." Less than a week into June and it was already midsummer sticky, even this late at night. I saw I was about to work up my second sweat of the evening, and in a far less attractive cause.

I was wearing one of my more daringly short dresses—sheer black silk—and Vince made no secret of giving my bare legs the once-over. "Big night on the town?" he asked.

"Almost," I said, not trying very hard to hide my general irritation.

"Poor Sandy. How'd he take it?"

"Like a man."

"That bad, huh? It's what you get for going out with civilians."

"You're married to one, Vincent."

"So are you."

"Only technically."

"Anyway, it's different for men."

"Most things are," I noted.

We'd reached the top stair landing. Vince pushed the doors open and led me down a hallway of yellowed and peeling plaster. He motioned me through the open apartment door. Two uniforms nodded as we went in. Neighboring heads timidly popped out from behind their own doors.

"I thought Cardenas and LaRocca were catching tonight," I said. Another uniformed officer who must have been first on scene was cooling his heels just inside. He looked pale.

"Boss wanted a woman's touch on this one," Vince said as we kept walking.

"Yeah, well . . ." I stopped short. "Oh, Jesus."

Lying face up on the glass-and-chrome dining table was a nude white female, probably late twenties or early thirties, but you could no longer say for sure. Her face, which may or may not have been pretty in life, looked as if it had been through a meat grinder. I thought I was going to lose it.

The only thing you could see clearly was a crude drawing on the girl's forehead that looked as though it had been done in black Magic Marker:

Not exactly your routine drug murder.

"Name was Sarah Hazeltine," said Vince. "Worked a couple blocks away on P Street in a gallery called Conway. Didn't come into work yesterday or today, and they had a show tonight, so one of the other girls got concerned. Sarah'd given her a key. She came over after the show, saw this, freaked, called 911. Voilà. First officer on scene was a rookie. Squad sergeant told him to stay put and beeped his watch lieutenant. Soon all the uh-huh birds flew in." He was referring to those higher up on the food chain with lots of scrambled egg on their hats who manage to show up at all the juicy scenes, follow behind grunts like us, saying "Uh-huh," and generally piss us off. Because according to the theory of transfer that all detectives live by, anyone who enters or leaves a room both brings and takes something with him. Routine fibers would be virtually meaningless at this scene now. Even the footprints would be worthless.

"You just missed the captain."

"Anything turn up so far?"

Vince shook his head. "Despite all the chopping, a very clean scene. No prints, no ligature marks, no sign of forced entry or struggle. Forensic evidence: *Nada*."

It was only then that I looked up long enough to register Jack Beauregard standing behind the table. "The brain was removed through the nasal cavity here at the front of the skull," he explained. The D.C. Medical Examiner was tall and broad and big in every way, but with a jarringly soft Georgia-accented voice that lent an instant sensitivity to his grim analysis. "We'd call that a transphenoidal excision. Whoever your perp was had to break through the nose and pull it out in pieces with a hook." Without missing a beat he turned to me and said, "My, but you're looking lovely tonight, Mansfield."

"Thanks, Jack," I replied. "Feeling lovely, too."

"Though I'd think you would have opted for nylons rather than bare legs. Women with relatively small bosoms are wise to draw visual focus to other areas. And as pretty as you are, with your tall, lithesome figure and long dancer's legs, there's no reason to have to focus on your chest. Don't you agree, Vincent?"

Vince, who had never once mentioned my bosom but was forever getting on my case for wearing my skirts too short, merely grunted. Vince thinks he's my father.

"I take it the brain is nowhere on premises?" I said, trying to shift attention completely away from my anatomy.

"Mobile Crime Lab's been all over," Vince replied. "Just can't seem to find the damned thing."

"You know how those things are," Jack quipped. He bellied up to the table and pointed to what was left of the nose. On each side, there were rows of tiny stitch holes where the skin had been pulled back together. "See this? Your guy took his time. Sewed the face back up."

When we see this much facial mutilation, conventional wisdom holds that there's a good chance the killer knew the victim, as if trying to obliterate some memory or connection through the destruction of her most identifying and distinguishing flesh. Maybe he was "re-creating" her to his liking. Or, if we were extremely lucky, maybe showing some guilt or remorse.

But I wasn't hopeful on that score because the rest of the body was just as much of a mess—split open all the way from sternum to pubis, with the skin neatly folded back and the internal organs removed. She looked like a medical school cadaver.

Those organs, by the way, were lined up, miraculously intact, in four large stainless-steel kitchen pots on an antique wooden sideboard. And over the years, I've seen enough of the insides of human beings to immediately recognize the contents of said pots as lungs, liver, stomach, and finally intestines.

I turned back to Jack. "So with all of this, what say you was the terminal event?"

"Take your pick," he replied, running stubby fingers through his damp, wavy hair. The apartment wasn't air-conditioned, and though all the windows had been opened during the search, the smell of ruined flesh was overpowering. "We'll know a little more when we get her back to the shop."

"And when did she fail the ultimate test?" asked Vince.

"I'm going to say Tuesday night. Can't give you any better than that."

The woman's eyes were wide open, as if in hideous, dumbfounded shock at what had been done to her. "God, I hate it when they're open," I said, and pressed down lightly with my thumb and forefinger. They didn't budge. "Rigor should be gone by now."

Vince bent down over the corpse and squinted. There were deep lines around his eyes from almost thirty years of squinting that way.

Jack directed his penlight onto Sarah Hazeltine's eyes and probed with his thumb. "Stitched open. Clean through the upper eyelid."

"Didn't we have another weird one a couple of weeks ago?" I said to Vince.

He nodded. "Fox in the First District. Captain's already made the connection."

"The woman near Capitol Hill with her heart cut out."

He looked down at the corpse and shook his head again, slowly from side to side. Then he pointed to the drawing on Sarah Hazeltine's forehead. "This mean anything to you?"

I shrugged. "Not unless it's some kind of satanic symbol. I'll check it out tomorrow."

He turned and addressed the room. "I want both these details under wraps. Everybody understand? Either of them gets out, I'll know it was one of you and I'll make sure your ass is fried. Got it?"

I watched silently as the ME's men wrapped Sarah Hazeltine's body in a white sheet and moved it to the stretcher to be wheeled out to the morgue wagon. There is always a searing finality to this moment that everyone involved feels, yet I've never really heard it articulated or explained. Maybe it has something to do with the transition from human being to piece of evidence. I'm not sure.

The uh-huhs had all gone, and things quieted down quickly. "Want to look around?" Vince asked me.

"Sure," I said.

"Want me with you?"

"No, I don't think so." We'd worked together long enough for him to know I was better at picking up vibes at a scene if I could do it by myself.

He went out into the kitchen to call the captain and organize the notes the uniformed officers had taken. I stayed and paced.

The furnishing was stark and spare, every piece chosen for its visual impact and to make the cramped space look larger and more dramatic. The walls and ceiling were all cool white, which is generally an excellent surface to pick up blood spatter patterns, but I didn't see any. There were several bold, semiabstract acrylics on the wall, not my taste. On loan from the gallery, I guessed.

The bedroom had a little more homeyness—stuffed animals arranged on a chair, photographs on the dresser of Sarah's parents and another of Sarah and her friends romping on the beach. It reminded me of my own life on the beaches of Southern California. She had been a pretty girl.

I took the stopper out of a frosted-glass perfume bottle on the dresser and sniffed. Obsession.

The bed was neatly made, but there were creases in the shiny blue satin bedspread, showing that it had been lain on. Despite all the trampling that had already compromised the scene, I could pick out nearly parallel depressions in the medium gray carpeting that ran like tracks from the bed to the dining room. Since there were no defense wounds on the body and no random foot patterns along the way, he must have neutralized her in the bedroom before he dragged her into the dining room. Since there was no blood spatter, he must have done all his cutting on the table. And since there were no impressions in the carpet from her rump or evidence he'd dropped her, he had to be pretty strong and powerful.

Sarah's clothes were piled on a chair next to the bed in the order they'd been removed—bra and panties on top, then panty hose, skirt, and blouse, and finally a silver Elsa Peretti pendant on a chain. The pattern of someone undressing willingly. The pattern of someone who knew her assailant and trusted him, who had no reason to fear him. A fuzzy blue teddy bear had fallen off the bed and lay forlornly on its ear. I resisted the temptation to ask it what it had seen.

The closet boasted a wardrobe any young woman would envy, including me—a row of neatly tapered dresses, short and stylish or long with dramatic slits, good quality, the better department stores or Connecticut Avenue boutiques. This was where a lot of her income went. The only thing she didn't have that I did was a couple of modest daytime black dresses. In her line of work, she wouldn't go to nearly as many funerals.

Sometimes it helps simply to "let go," to stop looking for any one thing and just let yourself be open to everything.

I walked around the place for several minutes, trying to do just that, trying to feel this woman, to absorb her life and her suffering.

And as always, that made me think of Gabbie.

———————

I finally made it home sometime after two in the morning, feeling sorry for myself and most of the rest of the world. I stripped out of my clothes and left them in a heap in the narrow front hall. I can do that because I live alone, in the English basement of a town house on 26th Street in Foggy Bottom. It's a nice, quiet little neighborhood tucked in between George Washington University and the Potomac River. And when I was going to school at GW, I always thought it would be a lovely place to own a house. I haven't made it that far yet. I rent from a lawyer just my age whose work happens to be much more lucrative than mine.

I was practically stumbling with fatigue. I hadn't gotten much sleep lately. Vince and I had gone out last night to Anacostia trying to see if a few house calls could get us anything more solid before the L Street Crew drug case went to trial. Sometimes people have more to say if you've woken them up and gotten them out of bed to say it. And then I'd spent most of the day in Superior Court, waiting to testify in the Frischmann case. The only overtime pay we get is for court appearances, so most of us pump it for everything it's worth. But it also means that the most industrious detectives are the most exhausted ones.

The light on the answering machine was blinking, and suddenly I got a hopeful stab in my gut that maybe it was him, calling to reschedule our date and pick up where we'd left off, so to speak. Or maybe he was just calling to say I'd left my perspiration-soaked panty hose in the middle of his living room floor and what did I want him to do with them? In either case, though, it would be an opening to further dialogue.

But my racing heart sank when I heard the first word and realized it was only Ted, calling for at least the twelve hundredth time: "Hi, it's me. How 'bout calling me when you get a chance. I miss you. I want to talk."

He always wanted to talk. I, on the other hand, wanted nothing more than to crawl into bed and sleep off whatever was left of the night, which wasn't much, considering I still had to answer roll call at six-thirty.

But first I had to shower, and not only because I was still hot and sweaty. I find I can't go right to bed or put on fresh clothing after I've been to a murder scene until I've washed my entire body: a similar ritual, I guess, to what I've seen of other women needing to scrub themselves raw after being raped.

We all have our little tricks for staying sane.

THE Homicide Branch of the District of Columbia Metropolitan Police Department occupies a long and ugly room on the third floor of the gray Municipal Center at 300 Indiana Avenue, N.W. It looks less like what you see in the movies than, say, the office of an insurance company that isn't doing terribly well. Under dingy white acoustical tile, two rows of black metal desks with simulated walnut tops give out onto a center aisle of pink linoleum. The black swivel chairs that go with those desks may not have been designed to torture their users to the point of giving up confessions, but that is their effect. At the end of the room near the captain's office there's a blackboard on the wall charting this year's murders compared with last year's, how many to date, each detective's clearance rate, how many cases still open. It reminds me of those charts you see in car dealer sales offices. And all this is illuminated by rows of harsh fluorescent panels that burn twenty-four hours a day, seven days a week, with no time off for holidays or good behavior.

Two floors below, during normal business hours, law-abiding citizens snake out into the hallways, getting totally pissed off as they wait endlessly to get their cars registered or driver's licenses renewed or any of the infinite petty details of life over which the government has control. I know, because I've had to wait in those lines, too.

But Homicide is where the real action's been in the building of late, and that chart tells the whole sorry tale. As those of us who live here know, Washington, D.C., is made up of many layers. It is the seat of government, a museum and cultural center, home to distinguished universities and scientific research institutions, a place where ordinary citizens live. But what seems to be the important point these days is that Washington is not only Our Nation's Capital, it is also the murder capital of the free world.

I staggered in a little before seven and was immediately met by a look from the shift lieutenant, Al Fahey.

"You're late, Mansfield."

"Yeah, well, it wasn't exactly like I was out dancing till dawn, and it wasn't exactly like it was even my shift, and—"

"Captain wants you in his office ten minutes ago."

So what have I done now? I wondered. But I didn't spend long finding out.

Captain Patrick Owen, commanding officer of the Homicide Branch, has a large corner office with paneled walls and a big desk of for-real walnut. There's a sofa and coffee table for visitors and an impressive view of the Mall. As I came through the door I spotted several of my colleagues—Marc Volmer, Joe LaRocca, Raphael Cardenas—and my partner, the aforementioned Vincent Robinson. Then I did a double take when I saw who was addressing this gathering: His Supreme and Exalted Excellency, Claudel Price, chief of police.

Owen, who packs every stress manifestation known to cops into a still muscular but underexercised body an inch or two shorter than mine, gave me the look of a teacher who's caught a kid sneaking late into class. In return I played the penitent, lip-biting schoolgirl, which I thought might keep my butt out of the fire, at least in the big boss's presence.

"You know the chief, Mansfield."

"We've met." Maybe twice in all the years I've been on the Job.

I sidled in next to Vince, whose eyes said "If I can be here on time at my age after being out half the night, why can't you?" I didn't say anything but liberated his coffee cup because I was desperate.

Chief Price has short, steely gray hair and penetrating brown-black eyes about two shades darker than his skin tone. Unlike Captain Owen, he's a big man, which is supposed to inspire public confidence, and he looks great in his fancy uniform or standing next to the mayor at press conferences. And though he is smooth as silk on television, he is known to come right to the point with the troops.

"My nuts are on the chopping block," he declared. "We've got two mutilation killings in two weeks. Either they're not related, in which case we've got a new 'alarming trend,' or they are, in which case we've got us a serial. Either way, we're stuck to a real tar baby.''

Translation: This type of crime would not be confined to the drug areas or the criminal underclass or the entire subculture that lives and dies by the gun. When they kill each other, no one loses much sleep. But this is the type of crime that undermines public confidence. It could happen anywhere, at any time. This is the type of crime people focus on.

It could happen to any of us.

''The mayor's taken a personal interest. I've instructed Captain Owen to assign his best people. That's why you're here. And I wanted to make sure you understood how important this is to all of us. That's why I'm here.'' The chief nodded meaningfully in my direction. ''As for you, Detective Mansfield, Pat informs me you'll be lead detective on this case.''

Who, me?

''I suggested to him that Vince might be a more . . . shall we say, 'logical' choice. But he has great faith in you, and I have great faith in Pat's judgment.''

The captain thanked him for taking time out of his busy day and all that. When Price was out the door, Owen leaned forward on his short, beefy arms, knuckles to the desk top, and looked up. ''So what have you got for me? Witnesses?''

Vince reported, ''We've got one description from tenants of a guy that didn't look familiar to them: white male somewhere in his twenties. But it's pretty vague, not enough for a composite. And we can't tie him to the building at the specific time.''

''Physical evidence?''

''We've got the lab trying to match hair and fiber against similar stuff they picked up at Fox,'' said Rafe Cardenas. ''No usable prints. Guy was very fucking careful.''

''ME says that Fox was alive when the asshole cut her heart out. Find out if Hazeltine was when he did her. Both girls have address books?''

Vince nodded.

''Cross-check for common entries. See if they knew any of the same people. Find out if they had *anything* in common—bank, cleaners, beauty parlor, video store, anything. Maybe they went to the same doctor or dentist. Maybe Fox came into Hazeltine's gallery. Just find out.''

Heads nodded silently.

"Okay, then, what do we know? No break-in in either case. So the killer either knew his victims or met them the night of the murder. We can rule out robbery. No money or jewelry appears to have been taken from either scene." He ticked off this last fact almost sadly. Any time you throw out a traditional motive, you've got one less element to fall back on. "What else?"

"The murders were probably pretty well planned," said Marcus Volmer. Marc was slight and thin and curly-haired, with a gracefulness about his movements that reminded me of a dancer. Since he's black and I'm a woman, most situations we would have found ourselves in together would have given us something in common. But here, I was the only minority. And if it weren't for my clearance rate, I'd be back out pounding a beat.

"In both cases, the weapon was brought to the scene, meaning the perp anticipated the need to use them," Volmer continued.

"And neither one was done with a gun," Vince added. "Both were up close and personal."

"You don't get much more personal than cutting out someone's heart," Cardenas offered.

Joe LaRocca—he of the blow-dried hair, shiny Italian suits, and perpetual smirk—was smoothing down the ends of his tapered mustache with his thumb. "If it had been a guy missing his balls instead, I'd put my money on Mansfield." I tried to ignore him as usual.

Owen paced restlessly behind his desk. "So the one thing we know about this guy is he likes to remove organs. We dealing with a cannibal? Do we have a Jeffrey Dahmer thing going here? Was he about to put those pots on the stove when he was interrupted?"

He addressed all these questions to me. "You've been through the FBI course, Sandy. What do you think?"

I shrugged. "Could be. I don't think we have enough information yet to come up with a good profile."

"The murders were exactly two weeks apart. It may be a coincidence, but it may not be."

"We'll know for sure in thirteen days," said Raphael Cardenas.

Owen glared. "Not if you do your job. Now, let's go out and play detective."

The others filed out of the room, but Owen put his hand on my arm and held me back. He has a way of keeping me seated while he stands above me, equalizing the height disadvantage. I knew what was coming.

"Make me proud," he intoned solemnly.

Translation: Don't even think of screwing up.

Being handed a case like this is either an honor or a setup, depending on your point of view. If it went well, Chief Price would look terrific and the department would get a lot of good press at a time when it desperately needed some. If it headed south, Vince and I were the sacrificial lambs. Careers are made and broken over cases like this.

Drug murders and grudge killings are the easy ones. People see things. People talk. So if you've got ways of getting information from the street, you can close them. Same with domestics. Someone is shot in their home, it's not hard to determine who was the last one to see the dear departed alive. Plus, you're working with a limited number of suspects. But like most things involving sex, sex murder is a lot more complicated.

I sat at my desk reviewing the Fox case file and comparing it with the little we had so far on Hazeltine—mostly crime scene photos. I began filling in the fifteen-page, 189-question VICAP Crime Analysis Report that would be fed into the FBI's Violent Criminal Apprehension Program database, hoping for an MO match with some other offender.

The common perception is that serial killing is a relatively modern phenomenon, beginning roughly around the time of Jack the Ripper a hundred years ago. This may be true. But it may, in fact, be older than we realize. Legends of werewolves, vampires, even witches and sorcerers, may have been their simpler times' way of comprehending and explaining a perversity of the human condition that we have come to take for granted. No one wants to believe that monsters could actually look just like us.

Julie Fox, age twenty-two, had been a dancer in a strip joint called the Touch of Class. When she hadn't shown up for work two nights running (similar to Hazeltine), another dancer she was friendly with named Bonnie Sharpless had gone over to her residence in a rooming house on Capitol Hill and had the landlady let her into Julie's room.

There they found the young woman's nude body facing them, tied to a chair, her arms pinioned behind her and a gaping hole in her chest where her heart had been. As with Hazeltine, there was no sign of forced entry and there were no other wounds on the body. The Medical Examiner determined that the removal of the heart had itself constituted the terminal event. Unlike Hazeltine's, Fox's clothes were deposited randomly around the room, more likely to have been removed by someone else. There was some suggestion that Julie Fox might have had sex with the killer, but nothing conclusive. Blood and tissue samples analyzed at autopsy were found to contain a high concentration of epinephrine, together with a liquid suspension of Dexedrine and xanthine, which is a metabolite of caffeine—apparently for the purpose of keeping the victim awake and conscious during the procedure.

He wanted her to watch, suffer, be an active participant in her own torture and death.

I shifted my gaze out the window for some momentary relief. I could see traffic and tourists and city bureaucrats who worked downstairs just coming in for the day. All the different strata, all the people who make up Our Nation's Capital, District of Columbia.

And somewhere out there among them was a monster. Someone so egotistical and self-centered and evil that he was willing to cut and torture and make other people bleed and give up their lives just to satisfy his fantasies and sexual urges. And I had to wait for his next move.

```
┌─────────┐
│         │
│    ③    │
│         │
└─────────┘
```

IF there is such a thing, it was a normal morning in Homicide: I'd just gotten to the office, I hadn't had my coffee, and my phone was already ringing. I've never been much of a morning person, and the repetitious jangling only accentuated the fact. I reached to silence it, in the process opening a gash just below my knee on the edge of Vince's desk. Nothing like physical pain to help you settle in.

"Homicide, Detective Mansfield," I barked into the phone, fishing through my desk drawer for a Kleenex or something to stop the bleeding.

"Someone must not have taken her happy pills this morning." It was Jerry Ashburn of *The Washington Post*'s metro staff.

"I've sworn off the stuff," I snapped again. "What in Christ's name are you doing calling me at this hour?" Jerry and I went way back together. I had just started in uniform and he was working night police, the traditional scut beat for young reporters. Among other things, Jerry got to compile the overnight crime report, the paper's daily listing of all the bad things people in this city had done to each other in the past twenty-four hours.

"Heard you caught the 'Damsels in Distress' case," he said.

"Oh, fuck, is that what they're calling it?"

"Not officially, but within the trade."

"How'd you find out already?"

"You're a detective, I'm a reporter. It's what we do. So what should I be writing about it?"

"I'd prefer you wrote nothing, but I know I've got more chance of winning the D.C. Lottery.'' I stopped the bleeding, but it had already matted my panty hose.

"I'm paid to uphold the First Amendment, you're paid to suppress it," he commented jovially. "Together we strike a balance."

"Off the record, Jerry, we don't have diddly, which on the record you can take as 'No comment.' Just give us a little breathing room. Is that too much to ask?"

"Of course it is. But in the interests of justice and fair play, I'll cut you as much slack as I can—just go with the basics." He paused for a reaction, but I didn't give him one. "The quid pro, naturally, is that as soon as you have anything, it goes first to your old pal Jerry. Deal?"

"I never make deals with reporters."

"I'll take that as a yes."

"Later, Jerry."

"I get your game, Mansfield. You're still holding out for my body. I thought you were past that."

"Am I that transparent?" I asked. Jerry was about three inches shorter than me, with wild curly hair, about twenty-five more pounds around his midsection than he knew what to do with, and an almost unnatural pride in his own schleppiness. If he weren't a reporter—and such a damn good one, at that—we might even have been friends, but that'd be the extent of it.

"And have I ever told you you're one of the cutest fascists I've ever met?" he said.

"Fuck off, Ashburn," I explained sweetly.

———————

Because of the way the process works, most murders that get cleared at all are closed in the first twenty-four to thirty-six hours. After that, evidence gets cold, people forget or get intimidated, weapons disappear, tracks get covered.

The Touch of Class was on 9th Street near Pennsylvania Avenue, one of those depressing little dives that exists in a different dimension from the shining sun. You had to walk down half a flight of steps from the sidewalk to get in, accentuating the image of descending into the depths.

I asked the Incredible Hulk minding the front desk where I might find Bonnie Sharpless, the girl who had found Julie Fox.

"Sorry," he grunted in a way that told me he wasn't actually. "She's working."

I flashed him my badge. "So am I."

This time he muttered and pointed toward the back of the dingy space, to a door near the stage. Behind it was a long narrow room with a back wall of raw brick, against which six or seven girls sat at cheap dressing tables with lighted mirrors. I recognized Bonnie Sharpless from the Polaroid a police woman had taken before driving her home. She'd just arrived and was still wearing her street clothes—tight, faded jeans and a loose-fitting cotton work shirt. I introduced myself and asked if we could talk. She said timidly that she didn't have much time before she had to go on but escorted me back to the dressing table near the end of the room. She pulled over the chair from the empty vanity next to hers. I realized it must have been Julie Fox's.

Bonnie was a little slip of a girl, possibly underage, and her eyes were wide with the fear that a first serious encounter with the law and bad things often brings out.

"Were you and Julie pretty close?" I asked.

She shrugged. "We didn't do much together outside of work. You try to keep this part of your life separate, if you know what I mean. But she was a real sweet, nice girl. We always got along real well."

I scanned her vanity top for any insight into her personality. But except for the makeup and cosmetics, it was completely unadorned, as if there were no point investing any real feeling or homeyness here.

"Bonnie, this may have been a random killing," I said, "but we think that the person who killed Julie might have known her, at least casually. Do you have any ideas about that?"

She shook her head.

"Did Julie date much?"

"Sometimes, I guess."

"Any particular men you remember seeing her with?"

Again, a shake of the head.

"Can you think of anyone who might have wanted to hurt her?"

She pursed her lips. "No, sorry."

"What about the customers? Some of them like to play rough? Have you heard about any who like to hurt or punish women?"

"Not that I know of. We try to pretty much stay away from the patrons—that's what the boss calls them." She glanced up at the wall clock at the other end of the room. "Umm, it's getting close to lunch. Is it okay if I get ready while we talk?"

"Sure," I said, and watched as she stood up and pulled the shirt over her head. As I'd suspected, she wasn't wearing a bra, though she certainly could have used one. In a few years she'd probably sag, but for now, I was envious. She undid her fly buttons and skimmed her jeans and panties down in one casual motion. Her pubic hair had been carefully trimmed to fit the rigid confines of her costume.

"Bonnie, did Julie ever mention knowing a woman named Sarah Hazeltine?"

She deposited her pants on the floor and said, "Uh-uh," as she slithered into a silver sequined thong that managed to show most of her charms in front and virtually all of them behind.

She turned halfway around. "Could you hand me that brush and compact, please?"

She took them from me and proceeded to rouge her breasts and nipples with a practiced air that left me thoroughly depressed.

"What do you know about Julie's social life in general? Had she ever been married? Any steady or regular boyfriends?"

Bonnie sat back down and began heavily rouging her cheekbones. I wanted to grab her and wash off her face and drag her out of there and back to her parents, if she had any. But that wasn't my job, and it wasn't my place.

"She's never been married far as I know," she said. "As far as dating, Julie pretty much kept to herself."

"She wasn't what my mom and dad's generation would have called 'promiscuous'?"

"Uh-uh. No. I know that prob'ly sounds strange to an outsider, seeing's how she worked in a place like this, but she really wasn't. And I know the next thing you're gonna ask me is if she ever turned tricks, and the answer is no, she never did anything like that."

That checked out with what Rafe Cardenas had put together. Except for the fact that she paid her way through life grinding her tits and ass, she was pretty straight.

"Did Julie like her work here?"

Peering into the mirror, Bonnie hunched her shoulders and fluffed her hair. "Maybe she used to at first, but I don't think so for a while. She had . . . what do you call it when you have a pain running down your leg?"

"Sciatica?"

"Yeah, that's it. She was always hurting, but she danced anyway. After you been at this a while, there isn't much else you can do unless you want to go wait tables."

The other girls had gone. Bonnie looked at me like a schoolkid who wanted permission to go to the bathroom. "I have to go now," she said.

I opened my purse and handed her my card. "If anything comes up, or you think of something else, please give me a call."

"Sure," Bonnie said meekly. I stood up to go, and she stood up with me, hooking her spangled bra. As I turned she touched my hand. There was a tear welling out of the corner of her eye, which she caught before it ruined her makeup. "I just don't understand why anyone would want to do something so terrible to Julie."

"Neither do I, Bonnie," I replied. "Neither do I."

As I walked up the entrance steps at 300 Indiana, I spotted them, but not before they spotted me. A TV crew from Channel 9. Shit!

"Detective Cassandra Mansfield," the reporter declared as he shoved his microphone tight in my face. I didn't even know his name, but he'd done an instant make on me. "We understand you've been appointed lead detective in the mutilation murders of the two young women. Could you tell us how the case is going so far?"

This is always one of those damned-if-you-do, damned-if-you-don't situations. You don't want to give anything away, but you don't want the department to look like it's sitting around on its hands, either. Mainly, though, you just don't want to be there at all.

"We're pursuing all leads," I stated succinctly.

"And are you close to an arrest?" I saw the camera lens zoom in on me.

"I don't want to say anything that could compromise the investigation."

"Is it true there are no suspects, Detective?"

"It's true that we're working diligently. Now if you'll excuse me . . ."

I pushed my way past the sound man. Behind me I heard, "That was Detective Cassandra Mansfield of the Metropolitan Police Homicide Squad, who was unwilling or unable to shed any new light . . ."

Still pissed off from the unexpected encounter, I went upstairs just long enough to meet up with Vince and pick up my messages. Someone was sitting on my chair.

Shit, I thought again as I got closer. Ted Monahan, my soon-to-be ex-husband, swiveled around to face me.

He stood up, at least having the decency to look sheepish and out of place. "Hi, the lieutenant said I could wait for you here. Hey, what'd you do to your leg?"

"Nothing. It's okay. How long have you been here?"

"I don't know. Half an hour, maybe."

I rolled my eyes at Vince, who only gave me a stern look in return. "What are you doing here?"

"You're never home. At least, you never answer my calls." That part was true. "Look, Cassie . . ."

Ted was the only one in the world who called me that, observing when we first met that Cassandra was the Trojan prophetess of doom. When we first started going together, I liked the idea of something special and private between us.

"Cass, can we just talk a minute?" he implored.

"I'm very busy."

"Later, then?"

"I'm not sure when. We're on a major case."

"I just need a few minutes."

"We're on our way out."

"I'll ride with you."

"Absolutely not!"

There was kind of a pathetic, desperate, calculated look behind his horn-rimmed glasses. I'd come to hate it when he did that to me.

A sudden perverse thought stabbed at me. Vince saw it coming and warned me off with his eyes, but I said, "Sure, Ted. Come on."

There's not much you can do to spruce up a basic white Ford LTD Crown Victoria, but there's a lot you can do to turn it into a pigsty, and the overnight shift hadn't missed a trick. The ashtray was overflowing with butts, and there were newspapers and fast-food wrappers on the floor and seats.

"Jesus, which pigs have this thing on overnight?" I said.

"Doesn't matter," Vince replied. "None of 'em has any pride anymore." Vince is old school: very big on standards.

The car's AC hadn't worked in two weeks, and I had no expectation it had been magically healed since my last shift. I grumbled as I rolled down my window. I was already pissed off before we even got going. Vince started the car and turned onto 3rd Street toward Constitution. No one said anything.

We'd been riding like that about ten minutes and were over around Eastern Market when I swung around to Ted, locked on to his eyes, and said, "Well?" I happen to be a damn good interrogator.

He hesitated a moment, then said, "Cassie, I want you to come back."

Vince glanced into the rearview mirror and said, "You sure you want me to hear this, Ted?"

He half smiled. "I'm not embarrassed . . . unless Cassie is." That's typical of the way he used to put everything back on me. I could feel my stomach squeezing.

"How was your date with Frank Kindler last night?"

"How did you know about that?"

"Cassie, why are you being so hostile to me?"

I tried to keep myself relaxed. "I'm not being hostile. I'm just not willing to be controlled."

"I'm not trying to control you."

"Then what do you call it?"

"All right, children, that's enough," said Vince as we pulled in through the main gate of D.C. General Hospital.

"What are we doing here?" Ted asked. "You talking to someone in the emergency room?"

"No," I said. "The morgue. You don't like it, you can get the Metro just outside the gate."

"Will you call me? Please?"

I finally nodded. He looked at me sadly for a moment. "You've really changed, Cassie."

"Yes, I have, Ted."

He turned, stuffed his hands into his well-worn khakis, and started to walk away. I stood there watching him. He may have sensed it, because after a few steps he stopped, looked back, and said, "By the way, I got turned down for tenure again."

I melted, as he must have known I would. "I'm . . . I'm really sorry," I said. "I'll call you." He nodded a little sadly and continued walking.

Vince was right behind me. "Sometimes I want to tan your backside."

I turned on him. "In case you've forgotten, partner: a, you're not my father; b, I'm thirty-two years old; and c, I don't get spanked anymore unless I want to."

But Vince, as usual, was not deterred. "What do you have to treat him that way for? You ought to be ashamed of yourself."

"Don't you see what he's trying to do to me?"

"I see what you're doing to yourself," he answered. "And with all the ugliness we see every day, it hurts me when I see ugliness in you."

We walked silently into the morgue. My cheeks were flushed hot with anger. I marveled at my own capacity to inflict pain. Maybe it was one of the reasons I felt so cozy inside the minds of psychopaths.

———————

The red-brick building of the Medical Examiner for the District of Columbia occupies a small corner of the D.C. General Hospital grounds. Outside, it is almost nondescript, except for the white marble lintel that proclaims its function. Inside, it is grim and gray and full of hard edges, as a repository of death should be. The ancient fluorescent lights cast a harsh yellow pall on everything, and no matter what the outside temperature, it is always cold.

Jack Beauregard was finishing up, still hovering over Sarah Hazeltine's nude body laid out on the steel dissecting table like a laboratory frog.

Sarah had ceased to resemble a person in any meaningful way. The top of her skull had been sawed off and lay next to her on the metal slab. The skin of her scalp had been pulled down like a rubber mask to allow the examiner access to the bone, obscuring half of the eye drawing. Inside, the grayish brown dura adhered to the surface of the hollow cranial cavity like old wrinkled parchment.

"I like the outfit," Jack commented as he glanced up. "The long, soft, unstructured jacket with the coordinated short skirt are your look, Sandy. And it was definitely worth the effort to lose those few pounds. You'd be amazed the percentage of body fat some women are carrying. Pathologists notice that sort of thing."

"I'm glad you approve," I said. It was sometimes hard for me to remember that this guy had put himself through the University of Texas on a wrestling scholarship. But I've always loved Jack, all the years I've worked with him. He's always treated me with that camaraderie and courtly protectiveness I've noticed in a number of gay men who are completely secure within themselves.

"Just one thing: You have such a pretty face that a little more shadow around the eyes could create a subtle but dramatic effect. And when you look tired, as you often do, it wouldn't be as noticeable."

Thanks for the tip. The one time I'd actually asked Jack for advice— about a vague but persistent pain I was having in my stomach—he'd said, "I can't tell anything for sure until the autopsy."

I noticed an impatient expression forming around the corners of Vince's mouth. "Can we get down to business?" he asked.

"As I was saying," Jack replied without missing a beat, "there's so much trauma that I can't give you a definitive on vaginal penetration. But in any case, no seminal fluid, and no abrasions of the type you'd expect to see in a rape. No evidence of anal penetration or sexually oriented mutilation. Some minor scratches on the buttocks, but I think they're incidental to positioning the body on the table. Fingernail scrapings reveal no skin, blood, or foreign matter."

Vince nodded. "Ties in with the lack of ligature marks or apparent defense wounds."

"Here's the interesting part," Jack continued. "The stuff your un-known suspect used to sew her face back together and eyelids open? Not your run-of-the-mill fishing line or anything from the local pattern store. This here's four-oh nylon suture thread, and after looking at the job under the scope, the puncture holes are all about the size a P-three steel surgical needle would make."

Vince studied the corpse, now so clinical and devoid of personality. "So what can you tell us from the wounds?"

Jack positioned himself next to the table, turned his body, and gestured with his arms. "Assuming he was working from the left side of the dining table as you come into the room, which is a pretty good assumption since the pots with the organs were on that side, the angle of penetration into the soft tissue tells us we're dealing with a right-handed individual."

"That narrows us down to about eighty percent of the population," I said.

"What about size?"

" 'Fraid I can't help you much on that one. I'm guessing he's a reasonably hefty boy from the way he carried her from the bed, but this cutting was done with precision rather than force. A woman your size could have done them."

"Fox's guy did his while she was still alive," I said.

"Not this one. This one got about ten grams of straight sodium pentobarbital."

"A sedative?"

"In a manner of speaking. In much lower doses, it's used as a surgical anesthetic."

"And ten grams' worth?"

"Only as a murder weapon. Injected intravenously, it would cause respiratory failure, then CNS collapse in seconds."

It didn't make sense. Fox's killer had gone to some trouble to keep her alive and conscious for his torture—a key trait of a sexual sadist. With Hazeltine, it was as if he wanted to kill her as quickly as possible so he could play with her body. One thing you learn in police work is that people's behavior doesn't change unless there is some compelling reason for it. So why the difference in the MO?

"Think we're looking for a doctor?" Vince asked.

"Leastwise someone with access to a hospital or doctor's office," said Jack. "And you don't cut this cleanly without some kind of practice. Now, from the pathologist's point of view, here's where the plot thickens."

He guided us both over to the foot of the table. "Look around the middle of the chest cavity," he commanded us. "Now, what do you see?"

"The heart," I said.

"And here and here?"

"The kidneys."

"Detective Mansfield passes Anatomy one oh one. So why does he take out all the other vital organs but leave those in?"

4

I was having trouble sleeping. I told myself it was just the normal jitters over finally breaking it off with Ted, but the truth was, my mind wouldn't let go of Sarah Hazeltine.

I kept tossing and turning and twisting my sweat-soaked T-shirt around me. I kept thinking of the dresses hanging in Sarah's closet, so similar in taste and style to what I wear. I kept seeing that drawing that looked like a sideways eye on her forehead.

So with the dark starting to close in on me, I turned on the light and reached over the edge of the bed to the bookshelf, grabbing my copy of Jung's *Man and His Symbols,* which I hadn't looked at since college.

I sat cross-legged on the bed, thumbing through page by page, hoping against hope I would see something similar. But I came up empty. Nothing looked even remotely familiar.

I got up and went into the kitchen, looking for something to eat. I opened the fridge to see what I could graze on. But all I saw was an old loaf of bread, a half-empty jar of Skippy, and several cartons of yogurt that by this point were probably more cultured than I was. Totally wired now, I went into the bathroom and stepped into the shower, but my brain still refused to let go. It played back what I thought we knew about this guy.

He'd probably be white, because the perpetrators of most sex crimes are white, the victims are both white, and these killers rarely target a different race. He'd be male, because for whatever combination of reasons, women don't commit these kinds of murders.

I'd been through the FBI's National Academy program down at Quantico, and their profilers—the ones who invented the science—divide killers into "Organized" and "Disorganized" categories. This one was highly organized, which meant he would probably be somewhat older and more experienced. These were methodical kills, not the opportunistic crimes you might expect from a disorganized offender. Nothing was out of place, the drugs and weapons were all brought to the scene. There was no sign of struggle, even with Fox, who was tied to a chair. So this indicated a sophisticated individual able to con his way into each apartment and . . . charm the victim out of her pants.

The hot water cascading over my body faded into background.

Generally, severe mutilation is associated with disorganized killers. So is not attempting to hide or transport the body away from the scene. But both these scenes were highly staged. The mutilations were very elaborate and graphic, so I'm guessing it was all part of a carefully planned fantasy that the killer had been developing for a long time.

I pictured the gaping hole in Julie Fox's chest. I tried to imagine what it would feel like to be that helpless, to be hurt that badly, to be subjected to that much pain for someone else's pleasure.

In the first case, he inflicts the most horrible torture, as if his buzz were wanting to see her heart being ripped out of her living chest. In the second case, he tears her up postmortem, but the kill itself is soft.

One of the key elements in sexually oriented murder is control. He got each victim into a situation in which he could totally dominate her. Maybe after the first kill, he thought about what he would have liked to do to the body. So it could mean the killer is someone used to exerting a lot of control in everyday life. Or it could mean it's someone who's frustrated by his lack of control, so he's created a fantasy situation that he can dominate.

He's targeting attractive, single white females. The fact that each one lived alone in a building without security might or might not be coincidental. But the fact that there was no attempt to hide the body is very significant. These scenes were meant to be found.

I clutched the bar of soap, lathering the same areas over and over again. My fingers and toes were already wrinkled up.

Is he trying to tell us something? Did some woman "cut his heart out," so he's getting back at all women, or women of a certain representative type? Did some woman "rip his guts out"?

What's he saying?

Is Captain Owen right—is he a cannibal? In the first crime, he makes no attempt to eat Fox's heart. But in the second, he takes the time to prepare most of Hazeltine's organs in kitchen pots before something interrupts him. So he is escalating.

And thus I welcomed the dawn.

———————

When I got to the office, it was already eighty-four degrees outside and almost that inside. Vince was there ahead of me, as usual. He and Norman Sidecki stood with their hands shoved into their pockets in front of the beat-up Zenith TV in the corner. Sidecki was in rolled-up shirtsleeves with his tie yanked down. Vince, as usual, had his striped tie knotted tightly at his neck, a perfect crease in his trousers, and exactly one inch of starched white cuffs showing beyond the sleeve of his perfectly tailored blue suit. Despite his years and size, Vince always dresses sharp. He shops in good places and chooses carefully. Having been on the streets as long as he has, he knows a man who dresses well gets a little more respect, and these days you play whatever card you've got.

"What's up?" I asked. Sidecki merely indicated the screen with his chin.

"Is it true there are no suspects, Detective?"

"It's true that we're working diligently. Now if you'll excuse me . . ."

"That was Detective Cassandra Mansfield of the Metropolitan Police Homicide Squad, who was unwilling or unable to shed any new light on these crimes that have sent a ripple of terror through the community. Back to you, Andrea."

"You look cute on TV," Sidecki commented sardonically.

"The captain's gonna bust a gut," I said gloomily.

"He already has," said Vince. "He read your friend Ashburn on the way to work."

"Make sure he knows I didn't talk."

"It ain't gonna make a rat's ass worth of difference whether you did or not," said Sidecki. Sidecki had always been one of the best detectives on the squad, but his problem was he remembered the old days too well. And with what'd been going down in this city the last several years, it was plain to see he'd lost his taste for the streets, at least the D.C. streets.

We walked away from the TV. "Anything new?" I asked.

"We found Hazeltine's brain," Vince said calmly.

I set my coffee cup on my desk. It splashed onto the open case files. "Fuck! I mean, where? Who?"

"Trash can in the alley between O and Newport."

"That's right near the scene."

"One of the uniforms canvasing the area stumbled on it."

"What did it look like?"

"Dried up and in pieces, just like Beauregard said. Wrapped up in plastic and one of those Styrofoam trays meats come in."

I took a bite of my doughnut and thought, I wonder if the guy tried to eat any of it.

In spite of where I live and the fact that it's my alma mater, it had been a long time since I'd set foot on the George Washington University campus. I walked up I Street and cut across the quad, where I saw the usual assortment of sunbathers and Frisbee throwers, interspersed with an occasional reader, this being a seat of higher learning.

I had on a short jersey dress. After years of having to wear a uniform designed for men, one that makes even the dorkiest guy look great and even the trimmest, most sophisticated women look like shit, when I went into plain clothes, I swore I was always going to feel good about what I was wearing on the Job.

My day was made when a tall blond jock Apollo in tank top and crotch-hugging shorts tried to pick me up. This is what I want for Christmas, I said to myself. Painfully, I reminded myself what I was here for and declined his kind invitation.

Dr. Edward Simpson O'Connor was thin and angular, with dry white skin and wispy blond hair. I put him in his late fifties, but he didn't look much different from when I'd had him in class more than a decade before.

His office on the fourth floor of Stuart Hall was linoleum tiled and painted cinder block and was lined with books on three walls. He sat with his elbow propped on his battered wooden desk, sighting down his nose at me over the tops of gold half-frames, and asked, "Do I know you?"

"I had you in class about twelve years ago." Apparently I hadn't made much of an impression. "You might remember my ex-husband, Ted Monahan."

I'm usually pretty good at reading reactions, but I couldn't read his. So I quickly moved on to my current area of interest and pulled out my badge. That seemed to brighten him up.

I explained what I wanted and handed over the photos I'd culled from the Hazeltine case file. He studied each one in turn. When he got to the closeup of Sarah's face, he gazed at it a long time with exotic fascination.

"It's an 'eye of Horus,' " he declared, "crudely drawn, but recognizable nonetheless."

"Horace who?" I asked.

"Horus, the falcon god of ancient Egypt. Were you in the habit of coming to class, Miss Mansfield? What grade did I give you?"

"I'm afraid I don't remember," I lied. "Refresh my memory, if you will. Did Horus have anything to do with murder?"

"In a way, you could say that. Stop me if I'm rehashing material you remember."

"To be objective, let's pretend I don't remember anything."

He peered down his nose at me once more. "We'll try to make that leap." He stared for several more seconds at the Hazeltine photo. "In one of ancient Egypt's primal myths, the evil god Seth kills King Osiris, then rends his body into many pieces and scatters them throughout the world, which, one would think, might be the end for poor Osiris."

With a wary smile, I took the bait. "It wasn't, then?"

"Not exactly. You see, the love of Osiris' wife, Isis, could not be broken. She traveled far and wide, and with the help of Anubis, the jackal-headed god, she found all the pieces and, with her own powerful magic, put them back together. Of course, that wasn't quite sufficient to make things exactly as they had been."

"I can appreciate that," I said.

"So Osiris became ruler of the underworld—that's why he's usually depicted with a green face and wrapped in a white burial shroud— while his heroic son, Horus the falcon, became ruler on earth. When each pharaoh died, he was thought to become Osiris, while his successor then embodied Horus."

"What exactly is an 'eye of Horus'?"

"It's perhaps the most central and potent of all the Egyptian mythological symbols. Technically, it's called *udjat,* meaning 'complete.' "

"Complete? In what sense?"

"When the ancient Egyptians said someone was complete, they

meant that he had all of the parts of his personality present and well balanced. That's why Jung found them so interesting.''

I nodded him an ''of course'' and said, ''So even back then, they believed a personality was made up of many parts.''

''The component symbols also represent the numerical fractions one-half through one sixty-fourth. But if you then add them all up again, as Isis did, you only come up with sixty-three sixty-fourths.''

''So where does the other sixty-fourth come from?''

O'Connor's eyes twinkled, and he stuck his bony finger into the air. ''Magic! The Egyptians understood that it takes a little bit of magic to make anything complete. And that was why the eye of Horus always accompanied the pharaoh's mummy on its perilous journey to the afterlife.''

Bingo! ''You mean in the preparation of the dead body?''

''Dead by *our* standards. It all depends on your frame of reference. *They* thought of it as preparing for eternal life.''

O'Connor obligingly described how the pharaoh's corpse was transported across the Nile to the high priests in the temple at the pyramid complex for seventy days of embalming. Then he came to the canopic jars.

He pulled a worn copy of *Man and His Symbols* from the shelf above his desk, opened it to the first chapter, and pointed to a picture of the jars across the bottom of page twenty-one. In my defense, the caption didn't explain what they were.

With his finger, he outlined the first of four stone canisters. It had a top shaped like a monkey's head. ''As the body was being prepared—mummified, if you will—the internal organs were removed and placed in these four canopic jars. This baboon-headed one held the lungs, the human-headed one next to it held the liver, the jackal-headed one the stomach, and Horus, the falcon—he got the intestines.''

Lungs, liver, stomach, intestines. ''Those organs were always removed?''

He nodded. ''If you wanted life after death, you had to play by the rules.''

I felt my pulse quickening. ''Those are four of the vital organs. What about the heart and kidneys?''

''A very good question,'' O'Connor finally allowed. ''Since the heart was thought to contain the essence of the individual, it was left in the body. And at that point in the history of science, the kidneys weren't recognized as organs, so there was no importance attached to preserving them.''

Okay, Professor, for the jackpot now . . . ''And the brain?''

Laugh lines formed at the corner of O'Connor's deep-set eyes and radiated out across his pasty face. ''Funny thing about the brain. They had no idea what it was for, so they just broke it up, pulled it out through the nose, and threw it away!''

———————

Vince met me for lunch at the Fraternal Order of Police lodge on Fifth Street, a couple of blocks up from the office. ''It doesn't have anything to do with cannibalism,'' I explained excitedly.

''Didn't anyone teach you not to talk with your mouth full?''

''Probably. I can't remember.'' I chewed and swallowed quickly. ''The two crimes are *thematically* related. And the theme is ancient death ritual. Hazeltine was Egyptian mummification and burial practice. The kitchen pots weren't to cook the organs. They were just the best he could do for canopic jars. With Fox, it was the Aztecs' human sacrifice. I chased that down in the GW library just now. So it's logical that Hazeltine was dead before he starting cutting her. The Aztecs, on the other hand, went to great pains to remove the beating heart from the living body of the sacrificial subject.''

The nice thing about eating—or drinking—at the FOP is that everyone else there is a cop or fellow traveler, so you don't have to worry about what you're saying or who's listening. The surroundings are pleasant—exposed brick, real wood bar and floor, creaky chairs and tables—the atmosphere is noisy and boisterous/raunchy, and the food is cheap and predictable. And you can run a tab.

Vince squinted at me like he always does when he doesn't quite buy what I'm telling him. ''I think you're making a little too much of all that profiling business they fed you down in Quantico. You know it's not a substitute for real police work.'' As I said, Vince is old school.

''It is real police work,'' I protested.

''So what do you plan to do with this stuff?'' he challenged.

''Just come up with a suspect,'' I replied.

5

I didn't waste any time going through channels with the FBI Washington Field Office. I called Jim Wright at Quantico and told him my theory. Wright is the special agent in charge of Investigative Analysis, part of the FBI's elite team of mind hunters and one of my mentors when I was in the National Academy program.

"So does it sound like anyone you've heard of?"

There was a pause on the other end of the line, and I sensed he was weighing his answer carefully.

"Well? Does it?"

"Yeah, it does sound like one."

"Who, Jim?"

Another hesitation. "Neville Ramsey."

This time the hesitation was on my end. I felt as if my breath had been taken away. "The artist from California? The one who killed that young movie actress several years ago?"

"He also did a female body builder, a prominent woman surgeon, a male porno star, and God knows how many others. It's the thematic nature of the crimes that really makes the case."

"A lot of serial killers use themes of some sort, something to tie their crimes together," I said.

"But Ramsey is the only one we know of whose themes were this complex and intricate. He's bad news all right."

"What about all the medical stuff—surgery, drugs?"

"Neville Ramsey went to medical school," Wright explained. "He didn't finish, but he learned what he had to. And he comes from a medical family. His late father was a famous neurosurgeon, Norbert Ramsey from New York.''

"I've heard of him," I said.

"And if my memory is correct, his brother is also a neurosurgeon, right in Washington!"

I called Jerry Ashburn at the *Post*. "Aren't you on the *L.A. Times* wire?"

"Yeah. Why?"

"I'll tell you when I get there."

He met me at the reception desk on the 15th Street side, signed me in, and escorted me up the elevator. The knot of his flower print tie was halfway down his chest, and the skinny end decorated his paunch a good six inches below the fat end.

The fifth-floor newsroom was buzzing. This time of day, just about all the desks in the endless uniform rows were filled with reporters filing for the early edition. The place was such a contrast to where I work—bright, energetic, nice furniture, and plenty of supplies. The classic contrast, actually, between a profit-making institution and government.

"So what are you looking for?" he asked as we zigzagged between the desks across the room.

I pulled him close so no one else could hear. "Whatever you've got on Neville Ramsey."

"Nightmare Neville?" His eyes grew wide. "Is he involved in this?"

"I don't know. But if you write or breathe a word before I tell you, I'll cut your balls off." Jerry and I enjoyed what you might call a "professional understanding."

He set me up at a carrel in the corner of the morgue and had the copy aide print out all the relevant clips. It didn't take long to fill in the story.

Neville Ramsey was an artist—a painter and a sculptor—and by all accounts documented in the file, a very good one. He had an international reputation, showed in tony galleries in New York and Los Angeles and was successful enough to have a house overlooking the Pacific Ocean at Big Sur, California. He lived there with his wife, Anthea, until she committed suicide. After that, he lived alone. Prior to the discovery of his crimes, a monograph had been published on his work, written by a leading art critic. After his trial, several more were published by leading forensic psychiatrists.

He went to Stanford Medical School, apparently at the insistence of his famous and domineering father, Norbert Ramsey, but dropped out near the beginning of his third year. Interestingly enough, it was the same year that his younger brother, Nicholas, was accepted. His art, according to critics, showed a profound understanding and appreciation of anatomy and the human form. Like many artists in the twentieth century, his work was also deeply influenced by the psychoanalytic movement and discoveries about the subconscious.

He was finally caught, like so many of them are, by accident, on a fluke. An officer on routine patrol in a back alley in West Hollywood had discovered the tightly bound corpse of a twenty-nine-year-old man. A wire cage with its floor removed was attached to the young man's buttocks. Inside the cage were two rats. In a panic to escape their confines, the rats had gnawed through his rectum into his body. At first, the police attached no particular significance to this gruesome torture. But Dr. Charles O'Shea, the psychiatrist who testified at the trial, identified it quite specifically as the psychoneurotic fantasy described by the "Rat Man," Sigmund Freud's most famous patient.

The young Los Angeles man had worked in a gallery on Melrose Avenue. When detectives discreetly attended the next opening, one of them happened to notice two small puncture wounds on the left hand of the featured artist, Neville Ramsey. A forensic dentist matched the wounds with the teeth of one of the rats recovered with the body.

Ramsey was apprehended in his hotel room at the Beverly Wilshire. The six arresting officers were backed by a fourteen-man LAPD SWAT team. He surrendered peacefully.

The widely covered trial lasted twenty-eight days. The jury deliberated for just under an hour and a half. Judge Thomas Schubert gave Ramsey one life sentence for each count of murder, to be served consecutively.

That had been eight years ago. Only eight years.

———————————

I slept a little better that night. The next morning, as soon as the rush-hour lemmings had all been absorbed into their offices, I ventured out across the Potomac and into genteel Virginia—that complacent land of luxurious shopping malls and inadequate, constipated highways, prosperous and conservative and fully convinced that a barrier of flowing water and three centuries of divergent history were enough to insulate it from the gritty evils of Washington.

And as a bonus, I got to spend some quality time with the one possession to which I'm truly attached: my 1968 MGB convertible—British racing green, English drive. It's got wire wheels with knock-off hubs and the old-style chrome bumpers, not those black rubber monstrosities that made the later models look like muzzled porpoises. Despite my loving indulgence, the lower body panels were finally showing some rust, the edge of the cracked brown vinyl seat cut into my rear end, and the electrical system had never been worth shit. But cruising down 95 South with the hot wind in my hair, my skirt hiked high so I could shift, and my hand on the stick, I felt gloriously alive.

So many memories were wrapped up in that car. Gabbie Hackett and I scraped together everything we had or could beg and bought it when we were in Oxford the summer after junior year, from a guy who was graduating. It had been handed down from generation to generation until it got to us, and it was so beautiful, we swore we'd keep it as long as either of us lived, the survivor retaining full ownership. I can't tell you how many warm English afternoons we blew off tooling those back-country roads, fighting about whose turn it was to drive, reveling in the sheer sensual exhilaration of speed and freedom. Shipping the car home cost almost as much as it had to buy it. And when we got back to GW in August, we looked all over for a place to live until we finally found an otherwise awful rat trap on F Street that came with a parking space out back.

Gabbie and I had met the first week of college and had hit it off immediately—she the sophisticated, jaded Bostonian and I the nature-loving Southern California girl. We were inseparable. We studied together, we played together. We cooked and we ate together. And when, after several months of living together, we realized our periods had become synchronized, we devised elaborate secret rituals surrounding the fact. We were like sisters without the emotional baggage of growing up together. We were telepathic: always knowing what the other one was thinking.

Gabbie has had such an important effect on my life. I met Ted through Gabbie. I met Vince through Gabbie, too. I met Ted second semester of freshman year when Gabbie came back to the dorm to report on this absolutely adorable teaching assistant in Intro Psych. I met Vince second semester of senior year after I had come home from a night at Ted's and discovered Gabbie's nude and violated body sprawled like a broken doll across our living room floor.

I drowned my memories in speed—punched the accelerator to the floor and tore down 95 as fast as I could flog the little green beast into moving.

———————

The FBI National Academy sits on a corner of the marine base in Quantico, Virginia, about an hour south of Washington. It's a fairly pleasant place as government facilities go, kind of a giant Holiday Inn, really—a collection of angular modern buildings connected by long tubes of glass, all set amid woods and rolling hills and marine firing ranges everywhere you look. Two years ago, when I moved across the hall from Sex Crimes to Homicide, I was sent through the FBI's National Academy program. I still have the unisex red polo shirt that distinguished me from the FBI agent trainees (blue) and the jackboot and black-shirted DEA paramilitary types who call you "sir" or "ma'am" when they pass you in the hall.

Within the complex that makes up the academy, all of the modern weapons arrayed against crime are tested, studied, and taught, from the newest firearms and ammunition to the latest laser imaging devices. But there is a segment of crime that defies this high-tech approach, that demands something much more primitive and basic. If you can't put yourself into the criminal's shoes, you have to find a way into his head.

That's what I was here at Quantico to do.

You reach the Investigative Support Unit through layers of normal, mundane institutional life, gradually peeled away. You pass Coke and candy machines, a lounge with TV and pool table, bulletin boards advertising bake sales and payroll savings plans, the schedule of the shuttle bus into Washington, the post office, and laundry. You pass a wall-size bronze plaque bearing the names of the academy's highest-scoring shooters. Then you turn a corner into the gun-cleaning room, full of gray metal tables and the familiar smell of Hoppe's gun cleaning oil, through the narrow passage where the world's most experienced hostage rescue team assembles its deadly gear, and finally to the creaky freight elevator in which you slowly descend into the bowels of the earth.

There, in a confining and windowless warren of rooms, ten men and one woman spend their days journeying into the very heart of darkness.

———————

Jim Wright is a big guy in his mid-forties, with steel-rimmed glasses and a walrus mustache that hides an upper lip his wife has never seen. He is tough enough to be sensitive, and every once in a while soft traces of his native Arkansas come out in conversation.

I stepped into his cramped office, crammed with police memorabilia from all over the world. My favorite is a cap from Oklahoma City Homicide that says, "WHEN YOUR DAYS END, OUR DAY BEGINS." Why can't D.C. come up with anything like that?

Wright sat at his desk, clasped his hands together, leaned forward, and said, "So what have you got?"

"I'll show you mine if you show me yours."

"Best offer I've had all week," he said. I handed him my file and began spreading out the FBI's Ramsey file in front of me. I don't know how much time passed, but soon I was absorbed in the narrative tale of a monster. I gazed at the photo of the gray body of a young woman who'd been completely drained of blood.

When I do this, I try to think not of dead human beings, but of pieces in a puzzle. But that has its limits. Certain types of sexual sadists, and there are many out there, so enjoy the act that they want to relive it over and over again. Once at Quantico, after sitting through a home video of a young woman being tortured to death in an Iowa basement, I staggered from the classroom as if I'd just been cut down from a whipping post. Looking at dead bodies is about the *effects* of violence, and if you're around that long enough, you do get used to it. But hearing or seeing it as it happened is about violence itself. And that, if you're at all human, you never get used to.

Jim was now standing over me. " 'Art is the transcendence of death,' Neville Ramsey wrote. His 'art' is about the best argument I can think of for the death penalty." He pushed another photograph in front of me, and I stared at what had been another young woman, reduced to a mass of charred bone and blackened ash, no longer recognizable as a human being: Ramsey's Joan of Arc scenario. All in the name of art.

There was one additional notation in the file. Several years ago, Special Agent John Douglas, chief of the Investigative Support Unit,

Jim Wright's immediate superior, and one of my personal heroes, had tried to interview Ramsey in prison for his ongoing serial killer study, which already included Charles Manson, David Berkowitz, and other celebrated monsters. Most convicted killers, egotistical, hoping for return favors, or just plain bored, are only too happy to talk. Ramsey refused, and when John asked why, he said he didn't want to give away any secrets; he might need them again.

I scanned through the autopsy protocols of some of the victims. Like my cases, these showed a proclivity for complex drug combinations and precise, almost surgical cutting. He'd gone from paintbrush and chisel to needles and knives. For Ramsey, it was a natural evolution from plaster and clay to human flesh.

I placed crime scene photographs from my two cases next to some of the ones from Jim's file. Even allowing for the differences of setting and angle, the similarities were eerie. I noted the way Julie Fox's wrists were bound behind her back. Wright slid a photo from the "Rat Man" case in front of me.

"Notice the binding around the wrists in your case and this one. The way victims are bound often gives us a signature aspect to work with, particularly if it's more elaborate than it has to be to do the job. But here, it's even more specific. I checked with our forensic pathologist. This is a typical surgical knot. Now look closely: you've got the exact same one used on Fox."

I took the magnifying glass he offered. "Too many things make sense." I put down the glass and leaned back from the desk. "Jim, this *has* to be our guy. And I just can't believe he's out on the street again."

"We've got him tracked as far as San Quentin. Call and verify he hasn't been moved, or . . ." He found his Federal and State Corrections Index in his credenza, leafed through to the right number, then handed me the phone.

I was surprised to see my hand was trembling. I took a breath, steadied myself, and punched in the number sequence.

I had to wade through several levels of prison bureaucracy before I reached the warden's office, and for a moment I had the rather uncomfortable sensation of waiting outside the principal's office. But when Warden Harry Sommers finally came on the line, his voice was disarmingly ordinary, more like the weary understanding of a guidance counselor.

"What can I do for you, Detective?"

"I need information concerning one of your inmates for an ongoing investigation."

"Very well." There was a noticeable pause, as if he were waiting for me to tell him which colleges I'd decided to apply to.

"Neville Ramsey."

Complete silence on the line. Apparently the name had the power to do that to people. I began squirming on my chair.

"I beg your pardon," Sommers said quietly. That was all.

Say something to me, damn it!

"Mr. Ramsey is no longer an inmate."

Score! I gave Jim the thumbs-up.

"He died about eight months ago. Here at San Quentin. He committed suicide."

6

I slammed down the phone in frustration. I was so tense I was trembling. Jim suggested we take a walk. We stepped out of the elevator, through the gun room, and out into the endless corridors. A troop of DEA recruits enthusiastically marched off to the firing range.

"Warden said he jumped a railing on an upper cell tier and fell to a concrete floor. Shattered his spinal cord. Died two days later without regaining consciousness. Talk about a great alibi."

"I know how you feel," said Wright. "But you've been at this game long enough to know the score. The good guys don't always win. And when they do, it's almost never fast enough. You're going to be angry and frustrated. Channel it. Use it. See where it takes you."

We passed through the large student lounge, which had been commandeered for the day by the Red Cross. Fifteen or twenty men and women lay on cots attached to flexible plastic tubes draining blood from their veins. Almost subconsciously I picked up my pace. I have always found something unbearably poignant in the idea of lawmen giving blood.

We turned the corner and went through the double metal doors and up the steep staircase to the dining level. There, tucked behind the main dining hall and the Marine Corps exchange, is the Boardroom, an informal gathering place where you can get sandwiches and drinks.

Wright bought us both strong coffees, and we sat at a table at the end of the room. "All right. What have you got to work with?"

"Nothing from the hair and fiber," I said. "Nothing from the forensics. Nothing from canvasing. Nothing from witnesses. No latents and no suspects, except the one with the perfect alibi."

Wright took the ever-present tobacco pouch from his jacket and found his pipe in another pocket. "So what are you left with?"

"A copycat?"

"We see a lot of copycats, particularly on the more flamboyant or well-publicized crimes—Zodiac, Hillside Strangler, that sort. But there's a difference between re-creating the gross details and getting all the nuances. Now, how likely is it that someone else committed these crimes?"

"Not bloody likely at all, unless . . ."

"Unless it was someone who wanted to be just like Neville Ramsey," Wright said, digging the pipe bowl into the leather pouch, "with the same fantasy systems, the same skills and talents and techniques available to him. Someone intimately familiar with his life and his methods and the unpublicized details of his crimes. You identify that person, and you may have identified your killer."

"You know what most cops think of behavioral science," I commented.

He lit a match and sucked deeply into the pipe. "You showed what it could do long before you came to us. Didn't you point the way to your roommate's murder when the cops weren't getting anywhere?"

"Sort of." I tried to banish the details from my mind. "So where do I go from here?"

"Our advice would be to get as far into Neville Ramsey as you can, all aspects of his life. Who knew him? Whom has he influenced? Who in his life would have the motivation and the means to do something like this? You have to get into his head to find out who else may be in there with him."

———————

There are varying levels of complexity in getting inside a suspect's head. A couple of weeks ago I sat in an interrogation room for three hours, squeezing a confession out of a seventeen-year-old dude with a rap sheet as long as my arm. He was in this time for pummeling a girl to death after he and his friends dragged her into the woods near Bladensburg Road and raped her. He displayed virtually no emotion regarding the young woman he'd destroyed or even the friends who'd helped him do it. In fact, the only time he truly became animated was when he described his .45 automatic—in the same loving words he'd used earlier to describe the bicycle stolen from him when he was nine.

Both were "my best friend, my pride and joy." Now it didn't take a Ph.D. in psychology to know where that kid was coming from, and unfortunately, every big city is full of them.

But then there are the Neville Ramseys of the world.

I could imagine what Vince would have said if he knew I'd asked Ted to have dinner with me, so I didn't tell him. I didn't need any lectures about thinking I could have everything both ways or not being able to keep my skirt down, which wasn't true and none of his business anyway.

We sat on the floor around the coffee table in my living room—me cross-legged in my cut-off jeans and him with his legs stretched out in his J. Crew chinos and sockless Top-Siders—opening up the cardboard cartons from the Great Wall, one of the better Chinese places in the area. Ted had that wide-eyed puppy dog look I once found so appealing, until I'd realized he could turn it on and off like a spigot.

He gazed around the room analytically. "There's so little of you here," he commented. "I find that depressing. Why don't you put up anything new? Aren't you a little old to keep that finger painting you and Gabbie did, especially up on the living room wall?"

"I like it," I said. "And I like it there."

"I'm not criticizing you," he assured me. "I mean, I can certainly understand why you'd want to keep it, but where you've got it shows a certain—"

"Let's talk about Neville Ramsey," I interrupted. "Why'd he do it?"

"Why do any of us do anything?" Ted replied with that way of his. "There've been a lot of theories. When O'Shea asked him why he'd committed the crimes, he responded, 'Why did Descartes seek the location of the soul?' "

"Sounds like a pretty fucking esoteric reason for burning someone alive or shoving a rat up their ass."

Ted forked the upper half of the kung pao shrimp onto his plate. I wondered if there'd be any shrimp left. They're usually all at the top. "The little bit that anyone's been able to come up with about Ramsey has to do with his being an artist."

"What do you mean?" I reached for the container to protect what was left.

"What artists portray are their interpretations of life—representations, if you will. Beauty, ugliness, passion, whatever. Apparently Ramsey reached the point where he was no longer satisfied with mere representations. He wanted to take it further. So for him, these horrible crimes were the ultimate expression of what art is all about.''

"Sounds like an excuse for sexual perversion.''

"There's always been a fine line between creativity and madness.''

This was starting to feel like the old days, the abstract philosophical discussions that went long into the night. He would turn me on with his brilliance and insight, preparing me for the next phase of his conquest.

"So what makes a Neville Ramsey?'' I asked.

"Shriber at Bellevue thinks it starts with something in the brain itself, which becomes active and dangerous when a combination of other factors come together—extreme impulsivity, paranoid misperceptions, a violent environment. There's the theory about the XYY chromosome pattern and the one about abnormal electrical activity in the brain causing psychopathic behavior. Other people have different ideas, such as endorphin production being linked to violent acts. Most of them seem to think childhood abuse has something to do with it.''

"Is there any evidence Ramsey was abused as a child?''

"Not that I know of. Unless you want to say having such a dominant, egotistical father was a form of abuse or warped him in some way. Then again, his brother, who was only a few years younger, was presumably subjected to the same environment, and he didn't grow up to be a serial killer.'' Ted used his chopsticks instead of the spoons I'd put out to expertly help himself to the beef lo mein. He was so good at insignificant things.

"Of course, the brother molded himself in the father's image rather than becoming an artist,'' I pointed out.

"Very good, Cass. You're still thinking like a psychologist.''

"Ted, let's not start that again,'' I said.

"What? Start what? I didn't say anything. I just gave you a compliment. What's wrong with that?''

It wasn't worth the struggle. "Nothing, Ted, nothing at all. Thank you.''

He passed me the carton. Even using the spoon, I managed to spill on my shirt. "Fuck!'' Just about the middle of my left breast.

Ted leaned over with his napkin and dabbed at the sticky goo. "Not too much damage done,'' he said soothingly. Then his fingers closed around my shirt button. All the while, he never took his eyes away from me. Just like the old days.

Just like the old days. There was the time he convinced me to let him hypnotize me because it would "free you up, put you more in touch with yourself.'' When he played me back the tape and I heard myself describing sexual fantasies of my adolescence and then details surrounding the loss of my virginity, I dumbly realized his game was about power and control and emotional manipulation.

I moved his hand. He looked stung and pulled away. "How much are you going to let this job take away from you, Cass, before it takes everything?''

"I don't know what you're talking about," I snapped, although I did.

"It's made you look for the worst in everyone.''

"Because I don't want you playing with my boobs? Can't we just be normal friends at this stage?''

He stood and pointed his finger down at me. "At this stage, your problem is you can't deal with 'normal' people anymore. Instead you have to keep your head full of the likes of Neville Ramsey.''

"And you teach about them.''

"It's not the same.''

"No, it's not," I agreed.

"Do you remember the times you used to take your clothes off in the hallway because you didn't want the smell of death in our apartment?''

"I don't know where this is leading.''

"Ever since you became a cop, it's like you've lost interest in everything else . . . in everything normal. You've never once asked how things were going at the university, for example.''

"I'm sorry. When you're trying to figure out who splattered a fourteen-year-old kid's brains over a junior high school playground, it's sometimes difficult to get all involved with who's trying to keep whom from getting tenure.''

"When is it going to sink in, Cass? Haven't you proven to yourself yet that no matter how many bad guys you catch, you're not going to bring Gabbie back? No matter how much you try to order the universe, you're not going to bring your father back. No matter how many times you stick your head into the buzz saw, you're never going to feel you've tested yourself enough.''

I got to my feet. "I thought we'd gotten past this," I said. "I'm sorry we haven't. I'm sorry I led you on. I'm sorry for everything. I could have used your help. I still could.''

"Then call me at the office," he responded as he left.

The Saturday mail was mostly bills, a quick perusal of which added up to more than I had in my checking account. Yet one more reason not to subject myself to the indignity of shopping for a new bathing suit. There was the usual array of junk mail: Ed McMahon eager to add me to the list of ten-million-dollar winners and possibly sell me a couple of magazine subscriptions while he was at it. You give me the ten million, Ed, I'll take every rag you've got.

Then there was a plain white envelope, standard business size, no return address, and my name and address typed in basic Courier 10. I hoped it wasn't a chain letter. I hate those things and curse the people who send them to me, but I'm not brave enough to ignore them. The one time I did, I tore a muscle in my calf and was on crutches for six weeks.

I ripped it open and started reading with the annoyance of anticipation. But after a couple of lines, my blood turned cold.

My dear Detective Cassandra Mansfield,

It's time we got to know each other, especially now that I understand you are looking for me. You are very beautiful, at least if the television may be deemed a reliable witness. I trust in the near future we shall come into face-to-face contact, and then I will be able to decide for myself. In the meantime, I hope you've been stimulated by my handiwork. I'm sure you were getting bored with all of those tawdry little drug murders. So tedious after a while. Well, bye for now, but rest assured we'll talk again soon.

Oh, and I like the way you dress—you know how to show off those great legs—but I'm anxious to see what's underneath!

I immediately dropped the letter onto the hall stand before it became any further contaminated with my prints. It wasn't signed, not even with one of those flamboyant nicknames. I'm not listed in the phone book. Where did this guy get my address?

My heart was racing. How much does he know about me? Has he been spying on me or following me? I can deal with things I can see. Things I can't see make me very nervous.

I shouldn't be surprised, I reasoned, trying to calm myself. As soon as they stuck that camera in my face and Jerry Ashburn printed my name in the paper, I knew what might happen. There's a long history of sexual killers communicating with the police, going all the way back to Jack the Ripper. And it's a well-known phenomenon that anyone who's put into a position of prominence, either by the department or the media, tends to become a focus for these psychos.

Still, I'd be lying if I said I wasn't feeling vulnerable.

┌─────────┐
│   7   │
└─────────┘

MONDAY morning I turned in the letter for analysis and was trying to catch up on paperwork when I heard, "Hey, Mansfield! Get your buns over here."

It was Joe LaRocca's eloquent voice from across the squad room. There was a small crowd gathered around his desk. Perhaps he was giving a seminar on etiquette.

Cardboard boxes were spread across his desk and that of his partner, Cardenas. "Evidence from the Fox scene," LaRocca explained to Vince and me. "Rafe and I been analyzing it."

"I'll bet you have."

"You wouldn't believe what was in this lady's underwear drawer."

"But if you can sweet-talk Joe into dropping trou for you, you can see for yourself," Cardenas offered. "He took a real fancy to the little black lacy number."

"Cut the crap, children," I said, "and just tell me why you've honored me with this invitation."

LaRocca gave me a solicitous frown. "I'm trying to help you, Mansfield, and you give me shit. Be that as it may, Detective, remember you asked for anything in either Fox or Hazeltine that had the name Ramsey attached to it? Well, voilà!" He handed me what looked like a white business card.

I took it from him. It was a doctor's appointment card. The filled-in lines showed that Ms. Fox had an appointment on May 14 at 3:30 P.M., an appointment that, for obvious reasons, she never kept. And when my eyes darted up to the top of the card, I saw the name:

NICHOLAS P. RAMSEY, M.D., F.A.C.S.

The Halsted-Washington Medical Center is a protected enclave of glass, steel, and concrete carved out of the urban decay that has festered for decades around 5th and K streets, N.W. It seems ironic to have this citadel of healing in the middle of what has become one of our prominent drug trading areas and minor killing zones, but there you are. Washington is a city built on irony.

I can tell you that Halsted's emergency room is almost always busy, and not generally with paying customers. But upstairs it's a different story, and people come from all over the country, all over the world. Among the most prominent of their departments, I had quickly learned, was the Neurological Institute. And that was where Nicholas Paul Ramsey, M.D.—Fellow of the American College of Surgeons, clinical professor of neurosurgery at both Georgetown and George Washington University medical schools, and brother to one of the most notorious serial killers of all time—hung his hat.

Vince dropped me off at the main entrance, manned by a phalanx of grubby panhandlers of all races hoping to cash in on the sympathy vote of those visiting relatives and friends. Almost like tossing coins in a wishing well or lighting a candle in a church, I suppose.

The glass-walled, open atrium main lobby looked more like a Hyatt Hotel. I used the information desk phone to call up to Dr. Ramsey's office, but his secretary said he was in surgery. I thanked her and immediately set about finding the operating area.

Inside the swinging double doors of the surgical suite, the pace was fairly intense. Gowned nurses and orderlies scurried in all directions. Wheeled gurneys were lined up against the main corridor wall. I buttonholed a very young-looking intern type as he sauntered past me. He looked too young to trust with a knife, but I figured he'd be okay for directions. "Excuse me, but could you tell me where Dr. Ramsey's operating?"

"Room number four," he said authoritatively. "Dr. Ramsey always operates in number four."

"And does that room have one of those viewing galleries?"

"Yes, but that's only for authorized persons," he said with even more authority.

Ho hum. I flashed him my badge. "I *am* an authorized person, pal."

Both of them are masked and draped, the patient and the surgeon, removed and protected from each other except at the one juncture at which they must interact. The surgeon's only exposure is the narrow slit of his upper face, between the green mask that covers his nose and mouth and the green cap pulled low over his forehead. The patient's only exposure is the right hemisphere of his brain. The skull portion covering it has been removed with a cranial saw and set aside by the scrub nurse on a steel cart covered by a white towel. Framed by a white perimeter of such towels and gauzes that have been attached directly to the surrounding scalp, the pinkish gray brain moves gently to the rhythms of respiration. There is one bright lamp shining directly onto the surgical field. Other than that, the room is dark and quiet, like an iceberg at night.

For a long time, the surgeon stares intently at the exposed brain, contemplating it, making no sudden or upsetting movements, as if he wishes to take it by surprise. At best, an operating room is only a semisterile environment, so he keeps his hands upright above his waist—the point at which sterility can be maintained.

He takes a step closer to the table. His movements are precise yet powerful, somehow delicate and assertive at the same time. He holds out his hand and receives from the scrub nurse a long, narrow instrument with a cord that looks like a small soldering iron. He pauses again, hunches over the living brain, this time as if paying it homage. Then he says, "How are you doing?"

"I'm doing okay," the patient on the table responds.

Jesus God, I thought, the patient's awake and conscious! He has half his skull removed, I can see his fucking brain, and he's lying there talking to the surgeon!

Nicholas Ramsey glances up briefly at the young men and women in the gallery, who are there to learn from him.

"Epilepsy is one of the earliest known diseases," he says. Even through the single microphone suspended above him and the small speakers in the gallery ceiling, his voice is deep and commanding. "Throughout history, an extraordinarily large number of creative people have been epileptics. Like many, if not most, things in medicine, we still don't exactly understand the reason for this. But it is true that the ancients often regarded epileptics with religious awe, which may have had to do with the visions some of them reported during seizures. From a medical viewpoint, St. Paul's celebrated vision on the road to Damascus has all the earmarks of a temporal lobe seizure.''

A slight drying of the mouth, a slight parting of the lips, a noticeable quickening of the heart, a certain sharpening of the senses. And yes, as Nicholas Ramsey eases the slender probe into the soft, receiving fissure, the tingling and moist warmth that has many sources, but a single origin.

"It wasn't until the last century that the British neurologist Sir John Hughlings Jackson began to increase our understanding of epilepsy in terms of minute lesions that can cause chaotic synaptic firing in the brain.''

. . . firing in the brain.

The first time I went out to qualify on the police firing range at Blue Plains. To prove myself. Legs spread, feet planted firmly on the floor, arms straight out in front of me in the standard firing position, grasping the Smith & Wesson .38 Chiefs Special with both hands. Holding my breath, feeling my index finger gently curling back, squeezing the trigger. Then the red-and-black explosion from the short muzzle, again and again and again. The slight kick and recoil each time, rippling my shoulder blades. And then suddenly it was over. The rangemaster flipped the switch and backlit the silhouette target to reveal five fine holes of light that corresponded to the skull holes through which the 124-grain copper-jacketed hollow points would have obliterated an actual person's brain. And I was surprised to realize at the moment that I'd gone wet from what I'd done.

. . . firing in the brain.

"This is a particularly severe case that has made the patient's life virtually unlivable, and it has not responded to medication or traditional treatment. However, we can still hope to help him through surgery, always a last-resort intervention, but one that we have determined is warranted in this case. Since we now know that epilepsy represents an electrical interference within certain specific areas of the brain, we will attempt to probe and map them out with this electrode so that we can alter them to conform with normal neural activity.

"What we are trying to do is to artificially induce a seizure by 'hitting the right button.' Then, once we specifically locate the area of the lesion with our probing and move out in minute increments from that locus to define its outlines, we will attempt to 'thread the needle'— to fully resect the lesion without affecting any contiguous tissue, thereby eliminating or mitigating the seizures while leaving no corollary deficits.''

We are not so different, Doctor, you and I. I carry a gun in my work. You carry a knife. Both of us come in after the damage has been done, and the most important thing we try to do is prevent more damage.

The scrub nurse handed him what looked like a tiny silver button with a wire attached. From where I was, it looked something like the electrode to a polygraph. Ramsey held it up to the gallery.

''Then we'll implant a tiny sensor-stimulator pack subcutaneously in the shoulder, with leads going up to the specific area of the brain. Many of you know a little about this device we've been developing here at Halsted, but in simplified form, we've borrowed existing technology from cardiology but refined it to the mircrotolerances of neurology. Just as when an implanted defibrillator senses an improper electrical impulse and stimulates the heart back into a normal rhythm, whenever ours senses an abnormal wave in its particular part of the brain, it will stimulate it back into the proper electrical pattern. We call this the 'neural modulator,' or NeMo. Combined with the next-generation EEG equipment, which allows us to localize the specific focus of electrical abnormality in the brain, we hope NeMo will eventually eliminate the need for a good deal of this type of surgery, thereby putting many of you out of work!''

There was a ripple of nervous laughter as members of the gallery contemplated the latest challenge to their high-income potential. This implanted modulator sounded fascinating. I wanted to know more about it.

''All right, let's review. As I touched various areas of the brain with my electrode, I affixed these little plastic numbers to each point. There was no response at point one, but at point two the patient experienced tingling in the left thumb. At point three there was tingling in the left side of the tongue, and at point seven we saw movement in the tongue. This indicates that three touched the somatic sensory convolution, and seven the motor convolution. Eleven, as we can see, marks the first temporary convolution below the fissure of Sylvius. You holding up okay, Mr. Cook?''

"I'm doing pretty well," the patient responded flatly.

"Now, let's go for all the marbles. Okay with you, Mr. Cook?"

"That's what I'm here for."

"Good. I'm now going to increase the electrode's power and continue probing deeper into what we call the interpretive cortex."

Dr. Ramsey held the probe in place. His hands were absolutely rock steady, and his face was completely calm. "Could you tell me what you're experiencing, Mr. Cook?"

"Ah . . . nothing."

"No? Okay, that was point seventeen-C." He moved the electrode. "What about now?"

"I don't think . . . anything. Sorry."

"Nothing to be sorry about. Eighteen. And now?"

"I'm like . . . it's like I'm . . . I can't . . . This is incredible."

I thought I detected a flicker of knowing triumph across the narrow exposed band of Dr. Ramsey's face. "Try to tell us what you're experiencing, Mr. Cook."

"Beach . . ."

"Beach?" Dr. Ramsey repeated.

"At the beach. Sand feels hot, hot and fluffy between my toes. Waves are cool . . . nice."

"You mean you vividly *recall* a trip to the beach."

"*No!*" For the first time the patient was insistent, almost urgent. "I'm *here* at the beach. Right now. Both of us. We're walking from the boardwalk over in the direction of that lifeguard stand over there. But, walk this way. Quick."

"Why is that, Mr. Cook?"

"Don't want to step on that jellyfish. It's a nasty sting."

"Yes, of course. But don't you know, Mr. Cook, that you're lying on a table in an operating room at the Halsted Medical Center in Washington?"

"Yes, I know that. *You're* operating on *me*. But we're also at the beach. I can't explain it, but it's true."

Dr. Ramsey nodded and looked back up at the gallery. "We call this mental diplopia, a presentation first described by Penfield in Montreal. As we deeply stimulate a specific memory area of the brain, the patient has an overwhelming sensation of being somewhere else, somewhere taken directly from his own experience and stored in the temporal cortex. This sensation has the power of reality. Depending on your definition of the term, it *is* reality. And yet, as we can see, this is nothing like a schizophrenic psychosis or hallucination or delusion. The critical ego remains completely intact.''

He took a step backward, as if assuming center stage. ''The patient you see here is in full control of his faculties. This is the edge. We have just crossed the mind-brain frontier.''

HE came out of the scrub room surrounded by his team of residents and nurses. He was still in his surgical greens, which hugged his muscular body like a designer sweat suit. There was a kind of resemblance to the mug shots of Neville Ramsey, but with higher cheekbones and a strong, angular jaw. Had to be in his forties, but not by much, with his sandy-colored hair just starting to turn gray. I had to admit, this was one hell of a good-looking guy.

"Dr. Ramsey."

The entourage stopped, and all looked to him. He was a study in arrested motion, an arrow half-cocked in the bow. His deep, alert eyes darted in my direction.

"Detective Cassandra Mansfield, Metropolitan Police Department. Do you have a minute?"

I could sense the gears turning as he tried to quickly evaluate the situation. I could sense a man used to quickly evaluating situations. A tuft of auburn-gray hair showed through the V neck of his blood-spattered tunic. "I have to see the family," he said.

"I can wait."

He glanced at his gold Rolex diving watch. "You know where the vending room is?"

"I'll find it."

"Basement level. I'll see you in ten minutes."

He turned, and his group followed. I watched them retreat down the hallway. Cops learn to infer a lot about people by the way they move, and Nicholas Ramsey moved with the swagger of self-confidence you expect in the top surgeons. It's not a job that encourages hesitation or rewards humility. And he had a sensational ass.

———

The vending room looked as though it belonged on a spaceship—in one of those cautionary science fiction flicks about how high-tech and inhuman the world has become. The area was fairly crowded, and no one looked happy. The interns looked exhausted. The support staff looked disgruntled. Family members of patients looked worried. And those actually eating the food from the wall of glass-and-stainless-steel machines looked unsatisfied.

I hadn't been sitting at the small white plastic table more than a few minutes when I became aware of a presence in the room. I looked up at Nicholas Ramsey.

He gave a few winks and smiles to passers-by. He exchanged a few sober and quiet thoughts with a colleague. An intense young man in surgical greens came over to him for advice. Then an earnest-looking young woman with a stethoscope dangling from her neck. An anxious, middle-aged couple summoned up their collective courage and approached him. Every business has its civilians.

He had a few reassuring words with them. He clasped the man's shoulder and received in return a look of awestruck gratitude, as if he could heal simply by the laying on of hands. I guess from their perspective, that's just what he did. They left his presence heartened and inspired.

He made his way over to my table. He was still in his greens. He smiled a world-class smile and the corners of his eyes crinkled up slightly, like a white hunter surveying the distant plain.

He said, "Hi. Sorry to keep you waiting." He extended his hand and, just as I took it, gave it a little twist so I couldn't get a firm grip, the way the queen does when she's got to shake a million hands. "Can I get you something?"

"A black coffee would be fine," I said.

"You don't mind if I eat, do you? I've been in the OR since early this morning and I'm starved."

I followed him over to the wall of machines. He fished an unruly wad of coins and dollar bills from his pants pocket, scanned the array of offerings, and fed several slots in succession. He watched as a gear turned and a plastic-wrapped tuna sandwich dropped with a thud to the bottom of the machine. A little glass door began to slide open, and Ramsey reached for his prize.

Suddenly, about halfway, the door lurched to a stop, then trembled a second or two as if it might snap shut again at any moment. Ramsey quickly pulled his hand away.

"Anything wrong?" I asked.

"Would you mind taking the sandwich out for me?" he said.

"I beg your pardon?"

"Would you mind reaching in there for me?"

Fuck it, I thought to myself, I wasn't going to make a point of it. I reached in and handed him the tuna sandwich.

He took it with a smile. "Thanks. These hands are my living. The insurance company doesn't like me to take chances."

We sat down and he said, "Well, Detective, what can I do for you?"

"I'd like to ask you about a patient," I said.

"Patient information is privileged and confidential. I'm sure you're aware of that."

"This patient is dead, Dr. Ramsey, so all bets are off. Her name was Julie Fox."

He shook his head sadly. "I heard about that." He could hardly have helped it.

"Did you ever see or treat a woman named Sarah Hazeltine?" I asked.

"No, I don't believe so."

"Why was Ms. Fox seeing you? She have some kind of brain problem?"

"Sciatica. Fairly severe and chronic."

I regarded him skeptically. "If she had a problem with her leg, why would she see a neurosurgeon instead of an orthopedist?"

"The pain is in the leg, but the source is in the spine. For all intents and purposes, the spine is an extension of the brain. You could go to an orthopod or a neurosurgeon."

"So sell me on your specialty, Doctor."

His deep blue eyes gleamed. "Orthopedists are used to being able to sew up their mistakes and no one's the wiser. Brain surgeons don't have that luxury. So we're used to not making mistakes."

"Doesn't that scare you, slicing into a live human brain?"

Again, that enigmatic smile. "Anyone who's not scared doesn't understand what he's doing."

"Had you operated on Julie Fox?"

"I hadn't decided yet if surgery was warranted. That's another thing about neurosurgeons: we think twice before we cut."

"Can you think of a reason anyone might want to cut her . . . for nonsurgical reasons?"

"The few times I met her, she seemed a quiet, nice person."

"Well, this quiet, nice person was practically turned inside out by someone who, aside from being a sadistic sexual psychopath, also knew his anatomy pretty well, favored medical tools and techniques, had access to hospital drugs, and possessed a rather sophisticated sense of the 'theatrical.' Someone very much like your brother."

I could feel the tide shifting. Suddenly everything had changed. He was livid. More than livid, ballistic. I thought those multimillion-dollar hands were going to clench right through the table or wrap around my neck.

"My brother is dead, Detective."

"Yes, I know."

"So anything he might have to do with your case would be purely academic."

"We don't know that yet."

"But you do know he's dead. I understand that's traditionally considered a very strong alibi."

"I've had that point suggested to me."

"If you're here to further your career or you want insight into the working of the brilliant criminal mind, you've come to the wrong place. I've already had every cop, every forensic psychiatrist, every FBI agent, every lawyer, every tabloid jerk who wants his pound of flesh. I think I've paid my dues and done sufficient penance for my brother."

He glared at me through those deep blue eyes, now steely cold, and all the charm was gone. "If you'll excuse me, I've got an entire afternoon of patients to see." He stood up, nodded, and turned to leave. I did notice that he quickly wrapped the uneaten half of his sandwich back into the cellophane and took it with him. Nicholas Ramsey was clearly an organized and calculating man with the ability to plan ahead and anticipate his needs and desires.

And as he walked briskly out of the vending room and disappeared down the hallway, I noticed again what a great set of buns went along with that brilliant mind.

I was about to get up myself when the good-looking guy who'd come in with Ramsey came over and stood above me. I read off the black nameplate on his coat. "Dr. Robert Fusillo, I presume."

"You can call me Bob," he said. "I'm not God yet, I'm still a resident."

Swell. "And what can I do for you, *Bob?*"

"It's more what I can do for you . . . Ms. Mansfield, is it?"

I nodded. "I'm all ears. Would you care to sit down?"

He remained standing. "Just a few words of advice. Dr. Ramsey is not the type you want to piss off. He can make things very unpleasant if he wants to."

"In what way?" I asked innocently.

"You'll just have to trust me, he can. You don't want him against you."

"Perhaps you and I could get together and talk," I suggested.

"I don't think that would be a good idea."

"And why not?" I persisted, still all sweetness and light.

"Because you'd obviously be expecting me to betray some confidence regarding Dr. Ramsey," he replied. "And if that's what you'd be expecting, then you'd be barking up the wrong tree."

"Thank you," I said, getting up to leave, now fully determined to shake that tree and see just what fell out.

9

A fundamental rule of detective work holds that people who don't want to cooperate have something to hide. It may not always be what you think, but there's generally something.

It didn't take long to come up with the name of Patricia Sunderland Ramsey. She agreed to meet me in the maternity ward of Columbia Hospital for Women. I was starting to spend a lot more time in hospitals than I thought was healthy.

She was pointed out to me when I got to the nursing station, a trim and attractive dark-haired woman in a shiny white lab coat, moving methodically among the rows of clear plastic cribs.

"You can go in if you like," the nurse said with a kindly smile. Here was the only hospital situation anyone ever wanted to be in. The only one I could think of where people were actually nice to you, where the joy outweighed the pain.

I went in and walked over to her. She was holding a tiny baby up to the light, as if examining it for possible defects or imperfections.

"Dr. Ramsey?" It seemed strange using that name in this context. "I'm Sandy Mansfield."

"Hello," she said with an infectious smile. "And this is Heather. Heather is three days old today, aren't you, sweetie pie?" The baby gurgled contentedly. She put the infant down and stroked her on the back before turning her attention to me. I followed her out of the ward, and as we walked down the high-ceilinged corridor she said, "I suppose this is about Neville."

"Yes, it is."

"I'd hoped that part of our lives was dead and buried."

"I'm afraid the dead have a way of coming back to haunt us," I said. "If they didn't, I guess I'd be out of work."

"You're no more likely to be out of work than I am," Patricia Ramsey observed. "People are born, people die. You accept that when you become a doctor. Fortunately for me, I'm on the happy end of the equation."

And for whatever reason, I'm on the other end.

"I thought of Neville when I heard about those horrible murders," she remarked. "It's almost as if someone's trying to copy him, to pick up where he left off. That's a dismal thought."

We reached her small and cluttered office. As soon as we sat down, she pulled a pack of Virginia Slims from her desk drawer. She shook open the pack and offered it to me.

"No, thanks."

She nodded knowingly. "Isn't it awful? Filthy habit. I know all the terrible things it does to you, and I make sure never to let my expecting mothers see me like this. But I just can't help myself. My soon-to-be former husband used to get on me all the time."

"This might be difficult, Dr. Ramsey . . ."

"Patricia, please."

"Thank you . . . Patricia. But I'd like to ask you some questions about your late brother-in-law."

She took a long drag and blew the smoke up in the air. "I guess none of us is ever going to escape Neville. The mirror into our souls."

"What do you mean?"

Another long drag, then she held the cigarette aloft and stared at it for several moments. "What do I mean? Let's see, what do I mean? I guess I mean that Neville, like any brilliant artist, brought all the under-currents up to the surface."

"Was he social, friendly . . . I mean, to people like you, family?"

"He was very charming to everyone. I know it sounds terrible to say, but he was—disarmingly so. Just like Nick. You've talked to Nick, I assume."

I nodded.

"He can charm the birds out of the trees."

Up to a point, I thought to myself.

"And yet Neville overwhelmed him. Neville dominated a room. I think that always bothered Nicholas. He never said anything, but I could tell. Neville was witty, stimulating, a terrific host. We used to love to visit him in California. You know, he built this marvelous house on Highway One at Big Sur. On a cliff six hundred feet above the Pacific. You could see thirty miles of the most beautiful coastline in either direction.''

She turned away for a moment, as if trying to decide what to pluck out of the memory for my benefit.

''In the garden—this terraced garden built into the hillside—were these two bronze figures he'd created: a man and a woman. Absolutely breathtaking. Nude, incredibly lifelike, twisted into these strange contortions. I'll never forget their faces. It was as if, somehow, he'd captured the agony of the human condition in their expressions. He'd had many offers for the pair of them, hundreds of thousands of dollars, but he refused to sell them. After he was arrested, we found out they were human bodies covered with bronze. Relatives were flown in to identify them.''

''Neville was a widower,'' I stated. ''His wife committed suicide.''

''That's the story,'' said Patricia. ''And it's probably true. I guess we'll never know for sure.''

''I'm not sure I follow you.''

''It happened in San Francisco. Neville and Anthea were there for a gallery opening. It would have been about the time of the second or third murder—when he cooked and ate the brains of the twin brothers.'' There was a momentary far-away look in her eyes before she brought herself back.

''What happened?''

''She jumped from the window of their room at the Mark Hopkins. They were just getting back from the reception. Neville told police that Anthea walked calmly to the window, opened it as though she wanted some fresh air, and then just 'stepped out.' ''

''Do you believe him?''

''As strange as it sounds, considering what we know now, I do.''

I've seen people do some awfully strange and sick things in the name of love, but I wasn't going to press the point. ''Not even to silence her,'' I suggested, ''if she'd found out about the crimes?''

''No, not even then. After he was caught—the rat cage—I understand they reopened the investigation of Anthea's death. But they didn't find anything. I knew they wouldn't.''

''Is there anything you know of in Neville's background that might indicate or explain what he became?''

"You mean such as late bed-wetting, fire starting, cruelty to small animals or other children? What we used to call 'the homicidal triad' in med school? I'm afraid it wasn't so clear-cut or simple. In real life, it seldom is."

After my father died when I was eight, I remember all the nights I woke up with soaked underpants and damp sheets. Also around that time, I remember my first serious spanking for impulsively setting fire to the trash can in the alley. I couldn't say why I'd done it. And though I never picked on other children or tormented defenseless animals, I do recall the sting from my distraught mother's hairbrush being supplanted by the confusing warm and excited feeling in my young loins as I ritualistically dismembered my naked Ken doll and buried his plastic parts in the flower bed.

Patricia stubbed out her cigarette, then meticulously mashed it in the ashtray, making sure it was dead and obliterated. She looked up at me. "I don't know how much you know about their background. Their father was Norbert Ramsey of the Goddard Institute in New York, probably the greatest neurosurgeon of his generation. Also an egotistical tyrant. Don't think it's by accident that Nick's and Neville's names both began with the same letter as their father's."

"Did Norbert favor one over the other?"

Patricia meticulously straightened a pile of papers on her desk into a neat, orderly stack. "They were very similar, actually—the two boys. Yet Neville was his father's pride. He worshiped Neville. So, from his own perspective, did Nick. But Norbert had little time or interest in Nick. It's very complicated; took me a long time to understand the family dynamics. So Neville grew up the fair-haired boy, the one who would one day take up the scalpel from his illustrious father. Neville was the one who protected Nick, who took an interest in him. Nick grew up confiding in no one but his older brother—a loner, an increasing risk taker, the kind of kid who would jump out of trees on a dare. Well . . . I'm sure you get the picture. Of course, the irony is lost on no one that Neville chucked the whole thing and totally rejected his father at the moment of greatest impact—when he was in sight of finishing medical school—while Nick grew up to become every bit his father's equal. By that time, though, Norbert was already dead."

"A heart attack, I read?"

"That's what they said. But there were rumors that he killed himself: some kind of injection that would be difficult to trace. I know that's what Nick believed. His mother had the body cremated before either of her sons got back to town."

"How did Nicholas react when he realized what Neville had done?"

"He was devastated. He couldn't deal with it. As I said, he worshiped Neville, even as an adult. He always wanted to be like Neville, to do what Neville did. He went to medical school not so much to prove himself to his father, although I'm sure that was part of it, but to be like Neville."

"You say that Nicholas worshiped Neville. What did Neville think of him?"

Patricia fumbled with her cigarette pack, finally wrestled one out, and lit it. "That's a toughie. Outwardly, it was wonderful; you wouldn't find two closer brothers. Nick thought Neville loved him, and I suppose in his own way, he did. But I always sensed Neville had a certain contempt for Nick—the same contempt he had for everyone. Everyone except Anthea, that is."

"I noticed that you and Nicholas separated last October—right after Neville's death. May I ask if it contributed to the breakup of your marriage?"

Patricia sighed and leaned back in her desk chair. "Sure it did. But you can't start there. Things were never completely smooth between us, right from the beginning."

"How so?"

"More than anything else, I guess you'd say it was a matter of outlook."

"Outlook?"

"The way two people look at life. We both went to med school at Stanford. That's where we met. He was handsome, athletic, charming, and even then you could tell he was destined for great things. He always marched to his own drummer and never cared what anyone else thought. It was always an adventure to be with Nick. Just when you thought you'd read his mood or had figured him out, he'd change. It could be exasperating, but it was one of the things I loved most about him. Right from the beginning, I knew I wanted to go into obstetrics, the most optimistic and life-affirming of all the medical specialties. Nick—his father's son—was relentlessly drawn to neurosurgery, the kingdom of lost souls."

"But there had to be more to it than that," I prodded.

Her warm, wonderful eyes turned sad. "There was always a part of

Nick I felt I never knew. I craved a kind of intimacy that he just couldn't give me. Surgeons aren't known for their intimacy in general, I realize, but it was almost frightening the way Nick would suddenly just go into himself. There was something there that scared me. I don't know any other way to describe it."

The intercom on her desk buzzed. "Mrs. Rawley's here to see you."

"Tell her I'll be just a minute."

"I'll let you go," I said.

But Patricia put up her hand to stop me. "Can I ask you a question, Sandy?" It was the first time she'd used my name.

I shifted back on my chair and crossed one leg tightly over the other. "Yes, of course."

"You must see a lot of killers in your work. I guess you see murderers like I see new mothers. Do they seem . . . different from ordinary people?"

"We want them to seem different," I said.

She swallowed hard, and the corners of her mouth creased downward. "I desperately wanted Neville to seem different when I found out. I wanted to see him as the personification of evil. But he just wasn't. Well, yes, of course he was. Anyone who did the things he did would have to be. But he was still Neville. If he wasn't, it would have been so much easier. Then I could have separated him out. Then perhaps I could have forgiven him."

———————

The office was pretty dead when I got back, except for Marc Volmer, who was on the phone, flailing his free arm around with too much animation for the conversation to be work-related. I waved, he held the receiver away and said, "Wondering where you were. Vince's in room three. He's got a confession in your case."

"No shit?" I felt a sinking sensation in the pit of my stomach. A jumble of mixed emotions swirled through me. Of course I wanted the asshole to be caught. But I hated to think he'd been caught with no help from me.

"Where'd he come from?" I asked.

"Blue bird," said Marc, and went back to his conversation.

I felt better and worse. In well-publicized cases we get a lot of "blue birds"—voluntary confessions that walk in off the street.

"By the way, the letter came back clean from the lab. No prints other than yours."

I was disappointed but not surprised. Anyone who could manage not to leave any prints at a crime scene wasn't likely to screw up on a simple letter.

I walked down to the end of the room, knocked once on the door, and let myself into interrogation room number three. Vince was sitting across the beat-up wooden table from a thin, curly-haired, and disheveled-looking white male, mid- to late twenties. Between them was a microphone, and mounted near the ceiling on the wall behind Vince was a video camera. We videotape all our interrogations now.

"This here's Elmont Cunningham," said Vince. "Detective Sandy Mansfield." Mr. Cunningham nodded noncommittally.

I wedged myself into a corner of the tight room and folded my arms across my chest.

"You say you live with your mother," Vince detailed. "Does she know you've come down here to give this confession?" The young man shook his head negatively.

Vince leaned in. "So as you were saying, Elmont, you went to the Touch of Class, you watched Julie Fox dance, you waited for her at the door, you struck up a conversation with her, she invited you home."

The sleepy-eyed Cunningham listened carefully to each step, then nodded his agreement. "Right."

"Then what?"

"She fixed me a drink."

"What kind?"

"Gin and tonic."

"You don't strike me as a gin-and-tonic man. What'd she have?"

"Same."

"So you two had drinks, talked a little bit, got to know each other. Then what?"

"I fucked her."

"Where?"

"Floor. Living room floor."

"Carpeted, rugs, bare floor, what?"

"Carpeted."

"What color?"

"Don't remember. Didn't pay any attention."

"She willingly complied. Let you make love to her?"

"Sure."

"I guess so, good-looking dude like you. Use a rubber?"

" 'Course I did. You got to be careful these days."

"No question. So then?"

"Then I tied her up."

"Just lying there on the living room floor?"

"No. In a chair."

"Right. She struggle much?"

"No, she let me."

"Why is that, you suppose? This some kind of bondage game?"

He shook his head. "Uh-uh. I don't play games."

"What then?"

"She had to be sacrificed. It was the only way. She understood."

"Afraid I don't."

Cunningham sighed at Vince's denseness but leaned in even closer, fixed his eyes, and explained patiently, "She had to be purified. It was the only way. Otherwise her soul would be lost forever. She would face eternal damnation. But if her heart could be redeemed ... You see now?"

Vince nodded. "I think I got you, pal. Tell you what: let's go on to the other one."

"Sarah Hazeltine," said Cunningham. He chanted the name like a mantra.

"Why'd you do her the way you did?"

"To get rid of the evil spirits that had taken over. They wouldn't come out on their own. It was the only way."

"Do you recall drawing anything on her body?"

The suspect thought a moment, stared up at the ceiling, as if waiting for a cue from the heavens. "Yeah, I think so."

Vince shoved a sheet of paper and a pencil across to him. "Could you draw it for me?"

Cunningham's tongue darted rigidly between his teeth as he concentrated on his artwork. Slowly and laboriously, he drew intersecting straight lines, then curving ones, and when he had finished, he had drawn a crude satanic pentagram in a circle. We've seen that one before, generally spray-painted on the walls of churches.

"And where did you put this, Elmont?"

"Between her legs," he said without hesitation. "The way into her soul."

Vince glanced back at me briefly. I shook my head slightly. I'd already decided this wasn't our letter writer.

Vince clapped him on the shoulder and stood up. "Elmont, my man, I think we've got what we need. We've got your number, we'll give you a ring if we think of anything else."

Cunningham blinked his eyes in confusion. "That's it? You're not going to arrest me?"

"No. But I am gonna give your mother a call and tell her you're on your way home now. I'll have a police officer drive you. And when you get out of the car, you be careful crossing the street now, you hear?"

Vince escorted him down the hall to the Patrol Division and handed him off. When he got back, he plopped down on his chair, thrust his feet up on the desk, closed his eyes, and kneaded his heavy brow with his thumb and forefinger. "They've started crawling out from under their rocks," he announced wearily.

Vince's phone buzzed. "Homicide, Detective Robinson." There was a pause as he listened. I tried to read his face. Another murder?

"Uh-huh, I understand. Hold on just a second, Mr. Taylor, I'm going to turn you over to my partner, Detective Mansfield."

What? I mimed. *What's going on?*

Before I could protest, Vince smothered the receiver with his meaty palm. He thrust it into my face and with barely disguised disgust in his voice said, "This is a Mr. Christopher Taylor on the line. He would also like to confess, and it's your turn."

10

YES, Mr. Christopher Taylor also wanted to talk, but unlike Mr. Elmont Cunningham, who had had the decency to come down to the squad, Taylor preferred that we meet at a location convenient to him, which happened to be over in Southwest. I wasn't expecting much from this encounter.

The one saving grace was that the location in question—Mr. Taylor's current place of business, as it were—happened to be the Arena Stage. And since I've been a theater nut ever since I was a teenager, the prospect wasn't completely horrible. Still, I didn't relish the idea of spending the afternoon with another fruit loop who'd gotten the Sunday paper wet and sticky thinking about what he'd like to do to a woman if he ever got up enough *cojones* to talk to one.

The Arena Stage is one of the leading regional theaters in the country. It's an impressive four-sided brick building that kind of defines the middle ground between the waterfront and the miasma of bland apartment blocks and town houses that make up the Southwest urban redevelopment. And for all the 1950s and 1960s designers' dreams about making this once blighted area into a new multiuse in-town mecca, the Arena remains the one reason a lot of people ever venture into Southwest.

It was, however, not far from where Julie Fox had lived on Capitol Hill. In fact, from much of the area, you could see the Capitol dome looming in the distance. It was also less than five blocks from the First District station, but that hadn't helped much in keeping Julie alive.

The theater marquee advertised John Guare's latest play, which had gotten terrific reviews all over, even from *The Washington Post*. But what caught my eye was the poster announcing the next offering: *Richard III*.

I walked inside and up the stairs into the spartan, brick-walled main lobby. I used to come here a lot when I got out of college and started earning money, but in the last few years I'd gotten out of the habit. Like so many other things in my life, it was just too much trouble to get organized.

The Arena, as its name suggests, is a theater in the round. A man who must have been the director was sitting in the first row on the near side. A small group of intensely focused actors hovered around him, listening. As I came in, one of them looked up, peeled off from the group, and waved tentatively.

I met him halfway down the aisle. He was of medium height, thin and delicate looking. He had narrow shoulders, kind of like the unfortunate Mr. Cunningham. He wore round metal-frame glasses and had sharp features that all seemed to come to a point. The kind of guy who'd just fade into the background in a crowd. The last guy I would have picked out as an actor, much less a serial killer.

"Hi," he said, extending his hand. "I'm Chris Taylor." He had one of those handshakes that simply gives you the hand and then lets you decide what to do with it. His smile was sort of weak-sad, but I didn't want to read too much into it.

He cleared his throat, a deep, guttural groan. "I'm sorry, I thought we'd be finished by now. But the director wants to do one more scene. You can sit here and watch if you like."

I smiled affably. "Which scene?" I asked.

"Seduction of Lady Anne," he replied. "I'm Richard."

Was he kidding? Maybe the most difficult scene to pull off in all of Shakespeare? Richard's got to somehow make this woman fall in love with him in front of our very eyes after he's just murdered her husband and father-in-law. And we're supposed to believe that this innocuous little guy is the most cunning and malevolent monarch in all of drama?

The actor cleared his throat again. "I'll see you in a little bit." I took a seat on the aisle. The young actress playing Anne was already on stage. She wore a bolt of material pinned at the waist over her jeans to simulate a long gown.

Christopher Taylor came on stage. And even before he opened his mouth, I could tell it was not the same Christopher Taylor I had just met. He wasn't wearing his glasses. His thin, straight body was bent into a hunchback's painful contortion. He lurched forward, dragging one foot behind the other. And when he tore away his ratty gray sweatshirt and exposed his hairless breast to Anne, challenging her to kill him with the sword he had just brazenly offered her, there was mad fire in his eyes.

> *But 'twas thy beauty that provoked me.*
> *Nay, now dispatch; 'twas I that stabb'd young Edward;*
> *But 'twas thy heavenly face that set me on.*
> *Take up the sword again, or take up me.*

At one time in my frivolous youth I had wanted to be an actress. It was the main reason I went to England that year with Gabbie. Real life and a somewhat more mature evaluation of my own gift made me give up that dream, but I still think that what we do in my business is in some ways very similar to what actors do. Both of us come to a scene— a scene in a play or a crime scene—"read" what's there on the surface, and then try to figure out what really went on among the participants. In other words, what is the *subtext?* Every scene makes its own sense and comes alive if only you can figure out the subtext.

I hoped I was as good at figuring out subtext in my business as Christopher Taylor was in his. He was literally breathtaking. In a few short and amazing moments, he had transformed himself from an unremarkable man who wouldn't stand out in a crowd into the king of evil. I felt my mouth drop open as I watched the lovely, weepy Anne swoon into his outstretched arms. I envied him his talent.

And then, when the scene was over, he was suddenly Christopher Taylor again. He came over to where I was sitting and with that sad, sheepish smile asked, "How was it?"

"You were wonderful," I said. "I can't wait to see the production."

"Thanks for coming by." I wasn't quite sure how to respond. He cleared his throat again. It made my own throat feel suddenly scratchy. "Do you mind if we go somewhere?"

We left the building, crossed Maine Avenue, and went down to the waterfront. A few small sailboats bobbed along the surface of Washington Channel, drifting lazily toward Hains Point and out into the Potomac. As we neared the docks, the pungent smells from the fish market hung heavily in the afternoon heat. I thought back to the floaters I'd seen pulled from the river. So many places throughout the city have memories for me.

"Tell me a little about your background," I said, trying to loosen him up.

"I knocked around New York for a while, did some showcases and off-off Broadway while I worked as a waiter and mover. I got some work at Playwrights Horizon, which Joe Papp saw, and he hired me for Shakespeare in the Park." He shrugged. "Things went pretty well from there."

"What brought you to Washington?"

"I went to Catholic University for their drama program. And being here, I'd always wanted to work at Arena."

"So you came to Washington for this role in *Richard the Third?*"

"No. I was sort of ill for a while. That's when I came."

I regarded him for a moment as we walked. I sensed I wasn't going to get any more out of him on this score. A nervous breakdown, my gut told me. I wouldn't be surprised if he'd been hospitalized.

We continued walking in silence. Within a few blocks, little rivulets of perspiration tickled me in all the awkward places, and my panty hose were glued to my crotch. God, I hate having to wear them. We were just approaching the Washington Marina pier when he finally looked up, turned to me, and said, "I read that story in the *Post* yesterday about the murders of those two young women."

At least he hadn't mentioned seeing me on television. "What about them?" I asked as we continued walking.

A deep-set frown creased his sharp features. He cleared his throat and pulled on the open collar of his blue denim shirt as if he needed more air. "I think . . . I may be involved . . . somehow."

I purposely averted my gaze. "You mean you think you did them?" During any possible confession situation, we try very hard not to use words that convey any sense of judgment. Words like "crime," "commit," and "murder" are definitely on the taboo list. We use "kill" if we can't avoid it, and then only with a lot of sanitation around it.

"I think I may have," he said.

"Did you know either of the women personally?"

"No."

"Had you ever met them?"

"I don't think so."

"One of them lived around here. Do you know which one?"

He shook his head.

"Ever been to a bar called the Touch of Class?"

"I don't think so."

"What about the Conway Gallery near Twenty-first and P?"

"I've been there, I think."

"So, these two women whom you've never met, do you remember killing them?"

He rubbed his head thoughtfully. "It's sort of like remembering a dream, I guess you'd say. In fact, I've been having dreams about it. Nightmares, bad ones."

"What do you remember from these dreams?"

"I remember the main story. Not all the details."

"Why would you have wanted to kill these women?"

He cleared his throat again, croaking like a thirsty frog. Funny that he hadn't had to do it while he was acting. "I'm not sure."

I wasn't buying this dream stuff. I almost never do. "Do you remember enjoying it," I asked, "what you think you did?"

"It just seemed so . . . so real, so normal."

I couldn't figure out where this guy was coming from. "Have you ever had feelings of aggression toward women—toward any woman in particular?"

He considered this a moment, as if genuinely trying to evaluate the question, then shook his head negatively. "No, it's more like . . . like I feel as if someone's controlling me, telling me what to do."

This is a fairly common cop-out among killers, conveniently getting them off the moral hook. But I still felt he was playing with me. I tried to get him to commit himself.

"Julie Fox worked in a bar where she took her clothes off and danced in front of strange men. Is it possible you thought this was wrong and she needed to be punished?"

"Everyone should be able to do whatever they want," he stated emphatically, "as long as it doesn't hurt anyone else."

I glanced casually across the channel. From where we were, you could just make out a couple of golfers hiking the flat public course in East Potomac Park. This was going nowhere. I said, "Let me ask you something, Chris. Why'd you come to us, rather than going, say, to a priest or a psychiatrist?"

He stopped walking and turned to me. "As a detective, your job is to get to the truth, isn't it?"

"I like to think so."

"That's what I want to do."

It was time to force the issue, ratchet up the tension a little. "Chris, I've got important things to do, and I think you're jerking my chain."

He turned to me, instantly indignant. "You think just because I'm an actor that I'm fantasizing." It was the same kind of quick change I'd seen come over Nicholas Ramsey.

"You said it," I replied, "not me."

"You think this was easy to do?" he shot back. "I'm telling you something extremely upsetting, and you're not even taking me seriously." He was very concerned with being taken seriously. Could he have written the letter? I wasn't ruling it out.

"Fair enough," I said. "You described the feeling as being like a dream. Could it have been a dream? A lot of times we dream things much more horrible than we could ever do."

"I guess it's possible," he allowed.

"As an actor, you probably put yourself in the place of a lot of people who aren't very much like you. Do you think you would have had this feeling of somehow being involved if you hadn't read about the case or seen it on TV?"

"Maybe not."

I indicated Chris to a nearby bench overlooking the water. I opened my bag, took out my memo book and pen, and handed them to him. "A drawing was left at one of the scenes," I explained. "Try to draw it for me."

He looked flustered and tried to hand the paper back to me.

"Try." He shook his head. "The first thing that comes to your mind."

He shrugged, cleared his throat, twisted his tongue between his teeth. I could hear him breathing with exertion. After a few moments he stopped drawing and passed the booklet back to me. He'd done the sorrowful mask of tragedy, one of the pair of age-old symbols of drama. And when he returned the pen to me, it was in his left hand, the one he had used to draw the picture.

"One more thing," I said. "Would you mind taking off your shoelace?"

"Huh?"

"Just tie it in a knot, whatever kind you want."

He shrugged again, then proceeded to come up with a standard sailor's hitch, the kind every scout learns.

"Thanks," I said. He hunched over to retie his shoe. "Chris, I think you can stop worrying. You didn't really strike me as the serial killer type, and now I'm even more certain."

He looked up. "You don't think so?"

I put my hand on his shoulder. "Not unless you give me the grounds. And so far, you haven't."

Elmont Cunningham and now Christopher Taylor. How many more, O Lord? I asked myself. How many more?

———————

Julie Fox's building was one of those gray-brick row houses built in the last century and lately broken up into apartments. Several of the neighbors had made attempts at nice little gardens on the tiny patches of earth in front, but there was no such attempt here.

I found the landlady in the basement. She was short, gray-haired, and birdlike, her head swaying from side to side in continuous disapproval of the world around her. She brought me upstairs.

The door to Julie's flat was sealed with yellow police tape. I used the edge of my house key to break it. Inside, the apartment had that musty, museumlike quality that indoor crime scenes always take on after a week or two. It was an L-shaped efficiency on the second floor, carved from a much larger room that looked out into a badly paved parking lot in back, obviously the cheapest room in the building. Julie Fox had put two bookcases together and covered their backs with bright orange fabric to create a room divider for her bed and dresser. The entire place was furnished in a shabby but almost anachronistically traditional manner, as if such homey touches as the "Welcome Friends" sampler at the front door could offset the dislocated life of a nude dancer in a cheap downtown dive.

Something terrible had happened in this room, and I strongly believe that changes a place. It's not something I can define or prove. I've just felt it over and over. After Gabbie was killed, I couldn't stay in our apartment. I moved as soon as I could. I don't know how many thousands of times I've driven past the spot on F Street in the years since, but I always get the feeling I can't breathe. Sometimes, if I can, I'll go several blocks out of my way just so I don't have to be there.

Like Sarah Hazeltine, Julie Fox apparently let the perpetrator in. She had opened a screw-top bottle of wine, and two glasses had been found. One had her fingerprints. The other had been wiped clean. Her shoes were found together near the sofa, so she'd taken them off because she felt comfortable. She was very comfortable with this guy.

Tracing the progression of the crime, I had to follow a zigzag course through the small apartment. Here was where the first articles of her clothing were found. Her blouse, unbuttoned. Then her bra, whose strap had been sliced through with a thin, sharp instrument, something like a scalpel.

I walked around the bookcases and over to the bed. Here he got on top of her, straddling her somewhere around the waist or hips. We know that from the creases on the sheets. This was probably where he overpowered her and forced her into the next act of his hideous scenario, judging from the depressions in the carpet and friction burns on her ankles, shoulder blades, and buttocks. It's unlikely she would have willingly allowed herself to be dragged across the floor by her feet.

And here was where she was sacrificed—the chair he'd tied her to, still sitting in the middle of the small living area. The nylon cords he'd used to bind her had been removed by the evidence team, but the twin stains on the rug underneath were still there—red from where his blade had pierced her chest, yellow from the spasm of fear that had made her lose control of her own bodily function. He brought the blade down accurately and precisely between the fourth and fifth ribs, through the pectoral and intercostal muscles, passing the juncture of the trachea and the left main stem bronchus. A subsequent blunt trauma blow, perhaps with a fist, cracked the sternum and caused mediastinal compression. None of that, however, told us what *really* happened.

Did she start taking off her clothes willingly? Did she let herself be tied up? Was it part of some bondage game that went sour? At what point did she realize she was in danger? At what point did she begin to feel afraid? At what point did she know she was going to die?

What is the subtext of this scene?

No one in the building heard anything. No one in the building saw anything. I walked over to the window to see from what other vantage points someone might be able to look in. There were the backs of other row houses across the alley, and if you were standing at the far end of the parking lot and looking up, you'd probably be able to see people in the apartment standing up within about eight feet of the window. I moved that far back to test my observation. Still, it was too much to hope that someone would happen to be out there at that particular time and happen to look up and witness anything unusual.

Just then something caught my eye, registering almost subliminally. I rushed back over to the window. I glanced down to see what it was. A figure stepped back around the corner of the far row house. Pressing himself flat against the building and still looking up, he gripped the edge of the brick wall, as if clinging to a ledge. As soon as he saw me, he withdrew out of sight. I caught only a glimpse of him.

But he looked an awful lot like a certain doctor of my recent acquaintance.

11

I bolted for the door, tore down the stairs, raced down the front steps, and ran around the side to the back of the building. I reached the parking slab, looked in all directions. I spotted the house I had seen him next to and went over to it immediately. Of course, he wasn't there.

I looked around quickly, then squatted down in the loose dirt and scrubby underbrush to see if there were any footprints or other physical evidence. I found nothing but the normal accumulation of cigarette butts, broken glass, and bottle caps. But it had been him. I was almost sure.

It was past four. I came back just to clean up some of my unending paperwork and make sure there were no fires to put out. The squad room was nearly empty.

On my desk I found a pink phone message slip—unsigned but in Marc Volmer's tight, meticulous handwriting:

Dr. Ramsey called. Wants to help. Call him.

Hmmm.

I called him right away. The nurse said he was seeing patients and probably couldn't be interrupted, but to hold on.

Then it was him on the line. "So you got my message."

"Yes."

"I'd like to help."

"So you said. Why the sudden change of heart?"

"It's not, really. I think we both want the same thing."

I decided to withhold judgment.

"When can we get together?" he asked.

"You tell me."

"You play racquetball?"

"Not lately."

"Good. I play all the time; helps me keep my edge. How about meeting me at the hospital?"

"When did you have in mind?"

"How about now?"

"I don't have a racket."

"I have two. What do you say?"

I wasn't sure what to say. So as always when that has happened, I said yes.

———————————

I stopped by my place. I went to the bedroom and rummaged around my closet to see what I could find. What I found was a large Rubbermaid basket overflowing with dirty clothes staring up accusingly at me. I hate doing laundry even more than I hate food shopping. Not having a washer and dryer in my apartment, I have to go to the laundromat up on Pennsylvania Avenue or crash one in a neighborhood apartment building. It's so depressing. But so is waking up for a morning shift and having to put on yesterday's underwear, a situation I've faced more than once.

This time I got lucky. I located a clean T-shirt and shorts, socks, and my sneakers. I threw them into my blue police gym bag and headed for the Foggy Bottom Metro station.

I took the train to Metro Center and cut through Chinatown to get to the hospital, feeling strangely lighthearted and exhilarated as I walked. I had to keep reminding myself that this was a potential suspect, not a date. I went up to Neurology and announced myself at the reception desk. The nurse told me to have a seat in the waiting room.

This late in the day, the room was empty except for an adorable little red-haired girl and her mother. I say "little"; she was probably ten or eleven. My heart went out to any child in need of the services of a neurosurgeon.

I also felt one of my momentary twinges of sorrow and regret about having nothing of permanence to show for my thirty-two years on earth. Most of the time, I couldn't imagine a kid coexisting with my lifestyle, but I couldn't deny that longing was still there, lurking somewhere below the surface, especially when I saw a child as delightful and appealing as this one.

The door to one of the examining rooms opened. Ramsey came out with an elderly black woman. "Looks good, Mrs. Clifford," he said to her. "I don't think I need to see you again for about six weeks. Why don't you make an appointment before you go?" He turned to the little girl, and his face lit up. "Samantha!" He held out his arms, and she ran into them.

He hoisted her in the air. "How's my favorite ballerina?"

"Gymnast," she corrected sternly.

"That's what I said. And when are you going to run away with me to the south of France?"

"Doctor, you can be so silly!" Samantha chided.

"I know," he admitted. "It's part of my charm." He turned momentarily to me. "Why don't you go in there?" he said, pointing me to another examining room. "We won't be long."

I went into the adjoining examining room and shut the door. It was the room next to Nicholas's office. There was a connecting door with a mirror mounted in its center. On the wall was a life-size chart of all the nerves in the body. On top of the gray metal cabinet sat boxes of bandages, swabs and ointments, and prepackaged disposable syringes. I put my gym bag on the sturdy, padded table and took off my shoes. I looked in the mirror and tied my hair into a ponytail.

As I stripped to my underwear, I suddenly felt strangely edgy and vulnerable. I couldn't help imagining myself in here for the room's real purpose, naked and exposed—probed and stuck and scrutinized to see if there was anything pathologically wrong with me. Tiny points of perspiration beaded along my arms and belly. I picked up my grungy sneaker as a talisman, reminding myself that I was merely changing to go play racquetball.

I recalled the familiar nightmare image: squeezing my mother's hand as she and a nurse with an eerie, plastered-on smile led me into the coronary care unit of UCLA Medical Center after my father had had his heart attack. I remember gawking at this gray, emaciated figure with its mouth open and eyes closed, connected to tubes and wires and surrounded by machines with little green television screens that made constant beeping noises. And as my little knees went weak, I thought to myself, This isn't my daddy, this isn't the man who picked me up from school yesterday and took me to Dodger Stadium last Saturday, who could still throw me up in the air and catch me in his outstretched arms, and who was known as a terror in the courtroom. This is some kind of sick joke, and why are they doing it to me, and when do I get my real daddy back? I had been told that normally, little girls weren't allowed in here and that this was something special. I learned quickly how special it was. My father died later that night.

There was a knock on the door. I gasped in surprise. "Ready when you are," came Nicholas's voice from the other side.

"One minute," I said, hopping into my shorts. I quickly checked myself in the mirror on the door. I willed my mind back to happier medical memories—Patricia Ramsey holding her cooing newborns, Samantha apparently cured of whatever her problem was as a result of Nicholas's ministrations. But once recalled, that final image of my father seldom left me quickly. And all the medical miracles from all the brilliant doctors in the world weren't going to bring him back to me.

12

W HEN I came out Nicholas Ramsey was standing outside the door, already changed and carrying two expensive rackets, which told me the game was a regular part of his routine.

His eyes traveled conspicuously from my sports bra–supported chest to the long expanse of bare leg. "You can arrest me anytime you want."

"I'll keep that in mind," I said. He looked pretty terrific himself, I had to admit. I could imagine him in the Jockey ads.

He took me down the elevator to the hospital's underground parking garage and led me over to a gleaming, charcoal-gray Mercedes 500SL sports car. He opened the passenger door, and the car's cream leather interior practically enveloped me. This beast could eat my little MG for lunch. As he backed the car out of the parking space, I could see his name stenciled on the cinder-block wall behind.

"I could fall in love with this car," I confessed when we were outside. The top was down and we were cruising up Mass Avenue at a reasonable clip, considering the time of day. Even in city traffic, it was elating.

"It makes me feel alive," he said. "With what I see every day, I need that. I'll bet you do, too."

True enough, but on what the city pays me, it's not going to be on wheels like this. He was so engaging, so affable and charming, so completely different from the side he'd shown me when I mentioned his brother.

Something makes you tick, Dr. Ramsey and Mr. Hyde, and I've got to find out what it is.

The weather gods were a little more generous than usual this evening. The humidity was down, and with the sun no longer overhead, a cool, almost comfortable breeze was soothing the air. As we rounded Dupont Circle I kept waiting for him to reveal his agenda for this invitation. But he said nothing. I've been with this type of man before, the kind who can be with you for hours but is so self-contained he doesn't find it awkward to maintain total silence. Just like his former wife said.

We arrived at Yates Field House at Georgetown University. This being Washington, the Mercedes felt right at home in the parking lot, along with other Mercedes, Jaguars, and Lexuses. In the lobby I noticed two senators, one cabinet officer, and a power broker lawyer I happened to know was under SEC investigation.

As we were walking downstairs to the courts, Nicholas glanced at me again and said, "I don't guess I'm going to have to hold back with you. You strike me as someone used to playing hard."

"What's that supposed to mean?" I asked.

"I'll bet when you were growing up, you were the kind of girl who didn't flinch when someone threw a football at your head. Those were the kind of girls I always ran after."

He had my number. "See this?" I said, pointing to the subtle crook in my nose. "Tenth-grade soccer."

"That had to hurt."

"It hurt more when the coach took me out of the game," I replied.

We stretched for a few minutes to loosen up. As he pushed off the side wall and bent his legs, I took in the shape and definition of his tightly muscled body. I loved the way his butt tightened when he tensed. And I must say that when I bent over to touch my toes, I was pleased to see him stealing so obvious a glance at my ass and legs.

Then we were ready to begin. He took his place behind me near the back wall. "Right," he said. "Give me your best shot."

"Okay." I shifted my weight forward for the serve. "What were you doing in an alley on Capitol Hill this afternoon?"

I aced him. Low and near the corner so he couldn't even get his racket under it. "What's that?" I'd been hoping to catch him off guard.

I served up another, a Z shot in the corner that caromed off the adjoining wall and whizzed past him. "Two–zip," I said. "What were you doing on Capitol Hill this afternoon?"

He recovered sufficiently to assume the proper defensive position, knees bent and feet apart, midway between the two side walls. "I presented a case at D.C. General, and on the way back I stopped to look at a property my accountant suggested I invest in."

"I didn't notice any For Sale signs in the area," I said as I served another ball right at him.

"Not listed yet." He met the ball squarely and bounced it off the ceiling. "That's why it seemed such a good prospect." It plunked right in front of me, and before I could back up it had taken its second bounce.

"Out!" he said exuberantly. "What were you doing there?" He assumed his position in the service zone and drove the ball low and hard, not more than six inches from the floor.

I rushed forward and scooped the ball up right as it came off the wall. "Official business."

He looked impressed. He charged down court, tucked into a shoulder roll, and knocked the ball into a diagonal spin. "You weren't following me, were you?"

I lunged into the air and managed to catch it with the rim of my racket. "Why? Were you sneaking around?"

"I guess I was," he responded with a smile, drilling the ball right over my shoulder. "One–two."

I hadn't expected that one. I prepared myself for his next serve. "Would you like to explain?"

He served a pretty straight shot. "If I was serious about the building, I didn't want anyone to see me or know I was interested." We rallied the ball evenly. I worked to the side and then gave his return a solid whack right back at him. He crouched and at the same time used a high overhand slice to send it down so low that there was no possibility of reaching it.

"Two–all," he announced with satisfaction.

Bear down, I told myself, you can get him. I took a deep breath and concentrated on focusing my energy.

He served a high lob. I backed up and tried to gauge the ball, then sprang off my toes and grunted as I smacked it down with everything I had. It stunned him, but he managed to recover and get under it, knocking it straight up to the ceiling.

But it was slow, and I had time to prepare. I shuttled back and to the side to set up a good forehand shot, swung strongly with a perfect arc, and directed the ball straight to his midsection. "Did you know the house behind where you were looking was where Julie Fox was killed?"

As soon as he saw it coming, he backpedaled furiously to get to the side of my shot and set up his return. For a split second I thought he was going to stumble, but then he recovered his balance and finessed himself to the side.

"Interesting," he called out as he got his backhand up and, with a slight twist and a light tap, lofted the ball just enough to kiss it off the side wall so that it banked to the front.

I launched myself off my toes, reached my racket far out in front of me, and dove for it, like Willie Mays in center field. I skidded forward on my belly and felt the skin tear away from my left knee. But it was all to no avail. The ball bounced to the opposite side wall about two feet from my outstretched racket, then skipped aimlessly across the court away from me.

"Are you okay?" He came over as I slowly got to my feet and surveyed the damage.

"I'll live," I replied, watching a droplet of blood dribble down my leg and stain the top of my sock.

He kneeled down and examined my leg, wrapping his fingers around my calf and lower thigh. There was a delicious sensuality to his touch. "Want to do something about that knee?"

"I'm fine," I responded. "Let's keep playing." I'd try to use the pain as a whip to focus me, to keep me sharp.

"Right," he said. "Three–two."

We played a complete match, playing hard and both playing to win. Nicholas's style was bold and dominating, just like what I'd seen in the operating room. When he saw a possible gain he'd always go for it, even if it meant risking the point. Sometimes his strategy was direct and obvious, sometimes it was tricky and elusive. His body position gave away no secrets. I was never quite able to predict what he was going to do or where the ball was going to go. At the same time, I realized he was anticipating my serve and moving to the right place before the ball arrived.

I played softball on the squad team, though I hadn't been to any games since this case started. In any event, it wasn't like this. And despite my conditioning and being ten or twelve years younger than him, he proved the adage we'd had drummed into us repeatedly at the police academy: A woman in good shape is no match for a man in good shape in terms of strength, leverage, or even stamina. We'd try, and I tried to compensate in every way I could, but after those first two surprise points, I was never really in control. Nicholas managed to establish his own rhythm for each game, sometimes stroking the ball into a series of nice easy lobs, content to rally as long as I cared to. Other times he made me work for every return, running me across the court and then back again, punishing me for my persistence with increasingly more difficult reaches and exhausting chases. As soon as I'd adjust to his drives, he'd change his pattern.

He had amazing hand-eye coordination. Whatever his brain willed, the rest of his body carried out flawlessly, just as in the OR. I, on the other hand, who had been trained to aim and shoot to kill at fifty feet, was already getting ragged. My hair was plastered to my forehead, my knee throbbed, and I tasted sweat whenever I swallowed, but I was determined he wasn't going to get away from me.

He took the first game 15–5. I fought back with everything I could muster and pulled out the second 15–13. I only got 2 in the third game. I downed about a gallon of Gatorade during the brief interval and psyched myself to somehow rob him of his self-assured victory.

We went for a second match. The first game, I got up to 14, only to have him snatch it away from me. At times I almost felt he was toying with me, letting me think I was in control, only to remind me at the last minute that he was still pulling the strings.

I felt the anger welling up inside me. I was royally pissed off, as I always am when my best isn't good enough. Breathing hard and struggling the entire way, I eked out two more points. But then it was as if his personality changed again. He became tenser, more serious and determined, fiercely focused. It was as if he had to see just how far he could go with me before retaking the offensive. By the time we finished the final point, I'd been thoroughly whipped.

A broad grin of satisfaction brightened his handsome face. I let myself collapse to a sitting position on the hard wooden floor.

He clapped me on the shoulder. "You play like a tiger. I like that." I just looked up at him and nodded, dripping, panting, and spent.

He gave me his hand, hoisted me up. I brushed the dust off my behind as we walked off the court and left the building for the parking lot. I didn't want to sweat on his expensive leather seats.

"How about we both shower and change and then dinner at the Jockey Club?" he suggested.

I was still smoldering with defeat, but I can't deny I was turned on. Something perverse inside me had enjoyed being dominated. For once, I wanted to be the hunted instead of the hunter, and I wanted him beyond all reason. I felt my breathing stop for a moment, and then I heard myself say, "Thank you, but I don't think so."

13

A FTER the game I took a cab home and jumped into a tub filled with the hottest water I could stand. I'd played two full matches with Nicholas Ramsey, and I still hadn't figured out his game. I don't know how long I'd been soaking in the tub, licking my wounds, letting the tension ooze out of me, caressing myself with my Swedish miracle body mitt, when the telephone jarred me back to reality. I waited for the answering machine to click on, hoping whoever it was would hang up and leave me alone. It was probably Ted.

"Mansfield, where the hell are you?" It was Jerry Ashburn's voice, even higher-pitched and more persistent than usual. "Don't play games with me, Mansfield. If you're there, answer the goddamned phone. I got people breathing down my neck, and I can't sit on this story forever. I'm at the *Post* now. If I'm not there when you get this, call me at home."

Damn, I thought, staring up at the bathroom ceiling. I treated myself to five more minutes of soaking, then stood up slowly and reached for the towel.

———

Jerry said he'd rather talk in person than over the phone, and he'd rather not wait. I told him I'd rather not go out again tonight, so he said he'd come over.

I pulled on a pair of cut-offs and my police academy T-shirt. I hadn't eaten, and neither had he. I was too tired to think about anything fancy, but my refrigerator still held the mortal remains of my aborted Chinese dinner with Ted and a six-pack of Coors Light. Nothing in the cartons too closely resembling penicillin, and I'd never known Jerry to be too particular about anything other than facts of a story. By the time he arrived, Cassandra, mistress of the microwave, had displayed her proficiency—the repast and all the beer were spread out on the small round dining table.

"So what's on your mind?" I asked as he gobbled what was left of the kung pao shrimp. He was amazingly nimble with chopsticks, or else he was just extremely motivated to get every last morsel down his throat.

"This isn't bad," he said through a full mouth. After he had scraped the bottom corner of the carton to retrieve the last remaining remnant of water chestnut, he put down the chopsticks, picked up his spiral-bound, green reporter's notebook, and said, "A real piece of work, this Neville Ramsey."

I moved on him menacingly with my half-empty beer bottle. "I'm gonna skin you alive, Ashburn! You swore you were going to lay off the Ramsey angle."

"Wrong! I swore I wouldn't print anything until I gave you time to check it out. In the meantime, *I've* been checking it out. You pitch me a name and a lead like that, you can't expect me to sit on my hands. Hey, what happened to your knee?"

"Nothing. I fell playing racquetball."

"Looks really painful. Did it bleed much?"

"Some."

He shuddered. "I hate bleeding."

"Good thing you're not a woman, then. Tell me what you found out."

"Okay," he said, taking a quick swig. "No sources, because that's none of your goddamn business. But when I started checking out Neville Ramsey and ran up against a dead end—literally—I started looking for other angles. That's how I came up with his little brother."

"Oh, great."

His eyes lit up. "We're thinking the same way."

"You'd make a good detective," I muttered.

"Doesn't pay enough, hours are too irregular, and you've got a better than average chance of being killed in the line of duty. But be all that as it may, Cassandra dear, you're dealing with a major player."

I thought back to my very recent experience on the racquetball court. "I know."

"Have you ever heard of the Ramsey neural modulator?"

"Is that NeMo?"

"Right. It's like a heart pacemaker-defibrillator, only smaller and more sophisticated."

"He was using one in the operation I watched. But I didn't know it was named after him."

"He developed it. I talked to our science editor. It's implanted in the shoulder with wires up to the brain, it monitors electrical activity in a specific area of the brain, and when it senses a rhythm disturbance, it corrects it. It's still experimental, but it can be read and adjusted from outside the body, and from what our guy tells me, it could be a major breakthrough. Ramsey worked with a team of electronic geniuses from MIT and Hughes. So aside from his surgical reputation, he's into leading edge medical technology. The animal tests have been very promising, and if it pans out in clinical trials on humans, he stands to make a fucking fortune."

"I don't get the impression he's exactly hurting as it is."

"Yeah, well, he could be hurting a lot less soon. But there are a lot of interesting aspects to Dr. Nicholas Ramsey. Are you aware he started his surgical residency at Hopkins?"

I hadn't been, but I didn't admit it. "What's your point?"

"My point is, he never finished. In fact, he hardly got started. After three months he left, saying the system was 'too rigid' and 'didn't allow for personal expression.' I don't know how much freedom of personal expression you like in your brain surgeons, but remember, this guy's just three months out of internship and he's bucking the most prestigious surgical training program in the world."

"So he's independently minded."

"You're independently minded. He's a fucking loose cannon. Let me tell you: He lands at Stanford, where he'd gone to med school, stays two years, and is asked to leave. People are kind of cagey about why, but apparently it has nothing to do with his competence; everyone says he's brilliant and shows tremendous promise and blah, blah, blah. He finishes up at the University of Denver and then becomes an attending at Mass General in Boston. Here's where it gets even more interesting."

For Jerry, telling a story and eating were by no means mutually exclusive. I grabbed the beef lo mein while there was still some left to grab.

"So anyway, he's at Mass General less than a year. Cut to the chase: He's brought up on charges before the hospital's ethics committee."

"For what?"

"For 'carrying out an unauthorized procedure.' That's the exact wording."

"Which means what?"

Jerry had the unnerving habit of answering your question by repeating part of it. "Which means, in this case, he transplanted fetal brain cells into a patient with severe Parkinson's disease. Remember, this was several years ago. So it would have been real early in fetal cell experimentation, which as you know is still highly controversial and a political hot button."

"So what happened?"

"What happened was that he was censured by the committee and told not to let it happen again."

"Anything else? Did it go before the state medical association?"

"Interesting question. Can I have another beer? No, it didn't, because lo and behold, the patient starts showing substantial improvement after everything else had failed. So young Dr. Ramsey kind of had them over a barrel. Are you going to eat all of the noodles?"

"You have the rest." I passed the carton across the coffee table.

"Thanks. The man is definitely marching to the beat of a different drummer."

I leaned forward and snatched the chopsticks from his hand. That got his undivided attention. "What are you saying, Jerry?"

Having no more reason to hunch forward, he sat back comfortably on the couch, cradling his bottle. "It just seems to me, you find yourself chasing a brilliant, talented psychopath—with some medical training, by the by—who gets his ego satisfaction mutilating people. Okay, then you've got a brother who's equally brilliant and talented—and closest living relation to celebrated serial killer—who's established a personnel file that reads like Sherman's march to the sea. Like a killer, he's totally self-absorbed."

"How can you make that connection?"

"I can't believe you're not on him like a heat rash in August. Someone's doing these women, and you haven't got anyone else. Am I wrong?"

"No, you're not wrong," I allowed.

"You don't have any other good leads?"

He took my silence for agreement. "And you must have already talked to Ramsey."

"We're following up on all reasonable leads."

"I'm ready to run with this story, Mansfield. I've played ball with you up till now, you've got to play ball with me. And give me back those chopsticks. I haven't finished yet."

"Have you talked to Ramsey?" I asked, holding out the sticks as a reward for his answer.

"On the phone," he said, snatching them from me.

"And what did he say?"

"Said he was busy and that he'd already talked to the police, which I guess means you."

"That was it?"

"No. I also talked to his chief disciple, Robert Fusillo. There's another piece of work. Dr. Charm."

"I know what you mean."

"So I did a little checking on him, too. He was investigated once by Halsted's Medical Oversight Board himself, you know. A patient died postoperatively on his shift for no apparent reason."

"So what happened?"

"He was eventually cleared. They ruled it a sudden stroke. But just take a guess who his chief defender was."

"Nicholas Ramsey?"

"Nothing gets past you, Mansfield."

Jerry was already in territory I didn't want him messing around in. "You didn't tell Fusillo why you were asking, did you?"

He held up his palms and gave me an injured look. "Did I tell anyone when I found out *Playboy* approached you for their 'Women in Blue' pictorial?"

"You better not have."

"It would have made a great little feature, local color, the whole nine yards. But was I willing to risk losing the cuddly and adorable Officer Mansfield as a source? No way, Jose. No offense, Detective, but are your boobs big enough for *Playboy?* This'll be deep background, I won't quote you."

"Give me a break, Jerry."

"I can see it now: a black leather G-string, your long athletic legs clad in motorcycle boots, a nine-millimeter strapped low around your shapely hips, and a police cap perched saucily atop your light chestnut tresses. They take any test photos?"

"Get real, Ashburn." I flashed him a withering glance.

"Let's both get real," he said. "This is a megastory, and I don't want to get scooped. You want me to play along, you got to play along, too."

I opened another bottle for myself. We were taking no prisoners tonight. "Look, Jerry: hold off a little longer and I promise you, all the inside dope."

He eyed me warily. "How much longer?"

"You must have noted a possible periodicity angle to the two murders."

"Both crimes took place on Tuesdays, two weeks apart. Coincidence?"

"Not sure yet. But all I'm asking is you hold off until next Wednesday."

He considered me with a horse trader's squint. "Exclusive?"

I took a deep breath and sighed. "Exclusive," I agreed.

14

W E were supposed to be off over the weekend, but Vince and I ended up in the office Saturday morning, going through the case files, talking to anyone we could think of, reinterviewing people who'd been in either vicinity who even subconsciously might have noticed something. We punched up every sexual homicide or assault in the computer to see if we could find even the remotest connection. Because unless the two-week interval was just a coincidence, come Wednesday morning there was a young woman somewhere in the city we were going to be staring down at on the medical examiner's table. Unless we did something.

The mail always comes later on Saturday. I don't know whether it's because there's a different mailman or maybe because the regular one just likes to sleep in on the weekends like I do. Whatever, when I noticed the plain white legal envelope addressed in Courier 10, I had the presence of mind before I opened it to put on the pair of rubber gloves I always keep in my pocketbook.

My hands were trembling as I used a steak knife to slit open the envelope. I read it as quickly as I could.

My dear Cassandra,

He'd dropped the last name. He was getting more familiar, feeling more comfortable with me.

It is gratifying to find so receptive an audience for my work. As an artist, one strives to achieve one's vision, but you don't really know how the public is responding. I'm so pleased the "reviews" have been so appreciative. And I cannot adequately express how satisfying it is that you, Sandy, dear,

He knew my nickname.

have become such a fan. Rest assured, I'll endeavor to live up to your expectations and not disappoint you. We can work so well together. After all, every artist needs a muse.

My hands were still shaking when I put the letter down and stripped off the rubber gloves. Since I work so much, most Saturdays I enjoy having alone to myself. But not today.

———————————

I was still thinking about the letter the next morning when my mother called. She always calls on Sunday mornings, figuring that's her best time to get me in. It's three hours earlier in California, and she was still up before me.

"So how is it with you and Ted?"

"It's over between me and Ted," I replied. "You know that."

"I always liked Ted."

"Then you can have him."

"If you're going to talk to me like that, Cassandra, we might as well hang up right now."

When she used that tone of voice and called me Cassandra, I was suddenly ten years old again and one step away from "young lady."

"I'm sorry, Mother, it's just that we've been through all this so many times."

"So who else are you seeing, then?"

"I've been very busy."

"I understand, but you know, you're past thirty now. There's only a limited amount of time that—"

I could feel my whole body starting to twitch. "Let's talk about you. Who are you seeing?"

"Me? I'm too old for that kind of nonsense."

It really bothered me to hear her talking like that. But she quickly shifted her attack. "You sound tired. Are you getting enough sleep?"

"I'm getting by, Mother."

"I worry about you all the time, Sandy."

"I wish you wouldn't, because you getting all stressed out over me just gives me something else to worry about."

"How can I not worry?" she said accusingly. "You're on the streets all hours of the day and night with the worst elements."

"I'm careful and I'm good."

"And how many times do I read about policemen . . . ?" Mom could never bring herself to say the words. "There was a case up in Los Angeles not a month ago. An officer twelve years on the force, a nice-looking man. A wife and two young children, and now they have no father. For what?"

Cops hate to talk about this, especially with loved ones. And nearly all our conversations lately had been the same. Within three minutes I would run the gamut from being the disrespectful, rebellious daughter to innocent sacrificial lamb to all the forces of urban evil. Obviously I wasn't going to tell her anything about the letters.

I could hear the catch in her throat as she went on, "You know, I worry all the time that what happened to Gabbie could happen to you. I'm sorry, that's what I worry about."

"The difference, Mother, is that if it happens to me, my fingers'll be around the trigger of a Glock seventeen semiautomatic, ready to pump seventeen Federal Premium Hydra-Shok Plus P's into the stupid fucker's brain. So please try not to worry."

I could almost feel her flinch on the other end. "Mother, I'm sorry if I upset you. I didn't mean to." It was so hard talking to civilians.

"When are you coming out for a visit? Your brother says he can't remember the last time he saw you."

"The planes fly in both directions," I said.

"At least try to take care of yourself a little better."

"I am," I said. "Really."

"Tell me."

I thought fast. "Just this past Friday after work I played racquetball with a doctor—a surgeon."

"You didn't beat him, did you?"

"No, Mother."

"Because men don't like that."

"I know."

"Well, anyway, it's a step in the right direction," she said cheerfully. "I knew you'd approve." It was gratifying that I'd finally said something to gladden my mother's heart.

Later, I went over to Vince's house in Northeast and had Sunday brunch with him and Dee and Lucinda. I always felt at home there, maybe because it was a real home and not just a place to sleep and hang your clothes like my place. Vince's life was so different from mine. He had a wife, a family, connection, a house that he owned full of middle-class colonial furniture and banal souvenirs of annual vacations.

Dee (her real name's Adelia, but nobody calls her that) has always made me a part of the family, and Lucinda has been like a little sister to me. For years her drawings adorned my refrigerator. But now she was becoming a teenager, and it saddened me immensely that I could feel that same gulf widening between us that was starting to disconnect her from her parents. Things that had meant nothing before were suddenly taking on huge significance in defining that gulf: I was older, I was a cop, I was white. No longer could Dee say, "Sandy, you talk to her. Maybe she'll listen to you." Vince is of the old school. He's always believed in respect and self-discipline and standards. Soon he would be competing with both her peers and the street for her body and soul. I knew this age was going to be hard on him.

That night, I had one bad dream after another. It used to be, when I was little and even up through my teens, my nightmares were always very bizarre and fantastic, full of monsters and aliens and elaborate threats of torture and defilement. Since I came on the Job, I've never had them again. Not once. My worst dreams now are faithful replays of things that actually happened.

This one I'd been having more and more lately. It went back to the time about six years ago when I was with Sex Crimes but had been loaned out to Narcotics for some undercover. There aren't a whole lot of young white women on the force, so we're always in demand for particular kinds of operations. The climax of the dream came, as always, in the motel room. Night Train Wilson, having already given me the elements for the bust, had just discovered the wire in my bra and realized I was a cop. He had the muzzle of a Smith & Wesson .357 Magnum pressed against the side of my cheek. He'd already hit me hard across the mouth with the back of his ring hand, and my nose and lip were bleeding. You didn't have to be an expert on ballistics to know that with a load of that caliber that close to its intended target, about one-eightieth of a second after he pulled the trigger, there'd be nothing left of my brain but scrambled eggs.

That moment was so crystal clear. I had filtered out his obscene tirade, had filtered out the raucous street sounds of New York Avenue below. All I heard were the faint rustle that rounded steel made against my skin and the tiny brushing sound of his finger itchily tickling the trigger. They became my entire universe as I prepared to die. I thought of Ted, brought in to look at a body that he might be able to recognize from a birthmark on the left breast but that would ultimately have to be identified through lower-jaw dental records. I thought of my mother and my brother standing over a closed coffin. I knew I was about to find out if there really was a heaven, and I wondered if I'd see my father there.

That's when the cavalry arrived.

"Touch one hair on her head and I'll blow your fucking face off!" yelled Tom McBride, unit commander of the Tactical Narcotics Team. We both turned around to see fifty guys in Kevlar vests, armed with everything from .38 specials to Uzis. At that point, Night Train wisely deferred to higher authority and firepower, and in the instant flood of relief that followed, I realized I had wet my pants.

Later, I found out how many men had had similar reactions. But it just goes to prove, none of us are quite as tough as we think we are.

———

Monday morning we threw ourselves against the wall again. We went over all the possibilities for Julie Fox and Sarah Hazeltine having known each other, or even met, but we came up with nothing. We looked for anything in witness statements that might have indicated the same person in either vicinity. Vince was out on the street, checking every store or service either woman might have used, but called in to say he'd found no commonalities so far. The only thing that tied them together was the tenuous link to Nicholas Ramsey.

I was just bringing back another healthy and satisfying meal from the lunch cart outside on the plaza when Norman Sidecki told me the boss was back and waiting in his office.

I came in carrying my hot dog with mustard and kraut and my diet Coke. Owen recoiled. "Don't get near me with that thing! Go sit on the couch."

Owen impatiently pushed his rolled sleeves as high on his forearms as the thick muscles would allow. "So you're still working the Nicholas Ramsey angle," he grilled me. I nodded. "That because you're strong on him or because you don't have anyone else?"

"Both," I admitted in midswallow. "He's been known as a loose cannon every place he's ever worked—"

"So have you," Owen interrupted.

"And I spotted him visiting the scene of one of the murders. That's classic postoffense behavior."

"He also may be telling the truth," the boss pointed out.

"If we could get a warrant, I wouldn't be surprised to find a scrapbook of newspaper clippings of the two crimes."

"So when Neville killed himself, this law-abiding citizen with nothing legally unkosher in his background suddenly gets the inspiration that he's got to continue his brother's 'work.'"

"Essentially, yeah."

"Why?"

"Could be any number of reasons. One explanation would be *folie à deux*, 'shared paranoid disorder.'"

"You're starting to sound like your husband. Keep it down to earth."

"Okay," I said with a sigh. "You have someone who's severely maladjusted, and someone very close who can't change him. Since the 'normal' person can neither change the abnormal person nor bear to reject him, he begins subconsciously conforming his own behavior to that of the psychotic."

"And you think he's the one communicating with you?"

"I can't say for sure, but it would certainly fit in."

"Those letters are starting to bother me."

You and me both, Captain.

"You've become too much of a focus."

I swallowed hard. "Does that mean you want me off the case?"

"Just deemphasize you. Maybe make Vince lead. For your own safety."

Suddenly I was on my feet and leaning forward over his desk. "Would you do that to a man?"

Owen shifted his gaze downward. "Of course I would."

"Look me in the eye and tell me that."

"Watch yourself, or I'll have you up for insubordination!"

But I persisted. "You know I'm right, Captain."

I stayed in his face. He leaned back and gave out with one of his long sighs of exasperation. "Tomorrow's the next witching hour," he said. "I don't suppose you have anything close to enough to bring Ramsey in and make a case the DA isn't going to spit back in my face?"

I retreated back to the sofa and finished the last bite of my hot dog. "No," I admitted.

"That's what I thought. So what would you do?"

I hesitated a moment. I knew he was going to squawk, and I'd already pressed my luck about as far as it was likely to go. "I'd put a tail on him and then stake out all the places he might show up at—his house, the various crimes scenes, et cetera."

"You know what you're talking about in terms of manpower?"

"I know it's a lot."

"Fucking A, it's a lot. You don't have to make out the overtime budgets."

"So what do you say, Captain?"

He didn't say anything, not for a long time. But I already knew he was going to agree. As he said, his nuts were on the chopping block and he was desperate to find something else to offer in their place.

15

THROUGHOUT my life, I've never found it easy to wait for anything, whether it was a birthday, or Saturday night, or a supposedly "routine" report from the doctor. So Tuesday morning was just about unbearable. Every ring of the telephone, every shout in my vicinity, every whoop out in the corridor, sent my heart racing. No matter what I did, I couldn't concentrate. I kept wandering from desk to desk until I was on everybody's nerves.

"Haven't you got anything better to do than disrupt the entire office?" Lieutenant Newcomb called out. "You, who owe me much paperwork."

"That's just diddly shit," I countered. "What good's it gonna do you?"

"It's gonna keep your ass planted in your chair," he replied. He had a point. I hate this stuff, but maybe I could find some peace in the dull and mundane and routinely depressing.

I had an absolutely heartbreaking case to write up of a fifteen-year-old who'd been killed by another kid for his new Nike Air Jordans. Right outside the school yard, the first boy had refused to take off his shoes and hand them over, so the second one, who wasn't much older, simply blew him away with a Glock 17, the same gun I carry. We'd been hearing about this kind of thing in New York for a while, but it was still new to D.C.

First thing I asked the little shooter—who'll be back on the street in about two and a half years, incidentally—was how he even knew the shoes would fit him. He couldn't give me anything better than a shrug. Sometimes I wonder if there's any hope at all.

I shoved the report into the To Be Filed box, where it became someone else's responsibility. I took out a stack of files and pretended to myself I was getting something done. Jerry Ashburn called for the second time. I blew him off, but not before he reminded me about our deal for tomorrow. Then I went down to the Sabrett's cart and picked a fight with some jerk from the public defender's office who tried to cut in line.

The afternoon was just as bad. It seemed as if nothing were happening in the entire city. No one was killing anyone for a change. I walked over to the radio desk and monitored the scout car frequencies. Even they were quiet.

I went over to the FOP for happy hour, but I wasn't very happy. Around six I wandered into Captain Owen's office. Normally he would have been long gone by then, but when something this big could be breaking, he always keeps the "death watch" himself.

"He's still at the hospital," Owen reported. "Cardenas just called in. You might as well go home."

I stood there with my thumbs hooked into my belt, unable to stay still. "I can't go home."

"Then go to the movies, dancing, pick up some guys. But get the hell out of here. Don't make me think you're a liability," he warned.

"Okay." I sighed. "Can I have a page if anything happens?"

"Yeah, sure."

"I mean it, boss."

"He so much as takes a leak, you'll be the first to know."

I went home and found nothing in my fridge for a change, but it wasn't much of a problem since I wasn't hungry anyway. I turned on "Jeopardy" but couldn't concentrate even on that level. I thought about taking a shot at "Wheel of Fortune," but we each have limits beyond which we refuse to sink, even at our lowest. So I ended up trying to escape into a paperback I'd picked up a couple of days before all this had started. It was part of a popular series about a woman private eye out in Southern California, and since that's where I'm from, I thought maybe I could relate to her. I've read a bunch of novels about private eyes, particularly female ones. A lot of them are good reads and depict a very romantic, exciting life. But the PIs I've met in real life are nothing like that. Real-life private investigation is all pretty routine and drudgy. They're often grungy low-lifes, and most of what they do involves marital infidelity and tracking down deadbeats. From my perspective, if you really want the kind of life those books describe, particularly as a woman, the only real action is the police.

The phone rang a little after eight. I swooped for it within half a ring. It was Vince. "He left the hospital about twenty-five minutes ago. He's just arrived at a house in three-D: Brandywine Street, block and a half west of Connecticut."

"They're sure?" I confirmed.

"Sure they're sure. Driving the Mercedes with the plate numbers you gave them. Pulled around back into the garage."

"Is he alone?"

"Far as I know. That's the whole report."

"Thanks, Vince. I appreciate it."

"Anything else happens, you'll know. See ya, kiddo."

I lasted about two more hours like that, cleaning the floors, shuffling through my bills, jumping out of my skin, that sort of thing. The phone didn't ring. My pager didn't beep. I couldn't eat. I couldn't relax. I was useless.

The hell with it, I decided, I'd had enough of waiting around. I put on my shoes, grabbed my bag, and headed for the Foggy Bottom Metro station. I transferred at Metro Center to the Red Line.

It was after dark, and the train wasn't very crowded. I was totally focused, but at Farragut North I became aware of three young dudes—two large and one small, a pilot fish swimming with his two sharks. All of them had gold chains around their necks and baseball caps reversed on their heads, and all wore expensive athletic shoes and fancy team jackets, in spite of the heat. I must admit the first thing I thought of was where they got them. The Nike murder was still fresh in my mind.

The three of them sat together at the front of the car and stayed there until the train left the Dupont Circle station for the long stretch up to Woodley Park. Then they stood up in unison. Roving slowly from one end of the car to the other, they eyed each passenger and each time were met with a downturned glance that yearned for noninvolvement. The subway was in danger of becoming like New York's. No place was safe any longer.

All three dudes' faces lit up as they got to me. The leader eyed my short skirt and tight blouse. He kept casually rubbing his jacket pocket as if he had a piece. "Hey, how you doin', sugar?" he asked. The other two slapped palms, as if he had just uttered something exceedingly clever.

He shifted his gaze upward from my chest, and our eyes met. My heart was pounding. I clutched my purse tightly and felt the reassuring shape inside. I tried to calm myself before I reacted. Then, very slowly and deliberately, I said to him, "You fuck with me, you're going to be very, very sorry."

There was a moment of silent confrontation as if he couldn't believe what he'd just heard. The passengers looked up, not knowing whether to be more or less frightened. The stunned young man considered his next move.

"Very, very sorry," I repeated without blinking.

He glanced back at his two friends, then around the car. Suddenly the eyes of every other passenger were focused on him. Miraculously, they'd found their courage.

"Shee-yet," he muttered with disgust. They retreated to the other end of the car and clustered together for security. When the train finally reached Woodley Park, I heard him say to the others, "Let's book outa here. This bitch ain't no fun."

We've all got to stand up to these little terrorists and take the streets back from them. Otherwise we don't have a city.

———————————

From Van Ness/UDC, I walked the couple of blocks up Connecticut Avenue to Brandywine. It's a peaceful, solidly middle-class neighborhood of trim little single-family Colonials on tree-lined streets with front yards and backyards and alleys behind, buffered from the avenue by massive brick apartment buildings. I spotted the cruiser lurking in shadow in an alley diagonally across the street.

I walked up to the car. Volmer was behind the wheel. LaRocca was next to him. I opened the back door and slid onto the backseat. It's amazing how cops never lock their doors. They both turned around in surprise.

"Boss know you're here?" said Volmer.

"Why?" I replied irritably. "You gonna tell on me? Anything happening?"

"Not so far."

"Is he alone?"

"Negative. He came in with a woman."

"Who is it?"

Volmer shrugged. "How should I know?"

"Did you see her?"

"Not up close, just in the car. But the passenger side was to us, so we actually got a better look at her than him. They pulled the car into the garage in back. They came through the backyard into the house."

"How do you know?"

LaRocca looked at me as though I were a stupid child. "I deduced it, Mansfield. Because two minutes after the engine stopped and the garage door went down, the lights in the house went on. 'Case you hadn't noticed, I'm a regular fucking Sherlock Holmes."

"How old?"

Volmer considered the question. "What would you say, Joe? Mid- to late twenties? Good-looking girl."

"Yeah," said LaRocca. "Like Mansfield, only younger. And friendlier."

"How do you know that?" asked Volmer.

"Who isn't?" He turned around to the backseat. "You aren't jealous, are you, Mansfield?"

I thought about choking him. I felt a sudden swirl of troubling emotions. Why should it bother me that Ramsey had a woman—I almost said to myself *another* woman—in there with him?

I slumped down with my knees wedged against the back of the front seat and tried to find a comfortable position.

He'd moved uptown. He was broadening his circle.

A half hour went by. Then forty-five minutes. The downstairs went dark. The only light was diffused through the curtains of one upstairs window. Volmer and LaRocca kept up their litany of idle chatter, moving from sports to office politics and finally to women, carefully skirting away from any subject in which I might have the remotest interest.

Waiting was always such a bitch.

After a while, when I couldn't keep myself from fidgeting and squirming, LaRocca handed me back the empty glass jar male cops invariably bring along on stakeouts.

"No thanks," I said. "I'll let you know if I get desperate." As a woman in this business, you learn to hold it in.

Just then . . . "You guys see that?"

"What?" LaRocca said sleepily.

"I saw a lamp topple over. Then the light went out." I leaned forward and slapped him on the shoulder. "There's something going on in there."

"Could be anything," Marc Volmer said.

"Exactly. I'm going in."

"We can't do that, Mansfield."

I grabbed my bag and opened the car door. "I'm not gonna sit by while he does number three."

They exchanged a quick glance, frowned, then bolted out of the car after me. I squeezed between two parked cars with Volmer and LaRocca right behind. We scrambled up the steps, and I mashed the doorbell.

Nothing. I rang again and pounded with the side of my fist. Come on! Answer the fucking door!

I put my ear against the heavy oak surface. Still no answer.

Okay, Doctor. I know you're in there, and I know you're not asleep. Probable cause? Dicey. But I can't take a chance.

I tore open my shoulder bag and fished out my lock-picking kit from the zipper compartment on the side. It had been a long time since I'd used one of these. Vince was much better at it than I was.

"Either of you guys good at this?"

They both shrugged. "You got the smallest fingers," said LaRocca.

"Fuck." I crouched down to eyeball the keyhole, then quickly picked out what looked like the right one of the nickel-plated implements.

I jammed it in and jiggled it around. Come on, damn it!

"Hurry up, Mansfield!" urged LaRocca, who'd still have been sitting on his butt left to himself.

I uncoiled the wire loop and fished it behind the bolt, between the door frame and the door. I turned the pick gingerly and pulled on the wire loop at the same time. I held my breath and put my hand on the doorknob. I twisted it and . . . Yes!

The door flew open, and we were through it. No alarm. Good. The Glock 9 mm was out of my bag and slapped between my hands. Volmer and LaRocca were right behind, but they understood, this was my lead.

The floor above us was creaking. I could hear shrieks coming from upstairs, high and shrill, alternating with whimpering, maybe pleading. Sweet Jesus, don't let us be too late.

Quickly I scanned the scene in front of me just like they taught at the academy. There was a short hallway with a low ceiling. Typical center hall Colonial with switchback stairs at the rear of the foyer. An arch leading to another darkened room, maybe the living room. Volmer and LaRocca took the two perimeter points. I raced down and turned the corner, skidding on a carpet runner. I regained my balance and looked up but couldn't see around the corner. Only one way upstairs. I grabbed the banister with one hand to pull myself around and up, took the stairs two at a time, the pistol always out in front of me. The two guys closed in behind me.

Lungs on fire, pumping adrenaline, I rounded the banister post at the top of the stairs, flattened myself against the hallway wall, trying instantly to consider all the possibilities. There was light spilling out of the door frame at the far end of the hall. Others were all dark. Didn't seem to be anyone in any of the other rooms, but I couldn't be sure. There hadn't been any other lights visible from outside.

I pressed myself tight against the wall and jumped quickly from door frame to door frame. Volmer followed, and LaRocca covered the end of the hall.

The door there was closed but slightly ajar. I moved rapidly but carefully toward it, trying not to be distracted by the pounding of my heart. The light-headed rush of fear and exhilaration. I could hear the floorboards creaking. The thumping and moaning were getting louder. She was still alive. Thank God. I kept a firm two-handed grip on the gun. One fluid motion. No second chances.

I turned my head back to the others and nodded.

Now!

I reached down and hiked up my narrow skirt a few inches for greater mobility, then shot my leg out high to the side and with my heel kicked open the door. Jumped into the open frame, coming down hard and flat with legs spread wide, braced into standard firing position, in the same split second, sighted down the barrel of the pistol.

"Police! Freeze!"

A woman's horrible scream.

Right in front of me, Dr. Robert Fusillo, butt naked on the Oriental rug, looked up incredulously, rolled off a good-looking woman with short tangled hair—also totally bare—and with a look of total terror, yelped, "God! Don't shoot!"

———————

"He set us up, Vince!" I said, sitting on the front passenger seat with my arms folded tightly and angrily across my chest. "He figured it all out! He knew we'd be tailing him, so he gives this guy his car and—''

"Fusillo told you: he doesn't have a car, and Ramsey lets him borrow one of his when he needs one.''

"And doesn't the timing seem a little too convenient? I mean, the night when Ramsey knows we'd be looking for him?''

"He's already established the pattern. Fusillo even has a set of keys to Ramsey's car.''

"So maybe Ramsey's been planning this for a while.''

Vince was unmoved, looking straight ahead with both hands on the steering wheel. "Now what in God's name was going through your brain, girl?'' When he called me that, it was like "young lady'' coming from my mother. We were supposed to be equals.

"Probable cause,'' I snapped. "Wouldn't you like to prevent a murder for once instead of just cleaning up afterward?''

"And instead you set up the department for breaking and entering, police harassment, God knows what else. That poor girl was terrified. It was her house you broke into.''

"She said she was a lawyer. Lawyers deserve to be terrified every once in a while.''

"She happens to work for one of the most prominent firms in town,'' Vince pointed out. Her name was Ashby Collier, and she was with Lazenby, Sherman, and Gray. I didn't like the sound of that.

"What should I have done, Vince?'' I demanded.

"What you should have done was stayed home like you were supposed to. Then this wouldn't have been an issue. You pull this shit all the time. How long you think you're gonna get away with it?''

"I'm lead on this case. I did what I thought was right.''

"Ramsey knows you. Even if he had been here, you would have blown everything if he'd made you.''

"I was trying to prevent a murder. And another thing: You totally humiliated me in front of other officers. It was LaRocca who called you, wasn't it?''

"And who knows how much more trouble you would have gotten yourself into if he hadn't?''

We rode the rest of the way to my place in icy silence.

16

THE phone rang at 5:47.

It was Vince. My adrenaline surged as I realized he must be calling to check up on me. And that, in turn, focused me on what I could expect from Patrick Owen when I got to the office.

"Just calm down and listen to me," Vince commanded. "We've got another case."

"Oh, Jesus, Vince." I shook the sleep out of my head to make sure I'd heard him right. "Where? When?"

"Call just came in. Battery Kemble Park in three-D. Guy walking his dog this morning found the body. Must have been last night."

"God. Who is she?"

"It's a *he* this time."

"A man? Sure it's related?"

"Seems to be. I've called Jack Beauregard at home."

Trying to think rationally. Bits of everything I knew about the cases spun through my mind. Neville Ramsey did do some men, so this could still fit in. Depended on what the specific behavioral evidence suggested.

"Throw on some clothes," Vince directed. "I'm picking you up in ten minutes."

––––––––––

I felt grubby and didn't have time to shower. I put on the skirt and top and panty hose I'd been wearing yesterday because they were still handy on the floor where I'd left them. Clean underwear and fresh deodorant would have to be my sole concessions to good grooming. Then again, I wouldn't look or smell any worse than whoever was lying out there.

Vince as at my door in nine minutes, and I was ready. With the bubble light flashing on top of the Ford cruiser, we raced down K Street, bobbing and weaving along the Whitehurst Freeway, already choked with commuters to and from Virginia. My heart was pounding. The traffic in our direction thinned out at Canal Road and up Foxhall to Reservoir. All the while I kept thinking to myself, I knew someone was going to die last night.

"You know if Ramsey ever surfaced last night?" I asked.

"Came home in a cab sometime after one."

I realized that Vince was also dressed in the same clothes he'd worn yesterday. "You went to his house last night, didn't you? You haven't been home."

Fingers locked around the steering wheel, he kept his eyes on the road and said nothing. We peeled off onto MacArthur Boulevard and careened around the steep uphill corner at Chain Bridge Road. The secluded street only runs for one stretch between MacArthur on the south and Nebraska Avenue on the north. And within that stretch lie the back of a private school, a hundred-year-old cemetery, dilapidated rural shacks, and million-dollar architectural masterpieces, all on one side of the heavily wooded road, because Battery Kemble Park—originally one of Washington's Civil War fortifications, occupies the entire other side. I'd been to the park a few times, generally with friends who wanted to let their dogs run free in peace and safety, and had always considered it one of the city's secret jewels. Apparently someone else did, too.

The Ford's tires spit pebbles and dirt as we bounced down the gravel drive that led off the road. A green wooden sign announced that the park closed at dark. The clearing in the center was a traffic jam of scout cars, cruisers, and mobile crime scene units. The medical examiner's wagon was already there. About two hundred yards off, near the mouth of the creek and where a trail through the dense woods began, was where everybody was milling around. I could see yellow police tape strung from tree to tree along a wide perimeter. I raced up to the scene and pushed my way through the crowd.

Oh, Christ.

Jerry Ashburn was hanging from the lowest limb on a towering oak tree, naked and lifeless, his arms and legs limp but frozen into place by rigor mortis. He had been secured in this position by means of a rope that ran across his chest and under his armpits. A second rope, attached in similar fashion, passed between his legs and bisected his groin and buttocks. His soft and moderately overweight body had been pierced by no fewer than twenty arrows, in a manner any attentive Catholic-school child or devotee of Renaissance art would recognize immediately as the punishment inflicted upon the early Christian martyr Saint Sebastian.

I noticed right away that the knots were of the same type Jim Wright had pointed out in the previous cases.

Jack Beauregard was going over the body section by section, examining each wound with a studied squint, then stepping back to look at the whole, much like a painter evaluating his art. He looked up, noticed me, and scolded, "You look like hell, Sandy. At your age, you've got to start taking better care of yourself."

"I promised I would talk to him this morning, no matter what," I said to Vince in an increasingly shaky voice.

A video photographer and a crime scene tech were working the site. A hunting bow and empty quiver, already tagged and dusted for latents, were resting against the side of another tree.

"His clothing was in a pile about twenty yards off," Rafe Cardenas told us. "Wallet and keys still in the pockets. Don't seem to have been touched."

"Nobody heard any screaming?" asked Vince.

Cardenas indicated the wad in Jerry's mouth. "Pretty good gag. He wasn't gonna make much noise with that in there."

"There's no sign of Ashburn's car," said Cardenas, "so unless one of them walked, they came here together."

Vince looked around and shook his head. "We can try getting a tire tread match, but with all the walking back and forth over the scene, I think it's pretty hopeless." The problem with most outdoor crime scenes and dump sites is that by the time the police respond and figure out what's going on, they've destroyed half the physical evidence. There were so many footprints in the area that whatever trail there might have been would now be all but obliterated.

"So let's say Ashburn agreed to meet our guy here," said Vince. "The park closes at dark, they both knew they'd be alone. Jerry was a pretty hefty guy. How's he get him under control?"

"Most logical answer is a gun," Cardenas said.

"He's never used a gun," I said quietly, staring down at the ground, my stomach squeezed tight in my gut.

"He's never done a man, either."

But Neville has, I thought to myself. I tried to keep my faltering voice strong. "Jerry wasn't chosen by accident."

I forced myself to look at him. Death had robbed him of all dignity, all privacy. His mouth was stuffed with some wadded-up fabric, possibly his own underwear, freezing his face into an eerily leering rictus. An icy spasm rippled through me as I watched my colleagues examine and analyze his body. Each arrow was embedded deeply in the flesh. The ones through his neck and left thigh had come out the other side. The blood had congealed to a sticky maroon syrup around each wound.

Suddenly my head was spinning. I couldn't stand it any longer. I was gagging and had to get away. An experienced homicide detective is trained to look at freshly dead bodies strictly as evidence—even if they were people he or she knew. I rebuked myself for reacting this way, but I couldn't help it.

I staggered off down the trail. When I reached the creek bank I collapsed to my knees, doubled over, and clutched an exposed root for support. I fought not to think of Gabbie and the scene that had greeted me as I opened the apartment door that horrible morning so many years ago. I tortured myself thinking of the agony Jerry had gone through while I was home watching television or sitting on my buns outside Ashby Collier's house last night.

I hung my head over the gently flowing water and retched quietly, turning my stomach inside out with each convulsion. Sweat beaded on my forehead. I waited a moment to see if I was done, wiped my lips and chin with my hand, then beat the clinging dirt from my knees and stood up unsteadily.

Slowly I made my way back, stumbling almost aimlessly along the uneven path. I couldn't bring myself to lift my eyes or look straight ahead, knowing what I was going to see. My mouth was as dry as cotton, and my eyes were wet with tears. My stomach was still rippling in my belly, and the acid taste of my own bile burned my throat.

I was about halfway back when I saw it: a dull orange object lying on a patch of dry leaves in the middle of the path. Something a hiker or jogger had dropped, or possibly part of a dog's collar. The woods were full of junk. I stopped and crouched down to look.

At first I thought it was a ballpoint pen. But when I got a closer look,

I could see it was actually a penlight—one of those little flashlights with a click button on the end that doctors use to look into your eyes. It had a metal pocket clip at one end and a drug company's name and logo in black along the side of the barrel. And even in my weakened and cheerless state, I knew better than to touch potential evidence with my bare hands.

17

I stayed with Jerry's body until they removed it and put it into the van. Then I let Vince guide me back to the cruiser, and together we drove down to headquarters.

"Make sure someone human handles next of kin," I said.

"I'll take care of it," said Vince. "But remember, Jerry worked for a newspaper. They're quicker at getting to relatives than we are." How many times had Jerry stuck his notebook into the face of some bereaved relative, looking for a good reaction? I'd always hated the kind of grief mongering that crime reporters inevitably put people through. Yet now that he was on the other side, I felt dismally sorry for him.

"And reporters don't have to play by the same rules we do," Vince continued, thinking out loud. "Now they'll all have picked up the blood scent."

When we got back to the office, Captain Owen's door was closed. Another powwow with the brass. It was probably Chief Price himself, and I wouldn't have been surprised to see the mayor and/or the publisher of *The Washington Post*.

However, I was surprised a few moments later to have the intercom ring on my desk. It was Owen himself. "Detective Mansfield, could you come in here, please?" Without stopping to speculate, I jammed my bag into my desk drawer and headed in.

But when I opened his door and let myself in, it wasn't the superchief or the *Post* publisher or the mayor in there with Owen. It was Dr. Nicholas Ramsey, sitting casually on the sofa. Dr. Nicholas Ramsey and his sidekick, Dr. Robert Fusillo, who had regained some of his dignity since the last time I'd seen him.

I wasn't asked to sit down.

I also noted that Vince hadn't been asked to join us. I knew a setup when I saw one.

"I believe you've met Dr. Fusillo," Owen intoned.

You could say that.

"And Dr. Ramsey." So what was he doing here?

"Dr. Fusillo isn't happy about the way things were handled last night."

"You bet your ass I'm not happy," Fusillo shouted, rising from the sofa. He began pacing back and forth, his finger thrust accusingly at me. "I just want to know where you get off breaking into someone's house like the fucking Gestapo, invading our privacy, terrorizing my companion and me half to death. . . ."

I jammed my hands into the pockets of my skirt. "I was trying to do my job as I saw it."

"I can only apologize for what happened last night," Owen said diplomatically. "My understanding is that Detective Mansfield rang the doorbell, and only when there was no answer did she—"

"We didn't hear anything," Fusillo stated. "But that doesn't give someone the right to barge in when we're . . . I was afraid she was going to shoot us."

"A very unfortunate misunderstanding," Owen intoned.

"Excuse me, Captain, but that's bullshit. Detective Mansfield is deliberately harassing Dr. Ramsey and me, I can only assume, out of her frustration in not being able to find the actual murderer."

I started to say something, but Owen shushed me with a look.

"A surgeon's got two things going for him—his skill and his reputation. Detective Mansfield and, through her, the entire police department is creating a cloud over both our reputations. And now she's also involved Ms. Collier."

Who has a very convincing bloodcurdling scream, I thought to myself. It was interesting to me that he was lumping himself and Nicholas Ramsey together, something I certainly hadn't done. Had Nicholas put him up to this, or was he just getting off on any kind of association with the great Dr. Ramsey? He did seem to be fixated with Nicholas.

"I'm sorry Dr. Fusillo ended up in the middle of this," I stated, "but it wasn't exactly as if it were accidental."

"Excuse me?" Nicholas finally spoke up.

I turned to him. "Where were you last evening between, say, seven and ten?"

"I don't believe that's the point of this meeting," he said.

"You set us up, didn't you?"

Owen looked as if he were about to have a stroke.

"You made a point of having me be able to ID your car, then you gave it to Bob here as a decoy to throw us off your trail."

"Are you saying you were following me?"

Owen quickly intersected. "A routine part of the investigation." Whatever that was supposed to mean.

In spite of the situation, there was an electric connection between us that made me feel hot and flushed. I shifted my weight. My legs prickled as I squeezed them together uncomfortably under my skirt. What was it about this guy?

Fusillo was about to start spouting again, but Nicholas put up his hand. Instantly little Bobbie was quiet.

"I don't think Dr. Fusillo is trying to break the department's back," Nicholas said, sounding oh so sensitive and reasonable. "We're well aware of the difficulties you're facing and appreciate the job you're trying to do. All of us want to be protected. And if there is anything any of us can do to legitimately help . . ."

Other than to tell us where you were and what you were doing last night, I said to myself.

"With all that's going on in this city right now, I'm sure this is not the kind of publicity you want for the department."

Ah, I knew we'd get to the veiled threat sooner or later.

"But I accept Detective Mansfield at her word that she was just trying to do her job, so if nothing like this happens again, perhaps I can convince my colleague here to let the matter drop."

He looked to Fusillo, who nodded grudgingly.

Owen looked relieved. I didn't know whether to be relieved, confused, or throw up. Of the three, confusion required the least commitment.

"Thank you both for coming," the captain said as hands were extended all round. I kept mine in my pockets and for once kept my mouth shut. "And please convey our apologies and deepest regrets to Ms. Collier." Then he turned to me and said, "Detective, would you mind staying a moment?"

When they were gone, he came out from behind his desk and said, "I hope you appreciate what happened just now. You dodged a bullet, Sandy. Or should I say, I just dodged one for you. Do you have any idea what it would mean at this particular stage of this particular investigation to have someone of Ramsey's stature file charges against you and the department?"

"He isn't exactly the aggrieved party," I said. "He wouldn't even tell us where he was last night."

"He isn't required to."

"I think this guy killed Jerry Ashburn, practically right under our noses."

"Would you care to argue the point before a judge with one of the high-priced lawyers Ramsey's sure to have at his disposal—possibly from the firm of Lazenby, Sherman, and Gray? The fact of the matter is, Ramsey can make us look very, very bad if he so chooses."

"Captain, I can't prove he's taken over his brother's career in crime, and I can't establish a clear motive. But I know he's hiding something."

"Maybe he is. Maybe he's just trying to protect his privacy. People have legitimate reasons for not coming clean on certain things. I mean, you can imagine how devastating something like this could be to his career."

"Particularly if he's guilty."

He looked away and said, a little too matter-of-factly to be spontaneous, "I'm thinking maybe I should take you off this case after all."

"Please don't do that," I said as penitently as I could stomach.

He leaned forward on his palms. "Then you gotta help me out."

———————

I was so unglued by everything that had happened in the last twenty-four hours that I decided to walk all the way home. I needed to burn up the nervous energy so I'd be able to sleep. Maybe I'd binge on chocolate-chip ice cream on the way. That usually helped.

Actually, I had to admit as I walked relentlessly through the oppressive afternoon, in search of the perfect hot-fudge sundae, it could have been a lot rougher. I was still on the case, and I hadn't gotten beaten up nearly as badly as I'd expected last night.

On the other hand, I hadn't expected Jerry Ashburn to be dead, either.

As soon as I got home, sticky from the humidity and sluggish from too much ice cream, I peeled off my clothes and left them in a heap on the floor. I was just about to step into the bathroom and turn on the shower when I noticed . . .

Had I left the bedroom window open? I often slept with it open when it was cool enough to forgo the air-conditioning. It faced onto the backyard, which was small and fenced in and relatively private. But I almost always closed it before I left for work. I'd certainly been rattled this morning, but . . .

I raced back to the front door, grabbed my bag from the mail stand, and reached inside for my gun. Still naked, but with the 9 mm out in front of me, I moved warily back toward the bedroom, sweeping the room as I stepped through the door frame. I sidled over to the closet and grabbed my robe, getting into it awkwardly with one hand so I wouldn't have to drop the gun. I searched every room until I was convinced I was alone.

Finally I started breathing a little easier. Am I just being paranoid? I wondered. I thought back. Yes, the front door was definitely locked when I turned the key. If someone had actually broken in, wouldn't there be more evidence of it? There was no indication of forced entry, and nothing seemed out of place. As a detective, you learn to pick up on subtle signals when things aren't as they should be. Maybe it was harder to be objective when it was your own home, but I wasn't picking up on anything here.

I laid the gun down, but not far out of reach. I opened all the closets and drawers in succession and did a quick mental inventory. Everything looked okay. With all that had happened today, I knew I had to guard against overreacting.

I walked over and closed the window, pushing the safety latch on top. Then I went back to the bathroom, put the stopper in the tub, and turned on the tap. I would take a long hot bath, during which I would try to turn my mind off and think of nothing. Then I'd get in bed, turn out the lights, and fantasize about what I was going to do to Jerry's killer when I caught him.

18

THE next morning, I skipped the autopsy. I skipped the squad meeting. I skipped all the things that responsible detectives are supposed to do. Being responsible hadn't gotten us anywhere so far. All it had done was get Jerry Ashburn killed, and frankly, I didn't have the stomach to watch Jack Beauregard pull arrows out of his naked flabby flesh and then slice him open and muck around his insides. I owed Jerry at least that much—not to be part of the violation. Vince could do what needed to be done for both of us. I called in and said I'd be out on the streets all day.

The papers, of course, were full of serial killer terror. Between that and the dismal economic news, the only positive thing I could find was a glowing review of *Richard III*, which had just opened at the Arena. Christopher Taylor had been singled out for praise by the *Post*'s normally ungenerous drama critic.

But that wasn't quite enough to keep the demons away. I had to get out. I had to get away. So I called Jim Wright at Quantico and asked him if I could come down again.

I finished getting dressed and opened the jewelry box on my dresser, looking for something in good taste but a little flashy. I needed sprucing up. Maybe the art deco cat pendant I'd bought at the antique stall in Camden Passage with Gabbie. That had a little flair.

But where was it? I rummaged through my meager collection.

Could I have lost it? I thought with alarm. The clasp was old and a little loose, but wouldn't I have noticed if it had fallen off? God, I hoped it wasn't lost. It was one of my favorites and reminded me of that magic summer in England.

I suddenly flashed on the open window last night.

I made a closer inspection of the room. Everything okay on the walls and shelves. I went back to the dresser. I started with the top drawer, did a quick perusal, then worked my way down. Just to be sure, I checked the clothes hamper in the bathroom, mentally reconstructing everything I'd worn since Saturday afternoon, when I'd made one of my all-too-infrequent forays to the laundromat.

Which reminded me—I'd never put away the clean clothes, which were still in the laundry basket in the closet. I sifted through them and could account for everything but a pair of blue string bikini panties I'd worn last week. I tried to recall if I'd taken them out of the dryer or if I remembered folding them and putting them into the basket.

Was I being paranoid? I was forever losing small items of clothing at the laundromat and had a sizable collection of single socks to prove it.

I checked with my landlord to see if there'd been any sign of a breaking and entering upstairs, but he said no. I decided not to dwell on it. You can make yourself crazy thinking too much.

———————

I buzzed Jim Wright from the front desk at the academy, and he quickly came out to meet me.

"I'm glad you brought everything," he said, leading down the hallway. "Here, let me take some of those from you." He held his ID up to the metal sensor on the wall, and the thick glass door clicked open. "I've asked John Douglas to take a look at your material. I haven't discussed the cases with him, so he can give us a fresh, objective impression."

I was surprised and touched. At any one time, a hundred departments across the country are vying for John's time and attention.

We turned the corner, and I naturally turned toward the gun cleaning room and the creaky elevator that would take us down into the bowels of the earth. Jim put a hand on my shoulder and steered me across the hall. "Elevator's broken for a change. We'll have to hoof it." Two long double staircases.

Jim ushered me into John Douglas's office. John stood up and came out from behind his desk. "Taking a day off from the D.C. shooting match?" John grew up in New York, and every once in a while it crept into his speech.

"You could say that," I replied. "How's it with you guys?"

"We'll never be out of work." He beamed. "Neither will you." John was one of those unusual people who looked equally natural with a broad grin or deep scowl, depending on the situation. He's tall and trim, with razor-cut hair. He was decked out in one of his signature tapered dark suits, with monograms on the cuffs of his starched white shirt. He didn't invent the art of criminal profiling, but he brought it into the modern world. Douglas was the first one actually to correlate what was going on in an offender's mind with what he left at the scene, a tremendous leap forward in the evolution of crime solving. Whatever any of us know about profiling, we learned from him or from people who learned from him.

John looked so good that it was hard for me to remember that during the Green River killings in Washington State in the mid-1980s, he was found by his colleagues comatose in his hotel room, near death. He spent two anguished weeks in the hospital with viral meningitis brought on by stress, deliriously convinced that the doctors and nurses prodding and sticking him were actually the serial killers he'd put away, torturing him to death. The Green River murders have yet to be solved.

John sat back down and got comfortable on his chair. He motioned us over to the blue leather sofa against the wall. "Sounds from Jim like you got a bad one up there, though he wouldn't tell me anything about it." When the ISU agrees to consult on a case, they want everything in your files except who you think the suspects might be. They don't want to be biased.

My eyes darted around John's office, paneled like a rec room and covered with photos and police memorabilia he'd collected from cases and consultations all over the world. There was a British bobby's helmet next to a Mountie's hat on top of the file cabinet. One of his bookshelves had been cleared off to hold a collection of hand combat weapons—brass knuckles, pugil sticks, numchucks. On his credenza was a diorama made for him by a former student of the Cock Robin murder scene. From the behavioral evidence displayed in the miniature room, you were supposed to be able to figure out who killed Cock Robin. I never could.

"So let's see what you've got."

"You sure I'm not keeping you from anything else?" I asked.

He half winked at Jim. "It's budget week." They both rolled their eyes. "Wouldn't you rather do murders than budgets?" But before I could say anything, the legendary profiler answered his own question.

"Of course you would. Otherwise you'd have become an accountant instead of a cop."

I opened up the file jackets and began verbally outlining the Fox and Hazeltine cases. At the appropriate points in each narrative I handed across photographs and crime scene diagrams. Douglas took each one in turn, grimly intuiting its secret messages and implications. I could see his eyes concentrating at the outer edges of each picture, working in a slow circular motion in toward the center. When I'd been here in the National Academy program, they'd taught us a detective can learn more from the edge than what he's looking at dead on.

John sat back on his chair, a felt-tip pen poised between his teeth. From time to time he would make brief notes on a yellow legal pad resting on his knee. Occasionally he would use the end of the pen to scratch the side of his head above his ear. Jim listened silently, breaking in only when I left out some point he considered important.

John made some final notes on the legal pad, then looked up. "This is an interesting guy you've got here, Sandy. Good thing most of them aren't quite this interesting."

"So what do you think?" I asked, a little more in control.

"Reads a lot like Neville Ramsey," he said offhandedly. "If he were still alive, he'd be the first one I'd think of."

Jim flashed me a look. There was an old-fashioned police billy club hanging on a hook on the wall, which he picked up and started playing with, shifting it back and forth in front of him like a metronome.

"Okay," said John, "let's take the easy stuff first. White male, at least mid-twenties but probably older, probably a college education or beyond, probably gainfully employed, socially active, not lacking for relationships. No prior criminal convictions, but a background of resisting authority. A very confident, resourceful individual. Goes his own way, follows his own rules, does whatever the hell he wants rather than what other people say he should. This is someone you'd expect to have a history of clashing with authority."

"You sure you're not talking about Sandy?" said Jim.

John grinned. "I just call 'em the way I see 'em. Anyway, I'm sure you came up with all that on your own."

"I was thinking in that direction," I claimed.

"Good, then let's look at what the three cases have in common. We've got a different means of killing and a different staging of each crime scene, but all in all, these are consistent, organized crimes.

There's no sign of a disorganized personality. Nothing is out of place. Everything is well planned, not opportunistic. There's a high degree of passion here, a high degree of ritual, but no frenzy. With all the mutilation, there is no slashing or beating or any sign of uncontrolled rage. These are all methodical, predatory kills, consistent with an individual with a refined fantasy scenario and enough intelligence and confidence to carry out those fantasies. This is someone who feels confident in his relationships with women. There are no defense wounds on any of the bodies, so none of the victims felt threatened until it was too late to react. In at least one of the scenes we have a victim who willingly removed her clothing, so we can conclude he is sexually attractive to women. We don't see any of the vaginal mutilation or anal assault we might expect from someone who feels sexually inadequate. There is no attempt to degrade the victim as such. What we have instead is a successful attempt to make the victim *participate* in a symbolic drama.''

John has a way of making crimes come alive again: a brilliant, though not altogether enviable talent.

"Most significant,'' he went on, "there is no attempt to hide any of the bodies. These scenes were meant to be discovered, which also speaks to a level of confidence and self-centeredness. So does the choice of victims. He's not targeting four-year-old girls or eighty-year-old women, victims who would be the most vulnerable and easy to control. He's going after more challenging individuals.''

He glanced down at his notes only long enough to trigger the next point. "There's no evidence he carries a gun, even as a backup. He uses knives and blades in the commission of the crimes. Why does he do that? Two good possibilities. First of all, as I said, we're dealing with someone supremely confident in himself. He doesn't think he needs a gun; he can handle whatever comes up without it. Second, and possibly interrelated, we may be dealing with someone unfamiliar with or uncomfortable with guns—upper middle class, probably; an intellectual, someone who doesn't come in contact with firearms on a regular basis.''

"I know a lot of sexual sadists keep collections of pornography to feed their fantasies,'' I said. "Think this guy is going to have a lot of bondage magazines at home? Whips and leather, stuff like that?''

John shook his head. "This guy is not a sexual sadist per se. He's more complicated than that. Certainly he wants to *dominate* his victims, and certainly he inflicted a lot of pain and suffering on them. But I don't think his *purpose* was to make them suffer. That's not what he got off on. So I wouldn't expect to see a pornography collection, for example, but I wouldn't be surprised by a collection of newspaper clippings about the crimes, probably very carefully organized, maybe even in a scrapbook. These events are very, very important to this guy, and those clippings are going to help him savor and authenticate them.''

John says ''very, very'' a lot, as if everything in his business needs to be described in extremes. ''That's why you might see him returning to the crime scenes,'' he continued. ''To relive his crime over and over again, to symbolically roll around in the mud. Murderers often return to the scenes of their crimes, but not out of guilt, as we used to think. They do it for the charge it gives them.''

I thought of Nicholas Ramsey darting around the corner behind Julie Fox's building and the ready-made explanation he'd thrown at me when I confronted him on the racquetball court.

''We sometimes find them going to their victims' funerals, or even leaving flowers on their graves.''

''So you think he's been planning these murders for a long time?'' I asked.

''At least the fantasy part of it, yeah, I'd say. But something specific will have made him finally decide to act on these fantasies. I'd expect to see some inciting incident in the days or, more probably, weeks before the first murder. The death of a loved one, breakup with a wife or girlfriend, loss of a job, these are the three most common things you'd look for. But with someone obviously this intelligent and sophisticated, we may be looking at something else.''

He reached for the basic shots of the Fox and Hazeltine scenes and held them up next to each other. ''There's no sign of break-in at either of the first two scenes. So, we have to conclude that he got to know these women well enough to get them to trust him, which also speaks to a sophisticated, intelligent, *manipulative* individual. Based on the refinement of the cutting and the use of complex drugs in both, I wouldn't rule out a doctor, even as rare as that is. Neville Ramsey went to medical school, you know,'' he said offhandedly.

Jim and I glanced at each other.

''Now, let's go on to yesterday's crime. We don't have the lab reports or autopsy protocols or all the evidence in yet, so we're going to have to be more speculative, but there are several conclusions we can still reach. What's the primary departure?''

''He did a man instead of a woman,'' I said.

"But with essentially the same signature aspect—this highly ritualized, almost religious-type scene. This is further evidence, I think, that we're not dealing with a sexually inadequate individual, or one who can only be satisfied in this way."

"So are you saying he's bisexual?"

"I see no evidence of that. Again, he's using the victim for his own purposes. The victim is an actor, a component of the artist's work."

"Art is the transcendence of death," Neville Ramsey had written.

"So why does he abruptly turn to a man this time?" Douglas asked rhetorically.

"To jerk us around?" I said.

He nodded. "That's what I think." He looked to Jim for corroboration. "And he knows the conventional wisdom that serials always do the same kind of victim, which is true and not true, depending on your perspective. He's trying to show you he's smarter than you are. He's rubbing your nose in it, saying to you, 'I already told you *when* I was going to strike again, and you still couldn't catch me!' "

He was right. The killer had practically announced when the next murder was going to happen, and he'd still slipped out of our grasp. And because of that, Jerry was dead.

"The next thing he might do is break the periodicity just as he moved to a man—start killing on another day to show you he isn't a creature of habit. He might diverge from the religious themes, though if he did, I'd expect him to substitute something equally imaginative."

That was a grim thought. The few things we had counted on were quickly disappearing.

John casually smoothed back his perfect hair. "Another thing I feel very, very confident about is that this individual will attempt to inject himself into the investigation."

"You mean, coming forward as a witness?"

"Possibly. Or it could be something more basic than that. He's already communicating with you. 'Catch me if you can.' Playing this cat-and-mouse game both enhances his sense of control and superiority over the police and at the same time lets him find out what's happening in the investigation. In the Atlanta child murders in the early 1980s, we'd predicted a police buff who would try to somehow involve himself with them on an official basis. And then we saw Wayne Williams actually show up at the crime scenes and offer to take photographs for the police. It all fit together. Arthur Shawcross, who killed the prostitutes in Rochester, New York, used to hang around the doughnut shop where the cops hung out, getting friendly with them and getting them to talk about the case. We've come to see this over and over again.''

Jim rested his head against the back of the couch. I could tell he wasn't surprised by anything John had said.

"So you think we're going to come in direct contact with him?" I asked, trying to summarize and put things in perspective for myself.

"I wouldn't be surprised if you already had," John responded frankly.

———————

Jim and I walked down the narrow cinder-block corridor, past the balky freight elevator, and up the stairs. "There's something you're not telling me," he said.

That was when I told him about the open window and the missing pendant and panties. "I didn't mention it with John because I didn't want to bring in anything extraneous," I explained. "And there's a good chance it's all just coincidence anyway."

"And there's a good chance it isn't," Jim said gravely. "Two of the most likely souvenirs for sexual psychopaths to take are articles of jewelry or underwear. You're missing both. Have you reported this?"

I shook my head in the negative. "I don't want to seem paranoid. Especially a paranoid female. And if Captain Owen thinks I'm in danger, he might pull me from the case."

"Sandy, I can't interfere in local police matters, but both officially and as your friend, I strongly suggest you tell them."

"Please, Jim," I said, "let me handle this my own way."

He shook his head in frustration. I seem to get that reaction a lot.

We reached the top of the stairs. He asked, "You have anything urgent right now?"

It was too late to worry about getting back to the office, and I was too wrung out to face it, anyway. I shook my head.

Jim ducked across the corridor into the gun vault and came back a few moments later with a box of Winchester 147-grain controlled expansion 9-mm Luger rounds. "Maybe it isn't anything," he said. "But just in case, let's make sure you've still got your edge."

He led me into the gun cleaning room, then over to the gray steel door at the end. He pressed buttons in sequence to open the cipher lock.

I loaded a full clip while he set up the cardboard target at the standard twenty-one feet. I put on the goggles and ear protectors, braced myself at the firing line, and emptied the clip. I loaded another and moved the target back to twenty-nine feet. Then I moved it back to the fifty-foot mark with the range lights off and nothing but the pulsating strobe to aim by. Every time I squeezed the trigger a beautiful yellow flame flared from the gun barrel, illuminating the darkness. I got the shots off in rapid succession, ejected shells spitting over my shoulder, arms almost locked, the Glock's gentle recoil becoming part of my body's own rhythm. I was feeling my juices flowing. For the first time in several days, I felt really good.

I removed my earmuffs and goggles and held the empty gun at rest. Jim pressed the button to bring the target back toward us. He flipped on the back lights so we could see what I'd done. Fifteen rounds—fifteen kills, all in a tight pattern around the heart.

"No one's gonna mess with you, kid," he commented.

"Thanks," I said, finally letting my finger relax. "I needed that."

19

I slept like a corpse that night and don't remember dreaming. I didn't wake up till the alarm went off at six. Bleary-eyed, I pulled back the light cotton blanket, squinted down at myself, and noticed my panties were stained red. So was the sheet underneath me. My period had started, at least a week early. It could have been all the tension and stress, or it could just have been, as I've always suspected, that God and Mother Nature have a strong sense of the symbolic and the ironic.

I went to the closet and pulled out one of my black dresses. Jerry Ashburn's funeral was this afternoon.

I showered, dried off, and put on my underwear. I opened a new pair of panty hose and crumpled the wrapper into the trash can.

That was when I saw it, just barely sticking out above ripped-up junk mail, makeup-stained wads of tissues, and empty toilet paper rolls. I bent down and fished it out of the trash.

When I realized what it was, a chill ran down my spine.

I tried to hold it by the edge. It was a snapshot of my brother, Tim, smiling and suntanned and handsome in his swim trunks, on Santa Monica Beach with the Pacific behind him. Or rather, it was half a snapshot, torn neatly down the middle. And the missing half was of me, standing next to him in a brief bikini, doing my best to look like the California surfing girl I once was. The picture had been taken the last time I'd been back home and had been stuck in the corner of my mirror. I guess I'd become so used to it there that I hadn't even noticed it was gone.

Someone out there has my pendant, my underwear, and a nearly naked picture of me. He knows where I live and has let himself into my apartment. He's most likely the same one who wrote the letters, which means he's probably the killer, which means . . .

———————

I managed to get to the office on time, fighting cramps and irritability and free-floating anxiety. After roll call and a critical visit to the coffee machine, Vince and I went back to our desks to get caught up with each other and plan the day. After some thought, I'd decided not to bring in the snapshot for dusting. I knew there wouldn't be anything on it, and I didn't want to tell Vince. If I did, he'd have Captain Owen yank me for sure. And the crime scene team would come to my place and discover nothing but the fact that I'm a lousy housekeeper.

"Lab report came in late yesterday on that flashlight you found," he reported, pumping powdered whitener into his cup.

"Anything?" I didn't take sugar this morning. I needed the uncut caffeine jolt.

"A couple of good latents."

"Well, that's a first." So far, our guy had made no obvious mistakes.

"But no match so far with anything in the files."

"Not surprising. Even if it did belong to our guy, the profile says he probably wouldn't have any priors. What else?"

"Manufactured by a company in St. Louis called Steinberg Novelties. They also make pens, lighters, that kind of thing. This penlight is in current production, and the last order from Shipley Pharmaceuticals was in August for ten thousand. I called Shipley in Minnesota. They give it out through their sales reps—they call them detail men—at medical and drug conventions, conferences, like that."

"Is it worth talking to the detail men in Washington?"

"We could, but there isn't a hospital or doctor's office that hasn't been visited on a regular basis. A lot of doctors or hospital people give them to patients, especially kids. Other people just take them. You know, like 'Property of U.S. Government' ballpoint pens."

"Anything on Jerry's actions or whereabouts?" I asked.

Vince flipped open his notebook, squinted, then pulled it nine or so inches farther back. "I hate this," he muttered.

"There's no shame in getting reading glasses, you know. They don't automatically sign you up for Leisure World."

"I don't need them. I couldn't get used to them, anyway."

"It's no big deal. We'll go at lunch tomorrow, Papa."

"I'm not your father," he said sternly. I thought about getting a signed statement. "Ashburn was at the paper all day, apparently working on the story. Unlike lawyers, reporters don't keep phone logs, and there's no electronic tracking of incomings, so there's no way of knowing if the guy contacted him. The people in the newsroom think he left for the night around six-thirty or seven. He has a desk blotter calendar, one of those kind that shows a month at a time. At the bottom of the Tuesday block there's a single word notation that stays 'Interview.' "

"What about notes?"

"They checked through his files on the computer and in his desk drawer. Since this was a capital case and since the victim was, in fact, the reporter working the story, their lawyer decided they could waive their shield law protection and let us see what he had. I went over there yesterday afternoon."

"And?"

"And a lot of detail, but nothing we don't know about. He had quite a bit of stuff on Neville Ramsey and Nicholas Ramsey, but it all looked like background."

"Does my name come up anywhere?"

He shook his head.

"Thank God for small favors."

I wrapped both hands around my coffee mug and held it in my lap. I found the heat comforting. "He must have gotten a call, a promise of a new break on the story. Probably told him to meet that night...."

Vince agreed. He reached for the autopsy protocols. The pink case file was considerably thicker than when I had seen it yesterday morning.

"So what about the terminal event?"

"No big surprises. Shock and internal bleeding."

"That doesn't say how the killer immobilized him. He couldn't pull the same stuff on Jerry he did on the women. Drugs again?"

"Nothing in the tox studies. Jack Beauregard said he thought it was this wound right here that did it." He passed me the whole body autopsy shot, then rooted through the stack for the best details. I put down my coffee mug at the far end of the desk where I was less likely to spill or knock it over. I still hold the squad record for most crime scene photos ruined.

I took the pictures and forced myself to look carefully. The problem with someone you know is you can't make that critical intellectual transformation from human being to evidence. Jerry Ashburn wasn't going to leave me alone until I'd learned more than he had.

Amid all the arrow puncture wounds was a vertical incision just above the navel, no more than an inch and a half in length, slightly ragged at each end, with oozing blood dried on the skin below. Vince pointed with his pen. "What's strange about this one, at least according to Jack, is that there doesn't seem to be any angle associated with the thrust. To make that neat an incision, the blade would have had to go straight in and out."

"Would have had to take him by surprise."

"Our guess is this is what immobilized him, at least to the point where the attacker could get control. From the look of the contusions, Jack says the ligatures were applied before the arrows were shot but after this belly wound was inflicted." He handed me an even closer detail shot.

I studied it for several moments, trying to process what Vince had said about the angle of entry. "What kind of weapon would make a wound like that?"

"Could be a lot of things. A thick kitchen knife, like a boning knife, maybe. But you'd expect a more angled incision as the wider part of the blade sinks into the flesh. If you ask me, I'd say some longer kind of blade, like a sword."

"A sword?" I said. "Have we ever had a homicide by sword?"

"Not exactly the weapon of choice for your run-of-the-mill drug pusher or street lowlife."

"It wasn't a scalpel or anything like that?"

"No. Definitely not a scalpel. That would have been an even cleaner incision: narrower, more like a slit. Or, if it was as wide as this, there would have been more trauma at the wound site, because it would have meant the blade was worked around once it penetrated the flesh."

"And they haven't found it?"

Vince shook his head. "We've searched the area, but woods are tough, and I wouldn't have expected him to ditch it, anyway."

"Any witnesses turn up, please God?"

"Just the guy who found the body. No one else happened to be lurking in the park in the dark. At least, no one who wants to admit it." He jogged the photographs together and slipped them back into the case folder. "So what did the folks at Quantico have to say?"

"That you don't get many serial killers who are doctors," I replied, "but that anything's possible."

———————

They didn't waste any time setting up Jerry's funeral. I was told his family was anxious to have it over with and get him back to New Jersey as soon as the medical examiner released the body. I could be cynical and say the paper also wanted it while it was still part of a breaking story, but today wasn't the time to harbor such misanthropic thoughts.

It was held at one of the big funeral homes up Wisconsin Avenue, but even that wasn't large enough. People were standing in the aisles, fighting for space with local TV crews. Their bosses were all there as official mourners, showing the flag for the city's media establishment. All the brass from the *Post* was there, and so were Chief Price and the mayor, both of them grim, and most of the city council. I felt so sorry for Jerry's parents, brother, and sister. They looked totally dazed and shell-shocked by all the hoopla. Who wouldn't be?

Lest I got too outraged or self-righteous, I had to remind myself that we had a video crew and a still shooter there ourselves, disguised with press credentials. After the ceremony, we'd try to identify and check out every face. In a perfect world, bereaved people should have a right to be left to their own private grief at times like this. But the fact that Jerry was lying in a fancy box at the front of the chapel rather than sitting at his desk in the newsroom attacking his keyboard attested to the fact that this was far from a perfect world.

It was a sad afternoon; I can't deny that. I sat over to the side, clutching Vince's shoulder and weeping softly as several of Jerry's colleagues got up in succession to talk about what a terrific reporter he was and how much he loved his work. They told stories and related funny incidents that made people laugh in spite of themselves. I kept wondering if my letter writer/panty thief was here getting his jollies, maybe staring at me this very moment. I was still having cramps.

One of the speakers decried the sickness rampant in our society, and one of Jerry's colleagues talked about the nobility of journalism and how the press is the front-line insurer of the democratic way of life and all we hold sacred. The minister finished up, rounding out the service with a text from the Bible: "Ye shall know the truth. And the truth shall make you free."

It sure made Jerry free all right.

We were filing out of the auditorium, my eyes still wet, when I felt a hand on my sleeve. I turned around. It was Ted.

"What are you doing here?" I said.

"I read about it in the paper and figured you'd be here," he said in that sheepish way of his.

"Oh, so you're stalking me, then?" For one wild moment it occurred to me that Ted could be the one who had broken in and was playing all these mind games with me. But, nah, I thought, that's not his style. And he'd be too afraid of getting caught.

He sighed. "More of your police paranoia?" I always felt as if he were analyzing me. "You won't return my calls, you won't agree to see me. What am I supposed to do?"

"You're supposed to leave me alone," I said under my breath.

"I just want to talk to you."

"I don't want to talk to you."

"Until you need or want something else from me. That's the way it's always been, hasn't it?" Ted had always had a gift for stinging me in all the most vulnerable places. It was one of his special talents.

"Let's get the car," I said to Vince. Ted finally got the message.

As we got outside, people were milling around on the sidewalk. I was trying to decide whether it was worth maneuvering to avoid Chief Price. I concluded it wasn't, since he probably wouldn't know who I was anyway.

We were just about to leave when I caught a glimpse of another familiar face through a momentary parting of bobbing heads. At least I thought I did. And then he was gone.

"You think you see Ramsey everywhere," Vince lectured as we walked back to the car. "Don't you think you're reading a little too much into this profiling business?"

"I'm telling you, Vince, it was him," I insisted.

"I didn't see him."

"Yeah, well, you need glasses, remember?" He gave me a withering look.

"Do you believe the balls of that guy!" I said.

"Who are we talking about now—Ted or Ramsey?"

"Ramsey, of course."

"Oh. It's hard to keep all the balls in your life straight."

"And what's that supposed to mean?"

"Nothing."

"No, I want to know."

"Forget it," Vince said. He opened the driver's door and flicked the central unlock button. I crossed my arms sullenly, stared straight ahead, and didn't say a word. The past few days and the past few moments had left me a combination of sad, hurt, angry, and frustrated. And that was before throwing in my period, never exactly a source of joy or comfort in its own right.

Since, as usual, neither of us was willing to blink first, we rode in silence all the way back.

As usual, I blinked first, in the elevator up to the office. I was never able to stay mad at Vince or bottle up what I was thinking very long. "He's jerking our chains," I announced. "It fits right in with the profile."

"Maybe so. But what are you going to do about it?"

"It's so blatant! He knew we would be there, and he knew we would see him. It's just like John Douglas said. He's playing this elaborate cat-and-mouse game with us. He's like a moth around a light bulb. He's so arrogant, he's almost defying us to burn him."

The elevator finally lumbered to a stop and opened on the third floor. Vince put his hand over the unpredictable door and held it for me. After my overture, I took this as a sign of truce. "I hope you're not planning to do anything stupid."

I didn't say anything.

"What do you have in mind?" he said, unconvinced.

I thought for a moment. "Play him off against himself. Throw it all right back in his face."

Vince looked at me warily as he punched the combination buttons that let us back into the squad room.

We were back at our desks with coffee when he said, "You'd better be more specific."

"I'm not asking you to go along with this."

"I had a feeling. All the more reason."

"It's probably better if I don't involve you."

"We're partners, Sandy. I'm not going to let you go off and do anything without telling me."

"You're not going to try to stop me?"

"Just tell me, for God's sake."

"Okay," I said, climbing out of the awful chair to sit on my desk. "You remember the John Wayne Gacy case?"

"The guy in Chicago, killed all the young boys and buried them in his house."

"That's the one."

"A building contractor. Active in politics, Jaycees, that sort of thing."

"Right. And when he wasn't raping and torturing young boys to death, he was donating his time to local hospitals entertaining terminally ill children."

Vince just shook his head. It was a sign of his unwavering decency that after all he had seen over the years, he could still be moved by the perversity of true evil. "A sick world it has become, kid."

"The police had informants who tied Gacy tangentially to some of the missing boys. They'd questioned him but didn't have anything strong enough to charge him, and Gacy knew it. He was so arrogant, he thought he was untouchable. Like he could walk on water."

"I know there's a point to this story," Vince said testily.

"The point is, the police didn't have enough to arrest him, they didn't have enough for a search warrant, but they knew he was involved. So they just started leaning on him—tailing him around the clock, not even trying to hide—letting him know he couldn't make a move without them watching. At first it was a game: 'I'll show these dumb cops!' Then little by little, he began picking up the bait and they started to get to him. They rattled him so much, they threw him so far off balance, eventually he led them right into his own house and twenty-nine bodies."

"And you think the captain's going to agree to have teams of cops hound Nicholas Ramsey until he finally loses it?"

"No, *I'll* hound Nicholas Ramsey until he finally loses it."

"San-dee . . ." His pitch went up ominously as he dragged out the second syllable of my name.

"The captain's desperate for an arrest," I said. "We all are. And yet he's totally spooked because Nick is influential and could make trouble."

"Nick?"

"Come on, Vince, listen to what I'm saying."

"I am listening to what you're saying. Which is, you don't have the elements, so you're going to harass him until he caves in and confesses. Look, the evidence you have on this guy is wildly speculative and circumstantial.''

"Which is why we have to do something to force his hand. If Volmer and fucking LaRocca had been more on the ball a couple of nights ago, maybe we would have had him and poor Jerry would still be alive. Do we have to wait for someone else to die?''

"You think he's going to stand still for this? You think he's not going to come complain to the captain and get your ass fried?''

"I'm hoping he'll think that for me to go out on a limb like this, I must have the goods on him.''

"I hope he doesn't know that you'll go out on a limb just because you like climbing trees. What if you're wrong?''

"I'm willing to take the chance," I said. "Someone's got to.''

20

I N our work or in our lives, we're all of us searching for someone or something.

Sometime after my father died, my mother bought my brother, Tim, and me a dog. Fluffy was her name. A golden retriever. It had to be a name like that after what we'd been going through. Fluffy and I grew up together and fulfilled deep needs for love and companionship in each other. Lying in bed late at night, or walking alone in the woods on a Saturday afternoon, I would tell her things I didn't feel comfortable telling anyone else. Fluffy would cock her head to one side as if she were trying to understand exactly what I was saying, and the pure, uncritical love that would pour out of that dog was enough to make my heart melt.

When I left home to go off to college, Fluffy, lonesome and morose in my absence, left home, too, and set off to find me. We never saw her again. To this day, almost fifteen years later, it still haunts me that Fluffy must have died, alone and far away, thinking I had forsaken her.

At the same time, that's what I feel I'm doing a lot of the time—searching blindly for something I desperately hope I'll find, and that if I do, it will complete things for me and bring some order back to the universe. This time it was a relentless murderer. And I had to nail him.

In pursuit of that goal, I became Nicholas Ramsey's shadow—at least to the extent that time, resources, and the logistical limits of only being one person would allow. I knew I only had a few days, because soon Captain Owen would start missing me. I couldn't take a scout car, because Vince would need the one assigned to us and stealing another that actually ran in our budget-strapped department was science fiction.

So I went on foot, by public transportation, or in the Green Hornet. And if I screwed up, or Nicholas actually had the chops to report me, I knew my butt was in the soup.

Unlike a real tail or stakeout, a lot of it was hit or miss. I decided to hit him first where he lived. And that's where I was, bright Saturday morning.

Nicholas Ramsey's house was on O Street, between 20th and 21st. This particular block has kind of a Gothic feel to it, lined with gnarled, twisted trees like the ones that grabbed the apple back from Dorothy in *The Wizard of Oz*. The large, gloomy, blood-red town houses that have been there more than a hundred years have peaked roofs that wouldn't look out of place sprouting gargoyles. The gallery where Sarah Hazeltine worked was around the corner. The alley where her brain had been found was practically behind the house.

I sat in the MG, parked across the street just after dawn. I watched as the wooden garage door (made to look like an old stable door) opened automatically and the charcoal-gray Mercedes roadster backed out. It straightened out and pulled forward, and when it passed me, I saw his eyes glance slightly in my direction. Whether he actually registered it as me I can't be sure, but at least the message had been planted in his brain.

———————

Monday afternoon I was in lecture hall 3C at the Georgetown University School of Medicine at two forty-five in the afternoon. Nicholas Ramsey seemed to have the same magnetic power there that he did in the operating room. As he walked into the hall, all the med students—men and women—sat up, charged on their seats. It was like the spark when a brilliant and charismatic actor makes his first entrance on stage. Was it the same power Neville Ramsey had used in luring so many talented, rational people to grisly deaths?

As he stepped up to the lectern, Nicholas noticed me sitting in the back. I thought I saw him wink at me. Then he started his performance, and we were all hooked. He gave his audience style and drama and wit. He moved decisively about the platform, gesturing grandly, demonstrating surgical techniques in the air, filling the space around him with an imaginary patient, an imaginary tray of instruments, an entire imaginary surgical team.

"But this raises an interesting question," he said, his finger in the air for emphasis. "With every other organ we operate on, we can see exactly what it is that organ does. The heart pumps blood, the liver purifies it, the stomach digests food. But we can't actually *see* what the brain does. We know it thinks, but we don't know exactly how or where it thinks. So when we operate on a brain, how do we deal with the fact that we're operating on the mind, too?"

Nicholas paused for dramatic effect. "We know a certain amount about which types of injuries and lesions cause which sorts of mental and emotional impairments. But most things can't be reduced to formulas, which is why the brain remains the last great black box of science."

He came around to the side of the lectern and leaned casually against it. "For example, where does memory reside? It has to be somewhere in the neural tissue, but where? If we transplant fetal substantia nigra cells into the brain of a Parkinson's patient, he doesn't end up with any new memory that wasn't his. But is that because memory doesn't reside in the substantia nigra, or is it because that fetus, with no experience of life, has no memory implant? We might as well ask where the soul resides. That's a legitimate question, too. But at this stage of our understanding, we simply don't know."

He went back to the lectern and pulled out a remote control on a cord, activating a large rear projection screen behind him. The screen brightened with the video image of long, thin worms swimming in a tank. What's this got to do with the brain? I wondered. As far as I knew, these worms didn't even have brains.

"In this experiment, flatworms were trained to respond to a certain type of light. They were then ground up and fed to other flatworms that hadn't been trained. Afterward the new flatworms responded to the light as if they'd been trained themselves, which has led some neuroanatomists to speculate that memory can be transferred in tissue. There've also been experiments transplanting embryonic chicken brain tissue into embryonic duck brains. When the ducks hatch, they instinctively peck like chickens. There are even more intriguing possibilities."

The scene shifted to a shot of an animal lab. The camera took in an overhead view of a maze. A lab person stood behind it. Then Nicholas Ramsey himself came into the frame, holding a white rat.

"Based on the theories of the British researcher Rupert Sheldrake, we set up this experiment."

On the screen, Nicholas put the rat down at the beginning of the maze. It poked its way through the corridors, hitting dead end after dead end until it finally just gave up.

There was a break in the video, and then the same scene came back on. Only it had to be another time, because there was a different lab person and Nicholas was in different clothing. Next to the maze this time was a cage holding four rats.

"The lab rats you see in the cage were taught in London to run this exact maze. They were then brought to Washington and put in proximity with our untrained rats."

Nicholas placed the rat down at the beginning of the maze. It took off immediately, making all the right decisions.

"As you can see, the untrained rat is now able to maneuver the maze much faster and more efficiently, and Sheldrake theorized it was strictly from being in immediate proximity with the trained rats. Why does this happen? We're not sure, but it's a scientific fact that it does."

The scene shifted to another part of the lab. Now Nicholas was apparently dissecting the rat's brain—a miniature replay of what I'd watched Jack Beauregard do so many times before.

"When we dissect and examine the rat's brain, we can't distinguish any differences on a physical level. Yet we know from our empirical observation that they must be there somewhere."

It was strange. I actually felt sad about the rat coming to such an ignominious end after triumphantly conquering the maze. I wondered if Nicholas had any such feelings. I doubted it.

"We also know that the brain generates electromagnetic waves— that's what the electroencephalograph measures. Sheldrake speculates that what we're seeing here is a phenomenon directly from classical physics—what he calls 'morphic resonance.' In other words, the untrained rat somehow morphically resonated with the trained rats. Or at least with whatever piece of their brains understood how to run the maze."

He had us all in the palm in his hand. Like a great actor, he knew exactly how to play an audience.

He switched off the video projector. "You know," he said as if he'd just thought of it, "this reminds me of the story of the Zen master meeting with his disciples. One of them said, 'Master, if two people who have both attained perfect enlightenment play chess together, who will win?'

"The master thought a moment, then replied, 'The better chess player.' "

When the laughter and chortling had died down, he called for questions. "Ask me anything," he challenged, sending another wink in my direction, "it helps keep me sharp."

One student raised his hand and said cockily, "You told us you would operate on any patient who came to you, even if other surgeons had said they wouldn't. What I want to know is, what's the point of operating on someone who's going to die anyway, to use up valuable medical resources and string a patient along, rather than just telling them the score and letting them come to terms with it?" There was a kind of smugness in this kid's eyes, the intellectual arrogance of someone who's always had everything going for him in his young and gifted life.

But Nicholas's eyes grew steely. Suddenly there was something very frightening there, what Patricia Ramsey had talked about but couldn't put her finger on. Before our eyes, he'd become a different person. He straightened up, like an alley cat who's been challenged in a fight. "What's your name?"

"Philip Buchanan," the kid said.

"Stand up, Mr. Buchanan." The kid stood, not knowing what to make of the order.

"Now get out of here."

"What?"

"You heard me, get out of here. Take your books, pack up, and get the hell out. And as soon as you do, I suggest you quickly make plans for another career. Because not only am I going to see that you're thrown out of this medical school, I'm going to do my best to make sure you never set foot in another medical school anywhere in the free world. Anyone who would ask that question clearly has no business being a doctor."

There was stunned silence in the room. You could have heard the proverbial pin drop. In fact, I think I could hear Mr. Buchanan's heart pounding in his chest. Smug as he had been, I felt terrible for the kid.

Buchanan slowly trudged up the steps to the back of the room. He seemed to be carrying the entire weight of the world on his shoulders. In only a few seconds, he had had his world destroyed. Nicholas had asked for questions. I couldn't believe he could be so cruel. Or maybe I could.

Just as he had his hand on the doorknob, Nicholas called out, "Okay, Mr. Buchanan. That's enough. Go back to your seat and sit down."

"But ... I ..." was all the kid could sputter.

"I have no intention of ruining your career. You asked an intelligent, important question, and I salute you for it. I just wanted you, all of us, to feel what it's like to have your hope taken away. All right, ladies and gentlemen. That's it for today."

The next morning I was sitting in the viewing gallery of operating room four at Halsted. Nicholas explained over the loudspeaker that he was resecting an acoustic neurinoma that was impinging on the seventh facial nerve of a fifty-eight-year-old man. All you could see of the patient was a small reddish hole surrounded by towels and gauze.

Things seemed to be going pretty smoothly as far as I could tell. Nicholas was in a relaxed, easygoing mood, joking with the other people around the table between his explanatory updates. There was a natural rhythm about the way he moved and the way the rest of the team moved in reaction to him. For me, there was that same drama, that same thrill, that same sense of power and sensuality, as the first time I'd sat here and watched him cut into a human skull.

Then he happened to look up into the gallery. Our eyes met briefly. Then they locked. I could see him smiling at me behind the mask. But something was different.

"Is something wrong?" the scrub nurse asked him.

"Retractor," he said stiffly.

She waited for him to turn up his hand to receive it, and when he didn't, she hesitated.

"If I wanted it tomorrow, I would have waited until tomorrow to ask for it!" he barked. She quickly thrust the instrument straight out in front of her. He snatched it away.

For the rest of the procedure, he spoke only to request instruments or give commands. His eyes were tight and cold above his mask, and the easy grace was gone. As soon as he had cut the tumor completely free, he held it up on forceps, then threw them down into the waiting steel tray. He turned to the resident assisting him. "Finish up." Then he walked abruptly out of the operating room.

———————

Maybe things were finally starting to come together or, rather, fall apart, I guess you'd say. The model I had in mind was a rubber band stretched too tight. Most assertive, control-oriented people are like rubber bands. If you flick the rubber band with your finger, it'll vibrate a little, then go back to the way it was. But if you keep stretching it tighter and tighter, after a certain point, you flick it again and it's going to react violently. And if you're sensitive to the outward manifestations, you can start to guess when and where the behavior is going to change.

I spent as little time as I could at the office, steering myself out of situations where Captain Owen might question me too closely about exactly what I was doing.

I went over to the Touch of Class, timing my visit for the end of the lunchtime show. This time, the behemoth in the front seemed to recognize me, as a dog might recognize a human who'd beaten him on their last encounter. He looked up at me and sullenly stepped aside.

I waited in the dressing area until the girls came off. Bonnie came over to her dressing table, heavily rouged and stark naked except for the glittery G-string. She looked surprised to see me, and not pleasantly so.

I handed her her robe. "Hi, Bonnie, you remember me?" She nodded timidly. "Can I ask you a few questions?"

"I . . . I guess so." She wrapped the robe around herself and sat at the dressing table.

"I'd like to show you some pictures."

From inside my bag I took out a manila envelope containing three black-and-white glossies of Nicholas. I'd gotten them from the *Post,* not as a police officer, but "disguised" as an interested member of the public. I didn't want to tip my hand. One of the pictures was a straight-forward head-and-shoulders publicity shot issued by the hospital. The other two were from neurosurgery conferences where he had demonstrated the Ramsey neural modulator.

I laid them on the dressing table in front of Bonnie. She studied them dutifully.

"Do you recognize this man?"

She considered her answer carefully. "I think so."

"Have you seen him here?"

"I think so." I read the fear in her eyes.

"Are you sure?"

She indicated the woman at the next table, who had been totally disinterested in our conversation. In a place like that, you learn to mind your own business. "Can I show her?"

"Sure, go ahead."

"Veronique . . . we ever seen this guy here before?"

Veronique, a statuesque black woman with lustrous hair down to her waist, took the photos. "Yeah, we seen this guy."

"Remember when?" I asked.

"Not exactly. Two, three weeks ago, maybe."

"Just the once?"

"No. Been here a couple of times, seems to me. Didn't seem like most of the other customers. Isn't that right, Bonnie?"

"Lunchtime is what I thought."

"Lunchtime, yeah. But once at night, too, I think."

"Was it before or after Julie Fox was killed?"

"Right around that time, I think. Little before, little after, I'm not sure," said Veronique.

"Yeah, sometime around then," said Bonnie.

"But you're both pretty sure it was this guy?" They both nodded. "He ever say anything to anyone—come on to you, try to pick you up?"

"Not me." Veronique shrugged.

"Me neither."

"Do you remember anything he said?"

"No, he was just . . . there," said Bonnie. "That's all."

"Now think back. Do you ever remember seeing him with Julie? Talking to her, anything like that?"

She shook her head. "No. Like I told you before, Julie pretty much kept to herself. You see anything, Ronnie?" Cute, I thought, Bonnie and Ronnie.

Veronique was nodding her head emphatically. "No, you're right about Julie. That girl kept to her own self. That's what you're doing, looking for who killed her?"

"That's right."

"Well, good luck, honey. That was one girl who didn't deserve to die."

None of us do or we all do, depending on your perspective. I stood up to leave.

"Thanks," I said. "I may call you again if anything comes up."

"Sure," Bonnie said meekly.

————————

When I got home there was another letter waiting for me.

Dearest Sandy,
   I hope you were impressed by my recent work. Please don't feel that since I chose Mr. Ashburn as my collaborator that I am slighting your fair sex. Nothing could be further from my mind. I just think it is better to keep us all on our toes. After all, foolish consistency is the hobgoblin of little minds.

He's breaking even farther out of the mold, I thought to myself. Just as John Douglas said he might.
   Then my eyes traveled down to the message he'd saved for the end:

   Oh, and one other thing, Sandy. When company might be coming, you really should make your bed.

21

I now had two witnesses who could place him at the Touch of Class. Not conclusive, but we were finally starting to move in the right direction. The key now was to fill in as many of the gaps as I could.

All in all, I was learning a lot about the day-by-day structure of Nicholas Ramsey's life: when he left the house and when he returned. When he began surgery and when he would finish up and begin rounds and when he would go back upstairs to see follow-ups. And it was there that I thought I first started to see the tiny crack begin opening into a gaping fissure.

I was sitting in the Neurology Department's waiting area late in the afternoon. I wondered how many of the people sitting around me today—some of them old and trembling—would consider themselves walking testimonials to the miracles of modern medicine and the sheer determined brilliance of Nicholas Ramsey, M.D. It was still difficult for me to resolve the godlike healer they were patiently waiting to see with the inhuman acts I was investigating. But then, John Wayne Gacy had divided his leisure hours between bringing laughter and comfort to dying children in local hospitals and raping and murdering healthy ones in his house. You don't go long in this business without developing a strong sense of the ironic.

The door to one of the examining rooms opened and Nicholas emerged. He had a stethoscope around his neck and a reflex hammer sticking out of the breast pocket of his lab coat. He held the arm of a seventyish-looking man. "I'm very happy," he said, placing his hand on the man's shoulder in what could have been either a gesture of manly camaraderie or a discreet attempt to steady him. "You're coming along fine."

"Without you I'd have been a goner," the patient said with a hint of worship in his shaky voice.

Nicholas grinned, obviously pleased. "I think you're going to live to be a hundred now."

Then he saw me sitting there. "Ms. Mansfield," he said with an exaggerated display of courtesy, motioning me into the vacant examining room.

The reception desk nurse called over to him, "Dr. Ramsey, I believe Mrs. Beasley is next."

"I'll take her in a minute," he said tensely.

I stood up and walked ahead of him into the room. He closed the door behind him.

"I don't get what you're after," he said with exasperation.

"Just a little cooperation," I replied.

"Cooperation with what? What do you want from me? My brother is dead! I'm entitled to be left alone."

"Once we're involved, no one is entitled to anything other than to tell the truth and have the truth told about them. I'm sorry, but that's the way it is."

"You're barking up the wrong tree. I've given you everything I can."

"I don't think so."

"I'm sorry, that's the way it is. As I said to your captain, I'm sympathetic with the job you have to do, but you're flirting with a harassment suit, particularly when you start involving my associates and their friends."

In any interrogation, rhythm and timing are critical. "Have you ever been to a club called the Touch of Class?" I asked.

"No."

"Are you aware that your patient, Julie Fox, worked there?"

"Maybe. I'm not sure."

"You go to any other strip bars?"

"None of your goddamn business," he said affably.

"Gay bars?"

"Same answer."

"Did you know Sarah Hazeltine?"

"You asked me that already. The answer's still no."

"You bought a painting from her gallery."

"Maybe I met her then, I don't know. I can't place her."

"We think whoever killed her was copying your brother or maybe 'carrying on' for him."

"They were highly publicized cases. I'm sure they captured the imaginations of a lot of psychos."

"Not who'd know all the specific details."

"That's like asking someone if he's stopped beating his wife."

"We talked to your wife. She didn't say anything about beating. Should she have?" He was fighting to keep control, but I could see his back teeth clenching.

"Let's be plain," I said, taking a step away from the examining table. "Someone's doing horrible things to people, just like your brother did. He's highly intelligent and well read. He's got access to drugs only found in a hospital. He knows anatomy. He knows details of your brother's crimes never made public. And one of his victims was a patient of yours."

"So?"

"So you tell me, Doctor. Did you attend Jerry Ashburn's funeral?"

"The reporter from the *Post?*"

"That's right." He knew damn well who it was.

"Why do you want to know? In fact, why don't you tell me what you've found out so far, if you're so sure I can help?"

This individual will attempt to inject himself into the investigation, John Douglas had predicted. Playing this cat-and-mouse game both enhances his sense of control and superiority over the police and at the same time lets him find out what's happening in the investigation.

"You know I can't tell you anything," I said.

"Then I'm afraid we've gone about as far as we can. I've still got a lot of patients to see, so if you'll excuse me . . ."

He came closer to me and took my arm, just above the elbow. But instead of moving toward the door, it was as if we froze in place for a moment, just staring at each other. A strange and compelling feeling came over me, as if our bodies were joined together. He was holding me firmly, more firmly than he had to simply to guide me out. There was seduction in his eyes and in his touch, and I realized I didn't want him to let go of me.

Was it this electricity, this magnetism, that won Sarah Hazeltine over? Was this what Julie Fox felt as she let him undress her and tie her to a chair? Sometimes it's difficult to empathize with or put yourself into the mind of the victim. This time, unnervingly, I was having no trouble at all.

The next thing I knew, the door to the examining room was open and he still had me by the arm, leading me out. He let go, then closed the door behind me, leaving me alone in the center of the room.

"You can send in Mrs. Beasley," I said to the nurse as I walked past her. "The doctor will see her now."

As I rode the elevator down to the lobby, it came to me in a flash: What better people to approach about a doctor than his patients? That would really infringe on his private space, really get him where he lived.

No one was just going to hand over this information to me. Patient information is considered confidential, the same as an attorney-client relationship. But you do what you have to. Sometimes you have to push the edge of the envelope to get what you need.

I stopped in the middle of the lobby. I had an idea. It was close to the end of the day. Judging from how many patients were waiting to see Nicholas Ramsey and how quickly he dealt with each one, I estimated he'd be done in about forty minutes.

I picked up a stack of *People* magazines from the lobby, went down to the vending room, got myself a cup of coffee, sat down, read, and waited. It would keep me up-to-date until my next visit to the dentist or gynecologist.

After about an hour, I went back upstairs. As I'd suspected, the neurology office was now closed. I put my hand on the metal doorknob and turned. Also as I'd suspected. Most hospital doors aren't locked. I let myself in and closed the door behind me.

Nicholas Ramsey's large black appointment book was right on the secretary's desk where I'd noticed it, opened in preparation to tomorrow's date. I picked it up, walked over to the copier, turned it on, and waited for the machine to warm up.

It only took a minute. Hospitals seem to buy only the best—unlike, say, police departments. Starting at the beginning of the book, I placed it page by page on the copying glass. Once or twice I glanced at a particular page. It had just the information I was looking for—names, telephone numbers, nature of condition.

As soon as I'd finished, I replaced the book exactly as I'd found it on the desk. Now, where would last year's book be lurking? I thought maybe in one of the desk drawers. It took a little hide-and-seek, but I finally found it in the front of one of the drawers of the lateral file cabinet. This one took a little longer to copy, but I got an entire year's worth of information for my efforts.

When the task was complete, I turned off the copier, refilled the machine with paper from the stack of reams right next to it, stuffed my treasure into my bag, and left. For a visit to the doctor, it hadn't been too unpleasant.

```
┌─────────────┐
│             │
│     22      │
│             │
└─────────────┘
```

THAT evening, away from the scrutinizing eyes of my colleagues, I spread out my newly acquired evidence across my bed. The television was on in the background. Channel four was doing a half-hour special about the murders. As pseudoauthorities droned on about what the average citizen could do to avoid being murdered and mutilated by a deranged monster, I sat cross-legged on the bed in my underwear and began sifting through the evidence of a year and a half in the professional life of Dr. Nicholas Paul Ramsey.

Just from the dry and dispassionate evidence at hand, the things I'd heard about him were true. He really would take on almost anything. Most surgeons, particularly brain surgeons, specialize in only one or two procedures. But Nicholas Ramsey had made daring and risky surgical assaults against all of the ills that plague this most vital and mysterious entity in the universe: aneurysms, epilepsy, neuromas, clots. Meningioma, laminectomy, subdural and epidural hematomas. All manner of gunshot wounds. Many times in autopsy have I witnessed the devastating effects of a high-caliber projectile as it rips through the delicate tissue of the human brain.

Then there was the depressing inventory of the malignancies known to grow within the skull, arcane scientific terms that sounded to my untrained brain like death sentences: astrocytoma, oligodendroglioma, medulla blastoma, glioblastoma multiforme.

There were notations next to the names of patients who had not survived. A few had evidently expired right on the operating table or shortly thereafter. More had died in the weeks or months following surgery. I began to realize, only now, that a neurosurgeon is very much like the hostage negotiator for a SWAT team. The mere fact he's given the case often indicates it's pretty near hopeless.

I had to keep reminding myself that each date next to a name, indicating the date of surgery, represented a kind of expedition or journey or discovery, a journey measured in millimeters or inches, yet as profound and scary as any on earth: an exploration into the physical neighborhood of the mind. The ultimate violation and yet the ultimate act of faith. I could make out from these records that in the last several months he had begun implanting the Ramsey neural modulator in selected patients, evidently as a way of monitoring their progress.

And as I pored over the copies of his appointment book pages, I had to keep reminding myself why I'd appropriated them in the first place—looking for names of people to interview to tighten the noose around the great Nick Ramsey's throat. But I just couldn't square that guy with the medical miracle worker who'd given all these people their lives back.

John Wayne Gacy divided his leisure hours between bringing laughter and comfort to dying children in local hospitals and raping and murdering healthy ones in his house.

Wearily, I massaged my temples and rotated my head in a wide arc, trying to relax my tense neck muscles. Could I have been misinterpreting the mountain of circumstantial and behavioral evidence that pointed to the living successor to Neville Ramsey, the California Angel of Death? Or had my judgment been clouded by my own longing and hunger, by the sparks he struck in me in the operating gallery or on the racquetball court or in the examining room or every time I casually thought about him taking me in his arms and transporting me to places I had only dreamed of? At Quantico, they taught us that it wasn't always possible to avoid personal feelings about victims and suspects, so the important thing was to be aware of them and deal with them as rationally as possible.

I had to take a break, chill out, get my head clear.

The best method I know for that was sadly unavailable. At the moment, there were no men in my life qualified for consideration. Which led to the second method: eating something really good and preferably cold—chocolate-chip ice cream topping the list. Which, in turn, suggested the third and most radical method, which was to work those calories off beforehand and counter feelings of being stale by feelings of being healthy. Extreme? Yes, but sometimes extreme measures are called for.

I rooted around the closet and found my sneakers and a T-shirt. My shorts, it turned out, were still in the hamper from my match with Nicholas, along with a growing pile of underwear.

It's too easy to let your life go to hell. I really had to get more organized and disciplined, not only about laundry, but about personal maintenance in general. As I stepped into the shorts and wriggled them over my hips, it seemed the wriggle was just a tad snugger than I'd remembered, and I didn't even have washing shrinkage as an excuse. Have you noticed how many policewomen have fat asses? Almost as great a percentage as policemen with enormous guts. Sure, it comes from a life of too much fast food, too much stress, and not enough exercise and relaxation. But I swore I was never going to let that happen to me, at least as far as weight. I had to get on the stick before it became noticeable to my mother, or Jack Beauregard, or any of the other folks in my life who feel it's their right and duty to critique my physical and emotional status quo.

I pulled my hair into a ponytail, went outside, and tied my shoelace around my house key. I bounced over and touched my toes a couple of times, then began pounding the pavement.

Before long my hair was matted to my face and I'd worked up a good sweat. I got into the rhythm of the run. I concentrated on the incipient cellulite melting away like magic from my hips and thighs. Maybe tomorrow I'd go out and look for a new bathing suit and not be totally traumatized. But block after block and step after step, the same single word kept pounding through my brain like a mantra: Why? Why? Why? Why?

What makes a brilliant, financially secure, world-famous, and godlike surgeon need to become a vicious killer?

Maybe he wanted to become a little more godlike.

And maybe so did I, which was the reason I was so determined to get to the truth and see justice done. Ted always told me I needed to control things, to impose order on the disordered world around me. He thought it had something to do with losing my father at an impressionable age, that the part of me that remained a little girl would never grow up. Could be.

I ran all the way down Twenty-third Street. I did about thirty loops around the Lincoln Memorial. I remember back in college when I used to come here for romance and drama after dark. Later, when I was in the Sex Crimes Unit, I worked the rape and slashing of a girl here with her high school class from Indiana. The Park Service seemed particularly perturbed about how to get bloodstains off the porous stone without damaging the surface.

———————

On my way home, I stopped off at the Federal City Market and bought my weekly Instant Lotto ticket but didn't look at it until I got home. That was part of the ritual. Between the store and my front door was the time I fantasized about what I'd do with all the money.

Once again I hadn't won millions of dollars. I downed what was left of the orange juice in the fridge. I showered but didn't have the patience to dry my hair. So with the towel still wrapped around me, I went back to my bed and the second installment of Nicholas Ramsey's guest book.

I decided to make a list of the people I'd try to talk to, based on the cursory information I had. I started writing down the names: Eugene Smythe, Henrietta Longfellow, Clark D. Washington . . . Annika Tamering, Loretta B. Edmonds, Alfred Levin. Here was Samantha Holleran, the little girl I'd seen in the waiting room. Then Isaiah Williams, Ashby Collier, Christopher Taylor . . .

What?

I dropped my towel on the bed.

Ashby Collier. Very interesting. Okay, so Dr. Bob the Stud Fusillo dates the cute patients. That one's easily explainable, and who am I to judge? But Christopher Taylor? How'd he get in here? Could it be the same guy?

I glanced at the clock. I dressed as quickly as I could—jeans and a shirt. With any luck, I could make the play before the final curtain fell.

23

I drove the Lean Green Machine as fast as I could without getting nailed by my law enforcement brethren. That's happened to me a couple of times, and it's no fun, particularly if you happen to run into a uniform like Joe LaRocca used to be. And since my MG's steering wheel is on the right, it tends to attract a lot of attention anyway, not all of it desirable.

I got to the Arena Stage just as the final scene was ending and the ushers were preparing to open the auditorium doors. I stood in the back of the house and watched as Christopher Taylor and the rest of the cast took curtain calls. From the enthusiasm of the applause, it was evident the audience thought as highly of his entire performance as I had of the small snippet I'd seen. For once the *Post* had got one right.

I asked an usher where the stage door was. She directed me out the lobby and around the side of the building, where I found my way back to the dressing room area. I knocked on the black metal door bearing a hand-lettered card, MR. TAYLOR.

A muffled voice shouted, "Come in." I've always found actors basically friendly people, unlike those in so many other professions you come in contact with. Doctors, for example.

I opened the door and found Christopher in a sweatshirt and shorts, his head defined by a wig of straight black hair with a pronounced widow's peak and his chin covered by a matching black beard that came to a severe point. It was a strange combination, almost as if his open, ordinary face were in bondage beneath this malevolent facade.

He stared at me for several moments, as if trying to place me. I guess the jeans and sneakers instead of skirt and blouse had something to do with it. Then the light of recognition dawned. I wasn't sure what to expect. It's been my experience that people don't often go all warm and gooey when they register that they're talking to a cop.

"Detective Mansfield. What can I do for you? Would you like a drink?" I was about to say no until he opened a small refrigerator and produced two bottles of Saratoga water. I accepted one gratefully and took a seat on the small ratty sofa adorning one yellow cinder-block wall. It must have been a prop from a previous production.

He turned the chair at his dressing table so he could face me. "I'm sorry I blew up at you when you came over to see me. That's really not like me. I don't know what happened." Then a quick segue into, "So how are you coming with your murder case?" The tone was so ingenuous, he could as easily have been asking about my needlepoint.

"We're still working on it," I said.

"Is there anything I can do to help?" He sounded almost too cooperative. But then again, a lot of actors who wouldn't think of hamming it up on stage tend to overplay real life.

"Chris," I began, "I know this may be somewhat sensitive, but I understand you were a patient of Dr. Nicholas Ramsey."

He blinked in surprise and prominently cleared his throat, just the way he'd repeatedly done at our last meeting. "Did he tell you that?"

"No," I admitted.

"Then how did you find out?"

"Let's just say there are ways. But please believe me, no one's betrayed any confidences, and I can assure you I haven't, either. No one even knows I'm here."

I couldn't read much in his reaction. He had every right to throw me out and refuse to talk.

"Well, what can I tell you?" he asked.

"Just tell me about Dr. Ramsey."

"What do you want to know?"

"Whatever you like. Whatever you think is important."

He looked straight into my eyes with that intense gaze actors are so good at and said, "Dr. Ramsey saved my life."

"Saved your life?" I repeated. I mentally ran back through the operative notes next to the names, the aneurysms and hematomas and tumors. Those were what I would have called lifesaving.

"He saved my career. And my work is my life. I'm an epileptic. I guess you know that if you knew about me and Dr. Ramsey. I've known since I was a kid. You can imagine how the other kids treated me.''

"I know children can be very cruel," I said. Because they learn from adults.

"It may have had something to do with my becoming an actor. I was always pretending or trying to be something other than what I was. For a long time, it wasn't too bad. At least we could handle it with medication. But the last few years, it got worse and worse—to the point where every time I went on stage I was afraid . . . afraid that it was going to happen.''

"A seizure?"

He nodded. "And it did happen several times. Not a fall-down, slobbering, foam-at-the-mouth fit. Very few epileptics are like that. I'd just sort of go blank, cease to exist. Sometimes for a just a second or two, but it breaks your whole continuity with what's around you, and on stage, that's devastating.''

"It must have been terrifying."

"The brain can be a terrifying thing. I lived in terror of losing the one thing in life that makes me feel most alive. And of course, once the word got around, I was afraid no one would hire me. It's tough enough to get work as it is.''

"It would be like me having my badge and gun taken away," I offered. The mere thought depressed me.

"I went from one doctor to another. Internists, neurologists, even psychiatrists. They tried different medicines, therapy, relaxation techniques, you name it. None of it worked. I even asked if there was a surgical solution. They told me that was too extreme for what I had, too experimental. Look, I'm not a star, I'm not making a million dollars. But acting is my life. And I couldn't do it anymore.'' He cleared his throat again. "Then I met Dr. Ramsey. I'd given up hope. I'd even thought about killing myself; it's true. But right from the start I could tell there was something different about him.''

"Different?"

"He had feeling. He had empathy. I could see in his eyes that he knew what it was doing to me. He understands what artists and creative people go through.''

I'll bet he does.

"The first time I came to his office, I'll never forget it. I don't know if I actually told him about my suicidal thoughts, but I guess he could see how desperate I was. He smiled and said, 'I think we can do something about this.' I couldn't believe it. It was 'we,' as if he and I were in this together. He was like a savior. I wanted to get down on the floor and kiss his feet.''

"So what did he do?''

He looked at me as if I'd asked a very naive question. "He operated.''

I thought back to the man lying on the table with half his brain exposed while he talked casually with the doctor. And I thought guiltily about the warm excitement that gruesome scene had caused in me.

"But here's the most amazing part, Ms. Mansfield ... Sandy. He said, 'You've come to the right place. Are you free tomorrow?' I guess I kind of shrugged and said, 'Sure, I'm free every day,' I wasn't in a play at the time. So he said, 'Okay, then, we'll operate tomorrow.' Can you believe it?''

"Pretty amazing,'' I admitted.

"Truly amazing, I thought, that he would put everything else aside for me. But that's the kind of man he is. Didn't leave me time to fret or worry. He just did it. He knew I was suffering, and he relieved it— the very next day!''

"What sort of operation did he do?'' I asked.

"I can't give you all the details. An experimental procedure he'd been thinking about for a long time, he said. The key was to cut out the area causing the problem, but then bridge the gap so there was no interruption in the electrical conductivity. That's about all I can tell you technically. But after the operation it was different. Right away, I was different.''

"Different?'' I repeated. The second time he'd said that.

"My life. Whatever he did, it worked. I had *me* back again. This is my first part since the operation. It's why I'm here in Washington. It's like a rebirth.'' He cleared his throat and kind of shrugged. "What else can I tell you?''

Well, for a start, how to explain the coincidence of your being a patient of my prime suspect and having come to me yourself to confess.

"I'm sure you've read about Jerry Ashburn, the reporter who was killed.''

"Unbelievable,'' he said sorrowfully.

"Did you happen to know him?''

He shook his head negatively.

"Met him . . . even casually?"

He shook his head again. "I'm sure I would have remembered if I had. Struggling actors don't usually forget press people."

I hesitated a moment, sat back on the sofa, and crossed one leg over the other. "Are you still having any of the feelings . . . the ones that caused you to call us in the first place?"

Chris smiled innocently. "No. I don't know why I felt that way, but once you reassured me, I've felt a lot better."

"Not even after you read about Mr. Ashburn?"

"Should I? Is . . . is there something you're not telling me?"

"No," I replied casually, trying to let any subtext filter into my voice.

"Okay," he said. I was hoping he wasn't going to ask me exactly why I was here, then. But fortunately, it seemed his comfort level didn't demand he know any more than he absolutely had to, as though he had no desire to rekindle whatever dark thoughts had brought us together in the first place.

"You've been very helpful, Chris," I said. "I hope you won't mind if I call on you again if anything else comes up."

"Sure," he stated affably, smiling warmly through his villain's beard.

"Thanks." I got up to leave. "And I'm really looking forward to seeing you in the play."

"Just call me. I'll make sure you get good tickets." He turned back around to the dressing table and faced the mirror. He picked up a jar of cold cream, started peeling off his beard, and said, "Well, it's time to go back to being me for a while."

I tried to make sense of it all as I drove home. The breeze over the top of the shallow windshield felt good against my forehead, but even a sports car convertible at midnight is no match for Washington's muggy summer heat.

What I was working on was a coincidence: that Chris had thought he was somehow involved in the murders and then it turns out he's a patient of Nicholas Ramsey—whom *I* thought was involved in said murders.

Could Chris Taylor be the killer? Could he have become obsessed with Neville Ramsey, which was why he sought out Nicholas for his epilepsy? Could he have contacted us for the thrill—to see how close to the flame he could fly and then pretend not to know the specific details? After all, Taylor was an actor. And John Douglas said our guy might inject himself into the investigation.

On the other hand, what if Nick was somehow setting up Taylor? Maybe through drugs or hypnosis or something else, he'd gotten Chris to believe he'd actually done the crimes. Then, of course, there was still the possibility it was just a coincidence: that Chris, who read about the crimes in the paper, had neither anything to do with them nor any connection to Nicholas Ramsey, other than the obvious one.

Possible? Yes. But do we believe that?

I suddenly realized I had been moving automatically and unconsciously through traffic, which always makes me nervous when I finally come out of it and realize what I've been doing. This time, I found myself stopped at the light where 18th Street turns onto Virginia Avenue. I was drumming impatiently on the MG's cracked vinyl dash when I happened to glance down and notice the bumper sticker on the road hog in front of me: HONK IF YOU LOVE THE LORD!

What the hell, I thought. With all the immorality and godlessness around today . . . Your mother would be proud. I hit the middle of the black-and-chrome steering wheel with the side of my fist and gave forth with two short high-pitched toots.

The guy in front suddenly leaned out of his window practically to the waist, turned around, and shouted, "What do you want from me, bitch! Can't you see the light's red!"

And a happy summer solstice to you, too, sir! I smiled and waved. People never cease to amaze me. Thinking about it, I'm not sure I would have been that ballsy, what with all that's going on these days, if I weren't carrying a 9 mm. But that's true of a lot of things in life.

By the time I got back home and wrestled up the MG's stubborn and mischievous top, I was so keyed up I felt like going out for another run. But I knew if I did, I'd feel dead in the morning. Dead. Dying for a vacation. I'll kill you if you don't call. It's funny how casually and thoughtlessly we use those expressions, even people like me who see real killed and dead people almost every day. Ted would say it has something to do with trying to take the mystery and horror out of it, a desperate attempt to make ourselves more comfortable with our worst fears. But Ted was always reading something profound into everything.

Why did I think of Ted so often this time of night? Aren't we past that yet? I scolded myself. Then I glanced over at the queen-size bed, empty save for the appointment book copies. I guess you didn't have to look too deeply for that one.

I took off my clothes, did my bathroom stuff, gathered the sheets of paper into a stack, and got into bed. I flailed around for a while on my back, then on my belly, scrunching my cheek into the pillow, trying to get settled, trying to clear my mind. But knowing there was someone out there fantasizing about my body and playing with my underwear, someone who'd been in my apartment and could get back in, I found it very tough to relax.

24

‘ ‘ T O what do we owe the honor of this visit?’’ Captain Owen asked me with a flourish shortly after roll call. We happened to be getting coffee at the same time. Another couple of seconds and I could have avoided the confrontation completely. That's what you find when you work Homicide for a while: life and death come down to a matter of inches and seconds.

Anyway, he caught me. ‘‘So how's it going, Sandy? I'm assuming the fact that we've hardly seen you in the office and the fact that you've given me nothing in the way of progress reports means that you've just been too busy.’’

‘‘You could say that,’’ I said.

‘‘Which means you're really on to something. And that we should have the results very soon.’’ The words were okay, but the tone was definitely on the snarly side.

‘‘I'm following up a major development today,’’ I said. I hoped it was true.

The captain crossed his arms over his chest and rubbed his shoulders impatiently. ‘‘Good. Because here's what I'm doing today: I'm on my way upstairs to meet with the chief, who, shortly after that, will be hiking over to the District Building to see the mayor, who happens to have her regular press conference this afternoon and will most assuredly get asked one or more penetrating questions as to the progress of this investigation which is on everybody's mind with the killer presumably poised to strike again and . . . Well, you get the picture, I'm sure.’’

I did indeed. ‘‘I do think we're getting close,’’ I stated. I came really close to telling him about the break-in, then chickened out at the last second.

He gave me a comradely clap on the shoulder and marched off with his coffee mug back to his office. I went back to my desk and picked up the phone. I called the Halsted Neurology Department and asked to speak to Nicholas. They said he was in surgery, which came as no surprise. I asked for a call-back.

By lunchtime I hadn't heard anything, so I called again. He was still in surgery. I left another message and this time added that it was critical he get back to me.

I was getting itchy, so after yet another nourishing and emotionally satisfying lunch from the old Sabrett's cart, I went over to the hospital. I went directly to the main OR desk and asked for a schedule update on room number four. A brief glimpse of my badge and subtly threatening body language got the head nurse over her concerns about my defilement of the "sterile envelope."

As luck would have it, the desk had already received the fifteen-minute call, announcing they were finishing up and the next team could begin preparations.

The OR suite at Halsted is built around two main corridors that come together to form a V. I guess the idea was that everything radiates out from a central point, making the running of the place more efficient. But operating suites are a lot like emergency rooms, and I've spent plenty of time in both, tending gunshot and stabbing victims who, depending how the course of their hospital stays went, would or would not become my clients. And I can tell you, the one group whose comfort and convenience these facilities are not designed around are the patients.

Wheeled gurneys bearing prepped and sedated patients lined the walls, stacked like so many cars lined up at a toll booth or planes waiting to take off at National. Two orderlies came by and unceremoniously pulled the lead gurney out of the holding pattern. Activity around me picked up. The air around me seemed more highly charged. A surgeon and several followers went into the scrub room. I heard some vague, good-natured banter inside. Within a few more minutes, Nicholas Ramsey emerged, again flanked by the engaging Dr. Fusillo. I resisted the temptation to mention Ashby Collier. No sense stirring up the hornets' nest right now, though I mentally held it out as leverage for Bob's cooperation in case Nicholas didn't know.

He stopped when he saw me. "What are you doing here?"

"I tried calling you several times this morning," I replied. "You didn't return my calls."

"I've been in surgery."

"Yes, I know. I need to talk to you."

"Can this wait?"

"Can I just have one minute of your time?" I said. He looked perturbed but made no move to leave.

I took a step closer and suggested, "Perhaps we should talk privately."

He reached out and put his hand on my shoulder. He guided me gently but firmly, about halfway down the corridor, as if I were a misbehaving child who had to be removed from a public place. I felt the sparks again when he touched me. We were between two gurneys whose occupants were fortunately off in dreamland. I glanced back. Fusillo was eyeing us warily.

"I just wanted to let you know about a new development," I said calmly. "We have a new suspect." I detected a slight shift in his eyes, as if he didn't quite know what to make of this information. I let the moment play. Then, when the time seemed right, I added, "His name is Christopher Taylor."

I wished I'd had him wired to a polygraph at that instant, or even an EKG machine, because I would have been able to read his reaction better. I thought I saw a slight flinch of the jaw, a flicker of surprise in those steel blue eyes. But then again, this was a man accustomed to reacting well under pressure.

"Why are you telling me this?"

I held his gaze. "He said he was a patient of yours." Actually, I had said he was a patient of Nick's; Chris had merely confirmed it. But no sense splitting hairs. "I'd like to talk to you about him."

"The physician-patient relationship is privileged."

"According to the Tarasoff precedent, the privilege does not extend to the possible commission of future crimes."

"What future crimes are you referring to?"

"It's time to stop being coy, Doctor. We have strong reason to believe the killer will strike again, and you could be charged as an accessory before the fact. Look, if you won't cooperate, all I need is a grand jury subpoena from any assistant U.S. attorney, and I know them all. I don't even have to go to a judge. So will you talk to me?''

He glanced around. Bob was still waiting at the end of the corridor. "Not here," said Nicholas. "Later." He thought for a moment. "I'll meet you tonight. My house at eight. You know where it is?''

"I'll find it," I assured him. So what was his game? I didn't think I could intimidate him with some vague legal threat. There had to be something else going on.

25

AT eight o'clock sharp I showed up at Nicholas Ramsey's house. I was wearing my raw cotton jersey dress, short and moderately tight—a reasonable compromise between jeans and a business suit that didn't look wrong without stockings. I'd worn it before when I'd had to deal with successful or influential men, and I'd been happy with the results. Up till now, Nicholas and I had managed to strike only glancing blows off each other. Tonight it was all on the line, and I'd use whatever I had and do whatever it took.

I walked up the steps to the front door. There was a little alcove with a doorbell and intercom. I pushed the button.

"Hello? Who's there?" came a brittle, squeaky voice from the speaker. I couldn't tell if it was a man or a woman. It didn't sound like a butler or a maid. Could I have missed the fact that he lived with someone? Irrationally I got a sudden sinking feeling in my chest.

"It's Sandy Mansfield," I said, "here to see Dr. Ramsey."

"Come in."

I waited for the door to open, but nothing happened.

"Hello? Who's there?" the voice from nowhere squeaked again.

"Sandy Mansfield," I stated, more firmly this time.

"Come in." But still nothing. Then, "Who's there?" in exactly the same tone and cadence. I could feel myself starting to tremble with growing anger.

"This is Detective Cassandra Mansfield! Metropolitan Police Department Homicide Squad."

No reply, but the door buzzed open onto a small vestibule. I stepped in warily. Cops are always sensitive to being trapped. My fingertips reassuringly grazed the outlines of the Glock 17 in my purse. Then a second door opened in front of me.

From somewhere around the corner I heard again, "Who's there? Who is it this time?" I jumped. For a second I had the instinct to go for my gun.

"Come in."

Then, as I turned back around, Nicholas was standing in front of me.

"Sorry about that," he said with a faint smile. "I was back in the kitchen." Then, "That's enough, Toby."

"Who's Toby?" I asked. He motioned me forward.

The entrance hall was like an atrium, an eclectic and inviting blend of styles dominated by a large skylight three stories above us. Around me, Chinese lacquer tables and trendy art complemented the house's traditional hardwood rails and accents. A white nineteenth-century phrenology head model occupied the place of honor on a high lacquer stand.

We turned a corner and came to a shelf of kachina dolls stretching across an entire wall. Opposite was an imposing carved oak staircase. And in the middle of the floor was a pole with a short crossbar at the top, on which perched a large gray parrot with red tail feathers.

"Who is it this time?" said the parrot. "Come in."

"I assume I have the pleasure of meeting Toby," I said.

"Birds can't talk!" Toby declared.

I grinned in spite of myself. "Does he know what he's saying?"

"I doubt he'd say it if he did. It's what Bertrand Russell would have called a self-disproving proposition, which could lead to what Ivan Pavlov referred to as a laboratory-induced psychosis. Although I don't think Toby's ever read Bertrand Russell, or Pavlov, either, for that matter."

There was that devastating sparkle in his eyes, simultaneously arrogant and charming and so difficult to resist. It made no promises but suggested a world of possibilities.

"Seriously, the answer is, we really don't know. But Toby is an interesting window into the neurologic function of communication and will. If he does know what he's saying, then he's got critical ego and a communication process similar to ours, which in turn suggests a higher brain organization similar to ours. If, on the other hand, he doesn't know what he's saying, he's still got the mental capacity to retain words and phrases and transform them into speech by association at the appropriate time and place, such as when he hears the intercom buzzer. In neurology, we would call this primary-level abstraction.''

''Very interesting.''

Nicholas pointed to the row of Indian dolls. ''The red tail feathers from birds like Toby were used by the Hopi tribe of Arizona to fashion the kachinas, representing their most sacred religious symbols. You can imagine how transcendent and unexplainable a talking animal must have seemed.''

We stood there in the hall just looking at each other. It was a strange atmosphere. I didn't want to come on too strong at first or push too hard.

''I figured you wouldn't go out to dinner with me,'' he said. He paused, waiting for a reaction. ''Did I figure correctly?''

''Umm, I guess so,'' I said, a little confused. I was trying to adjust my temperature to meet his, but so far he was giving me no clues.

''But I thought perhaps you'd join me here.'' He indicated the dining room with a wave of his hand. What could I say—''No, I'll talk to you, but I won't eat''? He had me captive. He was calling the shots, just as he had in racquetball. Out on the street, in a stakeout or firefight, I know what I'm supposed to do. The variables are limited, and the responses are basic. But here, anything could happen.

I followed him through the dining room. The table was already set for two. As I had in the hospital, I caught myself studying and admiring him from behind, speculating somewhat more than casually what he'd look like without his clothes.

I began picking up an incredibly inviting aroma. I followed him into the kitchen, which was large and bright, with a butcher block island in the middle almost as large as my entire kitchen. The back wall was all glass, built like a greenhouse into a lovely and well-cared-for garden. When my eyes landed on the restaurant-quality stove, I saw the reason for the wonderful scents. Simmering on the burners were several skillets and saucepans, one with some kind of meat cut into strips and another with mushrooms, shallots, and a light brown sauce. He looked as at home here as he did in the OR. A set of Sabatier knives lined one counter.

Nicholas assumed a natural position at the stove while I leaned over the island, resting my elbows on the well-used oak surface. He turned around and began nimbly peeling small potatoes with a scalpellike paring knife. He worked with mesmerizing speed and precision.

"You must enjoy cooking," I said.

"I do." Each potato was sliced into identical thirds. "It's something like surgery, but with a lot less at stake. Before I start, the subject is already dead. That's what makes it relaxing."

And after Neville cut off Terry Tyler's head, he saved her skull and kept it in his studio for inspiration.

Yes, Nicholas seemed to dominate the kitchen the way he dominated the operating room. I'd always found something really sexy about men who cook, especially lately when my own fridge was almost always barren. His hands darted assuredly between the various pans, adding more onions, sprinkling parsley, throwing in a pinch more tarragon, stirring the rich heavy brown sauce. He bent over and sniffed in the aroma almost as if he were taking in the scent of perfume on a woman's neck.

"Okay, that's under control," he announced. "How about a drink?"

"Whatever you're having," I said.

"Fair enough." He placed two glasses on the counter, then opened a well-stocked liquor cabinet and poured from a half-empty bottle of Glenmorangie. He reached inside the freezer and took a large frozen chunk from a bag of store-bought ice. He laid it on the counter, opened a drawer and took out a gleaming ice pick.

As he raised it to shoulder level, I was suddenly seized by an image of Julie Fox, tied helplessly to the chair, wetting herself in terror as the gleaming point descended before her open, screaming eyes. It must have seemed like eternity as the blade came closer and closer to her naked chest. Closer and closer in an ever-decreasing arc, until—

Crunch!

I jumped.

Nicholas jabbed brutally into the block of ice, sending tiny shards flying across the kitchen.

"An interesting irony," he mused, turning the pick's point toward himself for contemplation. "This crude instrument is the symbol of this century's most significant attempt at surgical manipulation of the personality."

"A rather misguided one," I commented.

"True, but brilliantly bold. Bold and daring."

I remembered Ted once telling me that Walter Freeman had used an ice pick specially gold-plated for him by Cartier for his first prefrontal lobotomy.

Nicholas handed me the glass and raised his. "Cheers. Here's to truth and beauty."

"I'll drink to that," I said.

"You should. You pursue the one and possess the other. That's a powerful combination."

"Would you be willing to put that in a *letter?*" I asked, looking straight at him to gauge his instantaneous reaction.

But he only said, "Sorry?" Not even a flicker of recognition.

"Never mind," I said. Either he genuinely didn't know what I was talking about or he had incredible self-control. Since I'd seen him operate and I'd seen him play racquetball, my inclination was toward the latter.

Our eyes were still locked, and there was definitely something happening between us. I felt charged, on edge, both the hunter and the prey. Here we were: two people, both separated, awaiting our divorce decrees . . .

"So what do you have to tell me?" he asked. "About the case, I mean."

I sipped my drink slowly, not wanting the effects of the alcohol to go straight from my empty stomach to my crowded head. I said, "Tell me about Christopher Taylor."

He began slowly, almost warily, as if trying to figure my game. "Twenty-seven or -eight, I think. Engaging personality, some indication of endogenous depression. Early adolescent onset of grand mal epilepsy, traced to the left temporal lobe, up to a point controllable with medication. Over the last several years the seizures apparently became more frequent and severe."

"He told me no one else could do anything for him, but then he went to see you and the very next day you operated."

"No sense screwing around."

"I've learned a little about the Ramsey neural modulator," I said.

"I didn't name it that, by the way," he noted with an amused smile. "Even I'm not that egotistical."

"If it regulates brain waves and epilepsy in a disturbance in brain waves, why didn't you just implant one in Chris?"

"We did," he replied. "It's in there right now. But so far NeMo's no substitute for surgery. You see, epilepsy isn't a disturbance in brain waves. It *causes* a disturbance in brain waves. With some petit mal seizures, the sensor seems to be enough. But with grand mal or the

Jacksonian march variety that progresses from one part of the cortex to the next, we've got to eliminate the problem or lesion causing the disturbance before NeMo can be effective. We've still got a long way to go."

"Okay, but why were you able to help when nobody else was?"

"You're asking what makes me *me*." He took a hefty swig of his Scotch and briefly studied his reflection in the glass. "Maybe it's that I'll take a chance on things other people won't. I say to myself, What happens if I do nothing? What's the worst that can happen if I try? You can't spend your time with your finger in the air testing the wind or getting all caught up with what your peers think—not if you're going to hope to rise above them. You know anything about medical research grants?"

"Not much," I admitted.

"They're supposed to be given for finding new answers to old problems. But if you're dealing with anything *too* new or different, then the person or committee judging your proposal won't get it. So the people who end up securing most of the money are the ones who are good at reinventing the wheel, at finding *old* answers to old problems. Like a bunch of crabs in a barrel: each time one climbs to the top, the others claw it back. That's not the way I operate."

"Christopher Taylor came to us," I said.

"What did he say?"

"He was afraid he'd murdered the young women."

There was an awkward silence. I let it go as long as it would. Finally he said, "Do you think he's capable of murder?"

"I think everyone's capable of murder. What do you think?"

He set his drink on the counter and cocked his head thoughtfully to one side. "Once a doctor starts making moral judgments about his patient, they're both in trouble. But why are you asking me? What are you going on?"

He was pumping me for information now. That fit in with the profile. "That's what I'm trying to figure out," I said.

He stared at me silently.

I stared right back at him. "So what I want to know is, what's the connection between this man who thinks he's picked up where Neville Ramsey left off and the fact that he's come into contact with Neville Ramsey's brother?"

"I could speculate," he said, casually adjusting the flame on one of the burners, "but I'm sure it wouldn't be any more valid than what you've already got." He picked up a spoon and stirred the mushroom-and-onion mix. It smelled so good, it was hard to concentrate.

"Have you ever done hypnosis?" I asked.

"From time to time."

"Lately?"

"Occasionally for a special purpose. Sometimes with my epilepsy patients . . ." He stopped himself short. "What are you suggesting—that I hypnotized Taylor to get him to take the rap?"

"I'm not suggesting anything," I said innocently. "Is there any reason you can think of why Chris might want to do you harm or make you look bad?"

He thought for a moment. "Patients sometimes have ambivalent feelings about their doctors, subconsciously resenting their control. But I really don't think that's the case here. I was hoping you could tell me something."

I'll bet you were, I said to myself. Meanwhile he turned around and emptied the two saucepans into the skillet. He lowered the heat and basted rich brown sauce over the succulent beef strips.

"So does this mean I'm no longer your prime suspect? Is that why you came here tonight?" He was amazingly cool.

I smiled ambiguously and crunched on an ice cube.

"Well?"

"Suppose some evidence turned up," I said in my most hypothetical tone, "fingerprints, hair, and fiber, could be almost anything—that linked you with the murders. I'm not saying it did, or that it will, but let's just suppose."

"Supposition means nothing in my business."

"But you do speculate. When a patient comes in, before you run the tests or look inside, you list all the things you think it could be. What do you call that?"

"A differential diagnosis."

"Right. So just think of this as my differential diagnosis. What would you say to that kind of evidence?"

It's a variation on a standard test question we ask: "We're not saying you did it, Mr. Upstanding Citizen, but if forensic evidence should happen to connect you with the scene, what would you say?" Generally, a guilty man will jump through hoops trying to come up with a logical explanation. An innocent man will vehemently chal-

lenge the very premise. ''If you find my prints there, then you fucking planted them!''

''So what do you say?''

Nick took a sip of his drink and shrugged at me. He had a crooked
smile on his face. ''I wouldn't know what to say.''

''Did you know Jerry Ashburn, the *Post* reporter?''

''The one who was murdered last week.''

I nodded.

''He called me. He was asking about the murders of the young
women. Must have made the same connection with Neville you did. I
said I'd told you everything I knew, so he should talk to you instead.
That was it.''

''So you never met with him?''

''No.''

''Never saw him after that?''

''No.''

''Never even spoke with him?''

''I said no.''

''We know that Mr. Ashburn also spoke with Dr. Fusillo.''

''He very well may have,'' Nicholas said.

''Do you know what they talked about?''

He shook his head.

''What's Fusillo's problem?''

''What do you mean?'' Nicholas asked.

''Does he always have such a big chip on his shoulder or is it that
he just doesn't like cops?''

''Bob came from a tough neighborhood on the outskirts of Chicago.
His mother was an alcoholic. He never knew his father. He was raised
by a promiscuous aunt who resented having the kid thrust on her. The
family had no money. He ran with a gang. Somehow, he still managed
to get into the University of Chicago on scholarship, working the whole
time for his spending money. Unlike most of us, he's had to struggle
for everything he's achieved. So I feel as close to Bob as any resident
I've ever worked with. When Neville died, Bob was tremendously sup-
portive. He was the only one I could really confide in. And if he's a
little bit brittle . . .''

And is it possible that as much as Bob might admire him, either
consciously or subconsciously he resents the golden boy, Dr. Ramsey?
I wondered.

"I'll bet he doesn't get straight A's in bedside manner." Not that many surgeons do.

"You've got him wrong," Nicholas insisted. "He leads one of our postsurgical support groups. Christopher Taylor's in it. Ask him what he thinks of Bob. The patients love him."

"One in particular," I observed dryly. "Is it considered standard form to sleep with patients—particularly the boss's patients?"

I seemed to have touched a nerve. "That's none of my business," Nicholas declared coldly. "I think you're reacting to the fact that he tends to be very protective of me. Most of my residents and colleagues are."

"Even the colleagues who asked you to leave Stanford and Denver and Massachusetts General?"

"They had no imagination," he stated definitively, "no vision."

"I guess there are a lot of people like that out there."

"Safe medicine isn't necessarily good medicine." Then out of the blue, he said, "I noticed you at Mr. Ashburn's funeral." I felt my pulse take a jump. He looked at me as if now trying to gauge my reaction.

"What were you doing there?" I asked.

He smiled. "Same as you."

"What's that supposed to mean?"

"Trying to see if I could learn anything about these cases. After all, you've gotten me involved. Isn't it true that murderers sometimes attend the funerals of their victims?" He laid the wooden spoon on the countertop. "He was a friend of yours."

"Yeah, I guess you'd say that."

"It must be tough on you, having to be personally involved."

"You learn to deal with it." The first out-and-out lie I'd told all evening.

He turned back to the range. *"Et voilà!"* he announced with a flourish, transferring the skillet's contents onto a serving dish, which he handed to me. "Here, you can put that on the table. I'll just put the dressing on the salad and we're ready!"

The dinner was as good as it smelled, maybe better. The meat was exquisitely tender and completely saturated with such a subtle and complex blending of flavors that I actually felt jealous I could never produce anything this wonderful. How many talents is it fair for one man to have? If I were Patricia, I would have kept him on for his cooking skills alone.

Everything about the meal was perfect, including the 1978 La Mission Haut Brion we killed off between the two of us. It had a smoky, sensuous quality, and combining it with the Scotch I'd downed in the kitchen, I felt my head going comfortably fuzzy and my body feeling easy and relaxed. From time to time I would steal my hand under the table and dig my fingernail into the flesh of my inner thigh, eliciting just enough pain to keep focused. I felt as if I were in the eye of a hurricane.

Nicholas didn't say much, but he kept looking at me, and there was something in those eyes that went beyond words. I was trying to figure out what I found so compelling about him . . . beyond the obvious rugged good looks and the terrific body.

I guess it was that most men have such tame, predictable lives—lawyers, businessmen, other doctors, even psych professors. And since no matter how desperate or socially starved I ever felt, I'd always been smart enough not to go out with anyone on the Job, my horizons had been somewhat limited. But here was someone else who seemed to look at life the way I did, who lived on the margins, who would take every chance and do anything not to be bored. Someone else who was always flirting with danger. Someone else who lived on his own terms and was willing to push the edge of the envelope to get what he wanted.

And doesn't that fit in quite neatly with the definition of the classic sociopath?

I felt that aching need deep inside of me. Here I am pleasantly having dinner with this man who may be a multiple killer, I thought, who may be the one taunting and terrorizing me with his letters, and all I can think of is how much I want him and how much I want him to want me. What have I gotten myself into?

Jim Wright would say to go with your feelings, see where they take you, use them.

When we finished eating he swiftly removed our plates. "Go sit in the living room," he said, indicating with his elbow. "I'll just clean up a little, then I'll be right there." This guy's amazing, I thought. He even cleans up after himself. I thought about trying to steal upstairs briefly for a little look-around, but it would be too obvious if he caught me.

The decor in the living room was cool and modern without being forbidding. It was a man's room, not a decorator's, full of wood and leather. A black leather sofa was large and richly padded, and it was balanced by two Eames chairs. But what immediately caught my breath was the painting over the sofa—a stark and stylized *udjat*.

He returned quickly and must have noticed me staring at the painting. "Neville did that. It was from a theme show he did in San Francisco of ancient religious symbols."

"The eye of Horus."

"That's right. So you've seen one before."

"Fairly recently," I said. Did he know where? We read for meaning in each other's eyes.

"Patsy and I flew out to the show. We both loved it. The idea behind it fascinates me—a transformation from one state of being to another."

"That's one way of describing it." Or a symbolic resurrection of the dead?

"A few weeks after we got home from the show, it arrived in a crate on our doorstep. A gift."

"You and Neville must have been very close."

"Look at this!" he said without responding to the comment. He held a plate out in front of him. "Chestnut-and-hazelnut chocolate torte!" It looked like something you'd see in a fancy restaurant or *Gourmet* magazine.

"Did you make that?" Please tell me you're not that superhuman.

"No, I bought it," he said, slicing a generous wedge. "But I've had it before. Here, sit down. Trust me, it's terrific."

"I'm sure it is, but I think I'd better pass."

"You don't have to worry with that figure. Just try it."

I held up my hands in protest. "I'm running miles just to keep my dress size."

"One bite."

"I really couldn't."

"I insist."

"Nicholas, please!" And I realized I'd just called him by his first name.

He sat down next to me on the sofa, picked up his fork, and nipped off the end of the slice. He held the morsel temptingly in front of my lips and smiled seductively. "Just one. Open wide, now. If you don't, I'm going to force your mouth open."

I sighed with resignation and opened my mouth. The delicate sweetness caressed my tongue. And with that, I realized, he had me eating out of his hand.

"I do have a confession to make," he said, moving closer to me on the sofa.

"You do?"

He nodded, nailing me with those killer eyes. A part of me remained detached, curious to see what he had in mind, an undercover agent studying the enemy's battle plans. The fact that I'm attracted to him should be saying something to me, I told myself. Let him give you his best shot. See where it leads. Use it. That's what you're here for.

"You do something to me."

"Could you be more specific, Doctor?" I said, suddenly feeling flushed.

"Everything about you turns me on."

"Is it warm in here?"

"The way you look, the way you are . . ." He paused, as if searching for just the right words. "The gutsy way you play racquetball, for example, how you move . . . how you sweat. What you did to me when you lunged for a shot or bent over to pick up a ball. The way you look right now as the light glints off your hair."

And unfortunately, the feeling seems to be mutual, I thought. Was this the rap he'd laid on Julie Fox and Sarah Hazeltine? I was feeling closer to achieving the detective's ultimate aim—of putting herself viscerally in the victim's shoes.

"I wanted to say something to you," he went on, "but under the circumstances, the way we happened to come together, it was awkward, unattainable."

"Which is why you kept blowing me off, is that it?"

He turned his body to face me. "I'm being serious, Sandy. You don't mind if I call you that, do you?"

"Not if I can call you Nick." And in my own mind, I already was. I let one shoe drop to the floor and folded one leg tightly under me.

He seemed to stare at me for several seconds, like an artist about to compose a picture. I wondered if Neville had looked at his subjects this way.

He said, "You're very beautiful, Sandy." Even without benefit of

NeMo, I felt that electric current ripple through me. "So . . . do you think there's any possibility?"

"There are always possibilities," I said.

He let the statement hang in the air. He put his hand on my wrist and held me that way.

I finally said, "You wouldn't want to get involved with me." Neither one of us was even divorced yet, both on the emotional rebound, still highly vulnerable. That in itself spelled nothing but danger and trouble.

"What's wrong?" he pressed. "We're both used to testing ourselves."

"I don't know if you could handle it."

He continued holding my wrist and looked straight into my eyes. "Try me."

Exactly where we crossed the invisible line, I'm not sure, but it was somewhere close by there. He moved his hands up my arms, near my shoulders. I stared into his eyes. I took in short, shallow breaths, and I didn't shake him off. He reached around my back with one hand and began undoing the top buttons of my dress while he cupped my breast through the jersey fabric with the other. My nipples stiffened to his touch. A million thoughts and images raced through my brain as my fingers found their way between the buttons of his shirt. The best thing that can happen and the worst thing that can happen are often so close to each other. If this was how he got Julie Fox and Sarah Hazeltine to go along with him, I was beginning to understand.

Soon his million-dollar hands were up under my skirt, then in my string bikini panties, cupping my buttocks, moving between my legs. It all felt so good and so right. I was wet as a river inside. And somewhere in the middle distance, I was vaguely aware of the beating of wings. Yes, Nicholas, yes.

Then a circuit tripped in my brain—one of those unwelcome but unavoidable epiphanies. I tensed. I can't let this happen, I told myself. I can't compromise the case, I can't jeopardize everything when so much is at stake. You've seen firsthand how he operates. You now understand what you needed to, and anything beyond this is your own agenda.

I grabbed his hands and moved them out from under my skirt.

"What's wrong?" he said.

"Nothing . . . and everything," I replied. "I'm sorry. I'm terribly sorry." I fingered the buttons on my dress, putting it back together.

I wasn't sure how he'd react. Would he accept what I'd just done? Would he think I was a tease? Or would he get violent, try to force himself on me? If he did . . .

But it was a smile, both sardonic and understanding, that crossed his lips. "Superegos can be a real bitch," he remarked, "can't they?"

26

I'M sure I was flushed a deep crimson. I could only nod. I stood up, still a little shaky, and smoothed my skirt down.

"Please don't leave," he said.

"I need to use the bathroom."

"Upstairs, halfway down the hall on the left. Take your time." He smiled a bit ruefully and added, "I'll finish cleaning up and put out the trash."

I retrieved my bag from the front hall stand, climbed the stairs, and located the bathroom. I didn't use the toilet yet or turn on the taps. I didn't want to tip him off I was finished. I hoped he figured it would take me several minutes to pull myself back together, to recover from his charms. Well, in a way that was true, wasn't it?

I tiptoed out into the hall, hoping I didn't rouse the stupid parrot. I wondered what kind of a witness he'd make. Probably better than most of the humans I deal with.

I found Nick's bedroom at the front of the house. I didn't risk turning on the light, but there was enough shadowy illumination from the street outside for me to make my way. I had a three-item agenda: my pendant, underpants, and the torn photograph. If I found any of the three, that would nail the fucker. At least in my mind.

Interesting choice of words under the circumstances, Cassandra dear.

I hunted around the room until I got my bearings. There was a sliding-door cabinet built into the walnut headboard of his bed. I opened it and fished around, thinking it might be a likely place to hide souvenirs, but I found nothing of interest.

On the dresser was a black leather jewelry box. I went over and opened it. Inside were a couple of heavy class rings, cuff links, a thin dress watch. It was too dark to read the name, but it looked expensive. But no pendant.

I slid open the top drawer of the dresser. Form-fitting briefs in different colors, I was pleased to note. I was sure they showed off his charms to great advantage. It would have been disappointing if he'd turned out to be a boxer man, but it was even more disappointing that I couldn't find out firsthand. Anyway, nothing of mine was in there; everything seemed to be of the masculine variety.

I looked everywhere I could conveniently get to in the room, even ducked into the walk-in closet. I'd known my chances of finding anything were pretty slim, but I was still disappointed. This didn't mean they weren't here. It just meant that with the limited time I had, I hadn't found them.

But I'd continue looking. Out into the hall again, I moved stealthily toward the back of the house. My heart was drumming insistently in my chest. Like having sex with your boyfriend in your parent's rec room or working an undercover narcotics sting, there's an undeniable high attached to risk, an illicit thrill when there's a prospect of getting caught. After a picnic once, I remember insisting Ted make love to me in a semisecluded glade in Rock Creek Park. I was so turned on that I could hardly contain myself. He was so uptight he couldn't get it up.

In the space roughly over the kitchen and dining room, I found another room that even in the dark had a different feel and aura. I slipped inside, closed the door, and felt around for the light switch. I flipped it on and found myself in a library or study.

An ornately carved fireplace mantel was flanked by dark built-in cabinets with bookshelves up to the high ceiling. The other walls were paneled in walnut or some other rich, dark wood. There was a tufted leather sofa facing the hearth, the type you'd expect to see in the reading room of one of the fancy clubs like the Cosmos or the Metropolitan. And in the center of the room, a table was piled high with more books and papers.

But it was the cabinets on either side of the hearth that commanded my attention. They had glass doors, and inside, the two shelves were crammed full of what must have been antique surgical instruments—knives, saws, drills, things that looked like large pincers. They were well made of brass and steel, and some had carved wooden handles. Most had tags attached written in florid nineteenth-century penmanship, as though they had once adorned some Victorian museum. But what they really looked like were medieval instruments of torture, implements designed specifically to tear the skin and break the bones of unfortunate victims. Implements capable of giving great pleasure and satisfaction to certain personality types.

Ever since I was a girl and first read about the Spanish Inquisition, I'd contemplated what it would be like to be tortured, how I'd react to that much pain I couldn't stop or do anything about. I looked once more at the cabinet displays and wondered how Julie Fox had reacted.

I scanned the books on the shelves. It was an eclectic mix—classics, scientific, historical—pretty much what I would have expected from a man as well rounded as Nick. On the table was a stack of journals waiting to be read—*Brain* and the *Journal of Neurosurgery*. Next to it was a small pile of books with numerous pieces of paper slipped in as place markers. The one on top was a library book titled *The Transmigration of Souls* by Martin J. Bell.

I sifted through the stack until, suddenly, my pulse quickened. There on the bottom were two more books, not from the library. The first was *Ancient Egyptian Funerary Practices* and the second, simply, *The Aztecs*.

I thumbed through the Aztec book. There was a long chapter on human sacrifice. One of the plates was an old engraving of the high priest in an elaborate headdress holding an obsidian blade above the bared chest of a bound sacrificial victim. The subsequent plate, by the same artist, showed the priest holding the bloody heart aloft, while behind him, the open-chested victim slumped dead against his bindings.

I turned to the Egyptian book and looked up *udjat* in the index. I turned to one of the bold-faced numbers, indicating a picture. There was the eye of Horus adorning the burial wrap of a royal mummy, just as it had appeared on Sarah Hazeltine's forehead and Neville's painting downstairs.

I was aware of my own heartbeat as my eyes darted around the table, looking for other clues. Nothing else of particular interest, so I gently opened the single drawer. Maybe I'd find my souvenirs here.

Amid the array of pens and pencils, rubber bands and paper clips, I saw a manila file folder. I reached in, pulled it out, and opened it. Inside was a collection of newspaper clippings. And by then it came as no surprise to see that they were all related to my cases, starting with Jerry Ashburn's stories on Fox and Hazeltine, then up through the coverage of his murder, including the short pieces in this week's *Time* and *Newsweek* about the macabre serial killer terrorizing the nation's capital.

Bingo! Wright and Douglas said the killer would keep a collection of press coverage to "authenticate" his adventures. And he'd ask questions and inject himself directly into the investigation, playing a cat-and-mouse game with the police.

"Sandy, are you okay?" Nicholas called from downstairs.

Uh-oh. I hurried back to the bathroom and called out, "Ah, yeah. Fine. Just took a while to repair my face. Be down in a minute."

I closed the bathroom door. I hadn't realized until now how badly I had to pee. For all his charms, Nick was evidently a man used to living alone—I had to put the toilet seat down before I could use it. But as I sat there, I had another inspiration.

There was his glass, sitting on the sink next to a toothbrush holder. If a particular person's prints didn't match with any of the ones on the orange penlight I'd found at Jerry's scene, it wouldn't necessarily mean anything; it's within the realm of possibility it was there randomly and not related to the killing. But if that person's prints *did* match up, that would be the acid test. Certainly enough to convince a judge that we weren't shooting in the dark. And here was that potential evidence right in front of me! All I needed was my mascara brush, a little powder, and a piece of cardboard and some tape.

But wait! I warned myself. Taking that print without a warrant constitutes "fruit of the poisonous tree." And if a judge finds out, even if we just use the information to guide us in the investigation and don't try to introduce it as evidence, it taints everything going forward. Even if it leads away from Nick and toward another suspect.

I pictured him one floor below me, what he'd already been able to do to me and how painfully it had stung when I made him stop. If I could show his prints weren't the ones on the penlight, that would actually be doing him a favor, right?

It was so tantalizing, knowing the evidence was right there in front of me. And even if we can't always have justice, what a good detective always wants is truth. Even if we can't always put the bad guys away, like detective novel addicts—we all have a constitutional need to know what really happened.

I finished, washed and dried my hands, and left the glass alone. When

I came back downstairs, Nick was in the kitchen, just completing the cleanup. It was now as spotless as an operating room.

"I should be going now," I declared. "It was a lovely dinner."

"You really don't have to," he said.

"No, I really do." Because what I found upstairs, I realize now, is not what I wanted to find. And in spite of that, if I stay here, I may not be able to prevent the kind of unprofessional behavior that has wrecked cases and ruined careers.

The look in his eyes suggested he knew exactly what was going through my mind. I felt both a secret thrill that we were communicating on that level and a sense of defenselessness and exposure that I was that transparent to him. What was it about this Nicholas Ramsey that he could conjure up all these conflicting feelings in me at the same time?

"Thank you for coming," he offered. "I've enjoyed it. I hope I was helpful."

"You were," I said, just standing there. More than you know.

I started to turn, then stopped and said, "Can I ask you something?"

"Sure."

"When you and Fusillo came to complain to the captain last week, why did you stick up for me?"

He took a step toward me, reached out and took my hand, then leaned over and kissed me. Not romantically on the lips, and not platonically on the cheek, either. But ambiguously, just on the corner of my mouth. "It should be obvious," he said. "Come on, I'll walk you to the door."

It was after eleven when I left. Nick stood in the door alcove and watched until I was at the corner. Then I heard the door close. And then, amid all the conflicting thoughts and ideas racing through my mind, I had one more. When I went upstairs to the bathroom, he said he was going to take out the trash.

I walked around to the entrance to the alley that ran behind the houses. I came to his and, before showing myself, looked up to make sure he wasn't watching. Then I stole into the area behind his back fence where the trash cans were kept.

Quickly, and as quietly as I could, I raised the floppy plastic lid. There was a white plastic bag on top, secured with one of those twisty ties. I opened it up and carefully rooted around inside. When I saw the wine bottle I knew I had what I wanted.

27

"Y OU'RE dumping trash on my desk!'' shrieked Bernie Colen, lieutenant in charge of MPD's Mobile Crime Lab, belaboring the obvious. He was a fastidious little man with a primal hatred of messiness. He was in the wrong business.

Reluctantly he pulled rubber gloves onto his bony hands and began sifting through the array in front of him. The crime lab is at 1501 South Capitol Street, S.W., above the police garage. Normally the mobile crime scene techs bring in the evidence, keeping the detectives out of the chain of custody. The fewer hands it's been through, the cleaner it is when the case gets to court. But it doesn't always work that way, and just the time I happened to stop by, it was my good fortune that Marc Volmer and Joe LaRocca arrived with something of their own— three tidy lock-seal bags of hairs and a lipstick-stained cigarette butt.

"Hey, Mansfield, what brings you to the office?'' said LaRocca. He looked at the pile on Colen's desk. "That yours?''

"Why can't you be neat like these two?'' Bernie chided me.

"It's one of my greatest failings in life,'' I conceded. "I guess I don't get my gold star for the day.''

"So what do you want?'' Impatiently now.

"Raise any prints you can—dust, scope, the works.''

"On everything?''

"If it's not too much trouble.''

"No trouble at all,'' he muttered, picking up the La Mission Haut Brion bottle and lifting it to the light.

"Someone's got good taste,'' observed Volmer.

"And the scratch to go with it,'' LaRocca added.

"Anyone we know?" Volmer asked me.

"Maybe it's a guy she thinks is cheating on her, so she's going through his trash to see if there're any prints other than his or hers," offered the ever-helpful LaRocca.

"Hell hath no fury like a woman scorned."

A snake of panic slithered through my gut. Had I touched the wine bottle? I quickly tried to replay the dinner, move by move. Let's see, first glass he poured. I drank, he kept topping me off ... Did I pick up the bottle to read the label, as I sometimes do? No, I was too distracted by other things. Anything else? Napkins? No, he used cloth, thank God. Safe by the tip of your nose, honey. But let this be a lesson. You can't afford to get sloppy or let down your guard.

———————

When I got to the office, Vince was at his desk going over the master witness list. He looked up as I sat down next to him, and I could tell right away it wasn't his normal good morning greeting. There'd been two messages from him on my machine last night, but by the time I'd gotten home I figured it was too late to call. If it had been really important, he would have called again this morning. Vince gets up before I do and has never been hesitant about waking me.

"What? What is it?" I asked.

"I called you last night."

"I got your messages."

"Where were you?"

"I was out till late. What's the difference?"

He stared down at his papers and shook his head. "No difference."

"What did you want?"

"It doesn't matter now."

"No, tell me."

"I said it doesn't matter."

"Vince, don't do this to me. Tell me why you were calling."

"Lucinda." He sighed, almost embarrassed.

"Is she all right?"

A long silence.

"Dee found a diaphragm in her purse. It was accidental, but she found it. She wanted me to talk to you before we said anything."

"Oh, well, I could still—"

"It's okay. I've taken care of it."

I could just imagine. "Is Lucy okay?"

"She will be."

My stomach clenched. Vince's expression was grim. I felt bad for Lucy. I knew what she must be facing. I looked straight at him, but he didn't say anything. "There's something else going on, isn't there?" I said.

He didn't reply.

"Tell me."

Vince looked up and cocked his elbow on the side of his desk. "Look at you. You've got that special glow."

I squirmed on my creaky chair. "What are you talking about?"

"You know exactly what I'm talking about."

I did know exactly. Like many of the best detectives—and a lot of sorority sisters, for that matter—Vince was very good at picking up the aura of recent carnal activity, even unconsummated activity. It often figures prominently in a case, and unfortunately the talent carries through into real life. I wouldn't have been surprised if that was what actually sparked the incident with Lucinda.

"You spent the night at his house, didn't you?"

"No!"

"Are you telling me you weren't there?"

"I'm telling you nothing happened." Compared to what I wanted to happen, that was true.

But I guess I've never been very good at covering up certain things . . . so to speak. I never misplaced a diaphragm, but when I was sixteen my mother once found my underpants in the backseat of the car. And she was a pretty good detective in her own right. Maybe that's where I got it from. Since I had my undies off, she concluded I'd been having sex. And since I hadn't remembered to put them back on again—generally considered a fairly standard procedure—she concluded I'd been drinking pretty heavily. At least I'd had the sense not to commit perjury when confronted by the physical evidence. Still, punishment was swift and sure. In addition to an array of the more odious household chores, she grounded me for a month during the height of the summer mating season. Meanwhile, I'm convinced she scoured the greater Los Angeles area searching for an Old World craftsman still making chastity belts.

My phone rang. Saved by the bell.

"Homicide, Detective Mansfield."

"I just wanted to say hello." Perfect timing, Nick! "And to say I hope sometime we can kind of pick up where we left off."

I glanced over at Vince and tried to keep a poker face. "Let me follow up on that," I said into the phone. I wanted him so much, it hurt.

"Is someone listening?"

"Exactly."

"I'll expect to hear from you."

"Right, I understand."

"By the way, I have a surprise for you."

A surprise? "What is it?"

"You don't think I'm going to tell you, do you?"

I'm not much good at surprises. The skill is a lot like waiting, which I'm also not much good at.

"Oh, and one other thing, Detective . . ."

"Yes?"

"You've got a terrific ass."

"Thanks, I appreciate that," I said in my most businesslike fashion.

"I'd like to see more of it."

I hung up the phone.

"Get up!" said Vince. Reluctantly I followed him.

He marched me into Captain Owen's empty office, closed the door, and turned on me. "Now what the hell are you trying to pull, sleeping with your prime suspect?"

"I'm telling you: I didn't sleep with him!" I came back. "But what the hell business is it of yours if I had?"

"It sure as hell is my business if you do something totally stupid that's going to jeopardize this case, not to mention your job and your reputation."

"Thank you, thank you! Once again Vincent T. Robinson selflessly takes on the role of the father I never had. Excuse me very much, but this isn't Lucy you're talking to now. I'm old enough to take care of myself."

"Not if you compromise the biggest case of your career, you're not."

"Compromise it? We were getting nowhere with it. Until I got things off the dime. I found out a lot of things last night, and I probably got a set of his prints to match."

"Without a warrant? You've tainted the entire case."

"No, I haven't. Courts have ruled repeatedly that trash put out for collection is abandoned property and therefore not subject to search and seizure laws.''

"You've got it all figured out, don't you?''

"I had other opportunities to get his prints, but they *would* have been tainted.''

"I'll bet you did,'' Vince remarked.

I realized I'd already said too much. So I just added, "I know what I'm doing,'' and turned away.

"A perfect justification. How selfless and professional of you letting him into your pants in the cause of truth and justice.''

I came painfully close to slapping him. "You're twisting around everything I've said.''

"Am I? Well then, suppose you tell me just exactly what it is you are saying, Sandy, because I don't get it.'' He grabbed my arm sharply and forced me to look at him.

"It wasn't like that, Vince. We didn't sleep together.''

"Are you telling me nothing happened?''

When I was a kid, they told us we had to confess sins of thought as well as sins of commission. I looked at Vince without saying anything.

"That's what I thought. Don't you get it, Sandy? You're already *thinking* differently. You're on that slippery slope, and if you don't get hold of yourself, there's only one way to go.''

"You've got no cause to talk to me like that. And another thing . . .'' I shouted as I stormed out of the room.

"I know,'' he called after me. "You can handle it!''

I was so angry, I was shaking. I couldn't go back to the squad room in this condition, so I strode out into the hallway and ducked into the stairwell. How many times was I going to let him do this to me?

Maybe I needed another partner. Maybe the time had come. Maybe we were too close and had too much history together. I thought about that every once in a while and had come close to asking the captain for a reassignment. But who was I going to go with, then? Sidecki, a burnout who hated the streets? LaRocca, God's gift to misogyny? They'd never pair me up with one of the other women on the squad. That was almost never done. I'm sure they were afraid our clearance rate would be too high.

I went into the ladies' room, splashed cold water on my face, redid my makeup, and went as calmly as I could back to my desk. Vince was already sitting back at his, methodically going through the witness statements. Why was he always so under control when I was always coming unglued?

"You aren't going to say anything, are you?" I asked tentatively.

"It's not my place to say anything. Like you say, you're a grown woman. You've got to take care of yourself."

A flood of relief swept over me. At the same time, I wanted to cry, to hug Vince and have him put his arms around me and hug me in return. But he just continued looking at me and said, "We're in this together, Sandy. Don't ever forget that. It's time to sober up and think like a professional."

Instead of a . . . what? I wanted to ask. But I decided to keep my mouth shut.

———————————

By afternoon I was worn out from the tension with Vince, and I was already thinking about a relaxing evening at home, maybe even with an actual nourishing meal that I would shop for and prepare myself, when Captain Owen came into the squad room, even more grim-faced than usual.

"Robinson, Mansfield: I want you to get over to Oak Hill Cemetery."

"Where's that?" I asked.

"It's the one in Georgetown—on R Street next to Montrose Park."

I turned to Vince. "I never knew that's what it was called." Then I turned back to the captain. "Why are you sending us? You're not taking us off our case, are you?"

"This is your case, Sandy."

———————————

By the time we got to the cemetery, a lovely wooded hillside between Georgetown and Rock Creek Parkway, the scene had been cordoned off and the adjoining Montrose Park closed down.

Less than an hour ago, a seventy-two-year-old man visiting the grave of his long deceased wife about halfway down the hill had come upon what looked to be a partially burned body. He went to the caretaker's shed, where they called the police. It doesn't take many ritual murders before the uniformed patrol officers begin to know one when they see one. And what tipped them off that this wasn't a routine case of trying to dispose of a body was that the victim was slumped on the ground, as if she had collapsed under her own weight, and she was leaning against the charred remains of what had probably been a fairly substantial oak tree.

Interestingly enough, the tree was one of the few positioned far enough from other trees so as to make a spread of the fire unlikely. It had apparently burned itself out before anything else caught.

The crime scene team was snapping away with the still camera and covering the entire area with video. Vince and I circled around the corpse, trying to stay out of their way. You can't always tell much looking at a burned body, even a partially burned one like this. But when he got to the scene, Jack Beauregard confirmed our grim supposition. The blackened, partially skeletized body was that of a white female, probably seventeen to thirty years of age, judging from the muscle tone on the remaining flesh. She had been dead less than eighteen hours. And worst of all—based on the wide and irregular rope abrasions on her wrists and neck, indicating frantic struggle—she had been burned alive.

The ropes, the young woman, the burning in a religious setting geographically close to the other murders. I didn't have much doubt this was meant to be the martyrdom of Joan of Arc.

And Nicholas had said he had a surprise for me.

Vince put on his rubber gloves and kneeled down close to the body. "What's this around her neck?" He looked up at me.

I bent down to see. It was my pendant.

———————

Vince spent the entire car ride back chewing my ass out for not reporting the burglary of my apartment, which turned out to be pretty good preparation for what the captain gave me in his office. But at least he couldn't take me off now. I knew too much. I was too involved; they'd lose too much time.

Everyone was low. John Douglas had predicted the killer might shift his MO, either in terms of theme or periodicity. Well, the theme was similar, but with the break in periodicity, all bets were off. He was escalating in violence, his cooling-off time was shortening, and we were staring into the abyss.

Tomorrow morning, when the photographs had been processed and the videotape duped, we'd begin examining the evidence in detail. ID'ing a victim this badly burned would probably take time. We'd have to start going through missing persons reports. And I was practically sure there'd be no usable prints.

God, I felt sorry for that poor woman. Vince's verbal flogging notwithstanding, what if I had stayed at Nick's house last night? Was he "showing" me? Getting back at me for leaving? What if I'd thrown my cautions to the wind and just done what felt good? Would this woman still be alive?

In fact, the entire time he was working on her he had probably been fantasizing about doing it to me. I wondered if the next one would be wearing my underwear.

———————

There was already a scout car outside my apartment when I got home, which didn't make me very happy, though I suppose, honestly, I'd have to say I did feel a little more secure. Still, the concept of violation breeds more than simply physical fear and vulnerability. There's an emotional component to it that all the guns and all the scout cars in the world can't neutralize.

But first and foremost, we had another horrible killing and were no closer to an arrest. By tomorrow morning the papers and TV would be full of it. I thought about calling Nick, out-and-out confronting him with the murder to see how he reacted. But what was he going to do— admit that that was the "surprise" he'd promised me?

I changed from my dress to cut-offs and a T-shirt, then foraged in the fridge until I found a plastic container with something in it that looked more like chicken salad than penicillin. I sat at the table with my haul from Nick's office. The appointment book had revealed the coincidence. Maybe there was something in it that would explain why it wasn't, in fact, a coincidence at all. There had to be a pattern in here. I just had to find out what it was.

I started outlining entries in red and listing them on a pad. Chris first went to see Nick on October 7. He was operated on, as he said, the next day. He came back for postoperative examination the following week. For three months after that, he was examined once a month.

Now, during any of those times when Nick examined him, could he have hypnotized Chris or planted some other "suggestion" that would have made Chris believe he was a murderer? And, of course, this would have been months before the murders actually took place, which in turn would have to mean that Nick had been planning them all along.

Or, to push the edge a little farther, was it possible that Chris, overwhelmingly grateful for his cure, developed some kind of all-consuming obsession with Nick, knew about Neville, and somehow took over as Nick's "darker half"?

I knew I was groping. There had to be something else in these records that would lead me where I wanted to go, wherever that turned out to be. The problem is that this kind of work is like looking for a cross street as you drive down a strange and unknown road. After a point, you have to decide: Do you keep on going in the hope you're still on the right track, or do you cut your losses and start again from square one?

Maybe it was that pressure, maybe it was my mixed feelings over what had and hadn't happened last night, maybe it was the vivid picture of that unknown woman burned to death, or maybe it was just the sudden burst of inspiration I'd been praying for, but when I came back to the name on my list of Fusillo's snuggle bunny, Ashby Collier, something started to click.

I rummaged back through the stack until I located Chris Taylor's entry again. October 8 of last year. Yes, it was. That was the same day he operated on Ms. Collier.

But so what? I thought. It can't be unusual for him to do two operations on the same day. You go through those records carefully enough, you're going to find a lot of match-ups, I said to myself as my fragile bubble of hopefulness burst.

But the coincidence. I went back to the copies, my eyes zipping down the dates with new focus. And within ten or twelve minutes I learned that Chris Taylor and Ashby Collier weren't the only ones he'd operated on that day. There was also one Mr. Zahedi Hawaas. Three major operations in one day—that had to be getting slightly unusual.

Even for a superman like Nicholas, that seemed like a lot. I started at the beginning and went through the entire stack of pages again, listing every date of every surgical procedure as I came to it. That took me more than an hour. But on no other date during the eighteen months covered by these entries did Nicholas do more than two.

The way cops look at things, when anyone diverges from a pattern, there has to be a reason.

```
┌─────────┐
│         │
│   28    │
│         │
└─────────┘
```

I couldn't locate a Mr. Zahedi Hawaas, but I did know where to find Ashby Collier.

In her I saw an idealized version of what my mother would have liked me to become. She was icily cordial and primly attractive in her tailored Burberry suit, striped oxford shirt, and perfectly tied collar bow. She had on just the right amount of makeup, expertly applied—quite a contrast to the last time I'd seen her—and I found my eyes snooping around the back of her desk for the inevitable designer satchel containing her Reebok commuting sneakers. Her short, silky hair was styled somewhere between perky and sophisticated to add a touch of sensuality when she moved her head, without giving proof of any real intent or compromising her professional status. And when she greeted me, she looked me straight in the eye and thrust her hand out as far as it would go for a firm and no-nonsense handshake. If she was in any way embarrassed or ill at ease, she wasn't letting it show. She was probably a terrific lawyer.

To be a senior associate at Lazenby, Sherman, and Gray, she must have gone right from Yale (the diploma was there on the power wall) to Michigan Law School (right there next to it). I scrutinized the photos next to the diplomas and on the credenza behind her desk. They boasted of breeding, sophistication, and privilege. And it was clear from that look in her eyes and the confident set of her jaw that Ms. Collier, esquire, had never held an adult job that didn't come with a secretary.

I tried hard not to dislike her or think about how much more money than I she was already making. I was willing to bet that unlike me, she had never seen the inside of a criminal courtroom.

"I'm sorry about what happened last week," I said, strategically deciding to bring up a sore subject. I was, too, and I'd had my butt chewed for it. At the same time, it can often come in handy to remind someone you've seen them in a situation they wouldn't necessarily want plastered across the front page of the *Post*. "I hope you'll believe me when I say I was just trying to do my job and possibly save a life."

She nodded, as if the less said about it, the better.

Don't worry, honey, I felt like telling her, I know what it's like to fall hard for a brain surgeon.

But what I actually said was, "I guess why I'm here is at least indirectly related: the fact that you were Dr. Ramsey's patient. I assume that's how you met Dr. Fusillo."

She nodded. "What you're asking about, it's not an aspect of my life I like to talk about very much," she confessed. "I don't mean my relationship with Bob. I figure I'm old enough to decide on my own who I want to go out with. But if that's why you're here, I don't think we have much to talk about."

"No, actually, it's Dr. Ramsey."

She instructed her secretary to hold all calls, then closed the office door and took the chair opposite the small sofa upon which she'd directed me to sit.

I tried to diffuse the tension. "I love that scarf you're wearing," I said. It was tied around her neck and contrasted dramatically with her blouse. I didn't think I had a single article of clothing as expensive. "Same one?" I pointed to one of the photos on the credenza in which she was actually wearing it on her head like a kerchief. How's that for pretentious?

"Hermès?" I asked. She nodded. "You have such exquisite taste." Then I cringed inside as I realized what I'd just thought about her.

"It was sort of forced on me," Ashby replied, not unpleasantly. "As you can see, my hair's still growing back." She smiled, as if to say, "It's okay, I'm used to it. Like everything else, I've learned to handle it."

For some reason, I just couldn't seem to get it right where this woman was concerned. Ted would definitely read something into that. "It looks like you've done amazingly well dealing with this horror," I retreated, trying to recover.

She shrugged. "I guess you do what you don't have any choice about. But thanks. Some of my friends say that deep down, I'm not dealing with it at all. But just because I haven't run to a psychiatrist or broken down and come unglued at the surgical support group meetings doesn't mean I'm not facing it. Maybe I just take things on a very practical and pragmatic level. It's probably why I'm a good lawyer."

It probably was. Ashby Collier suddenly struck me as someone who knew her own mind better than any well-meaning relative or friend possibly could. And my initial dislike of her washed away in a flood of guilt.

"I was wondering if you could tell me something about the day you had surgery," I said.

She crossed her legs in a beguiling yet professional manner and tented her hands under her chin. "I'll try, but I'm not sure I remember much. One of the drugs they give you in the anesthesia is to make you forget everything."

"Was the operation planned some time in advance?"

"Mmm," she murmured, thinking. "I don't believe so."

"So they just called you up one day and told you to check into the hospital?"

"I was already in the hospital."

"Yes, of course. I'm sorry." Very good, Sandy.

"It's okay. From what I remember, Dr. Ramsey came to my room and said he'd like to try an operation that might help."

"Did he say what type of operation?"

"Something very innovative and radical. With normal surgery, no matter how much of the tumor was cut out, it was going to come back. But he said he had been experimenting on animals with a procedure that interrupted the chemical messages between the cells. At that point, I would have let him try anything."

Ashby's speech suddenly grew even more careful and precise. "You have to understand, Ms. Mansfield, I was dying. I'd already come to terms with that. I had what they called a grade two astrocytoma. They were already giving me radiation but said the most that would probably do was buy me some extra time. The ward was full of people with conditions like mine, some more advanced. It still gives me chills to think about them."

I thought of this attractive, beautifully groomed woman with her confident manner and perfect suits and fancy diplomas, lying naked beneath a bedsheet with her head shaved, waiting to be wheeled into a sterile room so a masked man could do battle with a monster lurking inside her skull. There wasn't much I'd seen that was more terrifying.

"Then Dr. Ramsey comes along trying for a miracle. And whatever he did, it worked. It was a miracle. Two months afterward, the CAT scan and MRI showed no evidence of the tumor. That sensor he implanted continues to show brain function is back to normal." She rapped on the wooden arm of her chair for luck. I leaned over and did the same, desperately grateful that this pretty young woman of whom I'd been so envious was still alive.

"And how long after that conversation did you have the operation?" I asked.

"I think it was a matter of hours," she replied. "I was grateful not to have the time to think about it." Then she changed the subject on me. "Would you happen to know if there are any leads in the murder of those two young women?"

"I'm sorry?"

"Sarah Hazeltine, and I think the other was named Fox."

I supposed it wasn't so unusual after all, her asking me. After all, it was front page of Metro in every morning's *Post*. It was what people wanted to know about, especially someone like her, who fit the general description of the two women and would therefore feel vulnerable while he was still on the loose. She'd feel even more vulnerable when she heard about the latest.

"Frankly, when you called, that's why I thought you wanted to talk to me."

"Why is that?" I asked.

"Because I knew Sarah. We were in the same exercise class—the one Dr. Ramsey recommended to me."

———————

When I got back to the office, Vince gave me one of those looks that implied he'd been doing real work all morning while I'd been out rounding up speakers for Nicholas Ramsey's testimonial dinner.

"Are you sure you're not subconsciously groping for evidence to prove how wonderful he is?" Vince challenged me.

"I'm working the case logically and objectively," I insisted. Though how do we know what our subconscious motives are? If we knew, then they'd be conscious.

"Anyway, we've caught one lucky break," he went on.

"Yeah? What's that?" I asked, eager to shift the discussion away from me.

"We've got an ID on the victim—hooker named Joyce Fabrizi, age twenty-nine."

I tried to recall if I knew the name from my time in Sex Crimes, but it didn't ring a bell. That wasn't surprising, though. New names and faces appeared all the time, and old ones were constantly fading away, either through age or choice or, just as likely, drugs, disease, or crime. Because of the nature of their work, prostitutes are among the most vulnerable people in all of society.

"She was working the Thomas Circle area Wednesday night. Another girl, Clio Allen, saw her get into a white sedan—no ID on plates— around midnight or half past."

Over an hour after I left Nick's house, I thought. And a white sedan could easily be a rental. He hadn't called me last night.

"Joyce owed Clio two bills, which she was supposed to pay back after this trick. When she didn't come back all night, Clio got pissed and reported her as a missing person, figuring this was the most benign way of getting the cops to look for her and get Clio her money. Ordinarily they wouldn't have lifted a finger, but we checked out every missing on file this morning. Dental records from a free clinic confirmed the ID."

Poor girl. I'd spent enough nights out on the street as a decoy in a blond wig and skintight hot pants to know it was a tough and unfriendly way to put food on the table.

"When's the post?" I asked.

"Three o'clock this afternoon. Captain wants the tox studies as soon as possible."

"We have crime scene photos yet?"

Vince reached across his desk and handed me a hefty stack. I went through them one by one, trying to absorb the entire scene and establish an overview in my own mind. From the position of the unburned bits of rope, it was clear that she had been tied upright to the tree in a complex crisscross pattern. I was absolutely certain about the Joan of Arc scenario.

I flipped back through the stack until I found one with what I was looking for: a closeup of the binding. "Vince, can I borrow your magnifying glass?"

He opened his desk drawer and handed it to me. I squinted into it, studying the photo at length. Then I pulled out the Fox photos and compared.

"That's what I thought. Look, Vince: it's not the same type of knot."

"So what?" he replied.

"This type here in Fox is the same one as Ashburn and the same one Neville Ramsey used repeatedly."

"So what?" he said again. "This crime required more ligature, and even your FBI guys said he could start diverging from the pattern."

"Yeah, but it doesn't make sense why he'd diverge in a detail like this."

"Maybe just to jerk our chain. I think you're reading too much into it."

"Maybe," I said. "But something about this just doesn't add up."

————————

I had a couple of hours before the postmortem on Joyce Fabrizi, and I'd already decided what to do with the time. I walked over to Halsted and passed through the lobby and into the first corridor.

I took the stairs all the way down to the subbasement level and prowled the corridors. Several orderlies in white coats and maintenance men in gray coveralls passed me. They either nodded perfunctorily or seemed to ignore me completely. You don't need police training to know that the secret of not being stopped is simply to look as if you know what you're doing and where you're going. The only preparation you need is to have been in junior high school and to have been stopped once by a teacher without your hall pass. What you want to create is a presumption of legitimacy.

Somewhere in the rabbit warren of corridors I found my destination: the hospital laundry. I stuck my head inside the swinging double doors and reconnoitered. Big white canvas-sided carts cluttered the receiving area. They were stenciled on the sides with what they were supposed to contain, separate carts for bed linens, towels, and clothing. Seeing no one in the room, I went over to the closest of the clothing carts and dug around the soiled uniforms and surgical gear for a set of surgical greens that might fit me. They always looked loose and shapeless, so perfect sizing wasn't a must.

I found one pair that looked pretty good, but when I pulled them out, the top was crusty with bloodstains. Somebody had hit a gusher at close range, from the evidence of the spatter patterns. Cops are pretty sensitive to blood-borne diseases these days, as much as doctors. So I tried to stay away from that set and bent way over the edge and rummaged down near the bottom. Ah, here were some that didn't look too bad.

I tucked the bundle tightly under my arm and walked hurriedly back down the corridor and around a corner to a ladies' room I'd already scouted. Fortunately it was empty, too. Other than laundry workers, most of the denizens of the lower depths of large buildings are men. Even so, I went over to the farthest stall and latched the door. I stripped down to my underwear, folding my skirt and blouse as neatly as I could and slipping them in my bag. Then I pulled on my new duds and tied the drawstring at the waist. Unfortunately, I wasn't wearing running shoes, the universal footwear of doctors in hospitals. But at least I had on flats, which could be disguised by the disposable paper booties if no one looked too closely.

I stashed my clothes and bag on the floor behind the toilet, after first removing my gun and holster and putting them on under my greens top. I'd have to be careful how I carried myself. Seeing a doctor with a 9 mm might cause a stir. I'd brought a clipboard from the office to give myself an added aura of authority. I came out of the stall, gave myself a quick fluff in the mirror, then put on the cap and mask I'd taken from the supply closet. I pulled the mask down around my neck and went back out into the corridor, then climbed two flights of stairs and hoofed down another corridor to the Medical Records Department.

Sadly, hospital security is incredibly lax. Snatching newborns from nurseries has almost become an epidemic.

Comfortable now in my well-creased uniform, I walked up to the young man at the computer terminal. He was either asleep or dead. If he was dead, he'd been this way for several hours because rigor had already set in. But when I came up real close and leaned my chest over the counter and cleared my throat loudly, he raised a single eye in my direction. I took this as a preliminary indication that he had not as yet failed the ultimate test. Jack Beauregard would have to wait for this specimen.

I made a show of checking my clipboard. "Can you pull up records on . . . lemme see here: Collier, Ashby; Hawaas, Zahedi; and Taylor, Christopher." I held my breath.

"Sure," he said without energy, not bothering to look up. "When do you want them?"

"Now," I said, gaining confidence, trying to sound like an arrogant surgical resident. "If it's not too much trouble, that is." Stay cool and look like you're used to being obeyed without question.

This time I got the entire raised eye. "You people don't always have to bust my hump, Doc. Just hang on a minute. Now give me those names one at a time."

At that, I lowered my eyes demurely and smiled engagingly, as I always do when I get what I want.

29

NORMAL posts are bad enough. Those where the body is partially decomposed, mutilated, or, worst—burned—can be pretty excruciating. What was left of Joyce Fabrizi's body lay on a steel dissecting table in the morgue, in marked contrast with another table holding the body of a twenty-one-year-old black male who had died relatively peacefully by comparison—of a high-caliber gunshot wound to the chest.

The autopsy confirmed what we had strongly suspected—that the young woman had in fact been burned to death. "Terminal event was massive shock as a result of burns," Jack Beauregard declared, "though there seems to have been a prior loss of consciousness and possible suffocation due to smoke inhalation."

There are a lot of ways to die.

Tox tests had shown evidence of cocaine and amphetamines, but so far there was no evidence of any drug introduced in the commission of the crime. Nothing to dull this woman's awareness or pain.

But as I stared at this corpse, replayed the entire gruesome scene of her death in my mind, visualizing my pendant resting on that hideously tortured chest, something kept repeating itself to me:

What's wrong with this picture?

"That's about it," Jack announced, filling out the last remaining entries on the lab form.

"While I've got you here, can you help me with something?"

"I'm always ready to help you," he said. "You might achieve a little more professional look if you cut your hair shorter."

"That's not what I meant, Jack, but as always, thanks for the tip."

I'd gone through the three medical records as best I could in what little time I had before coming to the morgue, and I'd noted some of the things I wanted explained.

"What can you tell me about a grade two astrocytoma of the right temporal lobe?"

"Nothing good," Jack responded.

"What about temporal lobe epilepsy? Or multiple sclerosis?" That was what Zahedi Hawaas—the Saudi businessman—had had. And according to the record, it hadn't been long before he'd been well enough to return home.

Jack stopped what he was doing and turned to me. "What, exactly, are you getting at?"

"I need some help on the technical stuff."

"Come over here," the medical examiner directed, leading me over to the other dissecting table. He removed the top of the victim's skull, which had already been sawed open, eased in his gloved hands, and removed the contents, which he held up for my inspection.

"Lesson number one: This is a brain . . ."

———————

"Three major, complex operations on the same day, and at least two he does practically on a moment's notice," I said to Vince as I pounded on the candy machine in the vending room, demanding either a box of Milk Duds or my fifty cents back. I was getting neither.

"I wonder what'd happen if I shot the fucker," I muttered.

"Ramsey?"

"No, the candy machine." But I decided against it. People get away with murder every day in this town, but if I assaulted a crooked candy machine, my butt would be in court tomorrow.

"Come on, let's get out of here before I turn mean and ugly," I said. Vince, tactfully, made no comment.

I followed him to the other side of the room, where the coffee and soda machines were. "This whole thing doesn't make sense," I persisted. "It says here Ashby Collier's surgery began at three thirty-two P.M. in operating room four."

"So?"

"And Chris Taylor's operation began at eight-nineteen P.M. in the same place."

"I don't see what you're getting at," he said calmly.

"Surgeons start operating in the early morning—six, seven o'clock. Usually, the only kind of procedure they'd start at night would be an emergency that couldn't wait till the next day—gunshots, aneurysms, that kind of thing. But there's no way Taylor's epilepsy is an emergency. Or Hawaas's MS, for that matter."

"Maybe Ramsey's just compulsive."

"Why would he be more compulsive that day than any other in eighteen months? And why would he start so late in the day, anyway, when every other day he's in there by six-thirty or seven A.M.?"

"You're sure he didn't have another one before that?"

"I've gone over every entry in the date book at least ten times. There are no other references to surgery that day, and yet he operates all night and into the next morning, finishing up with the Arabian guy. If you ask me, I think Nicholas must have spent the morning preparing for the rest of the day."

"It could still be a coincidence," Vince pointed out.

"What about Ashby being in Sarah Hazeltine's exercise class? You think that's a coincidence, too?"

"You said it yourself, it's the one Ramsey recommends to his patients," Vince said coolly.

I slapped the back of one hand into the other palm. "We've already got a connection between Nicholas and Julie. There's our connection between him and Sarah!"

Vince was noncommittal. He removed a Dr. Pepper from the perfectly behaving soda machine. There must be something these metal beasts don't like about me.

"So what about the guy from Saudi Arabia?" he asked.

"I've got the FBI trying to track him down, but so far I can't find him."

"That one doesn't sound like a last-minute fill-in."

"You're probably right." I sighed as we climbed the stairs toward the squad room. "So what've you been doing?"

"Working on your break-in."

"What's wrong? You bored with homicide?"

"No. But if we can get the guy who broke into your apartment, we can attach him directly to this latest murder. It's called detective work, Sandy."

He had a point.

When we got back to the squad room, my phone was ringing. I had to dive to catch it. "Homicide, Mansfield."

"Lab. Colen."

"Bernie. What have you got?"

"We were able to raise a number of prints from that mess you dumped on my desk."

"I'm sorry about that."

"I'll bet you are. You owe me big time."

"Get to the point, Bernie."

"Cool your jets, Sandy, I'm trying to give you a complete, responsible report. You know, it's true what they all say about you. Anyway, we do have a match with the specimen print from the Ashburn penlight."

"We do?" I stated blankly. This is the smoking gun, I realized, and suddenly I felt numb.

"Don't thank me or anything for rushing it through and busting my entire department's hump," Colen grumbled. "And if Owen happens to ask, tell him it was because I'm a dedicated public servant committed to the cause of truth and justice and had nothing to do with your charm." Everyone wants a medal these days.

"Thanks, Bernie," I said belatedly. "I won't forget this."

"No," he grumbled again, "they never do."

I hung up the phone and just stood there a moment with my heart sinking. I said to Vince, "We've got a match."

One minute later we were standing in front of Patrick Owen's desk with the door closed.

"You tangle with someone like Nicholas Ramsey, you'd better be damn sure you can get it to stick," the captain warned.

"That's why we want to do a secret search," Vince explained. "If we find what we're looking for, we've got enough to charge. If we don't, then we haven't publicly stepped in shit. The matching prints give us probable cause for the warrant, and we tell the judge if it's not done discreetly, we have reason to believe he'll destroy evidence. And that way, His Honor knows he won't be dragging a distinguished citizen through the mud unless and until we can prove he's a murderer."

Owen drummed his fingers on his desk and turned to me. "You say you got this print match from Ramsey's trash?"

"That's right."

"What were you doing over there?"

"Asking him about the case. The Christopher Taylor connection."

"He was cooperative?"

I could feel Vince's eyes on me. "Reasonably so."

Owen pursed his lips and let a thin column of air escape between them. "This is what we've been waiting for. Let's not blow it. Get your shit together and come up with a list of things you'd expect to find. I'm gonna call Judge Blake and see if she'll see us tonight."

I wondered if Owen knew how good an idea I already had of the things we expected to find.

"And Sandy . . ."

"Yes, boss?"

"Make it look real."

———————

We spent the next hour getting our request together. I called Jim Wright at home. He coached me through the rationale for the kinds of things one might reasonably expect to find and the arguments about why it was important not to tip off a potential suspect in advance.

As I hung up the phone, Vince leaned across his desk and said, "I know how you feel."

"Yeah, well, good," I scowled, "because I don't."

"I'm proud of you for putting the Job first. I know how you feel about this guy, and it would have been easy not to go for the prints."

"Well, it's a shame it couldn't have worked out. But, hey, the guy's a murderer, what can you do? Know any nice accountants?"

For the first time since I could remember, Vince smiled.

———————

Shortly after seven, Captain Owen, Vince, and I showed up at Judge Blake's house in Cleveland Park. Vince presented her with the circumstantial evidence and the fingerprint report, and I gave her a profile-based explanation of why we would expect to find such items as a scrapbook or clipping file, material on mythic ritual, or some indication of sadomasochistic interest or behavior. Then Owen made his case for why the search should be conducted without advance notice, a tactic more often allowed in drug cases than murders.

As far as motive, we couldn't say much more than that some perverse inner drive must be compelling him to continue his brother's crimes. But since motivation is more the bailiwick of psychiatrists and priests than it is of cops, we knew that wouldn't figure into her evaluation of probable cause.

In the end, I think Owen pegged it right. Sensitive to the detrimental publicity that could accrue to all parties concerned if, contrary to available evidence, we had in fact committed a royal fuck-up, Judge Blake granted the search warrant. We'd go in tomorrow morning.

———————

I came home, changed, then went out and ran about four miles hard, trying not to think about anything. I got back wringing with sweat, stripped, and showered. I wasn't very hungry. I dug out tapes I hadn't listened to in years that were evocative of my formative teens and twenties, and as Mick Jagger warbled and crooned out "Satisfaction," I did my nails for the first time in modern memory. When I finally went to sleep, I dreamed of my father. Then I dreamed of Gabbie.

Then I dreamed of Nick, one of the most exciting, sexually fulfilling dreams I've ever had. I woke up tingling, trembling, and wet with desire. And all I could think of was, What was there left to lose?

———————

We arrived at Nick's house about nine Saturday morning—me and Alex Klein, one of our best crime scene techs, and our distinguished colleague, Norman Sidecki, who, while terminally jaded and decidedly long in the tooth, was still about the best man on the squad for getting himself into places that didn't particularly want him. You'd be amazed if I told you some of the houses in Washington old Norman broke into over the years with their owners and security companies never the wiser.

We were dressed as telephone technicians, which doesn't require a particular uniform, hardly ever arouses much interest, and allowed Alex to carry his equipment in unremarkably. Precinct police had been surveilling the street for the past two and a half hours, and they had confirmed when Nick's Mercedes pulled out of the garage.

Meanwhile, Vince had made an appointment to talk to Cynthia

Andrew, the woman who ran Ashby Collier's exercise class and who knew Nick professionally.

I thought Sidecki looked cute in his telephone costume. I was careful to get all of my hair underneath my hard hat. We made the ceremonial knock on the door, and when there was no answer, Norman proceeded to get us into the house quickly and cleanly. We were turning the corner into the main hall when a high-pitched voice squawked out, "Who's there?" Sidecki nearly jumped out of his skin.

"It's only the fucking parrot," I whispered.

"You got to tell me these things, Mansfield," he whispered back, clutching his chest.

As Toby looked on in curious silence, we prowled around the house. We went down to the basement, which was mainly given over to a large playroom. There was a cushy sectional, an expansive-looking sound system with speakers all over the place, a projection TV, a real arcade version of Pac-Man, a pinball machine, and a Vegas-style silver-dollar slot machine.

Yes, Nicholas Ramsey was a bit of a gambler.

When we'd finished with the basement, we made our way systematically through the first floor, then up the stairs and into the bedroom. Sidecki made a thorough search, examining anything his decades of experience told him might pay off. Alex created his own video narrative, punctuated at appropriate junctures by still detail shots.

"We're coming out of the kitchen and proceeding through the dining room, along the right side. You can see the sideboard and the china cabinet as I pan around. We are now facing the door frame leading to the hall and living room . . ."

And all the while I was thinking, Here's where we ate dinner, and here is where he got his hands inside my pants and caused for me one of the greatest character conflicts of my adult life. Oh, and the bathroom upstairs—that's where I considered tainting all future evidence in the investigation.

We hope you've enjoyed our little tour, and please come again soon!

Upstairs, things were pretty much as I'd left them, only the toilet seat was back up. I went into the bedroom and, just for the hell of it, went through his underwear drawer at greater depth. But I still didn't find what I was looking for and achieved no particular satisfaction from the search. I think men must get off on that much more than women do. At least it's usually the first target in a woman's bedroom most male detectives go for.

When we got to the study I tried to be as nonchalant as I could, waiting for my colleagues to discover the treasures for themselves.

"Quite a collection," Sidecki commented, eyeing the display cases.

On the bottom shelf of the built-in bookcases we found a set of photo albums, going back to the time when Nicholas was a little boy and chronicling his growing-up. I thumbed through them. They were too perfect: a 1950s *Life* magazine family. Here was the backyard swing set, the vacations at the beach, the Christmas Eves and Christmas mornings. There was no denying, Nick had been an adorable child. But the boys seemed more like objects, less living children than a proud man's trophies.

Perhaps the most interesting picture was of the eminent Norbert Ramsey, already an internationally respected figure. He was posing in the operating room in full surgical garb with his two boys—Neville maybe ten and Nick maybe eight—standing on stools next to him, similarly attired. It seemed grotesque somehow, a perversion of nature. If I had to conjure up a generic worst nightmare, it could very well be having a happy-go-lucky eight-year-old operating on my brain.

The photos of the two boys together seemed to confirm the portrait Patricia Ramsey had painted. Here was Neville with his arm wrapped protectively around his younger brother's shoulders. It was almost as if he were protecting little Nicholas from the rest of the world. Then here was Nick in another one, gazing up admiringly at his older sibling as he climbs behind him up the tree. In fact, as I flipped through the pages covered with yellowing plastic, I could find scarcely a single image of either of them without the other.

And there was a group shot. I had to look closely because it was small. A bunch of kids, obviously at a Halloween party, since they were all in costume. There was a witch, a ghost, a ballerina, a cowboy, a little girl dressed as a policewoman. Good for her!

I scanned until I spotted Nick, a red devil with horns, a tail, and a pitchfork. Okay, a fairly typical costume; let's not read too much into this. But next to him, to his right and about a head taller, was Neville. He had a long white beard and a long, flowing robe, sandals, and a tall staff in one hand. What was he supposed to be—Moses? Then I noticed the zigzag, foil-covered piece of cardboard in his other hand. A lightning bolt. I realized what he was supposed to be. God.

Portrait of the Artist as a Young Man.

Alex took closeups of a few pictures from the album. I put it back on the shelf and moved on to the center of the room and made a show of looking through the stacks of books on the table. When I ''discovered'' the ones on the Aztecs and Egyptians, I called Alex over to detail them. Then, with rubber-gloved hands, I opened the table drawer and extracted the clip file from the table drawer.

''Hey, hey, hey, looky here!''

Sidecki came over and took the open file folder from me. ''Truly amazing,'' he said with a conspiratorial look.

Rather than reacting, I continued to poke around in the deep, shallow drawer, in the hopes that I might find something else equally enlightening. I didn't want to look too rehearsed. And it definitely helped my credibility that at the very back of the drawer, I did feel something else. It was hard and plastic. I pulled it out. It was a videocassette.

I looked for some identifying marking, but all I could see was a date—September 12 of last year—hand-scrawled on the label. Something he'd seen on TV? I handed it to Alex. He tagged it and put it in his bag of tricks.

I made a special point of looking for the sword Jack Beauregard speculated might have been used on Jerry Ashburn, but I found nothing remotely close. I even went through his kitchen knives one by one, but none would have made that particular character of wound.

We were wrapping up when my pager went off, telling me to call in. Rather than use Nick's phone, I waited until we were out of there and back in the cruiser. And imagine my delight when the dispatcher told me that I was due in court in half an hour. The David Cicero case, which was supposed to have been continued, had suddenly come to trial. And since it was a major drug murder and the jury was being sequestered, they were holding court on Saturday. I had to be there to testify.

I had Norman drive me home and wait while I hurriedly changed so I wouldn't be late. Nothing pisses off a judge faster and gives the defense a needless advantage than when a detective is late or fails to show.

Shit! Normally I don't mind waiting around in court. It's easy money, and I can usually sleep. But today I had better and more important things to do.

30

A S I'd suspected, I ended up cooling my heels at Superior Court most of the afternoon. It was a messy case, and frankly, I had my doubts it was going to amount to anything. One Elvert Jackson, who had information about a drug murder and who was himself no choirboy, had been gunned down in a drive-by shooting by persons unknown who presumably were unhappy about his decision to share said information with the MPD and our colleagues in the district attorney's office. Enter one David Cicero, well known in certain lowlife circles, who we did not believe had actually participated in the aforementioned shooting, but whom we nonetheless postulated had material information regarding it (in much the same way as the decedent, Mr. Jackson, had had information about the previous one), had himself a series of nasty legal difficulties to contend with, and . . . well, you get the idea. Sometimes I think of crime and punishment in Washington as a game of dominoes. And with the rules of the street as they are now played, it is often an incredible bitch getting that first domino to fall before someone takes it out of the set.

Anyway, by the time the judge and all attorneys had sorted through all the details and finally got to me, the day was practically shot. It was almost five by the time I got back to the office. The only good thing was the overtime. If they want to waste my time, they can waste their money, too.

As I came in the door, I noticed a stocky, middle-aged man emerging from the captain's office. He noticed me, too. He looked exactly like the captain in every respect save one. He was wearing a broad grin. I moved closer to make the positive ID. Sure enough, it was the captain.

"No offense, sir," I said, "but are you currently in your right mind?"

"That is the case," he confirmed. "The reason being that my ace detective second grade, Cassandra Lynn Mansfield, has finally put together the elements. Monday morning the press buzzards are going to start the countdown for the death watch. And by Monday afternoon, in time for the six o'clock news and the *Post*'s first edition deadline, you and I and Detective Robinson and the Honorable Claudel T. Price will appear at a news conference announcing the arrest of a suspect. How's that for timing!"

"You think we have enough?"

"Between the methodology, the behavior, the prints, and the fruits of the search, we've got more than enough. The books were nice, the clip file was terrific, and the video was really the clincher. Then we've got all the little extra goodies like Julie Fox being a patient and the other stripper recognizing his photo. I know I've given you shit, Sandy, but I'm proud of you."

Which can be a bigger burden than having someone pissed off at you, I knew. Because when you're at the top of the heap, there's only one direction to go.

"What was on the tape?" I asked.

"It was the brother, Neville, waxing eloquent—definitely a primo psycho—essentially a how-to for the Ashburn murder."

"Where's Vince?"

"In there with him now. Room number one."

"What?"

"That's right. Dr. Nicholas Ramsey, his personal self."

"How long's he been here?"

"About twenty minutes."

"You book him?"

"No. Asked him to come in for questioning. I suggested he might want to bring an attorney along, but he said that wouldn't be necessary—he could take care of himself. Once he was here and in the box, Vince Mirandized him. He still didn't want a lawyer. Guy's got balls, I'll say that for him."

"What's he said so far?"

"Said he wants to talk to you. Alone."

"He did?"

"You'll probably want to watch the tape first."

I nodded, not sure what to make of all this.

Owen gestured to the other end of the squad room. "All set up for you in room number three. I think you'll find it quite enlightening."

I nodded again and headed off in that direction.

"Sandy . . ."

I stopped and turned around.

"Are you okay? You don't look so great all of a sudden."

———————

I went into room three and closed the heavy metal door behind me. The table was littered with Styrofoam coffee cups and tinfoil ashtrays heaping with butts. I was agitated to begin with, and that just pissed me off even further. Men are pigs. It never occurs to them to clean up after themselves because most of them don't give a shit if their immediate environment is a pigsty. I pulled the gray metal trash can over to the side of the table and swept everything into it. Now, would that have been so challenging for one of those bozos to think of?

Just two rooms over was Nick, and he'd asked for me. I got a warm and tingling feeling in my groin. It was quickly replaced with a cold and twisting feeling in my stomach. Everything I'd worked for for almost a month now was coming together. And I was feeling empty and sick.

I imagined the conversation in there running something along the lines of "Could it be possible that when your brother died, a little part of him stayed alive inside you?" But I hardly expected him to fold that easily under Interrogation Tactics 101.

The VCR and monitor were set up on the metal table against the wall, positioned so that the detective could see the screen but the suspect being questioned could not. I popped the cassette into the slot and sat backward on one of the two padded chairs, hitching up my skirt so I could straddle it. I put my hands on the chair back and rested my chin on them.

I reached out and picked up the remote control. I pressed the play button. Then I sat back, watched, and listened.

The scene was the deck of Neville's Big Sur house with the majestic blue expanse of the Pacific behind him. He was sitting on a wrought-iron chair, his legs comfortably crossed, dressed in an open-neck white shirt and khakis streaked with paint. He was a little more gaunt than Nicholas, his features somewhat sharper and not nearly so handsome. But the resemblance was obvious. And eerie.

The voice, when it came on, was also vaguely like Nick's, but with a higher, more intense quality and more sardonic, too, as if a sneer were wrapped around every word.

"Transcendency," he began. "The quest for something beyond ourselves. That's what we're talking about—the entire basis of religion in a nutshell. The search for that which will deny us our nothingness. The saints and martyrs understood this. Oh, yes, else why would they have so joyfully embraced the cross, the scourge, the flame?"

It was one thing to study the files, to read the stories and reports, to see the crime scene photos. But seeing the man and hearing the voice— the directness, the primal, elemental intimacy—I felt as if I had just taken one step farther into the mind of the monster, into the heart of darkness.

"We have only to look to the Renaissance painters for confirmation. They understood the true purpose of art. They knew how to capture that fervor, that delight, that pure erotic ecstasy. Just look into the eyes of their subjects.

"Saint Sebastian. Now there's one I'd like to do myself. I remember that magic time in Vienna. Anthea and I were on our honeymoon and so full of life and joy. We were wandering through the Kunsthistorisches Museum and came upon Mantegna's magnificent painting. I was transfixed. It is about nothing short of apotheosis. I'm sure Anthea could see it in my eyes."

He used his hands evocatively. "That splendid naked musculature. That wonderful pose: the hands tied painfully behind and the hips jutting provocatively to the side. The arrows piercing through the luminous skin and the exquisitely thin trickles of blood emanating from each wound. The mouth—tense but brave, the lips slightly and suggestively parted. And the eyes—those ecstatic eyes looking beseechingly heavenward. The ecstatic, open eyes looking to something beyond, looking up to no less than the supreme being of the universe."

I felt as if I were back at Quantico, sitting through a session of those torture films.

He cleared his throat—a rasping, barking "achemmm."

"How I wished at that moment I could ever achieve such greatness in art, that somehow I could live up to the example set by the great religious ecstatics. But in our secular age, how can we possibly hope to recover any of that fervor, any of that ecstasy, any of that delight?"

He stood and held his finger in the air, just the way Nicholas did.

"The ecstasy of religious ardor, that's what I'm after. The pure, orgasmic energy of eternity. The saints understood this. Ordinary men cannot possibly. For how can one relate the fleeting pleasure of ejaculation against the ecstatic agony of martyrdom? The shuddering to climax of the most exquisite female loins is base and meaningless when compared with the passion of little Joan of Arc as the flames whipped around her breasts and consumed her living flesh. What unimagined joy that simple farm girl must have experienced as the unbearable and unvanquishable pain carried her into eternity! A joy which remains with us unto this day."

Yeah, you tell us, Neville. And then tell Joyce Fabrizi's family.

"In the right context, it is possible to live forever! But it may be no more possible for our age to recapture that than for a modern real estate developer to hope to build Chartres. But it is up to those few brave explorers among us to try."

And another deep, guttural rasp.

Then the screen went snowy. I felt a bead of cold sweat form between my shoulder blades and slowly trickle down my spine. It reached the top of my buttocks and made me squirm on my chair.

I pressed the stop button. Then I got up and walked two doors over and opened the door of room number one.

Just as I'd visualized it—there weren't many variations on this theme—Nick sat across from Vince. They bore the weary expressions of two negotiators stalemated on an intractable point. And just as I'd visualized, the room was adorned with spent cigarettes and empty coffee cups, most likely from the previous users. Still, the ventilation system was no better than any of our other facilities, and a gray haze hung in the air.

I thought Nick's eyes lit up when I came in, but he didn't say anything.

"What's going on?" I said.

"Just asking the doctor a few questions," said Vince. "But he doesn't seem to have much new to contribute. Perhaps he'll be more forthcoming with you."

As soon as Vince was gone Nick said, "Is that camera on?"

I said, "No. It's used for confessions. Are you telling me I should turn it on?"

He slammed the table with his open palm. "I trusted you, and you led me on. I thought we had something."

I pulled out the chair and sat down across the table from him. "I can't deny that," I said.

"I didn't do it!" he shouted. "I'm innocent!"

"Believe it or not, it's been my experience that that's what most guilty people say."

"I've devoted my life to saving lives. Why would I want to take them?"

"I could come up with some possibilities, but they'd all sound like pop psychology. Why don't you tell me?"

"I am telling you. I'm not your man!"

"You collect instruments that look like a sadist's wet dream."

"Historical curiosities. They show how far my profession has come. You don't know policemen who collect antique guns?"

"Yeah," I said, "and they're all weirdos. And what were you doing with the books on the Aztecs and the Egyptians?"

"You said it yourself—the murders of those two women were very similar to what Neville had done. When I visited him in prison, he said something about the Egyptians' triumph over death. As an artist, it was one of his favorite themes. Once I figured out the Egyptian theme, the Aztec wasn't that difficult—not if you knew the way Neville's mind worked. I wanted to learn more."

"What about the clippings?"

"I wanted to know as much as I could about these crimes, particularly after you involved me."

"The file was started before I came to you. You're going to have to do better than that, Nick."

"I can't do better than the truth."

"And what's the truth about the penlight from the drug company found at the Ashburn murder scene with your prints?"

He seemed to withdraw slightly. "I don't know. Maybe someone planted it."

I leaned away from the table, crossed one leg high over the other, and flexed my fingers behind my head. "Have you been writing me letters?"

"What are you talking about?"

"Have you ever been in my apartment?"

"I don't even know where you live."

"What about the 'surprise' you said you had for me?"

"If you must know, it was a racquetball racket, along with an invitation to play again."

"Not Joan of Arc in a Georgetown cemetery?"

He turned away from me. "This is preposterous!"

I clasped my hands together on the table in plain sight—symbolic of being completely open. At least, that's what they teach you in the basic interrogation course. "Nick, is it possible we're actually dealing with two entities here?"

He didn't respond.

"Obviously, the Nicholas Ramsey who saves lives and takes on cases no one else will attempt is incapable of what has happened." I stood up and began circling around the table. "But something's very wrong here. Something doesn't add up. On the one hand, we've got a brilliant, caring surgeon. And on the other, we've got a tremendous amount of evidence—both forensic and behavioral—which points to an out-of-control sexual psychopath, an individual very much like—no, uncannily like—your late brother, Neville." I stopped, gripped the corner of the table, and leaned far in to him, violating his space. "Now which one are you?"

"How many times do I have to tell you?"

"Let me ask you this: Can you imagine what it would be like to do what your brother did?"

"On a certain level. So can you."

"That's true," I said. "I can relate to that." I began pacing again, circling in for the kill. His eyes followed me around the cramped space. "In a way, it isn't much different from what you do every day!"

"It's completely different!"

"Let's think about it. I mean, you've got a helpless patient on the table, you cut into her, make her bleed. Okay, sure, she's there willingly and you're doing it for a 'good' reason. But didn't Neville think what he was doing was for a good reason? He must have. Transcendency of art and all that swell-sounding stuff. And at least at first, the victims went with him willingly. I'm not saying it's exactly the same, but when you think about it, it's pretty fucking close."

"Maybe in your mind."

I retreated to the far corner of the room so I could project more—that old drama training. "And what about the power? Life and death. Can't get more basic than that. What would it feel like to have Julie

Fox tied to a chair in front on you, naked, helpless, subject to your mercy, to your whim? You get to control her completely, to dominate her, to create the new reality between you.''

I was revolted by what I was saying, I hated myself for saying it. But there was no holding back. It was more important than anything else. I moved up close and began miming every action. ''You take that scalpel—after all, who's better with a scalpel than you are—you take that scalpel and you cut: so precisely, so artistically. With all his talent, Neville never could have done it as well. A few quick strokes since you know just the right places . . . A few quick strokes and you've got her heart in your hand.''

I held the imaginary heart up in front of me, like Hamlet contemplating Yorick's skull. ''In fact, when you first touch it, it's still beating! That's a hard one to top. What does Neville do? He has rats crawl up a guy's ass. But you, you've got the living, breathing heart of a beautiful young girl.

''What did it feel like,'' I asked, subtly shifting tense and case, ''what did it feel like to hold that bloody heart in your hand? Did you panic? Did you panic, or did you get a feeling of exaltation, of fulfillment?''

''I wouldn't know,'' he shot back, glaring at me with rage and disdain.

''Was it that easy getting Julie Fox to fall for you?'' I pressed on. ''I wouldn't think it would be too difficult. Here she was, this shy, vulnerable kid living by her tits and ass, showing them off four times a day to a roomful of creepo businessmen. She comes in to see you in your office, tells you about this pain she has in her leg. Let's see, she either takes her pants off or lifts her skirt to show the doctor where it hurts. Which was it, Nick?''

''Stop baiting me.''

''No, you're right, it's not important. But here's what is important: I'd imagine a wealthy, sophisticated doctor would have no trouble sweeping little Julie right off her feet.''

''I don't behave that way with my patients.''

''I'm a law officer, and until Wednesday night, I could have said the same thing.''

He started to protest, but I cut him off. ''Now, let's see. Sarah Hazeltine would be a little more difficult. More refined, knows the world of art, hangs around with a different crowd. But you are one attractive guy, and you learn as you go along, you work your way up from one to the other until finally . . .''

"Until finally I get to you?"

Of course. That was what I was saying, wasn't it? I put my hands out, palms upward. "I can't deny it. Pulling myself away from you was one of the most difficult things I've ever done. Nick, I dreamed about you last night. And it was great! I really mean that."

I really did. Even as I stood here trying to wring a murder confession out of this man, my yearning for him and his touch was all but overpowering. Since Wednesday night, I hadn't been able to shake it. It had been like a semiconscious overlay on everything I'd done and thought.

I felt like a participant in a rape, both as attacker and victim. But I kept going, kept hammering at him, kept hammering at myself in the process. It was as if I had become someone else. I wondered if this was how Chris Taylor felt every night when he transformed into Richard III and brought the hapless Lady Anne under his power.

I paused. It grew quiet. And in that moment, I realized my body was trembling and that under my blouse I was covered with a thin film of perspiration. I coughed from the bad air.

I grabbed the chair from behind and slid back onto it. "Nick, let's talk practically," I said, consciously softening my tone. "Let's look at the situation from both our points of view. I've got a series of horrible murders. They bear the evidence of your brother's hand, right down to the eye of Horus hanging on your wall and the types of knots used in the ligature." I didn't mention the interesting divergence in the latest one. "I want to believe you. I really do. But all the evidence—every shred of it—points to you."

"You can't get a conviction."

"Maybe I can't and maybe I can. But you know as well as I do this case is going to make international news. Every TV tabloid show in the country is already yapping at our asses. Can you imagine if we hand them Nightmare Neville's brother, the famous, brilliant lifesaving brain surgeon? What's that going to do to your career? What's that going to do to the confidence of your patients? What's it going to do to the scared and gutless bureaucrats who know the programs you've already been thrown out of? Face it, Nick. No matter what happens from this moment on, you lose."

His eyes flashed. He stood and leaned forward over the table. "You want a suspect? I'll give you a suspect!"

My heart quickened. This is the moment in every interrogation that you work for, wait for, hope for—they're about to go over the edge, and sometimes you just have to hold your breath while they finally tip.

He leaned in even farther and waited until I had leaned in so close that our heads practically touched. "You've got to promise me that whatever we say is just between us."

"What?"

"You can't tell anyone else anything, at least for now."

I sat back and slapped my hand down on the table. "Nicholas, you're about to be arrested for murder. You're not exactly in the strongest bargaining position."

"There's a lot at stake here," he said.

"Of course there is."

"More than you know. That's why you have to trust me."

"No, Nick," I said, leaning in hard again, "you're going to have to trust me. Now, point-blank: Are you responsible for those murders?"

He looked straight at me, and almost imperceptibly, he nodded. "I guess you could say I am."

I felt a flutter in my stomach, and simultaneously the air drained from my lungs. The climax of the drama.

"But I didn't kill them."

"Cut the shit," I said angrily. I hate being jerked around by a suspect—any suspect. "We're past 'the bad Nick did it, but the good Nick didn't know anything about it.' I offered you that option. You turned me down."

"That's not what I mean."

"Then what do you mean? Which is it, Nick?"

"Both."

"Okay, if you didn't kill those people, do you have any idea who did?"

"I think so."

I stood up suddenly and bent over the table on my palms. I whispered, "Then who in the fuck was it?"

He looked up at me again. He rubbed his hands together, like Lady Macbeth trying to rub out the blood. He opened his mouth several times without actually uttering a word. I'd never seen him like this. Finally he did manage to speak. "Christopher Taylor."

"Then it was Christopher Taylor who stole the penlight from your office and planted it in Battery Kemble Park?"

"I guess so."

Now I was really pissed. Couldn't he come up with something cleverer than the name I'd brought to him? "Why would Chris Taylor recreate *your* brother's crimes?"

"Because I gave him a piece of *my* brother's brain."

31

A S we move through life, there are certain revelations that forever alter our perceptions of reality: that there is no Santa Claus; that babies form and grow in women's bellies; that life has an end; that time contracts and space bends in upon itself.

For a moment, it almost passed me by. Then I thought I must have heard wrong. Then I responded to what Nicholas had just said with the same incredulity with which I had greeted, at the appropriate time, every other preposterous notion that had assaulted my rational mind.

"That's absurd," I said, because I couldn't think of what else to say.

"Hamlet to his best friend: 'There are more things in heaven and earth, Horatio, Than are dreamt of in your philosophy.' "

"But it's not possible."

" 'Discarding accepted ideas of what's possible can make it easier to take new ideas more seriously.' Murray Gell-Mann, Nobel Prize–winning physicist. The impossible is always absurd until it's done. Then it's possible, and after that, it's ordinary. If you'd described electricity to a fifteenth-century pope, you would have been tried for witchcraft. If you had told a nineteenth-century doctor that the answer to the scourge of infectious disease lay in bread mold, what do you think his reaction would have been?"

"Tell me exactly what you're talking about."

"Then I have your word this remains between us?"

"Just keep talking."

"Do you mind if I stand? I've been sitting a long time."

"You want a Coke or anything?"

"No." He stood, braced himself with his hands against the side of the table, and stretched. He flexed his elbows and knees, as if getting ready for a race. There was that catlike grace to every movement.

"Late October, the warden of San Quentin called and told me what Neville had done, that he'd jumped over a railing and tried to kill himself. He told me they'd taken him to Letterman—it was the closest military hospital, and Neville was still considered a security threat. I spoke to the doctors there. They told me he wasn't going to make it. Between them and the warden, they agreed to let me bring Neville back to Washington. I arranged for an air ambulance and had him brought to Halsted."

"Why?"

His eyes were misty. He bit his lower lip and almost shrugged. "To see him one more time. So he wouldn't die alone. So I could salvage some good out of his life."

"You mean . . ."

"I notified the transplant team and had them harvest everything they could—kidneys, liver, heart, corneas. They even took most of the bowel. That's the one good thing about a fatal spinal cord injury: the vital organs are generally in good working order. There are people walking around today who wouldn't be if it weren't for Neville."

And a lot more who still would be if not for him. "And Chris Taylor?" I asked. "How does he fit into this?"

"I resected a small part of his left temporal lobe and 'replaced' it with a similar piece from Neville's brain."

"But how? Neville was dead. His brain was dead."

"Not quite, or just barely, depending on your interpretation. In modern medicine, death has become a subjective state."

"Has . . . has anything like this ever been done before?"

"Not to my knowledge. But I wasn't flying completely blind. There's been a lot of work by a lot of people, including White at Cleveland Clinic. We've done a lot of animal studies. I've been thinking about it, studying the possibility, for years. I'd already done a couple of fetal tissue grafts for advanced Parkinson's. The trick was to accomplish the same thing with mature, differentiated neural tissue and have it remain viable. In a way, whether I knew it or not, my whole career had been building up to that moment."

I recalled what Jerry Ashburn had told me about Nick's checkered past with hospital administrations. So this was his secret agenda.

"There's even some indication my father tried it, or at least thought about trying it. I went through his papers after he died. They were rather mysterious on the subject.''

"What did the people at Halsted say about this?'' Even if what he was telling me was possible and true, I couldn't imagine a lawsuit-conscious administrator allowing him to do it.

"They didn't say anything because they didn't know.''

"You didn't tell them?''

"What was I supposed to do—take it before the ethics committee and have it tossed around for days or weeks by a bunch of careful, responsible cowards, while the tissue rotted? Forget about doing it? That would have been the 'prudent' thing. That would have been the safe thing. But the great breakthroughs in science are never safe. They're bold, they're daring, and they're risky. Nothing worthwhile is ever achieved but through risk. The great breakthroughs, the things that save countless lives and change history, have never come from committees or panels or conventional wisdom. They've never come from playing it safe. I had about an hour and a half to decide, plan a strategy, and get it started. Not days, not weeks. An hour and a half.''

Then that was why Chris and Ashby were both prepared for surgery on such short notice. And that was why he did three operations on the same day, and that was the significance of the date—two days after Neville jumped.

So many things were racing through my mind. I couldn't sort it all. I couldn't handle it. "Chris Taylor,'' I said, "the way he talked . . . I mean, that thing he did—the way he cleared his throat all the time. I heard the same thing on the tape of Neville.''

"A neurological tic, you might call it. I remember Neville had it since he was a little boy. It became more pronounced whenever he got excited.''

"So that's why you think it was Chris Taylor.''

"That and what you told me. Unless it was Ashby Collier.''

"Or the businessman from Saudi Arabia,'' I reminded him.

He nodded but didn't say anything.

"Did they know what was being done to them?''

"I prefer to think of it as what was being done *for* them. They knew I was doing surgery to help them, especially Ashby. If it weren't for this, nothing short of the hand of God would have kept her alive. And now, as far as we can tell, she's cured.''

"You didn't tell these people what you were doing?''

"They couldn't have handled the details."

"So you just asked them to trust you with their lives. That's a pretty fucking big responsibility."

"I'm used to pretty fucking big responsibilities."

"Does anyone else know about this?"

"Pieces of it. Some people know I had the brain removed 'for study.' Others knew I'd sectioned it off in a laboratory. The few people in the OR knew I was trying some kind of experimental procedure involving a graft. I also implanted a NeMo in each one, so the surgical team probably focused more on that since they know we're going through clinical trials. Anyway, brain surgery isn't big or showy. You only need an anesthesiologist, a good nurse, and maybe a resident to assist. And they don't have to know exactly what you're doing. No one else knew the whole story . . . until now."

I folded my arms across my chest and paced back and forth in front of the table. It was as if my perception of reality had suddenly been knocked askew. "You're asking me to believe you could transplant one person's brain into another person's body, like Dr. Frankenstein."

"A *small piece* of one brain to positively influence another brain. It was theoretically plausible. The brain is the one part of the body that does not recognize foreign tissue and reject it. I had the opportunity. People could be helped. I had to try."

"How do I know what you've told me here is true?" It seemed an obvious question. "You've had a lot of time to come up with this story to cover yourself."

"Do you believe I'm telling the truth? What's your gut reaction as a homicide detective?"

"I want to believe you're telling the truth. And that's why I'm wary of my own judgment. I want desperately to believe that Dr. Jekyll isn't Mr. Hyde."

"Dr. Jekyll created Mr. Hyde and then tried to make up for it. That's what I still have to do. And I need you to help me."

"The evidence still points to you," I stated. "Where were you the night of Jerry Ashburn's murder?"

"I was working late at the hospital."

"Can anyone verify your presence?"

"I was working alone, going over my notes, trying to figure this whole thing out."

"Why did you give Bob Fusillo your car?"

"I often loan him my car when I won't be needing it. He likes driving it. It's a nice car. It impresses women."

Including me, but it wasn't much of an answer. "If you are telling the truth," I said, "then why did you keep trying to throw me off?"

"I thought I could handle it myself."

"Surgeons really do think they're gods, don't they?"

He cracked a faint smile. "That should be obvious by now."

"And why were you really at Jerry Ashburn's funeral?"

He shrugged. "Same reason as you. I wanted to see if any of the 'suspects' showed up."

"And did they?"

"No. Same about going to Julie Fox's club."

"You keep asking me to trust you. Why didn't you trust me? Why didn't you just tell me, Nick?"

"Tell you what? That someone was copying my dead brother's killings? You figured that out on your own. But that I had nothing to do with it? You wouldn't have believed me. You don't know if you do now. And since, if my suspicions were right, I had caused what was happening, I had a responsibility to my patients. I still do."

"But you're saying one of them is a murderer."

"One of them *might* be a murderer. We don't have proof of that, neither one of us. Until I know for sure, I can't take a chance on ruining their lives. And if it gets out about Chris, the others will know, too. It'll destroy them."

"I can't take a chance on someone else getting killed," I countered. "What are you saying you want me to do?"

"Let me go."

"Just like that?" I turned around and thrust my hands into the patch pockets of my skirt. "The captain will love it."

"You can keep me here as long as you want. But it won't stop someone else from getting killed. You've just had another."

Which still bothered me. And if the divergence from the knots bothered me, then the divergence from the cycle did, too. "Do you have any idea what the significance of Tuesday is?" I asked him.

"I have no idea,"

"They have any special significance in Neville's mind?"

"He was married on a Tuesday, I think. I'm not positive, but I think Anthea committed suicide on a Tuesday. Wait a minute! It was a Tuesday last October when he jumped. Do you think that's it?"

226 ——————— THE EDGE

"Good chance," I said. "We haven't come up with anything better. What about the two-week periodicity?"

"I don't know. What I do know is that I need your help."

I couldn't help thinking that if he'd decided he needed me earlier, Jerry Ashburn might still be alive, not to mention Joyce Fabrizi. "Then you have to tell this story to the rest of the squad," I said.

"No! Once it goes farther than you and me, it's out of control. What if I'm wrong? That'll destroy Chris's life."

"If you're telling the truth, then there's a larger issue here, Nick."

He sat on the edge of the table. "You want to talk larger issues? Okay, try this one. This is a field so theoretical and experimental that most people—most doctors—don't even know it exists, but with the right support and development, it's going to stretch the limits of medical science and help countless people. It's going to help us define how the brain works—how we think. The implications are incredible. The wrong kind of attention or fear will kill it or hold it back for twenty, maybe fifty years. Sandy, this is what I've been working up to my entire career. It's what I've been put on earth to do. And it's only the beginning!"

My head was swimming. I was still trying to sort it all out in my own mind. The tiny room was growing increasingly claustrophobic, as if we'd used up all the available air. Normally I use this to my advantage in an interrogation. Now I felt as if I were the one who had to get out.

"How can you say it's the beginning? Look what's happened!"

"Look what happened when Barnard and Shumway started transplanting hearts. Look what happened when Starzl started transplanting livers. There are always problems to be solved."

"Yes, of course," I said. " 'Excuse me, Dr. Frankenstein, sorry to bother you, but we seem to have a little problem here.' "

"There is no progress without pain and sacrifice and suffering. Don't you understand? Tell your captain you're keeping me under surveillance, I don't care what you say. You carry a gun—if you think I'm dangerous or threatening, then shoot me. With all the evidence you've got, you'd be in the clear. But if we don't get to the bottom of this in the next few days, there are going to be more murders, regardless of what you do with me. I think you know that."

He put his hand on my shoulder. "What do you say, Sandy? I know you make deals all the time, and I'm asking you to make one with me."

"Or with the devil," I said.

We all face our moments of truth, when all the extraneous material of life moves to the side, when we have to reach as deep inside as we can go and decide just exactly what it is we believe and believe in. And when that moment comes, you hope not to be corrupted by anything tainted or impure. As police officers, we're supposed to believe in truth and justice. But justice is often elusive, and truth is a moving target. You make the best choice you can, knowing you will have to live with the outcome from that time forth.

Without saying anything, I turned to the door and left the room. I closed the door behind me and walked the length of the aisle down the center of the squad room. I could feel all eyes on me, but I didn't stop or turn around. I passed the entrance door, I passed the lieutenants' desk, I passed the coffee machine.

The captain's door was open. Vince was in there with him. When I came in, Owen stood and looked at me expectantly.

"Ready to book?"

"Let him walk," I said.

32

PATRICK Owen recoiled back onto his chair as if he'd been hit by a baseball bat. If he'd had one available, he might have used it on me.

"What!"

It was only one word, but I thought he would choke on it.

"I'm not convinced he's the guy now," I said as calmly and evenly as I could.

"You've spent almost the last month convincing yourself he was. And then you convinced the rest of us. What gives?"

"Another suspect."

"What's his name?"

"Christopher Taylor."

"And who the fuck is Christopher Taylor?"

"You must not go to the theater very much, boss."

"Spare me, Sandy."

"He's an actor."

"And you've got him playing the role of serial murderer?"

"He's one of the ones who came in to confess," Vince explained. "Sandy interviewed him. Thought he was a mixed-up kid looking for attention, just like all the others. Didn't have any of the key details."

"So what's changed?" the boss asked impatiently.

"For one thing, he's a patient of Nick's . . . ah, Dr. Ramsey's."

Owen and Vince exchanged glances. I had to watch myself.

"Then there's some other things I need to check out." I tried to be as vague as I could. I turned to Vince. "Anything pan out on Cynthia Andrew, the exercise lady?"

"Nice woman, great figure—Ramsey's sent her a fair number of his patients who needed some sort of rehabilitation. But he's never visited the class personally, and she doesn't know how he would have known Hazeltine. I'm going to talk to some of the other women."

"You said Taylor came to us," Owen broke in. "Why would he do that if he was the actual perp? Vince just said he didn't even know the details."

"He may have been testing us to see what we knew or how he'd react," I said, "how safe he was. These people can be very manipulative. And a lot of them flirt with being caught; it's part of the kick. Don't forget, he is an actor, and a damned good one. Or it might have been a subconscious cry for help, to stop him from what he was doing."

Owen leaned forward and began hammering his desk, began hammering me. "You say it is Ramsey, you say it isn't, it is, now it's another guy. What, Sandy? What? We don't even have enough to get a search warrant on this guy, Taylor. I still don't understand why you soured on Ramsey."

"I've just got serious doubts. I'd hate to take it to a prosecutor and have it blow up in our faces. Or worse yet, put Ramsey on ice and still have someone else killed Tuesday."

"I thought we were off that now with Fabrizi."

"I'm not sure."

Owen threw up his hands in exasperation.

"You've just got to trust me, boss." There was that word again.

"God, I hate this," he declared to no one in particular. "So what's your bright idea?"

"Tail Chris Taylor," I said. I hadn't told Nick this would have to be part of the deal. Things were messy enough already. "You can start right now, begin picking up the evidence we'll need for a warrant. He won't be difficult. We know he'll be at the theater in the evening. My guess is the critical time is going to be right before or right after the show on Tuesday."

"If we don't have another dead body before that."

"If we do," I asserted, "it won't be in this series."

Owen turned and walked back behind his desk. "Sometimes I wish I understood how your mind works," he muttered.

"We could have Sandy get more 'involved' with him," Vince suggested. "If he's the one writing her letters and who broke into her apartment, that might draw him out."

Owen shook his head. "I don't like that; could seem like entrapment. And she's said nothing to convince me so far, anyway." He turned back to me. "So what do we do about Ramsey? Even if I decide to humor you, as far as I'm concerned, he's still our prime suspect."

"I can keep tabs on him."

"He's not going to do anything if he knows a cop is watching him all the time. Even the most compulsive sexual killer isn't that compulsive."

"But that's just the point. If it is him and he really does have the need to kill on this particular night, he'll do anything he can to ditch me. Then we'll know. Meanwhile, we'll have Chris Taylor covered."

Owen wearily rubbed the back of his neck and then leaned heavily against his desk chair. "So you've developed something of a 'relationship,' shall we say?"

I nodded, purposely not looking at Vince. "We try to develop relationships with a lot of people."

"Yeah, but a two-bit drug dealer's a lot different from a prominent brain surgeon." Implying the first is okay, but the second is a no-no? If my mother could only hear this.

"You know you're playing with fire, Sandy."

"I think I have it under control," I said. I was curious myself to hear how it sounded from my own mouth. "I had to get close to him and get him to trust me."

"And I'm trusting you to know where that magic line is and not to cross it." Owen now looked as if his stomach were bothering him. "Okay," he said without enthusiasm, "if you think there are flaws in the Ramsey case, he walks. But you're responsible for him. He belongs to you."

"I understand."

"I'm warning you right now, any fuck-ups and you are the sacrificial lamb offered up at the feast of public remonstrance. *Comprenez?*"

Did I have any choice? As I said, a case like this will make or break you, particularly if your instinct for covering your own ass is as underdeveloped as mine seems to be.

"Okay, that's it," Owen announced. "It's not often the same person can make your day, then ruin it on the same day."

Vince and I left together. As soon as we were outside the office, he turned to me and said, "I hope you know what you're doing."

"Me too," I agreed readily.

I went back to the interrogation room and told Nick he was free.

"You did it," he said with relief.

"You're not out of the woods," I warned him. "Neither am I."

When we got outside, there was a ticket under the Mercedes' single sleek wiper blade. He tore it off casually and threw it in the back. When you make as much money as he did per minute, I guess twenty bucks isn't that big a deal. Either that, or a parking violation palls next to a possible murder rap. But you'd be surprised how many killers and armed robbers we pick up after tracing them from parking tickets. Just goes to show, people who have no respect for the big laws have no respect for the little ones, either.

"Can I take you somewhere?" he asked.

"Like where?" I said skeptically.

"Why don't you leave that to me?"

"You mean, like trust you?"

We stopped off for dinner at Primi Piatti, a welcome change from the Sabrett's cart and my eternally barren fridge. It seemed I got my best meals lately from Nick. The restaurant was a good choice, actually. Besides the excellent food, it's difficult to be overheard, even a single table away.

The maître d' recognized Nick and ushered us to one of the best spots. Nick ordered a bottle of red. I was grateful for the brief respite and diversion the dinner represented, but I couldn't forget why we were here together or what had to be done.

"You said you did three operations using Neville's brain," I said, crunching on one of the famous breadsticks. "Isn't it possible it's one of the others?"

"It's possible," he said. "But who else would it be? Ashby? She wouldn't be physically capable."

He was right about that. Whoever did it had to be strong enough to drag Julie Fox's body from the bedroom to the dining room without letting her behind hit the carpet.

"And didn't you say there was some indication of intercourse?"

"There was some. But without evidence of semen, that doesn't rule out a woman." What other profession boasts such scintillating dinner table conversation? "What would," I said, thinking out loud, "is that women rarely, if ever, commit these kinds of crimes, certainly not against other women. Of course, women rarely, if ever, carry around pieces of men's brains in their heads, either.''

"What about this Hawaas?" I asked.

He took a sip of wine. It almost seemed like a hesitation. "He wasn't much bigger than Ashby. And as far as I know, he hasn't been back in here since then. He hardly spoke English.''

Nick retreated conveniently into his menu, but I could see I had hit home. The waiter came with a bottle of Chianti. He poured a sample, which Nick judged to be acceptable.

"I guess Chris still looks like our prime suspect,'' he said, swirling the wine in his glass.

"If we rule out you,'' I said dryly. He made a face. "I'm going to ask you one more time: Did you break into my apartment and take my jewelry and underwear?''

"As you've seen, when I want to get to your underwear, I'll take a more direct route. What kind of guy do you think I am?''

"I don't know what kind of guy I think you are!" I declared. "That's what's driving me crazy.''

"What is it going to take to get you to fully trust me?''

"I wish I could tell you,'' I said. I sipped my wine.

"Let's get back to Chris,'' he said, clearly anxious to get off this tack. "He's the one with the most physical skills. He's a good-looking, personable young man. He'd be the one most attractive to the women.''

Except, perhaps, for a rich, handsome, and famous brain surgeon.

But back to work. "The ME said Jerry Ashburn might have been stabbed by a sword,'' I mentioned. "As a classically trained actor, Chris would be one of the few people left in society who still knew how to use one.''

"Makes sense.''

"What about the medical knowledge the killer demonstrated?''

"I can only assume he got that from Neville . . . I mean, from Neville's brain.''

"Is that possible?''

"Theoretically, yes, though it's never been proven in humans.''

He reminded me of the flatworm experiments I'd seen in his lecture—the one where learning was actually physically transferred. "But it's a bit of a leap from flatworms and chickens to human beings,'' I said.

"Great science is always a leap, a leap that begins with an intriguing premise."

"I feel as if someone's controlling me; telling me what to do," Christopher Taylor had said to me. So it was true, then. Someone else was controlling him. The late Neville Ramsey.

I stared down into my wineglass. "So Chris got the unlucky piece of Neville's brain, the one that made Neville what he was."

"Not necessarily. As we saw from our rats who seemed to learn the pathway through a maze simply by being near rats who already knew it, the brain is an incredibly elastic organ. Physical changes in the brain can cause emotional changes in the personality. Emotional stimuli can cause physical changes in the brain, and on and on. Chris is an actor. He has an artistic temperament like Neville. It's possible that it was the combination of the physical brain tissue and the ineffable sensibility that did it."

"You mean a combination of hardware and software?"

"People are always using the computer analogy. It works up to a point." He thought for a moment. "It's also possible that the introduction of new tissue has altered brain chemistry and changed neurotransmitter uptake in some subtle way."

Sure, it was possible, I thought to myself. I was beginning to believe anything was possible in this brave new world of medical miracles. And if some of it happened to lead to violent death, well—there's no progress without pain. Wasn't that what Nick had said?

After dinner, we walked in silence along Pennsylvania Avenue, heading nowhere in particular. It was dark enough now that the fireflies had come out. First we'd see one and then another, blinking their tiny electric tails in random sequence. Then we saw more, swarming together, clicking on and off, on and off, as if in some elaborate mating ritual. And then, before we knew it, it was as if the swarm had gotten its collective act together, resonating nearly in unison, as if each bug were only a tiny piece of the collective mind of God.

"I understand what you were trying to do for these patients," I said, "but when you transplanted those pieces of that brain, didn't it occur to you that maybe you were also transplanting what that brain was . . . thinking about?"

Nick looked straight ahead as we continued walking. We crossed with the light at 17th Street. Lafayette Park and its constant phalanx of protestors came into sight.

"That's not a framework a surgeon considers, ever. Strange as it may sound, when a surgeon thinks about a brain, he doesn't think about 'thought.' He can't afford to. What he thinks about are lesions and deficits, not moral points of view. That's for philosophers and priests, not doctors.

"You have to understand, the test of success for a brain surgeon isn't whether the patient suddenly decides to help the widows and children of the world; it's whether he stops having seizures or regains his reasoning ability or stops forgetting. Chris and Ashby had NeMos wired to the exact point of the transplant. And I can tell you, their readings since the surgery have been consistently normal. That's a cure in my book!"

"Tell that to Julie Fox and Sarah Hazeltine," I said. "But you must have considered this. You must have allowed for some contingency."

He stopped and turned to me. "You still don't seem to get it, Sandy. An internist, a pediatrician, a radiologist, they can all hedge their bets: 'consistent with . . . indicative of . . . suggest further study and follow-up evaluation . . .' Not the surgeon. You decide what you're going to do, and once you cut open your patient, that's the moment of truth."

And unless we do something pretty fucking quick, I thought, Tuesday is when we face ours.

————

With all our talk, with all the twenty-twenty hindsight of that night last October, that was the one question that remained unanswered. *The* question: What were we going to do about it?

"If you made him that way, can you unmake him?" I asked.

The answer came back at Nick's house. I went up to the second-floor bathroom to take off my infernal panty hose and try to repair the ravages of a day of stress and a soggy blanket of humidity. When I came out, Nick was in the den on the sofa, a double Scotch in his hand, staring at the television.

"Watch this," he said grimly.

Chris Taylor was dressed in ordinary clothes and sitting in an orange plastic stacking chair against a neutral background. Another look and I realized it was one of Nick's examining rooms. There was a running time code across the bottom of the screen, the same as when we tape confessions. Chris was talking, apparently answering a question, when all of a sudden he just stopped cold and zoned out. His mouth hung slightly open. His eyes had a blank, otherworldly stare. It was as if Nick had just pressed the pause button on the remote control or the entire scene had been suspended in time. Then, just as abruptly, he resumed the conversation, a little fuzzy, but basically where he'd left off.

The exchange continued. The content was almost incidental—the weather, recent good movies, how the Redskins were doing early in the season. The other voice was Nick's. Then it happened again, no more than two or three minutes later. Chris just ''left.'' This lasted maybe thirty or forty seconds, and then life returned.

''That's creepy,'' I said.

He looked up morosely. ''This is what Chris Taylor was like the day before I operated on him . . . the day after Neville jumped. And what he'll be like after I operate on him again. Or worse.''

''What are you talking about?'' I asked, his final words still hanging ominously in the air.

''You asked what I can do about it. I guess I've known for a while. I don't have any choice.''

He unfroze the frame, and again Chris Taylor froze up on his own. ''I've got to go in again and reverse what I've done.''

''What?'' A part of me knew exactly what he was talking about. ''How?''

''I've been thinking about that, too. I'll call him to come in for a follow-up visit. I'll do some tests—an EEG, a head CT, check the NeMo readouts—then I'll analyze them and regretfully tell him that he needs further surgery.''

''Is that ethical?''

''You tell me,'' he challenged. ''And then tell me how many angels can dance on the head of a pin. Ethics are a set of moral standards applied to a particular situation or type of behavior. Ethics grow out of a need, and the need is the situation itself. You didn't need a code of ethics for people in renal failure until it was scientifically possible to keep x-number of them alive on dialysis. And then you didn't need a policy on which of them got new kidneys until it was scientifically possible to transplant an organ from one human being to another. If you go by the basic maxim we've all had ingrained in us since medical school, 'First, do no harm,' then we're already past that. We're in uncharted territory. But I can't let him go on murdering.''

''You could just tell him the truth.''

''What do you think he'd say? Do you think he'd agree to the surgery? And if he didn't, then what? There are people still undergoing intense psychiatric care just because they posed for Neville.''

"What exactly would you do?"

"I'd open up his head, locate the vector in his temporal lobe where I introduced the transplant, resect it, and get the hell back out."

"Would you just be able to get the transplant and nothing else?"

"I doubt it."

"So what would be the effect?"

Nick shook his head with uncertainty. "We can't be sure. But it won't be good."

———————————

It was after twelve when I got home. I lay in my tub soaking, as stretched out as my long legs would allow, my head resting against the hard porcelain rim. There is something purifying about being naked and clean and wet and warm. I kept thinking about everything that had happened today, the implications and the nuances, and what it all meant.

Nick wanted me to believe everything he'd told me, to take the law into my own—our own—hands, to break the rules in a major way. Nick wanted to alter Chris surgically, to try to take out the part we thought made Chris a killer.

Could I go along with it? What would it do to Chris, and how did we know it would work? If Nick was right that it was the combination of Neville's brain working on Chris's sensibility that had created the monster, how could we be sure that even if Nick could take out the "Neville" part of Chris's brain and very little else, that evil influence would be gone with it? The fact of the matter, as Nick grimly but readily admitted, was that we couldn't be sure. We couldn't be sure of anything.

"Science doesn't have an explanation for everything," Nick had said to me. "How, for instance, does science account for our memory of dragons?"

The memory of dragons.

What if it's not Chris, but this mysterious Saudi who's disappeared into thin air? The evidence pointed to Chris. But this was all new territory, so what did any of it mean?

The more I considered all these possibilities, the shakier I started feeling. It was what Ted used to call "thinking disease." The mere act of thinking too hard about something becomes a morbid exercise. And the more you think about it, the worse it gets.

Thinking disease.

And the memory of dragons.

33

I slept late Sunday morning, and even after I woke up, I lay in bed searching for direction and comfort, trying to make sense out of everything.

We talk about environment, we talk about heredity, we talk about upbringing and nature versus nurture. But seeing the things I have over the years, what it always came down to for me was this: Is all human behavior merely the movement of electrons and molecules through the neural and chemical pathways of those three pounds of brain tissue I'd seen so many times in autopsies, or is there such a thing as evil in the universe? Did the answer lie in science or in something deeper and more primal that science could not explain, any more than it could explain the memory of dragons?

Where had Neville Ramsey come from? And was his brother from the same place? If what Nick had told me was true, what was his real reason for transplanting those pieces of that brain? Was it to help those victims of life's deadly caprices, or was it to keep alive the beloved brother and protector from whom he could never truly separate himself?

Or was the entire story of what happened at Halsted the night of October 8 merely a metaphor for something else Nick had done: for keeping Nightmare Neville and his art alive through Nick? What if this transplant business is all made up? I confronted myself. What if it is just Nick's elaborate fantasy to avoid guilt, detection, and punishment?

Think about it! If he is the murderer, then it makes perfect sense. What if he's using me, the department, Chris? What if he's planning to kill or incapacitate Chris on the operating table to cover up for himself? If he can blame the murders on Chris, use me for his bona fides, and then the killings stop, he's gotten away scot-free. He's committed the perfect crime!

And if that was what it was, then what did it say about me that I was so totally and overwhelmingly consumed with him?

I finally got up, showered, and dressed and on my way out the door realized I hadn't bothered looking at yesterday's mail.

There was another letter. I felt a stab of panic in my gut. My heart started to beat fast. I tore it open without worrying about prints or evidence.

Dearest Sandy,

I hope you appreciated my latest offering to you. I was hoping you'd at least go on television to thank me personally. Jung would say that to be what she was and do what she did, Joan of Arc must have possessed both the anima and the animus—the female side and the male. So do you, Sandy, dear, which may explain why I find myself so attracted to you.

Rest assured, my pet, it won't be long now. It won't be long.

I'd just showered, brushed my teeth, and put on fresh clothing. And already I felt unclean.

———————

In the afternoon, Vince and I hit the pavement again. The idea of a full day off was becoming a rapidly receding memory.

We went back to Julie Fox's Capitol Hill neighborhood and showed Chris Taylor's photo around. I'd gotten it from the Arena playbill and run off several hundred copies. As a control, we showed them Nick's photo at the same time.

We came up with a few who vaguely remembered having seen one or the other of them, which is about what you'd expect if you took any male photo at random and showed it to enough people in a given neighborhood. It doesn't mean they weren't there, it just doesn't give you anything conclusive to go on.

We tried the same thing with the girls at the Touch of Class. We still got the same positive ID on Nick, which he'd already canceled out by explaining that he'd been conducting his own investigation. None of them, however, recognized Chris.

The truth was, we hadn't been able to establish any material connection between Chris and either of the women. We'd played with the fact that he and Fox had both been patients of Nick's, but going through the appointment schedule, we couldn't come up with any time they might have intersected. And we were drawing a complete blank with Chris and Sarah Hazeltine, too.

When we got to Sarah's neighborhood and the area around her gallery, the reaction was a little more positive, but not necessarily more indicative of anything. After all, it was the neighborhood where Nick lived, so it was natural people would recognize him. We got almost as high a response to Chris's photo, including several people who were pretty sure they'd seen him in the area late at night.

"Finally we're getting somewhere," I said to Vince over coffee and ice cream in the crowded café at the back of Kramerbooks on Connecticut Avenue. He sat as far from me as he could in the expectation I might spill.

"It might even say that Taylor was obsessed with Ramsey and was stalking his house," said Vince.

"Yeah, but there could be another explanation," I said in sudden realization. "The Dupont Circle area has one of the highest concentrations of the trendy and with-it gays in the city, right?"

"Taylor's one of them?"

"Come on, Vince. I hate it when you talk like that."

"Like what?"

" 'Us,' 'them,' Like they're different."

"They are different."

"I'm different, you're different. Different from what? There's no normal. You've got to be open to new ideas." Now I sounded like Nick.

"Sandy, I don't need a lecture from you about oppressed minorities," Vince said with irritation.

But if I could cash in all the time I'd spent being lectured by him over the years, it would have added up to a six-week vacation. Sometimes I think things won't change until the older generation dies off completely. But then, hasn't every generation in history said that? And haven't they all been right?

34

WHEN I got to the office Monday morning, Vince wasn't there. Neither were Volmer and LaRocca. I wondered if something was going around. If it was, I'd get it soon. I always did.

"You know where Vince is?" I asked Norman Sidecki.

"Superior Court, picking up an arrest warrant."

"For who?"

Sidecki shrugged and went back to his desk work. "Search me."

"I wonder why he didn't say anything to me."

"You'll have to take that up with your partner." It was all too pat, as though he didn't want to tell me.

Something was going on. The place was like a ghost town. It was making me edgy, edgier than I was already.

Between operations, Nick called me. "Well, I did it," he reported grimly. "I called Chris Taylor, told him I wanted him to come in as soon as possible for a follow-up."

"And . . ."

"He'll be in this afternoon."

"So will I," I said.

———————

It was almost eleven when Vince finally showed up, accompanied by two uniforms who in turn were escorting a white male in handcuffs—late twenties to early thirties, dirty blond hair, medium height, and slightly pudgy. And as if by magic, Captain Owen returned to the squad room at precisely the same moment, beaming broadly. That always made me nervous. Something was definitely going down, and I wasn't part of it.

"You ever seen this guy?" Vince asked me.

I took a long look, having no idea what he was getting at. The guy returned my stare with a curious leer that gave me the creeps. Owen was studying my reaction. "No, I don't think so," I said.

"Put him in the interrogation room," Vince directed the uniforms. "I'll be there in a second." When they'd taken him away, Vince announced with a flourish, "That there is the dude who broke into your apartment. And therefore, by implication, our killer!" He clapped both fat hands on my shoulders. "Your instinct was right, Sandy. If we'd held Ramsey, we'd have had a lot of egg on our faces this morning."

"But . . . I don't understand," I said with genuine confusion. "Who is this guy? Where'd he come from? And how come I wasn't in on this?"

"I watched your place yesterday morning," Vince explained. "Just plain old-fashioned detective work." Was this supposed to be a lesson to me?

"I didn't see you."

"You weren't looking. I talked to about twenty people to see if we could get any witness descriptions. This guy came by, seemed real interested in your house. When I asked if he'd seen any strange or suspicious people in the neighborhood, he was all too willing to cooperate; you know the type. Seemed very interested in the murders, wanted to know how we were coming along. Also seemed to get off on the scout car parked in front of the house. He gave me his name—Russell Morgan. I checked him out. He'd been seen by other neighbors hanging around since about the time the first letter came."

"Who is he?"

"A process server who does work for a lot of lawyers in town, including your very own landlord. Most of these guys have pals on the force so they can get unlisted phone numbers and addresses. He also applied to the police department twice and Metro police once. You guessed it: turned down across the board. Process serving was as close as he could get to law enforcement. Real spooky guy, smart but low self-esteem, couple of misdemeanors. Probably has a tiny dick, too, but I didn't check. He lives in a one-room apartment on Capitol Hill."

Near Fox, I thought. But still not much to go on.

"Judge Wachtel issued a warrant this morning."

"Based on what?"

Vince opened his jacket and pulled out a glassine evidence envelope. Inside was the bikini shot of me at the beach. "I finally asked him for some ID. When he opened his wallet, guess what fell out. You know, some of these guys just want to be caught."

"Volmer and LaRocca are searching his house even as we speak," Owen reported.

I was flabbergasted; more than that, I was infuriated. "All this is going on around me—why didn't you tell me? Why didn't you include me?"

"What? And have you surveil your own apartment?" Owen retorted. "The important thing is, we got our guy, and you were a critical part of the team."

"Yeah," I said, "the bait."

"This is going to look very good in your file jacket."

I turned to Vince. "That's not good enough."

"What should I have done? You were pursuing your leads, I was pursuing mine. I didn't want to distract you from what you were doing if this came up empty. And you were emotionally involved. After all, it's you he's fixated on. I just worked with that."

I still didn't like it. "You were trying to cut me out, go around me."

He reached out to put his hand on my shoulder, but I pulled away. "Sandy, you're making too much of this," he said.

"I don't think so," I replied, trying to make the hurt sound more like anger. Well, what was I going to do? "Has he admitted anything?" I asked.

Vince shook his head. "His attorney's on her way over."

"Who?"

"Dana Bazelon. She's one of the lawyers he does work for." Dana Bazelon was tough, smart, and attractive, the kind of defense lawyer who gives the police and prosecutors fits. It wouldn't be an easy interrogation.

"We've already picked him out of shots at the Ashburn funeral. He's doing what your profilers said he would."

The shock and surprise had worn off, and my anger and outrage were shifting their focus. Before Bazelon arrived, I wanted to go into the interrogation room, shut the door, and do something to him. I didn't know what, exactly, but something painful, something extremely painful. I wanted to give this maladjusted little pervert just one small taste of the hurt he inflicted on innocent people. He's a fan of Neville Ramsey's "art"? I'll show him art.

And if I'd been a civilian, that's exactly what I would have done, regardless of the consequences. But we'd worked too hard on this case and put too much into it to jeopardize it for my personal satisfaction. I wouldn't let the anger cool. One way or another, I'd send the message to this little shit.

Just then, Volmer and LaRocca came bounding in along with Alex Klein, the crime scene tech. LaRocca spotted me and held up a plastic evidence bag. "These look like yours?" he called out. The bag contained my stolen panties. I flushed instantly and tried to snatch them away.

"Whoa, Mansfield," he taunted, pulling it back. "Evidence."

"Where'd you find them?" I inquired frostily.

"Under his pillow," said Volmer.

"Great." Now I really had the creeps.

"And look what else we found," said LaRocca, holding up another bag containing a lock-picking kit. "This explains how he got in."

Volmer added, "We also found a picture of you cut out of the Sunday *Post,* a paperback about Neville Ramsey, and an extensive collection of bondage pornography. Maybe there's something to this profiling business after all."

Dana Bazelon showed up and immediately challenged the propriety of the arrest and search warrants, stating her client claimed to have found the torn photograph of me on the sidewalk, where I no doubt had inadvertently dropped it.

"Have you perhaps recently had a fight with your brother, Detective?" she suggested. I suggested in return that she look closely to see if her client had hairy palms. Then she and Vince went into the interrogation room to lock horns. He specifically did not want me in there with him. It was messy enough already with me being the victim and a possible witness.

"Don't worry what Bazelon says," Captain Owen declared, putting a hand on my shoulder and taking me aside. "Your possessions were found both in Morgan's apartment and staged at the Fabrizi scene. That ties it all together. Vince'll get a confession out of him. Then we'll tie him to the other three, and we're home free. You were so right about Ramsey. You'll be part of the press conference, of course."

"Captain . . ."

"This is going to look very good for the department at a time we really need it."

"Captain . . ."

"What, Sandy? What is it?"

"This asshole did Fabrizi, but I don't think he did the other three."

Less than a minute later I was in the captain's office with the door closed. Owen had interrupted the interrogation and brought Vince in, too. Owen sat behind his desk. Vince leaned on the side. I felt as if I were the one being interrogated.

"You get us off Ramsey, now you get us off this guy," Owen stated accusingly. "We know he's been stalking you, it's the same pattern and MO. Why don't you think it's him?"

"Because it's not the same pattern and MO," I responded. "I've been thinking about this, trying to figure out what was wrong. First of all, the knots are different."

"Okay, I know, but that's pretty subtle. When I go camping I don't tie my tent down the same way I tie my shoes."

"But up until now, they've all matched. Also, the body was only partially burned."

"Most people don't realize how hard it is to burn a body," Vince pointed out. "They think they're going to destroy the evidence, and all they do is leave more to implicate them."

"Yeah, but our guy would know," I argued. "He . . . Neville Ramsey, they've both known exactly what it took to achieve every effect they've wanted to. These have all been carefully researched, carefully planned scenes. If our guy had done this one, he'd have known exactly how much wood and how much fuel he'd need to completely consume the body. And since we know Morgan did this one, I say he didn't do the others."

Owen rubbed his neck. "You're really going out on a limb here, Sandy."

As usual, I couldn't help pacing back and forth as I talked. "Now we get to victimology. Joyce Fabrizi was a prostitute, which makes her an easy, vulnerable target. All of the other victims were more difficult, more challenging. It doesn't make sense that he'd regress. If anything, killing Jerry Ashburn shows he was moving in the other direction, toward increasingly demanding kills."

Owen and Vince exchanged glances. Vince gave him a "could be" look.

"And another thing," I went on. "Neville Ramsey already did a 'Joan of Arc,' and he never repeated the same scene twice. Morgan is a copycat. The two-week periodicity still holds up."

Patrick Owen was not a happy camper. "So you're still hanging with

Christopher Taylor as your number one?'' I nodded. ''Taylor and not Ramsey.'' I nodded again. ''And you still don't have the elements on Taylor.''

''No, but I hope to soon,'' I said.

''It better be damn soon,'' said the captain, removing a bottle of Maalox from his desk drawer.

''So what's the drill?'' I asked.

Nick and I were alone in his office with the door closed.

''I'll talk to Chris,'' Nick outlined, ''take a history since the surgery, a physical. I'll analyze the MRI and CT's and NeMo readings. I can even adjust the neural modulator to show an abnormal reading.''

He was the commanding general again. Any business involving as much death as ours do requires a certain resilience. Without it, you start dying yourself.

''Then what?'' I asked.

''Then I'll tell him it's my clinical opinion that he needs another operation or his symptoms are going to return. I'll schedule it for as soon as possible, and God help me.''

''God help us all,'' I said. ''But there's one more thing I want you to do in this.''

''What's that?'' I thought I detected a slight smile, as if he were amused a layman would suggest a medical protocol.

''Hypnotize him.''

''Why?''

''We've jumped through a lot of hoops to figure out whether Chris is the one carrying on Neville's crimes. Before we do anything extreme or irreversible, why don't we ask him?''

The vibes Nick gave off told me he was not happy about this request on my part, but I didn't give him a convenient way out. If he was serious about getting at the truth, then he had to use every means at his disposal.

And so it was on Monday afternoon that Chris was ushered into examining room A, the one in which I'd changed the day we played racquetball. From the office side, I realized the mirror set in the door was actually a one-way glass. ''So that we can objectively observe neurology patients without inhibiting them,'' Nick explained.

"You wouldn't have happened to observe me while I was changing, would you?" He merely smiled enigmatically.

There was an intercom unit on the adjoining wall. "You'll be able to hear everything we say." He opened the door and went in.

I watched as he worked through all of the standard parts of a neurological exam—reflexes, eyes, everything. Then he had Chris remove his shirt. He picked up a small metal box connected by wires to a portable computer, not much bigger than a laptop. He held the box against Chris's skin, on the top of his shoulder near his neck. That must be where NeMo's generator pack was implanted, I thought.

Almost instantly, rows of jagged lines appeared on the computer screen. Nick studied them for several moments, then pressed several buttons on the keyboard. I noticed the second and fifth rows changed their rhythm. He pressed another series of buttons, and they returned to their previous pattern.

Nick excused himself a moment, came back into his office, and closed the door.

"What were you looking for?" I asked.

"Evidence of abnormal thought patterns," he said.

"You can see thought patterns?"

"No, but you can infer them from brain waves. There are a number of patterns that have been linked to sociopathic behavior, such as the repeating 'fourteen and six spike' frequency.

"And did you see that in Chris?"

"No," he replied almost glumly. "And his alpha wave, which synchronizes all the cells in the brain to work together, is a standard ten per second. As far as all the physical tests can show, he's completely normal."

That didn't necessarily mean he was, though, I knew Nick would be quick to point out. The brain fights tenaciously before giving up any of its secrets.

Chris remained calm throughout the examination. And even when Nick delivered his "findings," he took the news stoically. But it was obvious he was freaked out, which was what turned out to give Nick his opening for my part of the program.

"I may be able to help you with that," he said soothingly. "I'd like to hypnotize you. It should help you relax and get through the next couple of days, and also deal with some of the underlying fears we all have.''

Chris agreed. Nick stood in front of him and leaned casually against the examining table. ''I want you to sit back comfortably, uncross your legs, and put your hands at your sides. Let the tension and pressure drain from your body. Close your eyes lightly, and as you hear me speak, start counting slowly backward from a thousand. Good. Nice and easy.

''Now, we're in a small boat, drifting slowly down a beautiful mountain stream. It's very peaceful. Weeping willows hang over the edge of the stream bank, just touching the surface of the water. The boat is rocking gently, which lulls you into a dreamy haze. Everything is serene . . .''

Within a few minutes, he was under. Nick asked a few preliminary questions. ''Now, Chris, I want you to tell me how you've changed since the operation.''

''I don't have seizures anymore,'' he replied slowly and softly. ''I can concentrate again. I can act. I feel alive.''

''Anything else?''

''No. I feel like myself again.''

It went on that way for a while. And as far as I was concerned, we were getting nowhere. It's possible under hypnosis to continue to hide things, and Nick's questions weren't getting us where we needed to be. Whether this was intentional on his part or not, I couldn't be sure. But the time had come to bring in the offense.

I rapped lightly on the door and then listened to see whether Nick had picked up the signal.

''I'm going to bring Sandy Mansfield in here now,'' he told Chris. ''She's going to ask you some questions which you're anxious to answer, which will help you get rid of your concerns. And when she leaves, you won't remember that you talked to her.''

I opened the door, came in, and sat on the orange plastic chair facing him. Nick stepped back behind me. ''Hello, Chris,'' I said. ''Do you remember who I am?''

''Sure,'' he said pleasantly.

''I'd like to help you. Is that okay?''

He nodded his head.

''Good. Now you remember when you read about the murders of

those young women in the newspaper. What did you think about them?''

He hesitated for several long moments. "It was bad," he said finally. "I wondered what kind of person would want to do something like that."

"What kind of person do you think it would be?''

He paused again, then said, "Someone who loves power, real power, the ultimate power.''

"You know this personally?'' I asked.

"Yes.''

"Can you imagine yourself doing something like that?''

"Yes," he said meekly.

I could feel my pulse jump. "How can you imagine yourself doing it?''

"I'm playing Richard the Third.''

My heartbeat gradually returned to normal. "Okay, let's try something else. "Chris, you came to us after reading about the murders. Why was that?''

"I dreamed about them. It scared me.''

"Because you were afraid you had something to do with them?''

He nodded his head intently, like a little child.

"You told me you felt as if someone were controlling you, telling you what to do. Do you know who that person might be?''

He shook his head negatively.

"Do you still feel that way now?''

"You told me I didn't have to. I believe you.''

"What about Jerry Ashburn? Does that name mean anything?''

"Uh-huh. A reporter.''

"Right. Have you ever talked to him?''

"I called him on the phone.''

"You did? Why?''

"After I read his stories in the newspaper. I wanted to ask him about the crimes.''

"And what did he say?''

"He said he wanted to interview me.''

"And did he?''

"Uh-uh. He said he would. He was going to come over to the theater. But then he got killed himself.''

I leaned back on my chair and tried to collect my thoughts. I didn't say anything for a while. I looked at him and tried as hard as I could to visualize a murderer, brilliantly seducing his own real-life Lady Anne. But it was no good.

Oh, well . . . people who worked with Ted Bundy at the Seattle rape crisis center couldn't imagine him raping and mutilating beautiful young women, either. Even as he marched to the Florida electric chair, they kept saying, "It can't be the same one. That can't be our boy who did those terrible things."

Maybe in our case, it wasn't. Chris Taylor had never met Jerry and now denied he'd had anything to do with the murders. But was it possible that someone else in there did have something to do with them?

In other words, could we be dealing with a multiple?

There's a lot of disagreement in the forensic psychiatric community about whether true multiple personalities exist at all. Part of this skepticism, I'm sure, stems from the fact that whenever we see someone claiming to be one, it's usually because he's trying to avoid punishment for a serious crime. Still, I've seen some tapes of sessions that are pretty convincing, especially of molested children who wouldn't have the sophistication or guile to put one over on the examining psychiatrist. And in Chris's case, if we were truly dealing with the introduction of someone else's brain tissue, then the case for a multiple personality diagnosis might be all the more compelling.

"Chris, you've been very helpful," I said softly. "Now, I'd like to speak with Neville, if you don't mind."

"Who?" he asked.

"Neville," I said firmly. "Neville Ramsey."

He scrunched up his face as if I'd confused him. "You mean Nicholas Ramsey?"

"No. Neville Ramsey," I repeated. "Nicholas's brother."

"I'm sorry," said Chris. "I don't know Neville Ramsey."

———————

Chris agreed to undergo the new surgery as soon as the run of the play was over. Nick told him it wouldn't cost him anything.

Except, perhaps, his conscious ability to function, I thought grimly.

When he had gone, Nick came back into the office where I was waiting. I wasn't sure whether he was frustrated, like me, that Chris had been so inconclusive, or relieved. He did a good job of hiding his emotions.

"So did you get what you wanted?"

"You know I didn't," I said. "But I'd like to take another stab at it tonight."

I saw a look of concern creep quickly over Nick's features. "You want to hypnotize Chris Taylor again?"

"No," I replied. "I want to hypnotize you."

35

"IT'S good to see you, Cassie," Ted remarked as I ushered him into my living room. "You're looking tired, though." I was still wearing my dress from work. I thought it might make things a little more formal.

"Ted, this is Nicholas Ramsey," I said. "Ted Monahan." The two men exchanged a grave handshake.

"Well, shall we get started?" I motioned Nick onto my most comfortable chair, a brown leather recliner in the corner of the room. It was the first time he'd been to my apartment, and he hadn't quite gotten his bearings yet. That was just the way I wanted it, with him in unfamiliar territory. Russell Morgan had been brought before a magistrate and denied bail, so at least the scout car was now gone from in front of the house.

Nick hadn't been any too pleased at my insistence he undergo this examination and had thrown up a barrage of defenses. But it had finally come down to the old standby: "What are you trying to hide?"

Whether or not he was trying to hide anything, surgeons don't like to be out of control. Neither do cops, for that matter, which is why both groups make such poor patients. But when I assured Nick I could find someone competent and discreet to do this who wasn't associated with either Halsted or the MPD, he reluctantly caved in.

"Are you comfortable?" Ted asked. Nick nodded.

"If you resist, we'll know," I warned.

"I won't resist," he said sullenly.

"Cassie, please, step back, let me handle this," said Ted. "All right, let's begin."

Nick went under with surprising ease, especially for someone as control freaky as a surgeon. Ted's technique was as good as I'd remembered. Ted had always been good at technique. It was the substance I'd often found wanting.

I waited impatiently as he got past the qualifying questions, then he said, "Nicholas, now I'm going to take you back to San Quentin Prison, to the first visit you had with your brother, Neville, after his trial. Do you remember that?"

Nick nodded. Ted and I had talked about key incidents or events that might trigger some insight into what made Nicholas tick. The trial itself was in the public record and luridly covered by the supermarket press. But this meeting might have been the crucial one, the first encounter between the brothers in which neither one had anything to hide.

"He's behind a thick pane of glass," Nick began. *We have to talk through telephones. "How have you been, Nick?" he asks me.*

"Okay, Nev. How have you been?" I ask.

He smiles at me. "A funny thing about our correctional institutions. The more heinous the offense they think you have committed, the more considerately and respectfully they treat you. If I had pistol-whipped an old man while knocking over the Big Sur Market, I'd be in the general population of some lower-rung state prison, being sodomized in the communal shower. But because of the majestic enormity of what I've done, I'm approached with respect bordering on worship. I am studied to see what light I can shed on the psychotically brilliant, anti-social mind. Don't get me wrong, I'd rather not be here if given the choice. But I do get time to think."

"And what are you thinking during this time, Nicholas?"

I'm looking for a stranger, but the only person I can see is my brother.

"Nicholas, did you ask him why he did the things he did?"

"You know, Nick, I've always suspected, and looking back over the catalog of my work has confirmed it, that I see things, feel things, know things, more vividly, more intensely than other people. That puts me on another plane of existence."

"And how do you respond?"

I say, "I can't accept that."

"Of course you can. You already do! Both of us, Nick, we exist in a realm that isn't defined or deterred by empty social conventions or

laws or even our so-called natural feelings such as fear or remorse or disgust. Tell me, Nick, do you experience disgust when you are in the operating theater with your hands drenched in blood? Of course not. You do it for your own satisfaction, just as I do. The ritual of surgery removes you, cleanses you. But don't try to deny the ecstatic thrill that must course through your body as you cut through the flesh and then plunge your fingers into the quivering, pulsating, living insides of a human being. We both know, there's no feeling quite like it. High drama. And when you come right down to it, there is precious little difference between what I do in my studio and what you do in the operating theater. But what we're talking about is the theater of the mind—the most potent drama of all."

And if Nick couldn't process that, couldn't reject what his beloved brother was saying to him, then perhaps subconsciously he had to become a part of it.

"If you did what you do anywhere else but the operating room, you'd be right in here with me. After all, you've buried more victims than I have. The biggest difference between us is that my victims came to me willingly."

"The biggest difference is that you're psychotic."

"In the night, when we sleep and dream, we're all of us psychotic. The difference is that some of us have the power and the will to make our dreams come true. Nicholas, the power you have to eke out a little more life is paltry and uninteresting when compared to the power I have to end it."

You could say the same thing about me, I thought, instinctively fingering the outline of the 9 mm in my bag.

"So that's when the idea of picking up Neville's career first occurred to you?" Ted suggested.

I grabbed him by the sleeve and yanked him backward toward me. "What the hell are you doing!" I said in a harsh whisper.

"I'm just trying to get to the truth," he whispered back.

"You're leading him! You could blow the whole thing."

He scowled. "You called me, Cassie. Are you going to let me do it my way or aren't you?"

Before I could say anything, he turned back to Nick. "And what did you say to him?"

I say, "Neville, why did you become like this?"

He shakes his head sadly from side to side. "Nicholas, Nicholas,

Nicholas. Have you become just like Dad? Has the human brain become nothing more to you than three pounds of fat and vasculature and connective tissue? Can you no longer glory in the brilliant chaos of the mind? I had such great hopes for you, and you've so disappointed me." He smiles cruelly. "But then again, I supposed I've disappointed you, too."

"Neville, you've killed eighteen people!"

"Twenty-two, just between us pals. Poor Nicholas. Perhaps I should have done you while I had the chance. You and the lovely Patsy. I can see it now . . ."

"How can you talk that way?"

"You remember the rabbit and the duck, Nicky?"

A look of childlike hurt and confusion came over Nick's face. "Tell me about the rabbit and the duck, Nicholas," Ted prompted.

Easter. Nev got a rabbit. I got a duck.

"How old were you?"

Eight. Nev was ten.

"Okay, we're going to go back to that time and place. . . ."

It's the next morning. I come downstairs and my duck is lying on its side. I come over and try to make it stand up, but it can't. I look to see what's the matter, and Nev's rabbit has chewed away the webbing on one of the feet.

"How do you feel?"

Mad. I start crying because I don't know why he's done it. Why would the rabbit do such a terrible thing?

"Then what do you do?"

I find Nev's rabbit and I take it into the kitchen. I put it up on the counter. I open the drawer and take out one of Mom's knives—a thin one, real sharp. I hold the rabbit down and I cut off the top of its head. It makes a shuddering motion, then it's still. I reach in with my hand and take out the brain.

"Then what happens?"

Then Nev comes in and sees what I've done. He runs out screaming and wakes up Mom and Dad. They come down and Mom screams, too, and Dad grabs the knife away from me. He starts yelling at me and slaps me and asks me why I did this.

"And what do you tell him?"

I wanted to look at the rabbit's brain and learn why he ate my duck's foot. Then he hits me again. Hard. I start crying. I don't understand why he's so angry. I've been to work with him. I know he opens up people's heads. I know he also took out brains from animals to learn from them. He'd showed me. I just wanted to find out. I just wanted to know.

I listened in horrified fascination, standing behind Ted, gnawing on the knuckle of my thumb. There is so much to know about a person, so much to try to understand. I was taking a big chance here. Hypnosis isn't truth serum. The critical ego, as psychiatrists call it, remains active throughout the process. If I pressed too hard, he could snap.

"Did you enjoy this—what you did to the rabbit?" Ted asked. "You liked it, Nicholas, didn't you? It felt good."

This time I grabbed him and yanked him out of the way. "What are you afraid of?" he whispered. "You're so intent on proving his innocence that you don't want to hear any of the rough stuff."

"I'm taking over," I said.

"I don't think that's a good idea," Ted remarked sharply. I just glared at him.

"Nick," I said carefully, "this is Sandy speaking. I understand why you did that to the rabbit. I can understand everything you've done, and I can help you. But you have to be honest with me. You have to tell me, did you kill Julie Fox and Sarah Hazeltine and Jerry Ashburn?"

I noticed his eyes fluttering, his jaw working up and down, a sudden rigidity to his posture. I held my breath for several long seconds, then he said, "Neville killed them."

"Did you have any part in it?"

"I made it possible."

Could it be possible he made up the story about the brain transplants but that he really believes it? I started to wonder. If he killed those people himself, then what he's done is so monstrous, he's had to construct a myth around it to absolve or mitigate his guilt. He acknowledges it enough to say that he used his power to "keep Neville alive," but that's as far as he can go.

"Let's go back to the hospital on October eighth," I directed. "I want you to tell me what happened."

I sit in my office all alone, studying the films, matching them up to the diagrams I've made. It's all planned out. Everyone's been prepped. Neville is on the heart-lung machine. The rest of the transplantation team is ready to take his organs . . .

He related the story in detail—the tests he used to examine Neville's brain, how he selected his transplantation subjects, how he planned his surgical strategy. If he were making the whole thing up, if it was all a conscious or unconscious fabrication, he had the story down cold.

He'd been awake continuously since the fateful call from California telling him what Neville had done. He'd made all the arrangements to bring him back to Washington, he'd notified the organ harvesting team and the national organ match, he'd run a computer search of literature through the National Library of Medicine. He'd gone to the animal lab for hasty experimentation. He'd notified the patients.

He started prepping for the first operation shortly before noon, and he and Robert Fusillo did all the surgery themselves. They didn't begin the last one until nearly dawn the following morning.

"This one is Mr. Hawaas," I said.

Bob.

"Dr. Fusillo is assisting you."

Not this one.

"Why not? He'd helped you with all the others. Was there something you didn't want him to see in this one?"

He's the one.

"What do you mean by that, Nick? The one what?"

His condition's getting worse. All those years of training wasted if it can't be turned around. Maybe a mature transplant of differentiated neural tissue can be better than fetal tissue if my theory of hormonal secretion is right. Maybe Neville's brain can cure him. I'm nervous about doing it on someone I'm so close to, but Bob insists. He says I can't deny him a chance.

"What about Zahedi Hawaas?"

No Hawaas.

"What?"

We made up the name, someone who couldn't be traced, who could disappear afterward; made up the story so no one would know about Bob. It's very important we keep that a secret. They'd throw him out of the program if they knew. No one must find out.

———————————

I had to get Ted to bring Nick out of the hypnotic trance, then I asked him to leave.

"That's it? I come running to you as soon as you say you need me, then as soon as I've served my purpose . . ."

I could have said a lot of things, but I didn't. "I've got to be alone with Nicholas now. Please try to understand. I'll call you soon, Ted. I promise."

He nodded sullenly. He held my wrist and said in a low voice, "When are you going to stop playing games and face yourself, Cassie? I'm the one person who's always seen you as you are. If you shut me out, you're just running away from yourself." Then he leaned over and kissed me. On the lips. I didn't resist or turn my head away, but I felt my stomach twisting in knots. Then, without saying anything else, he left.

I controlled myself just long enough. When Ted was gone, I walked back to the living room, where Nick was still sitting on the leather recliner. He got up when he saw me come back and held his hand out to touch my arm.

I hauled off and punched him in the stomach.

"Oof!" he gasped meaningfully. "What was that for?"

I slapped him across the face. His eyes registered shock and surprise, and his cheek turned bright red. Then I started beating on his chest with the side of my fist. I guess I ended up resorting to the girl stuff because if I'd relied on my real training, I could have really damaged him.

He finally managed to grab my hands.

"You asked me to trust you!" I screamed. "You ask me to lay my career on the line for you. And you're still lying to me!"

"What are you talking about?"

"Zahedi Hawaas, or rather—shall we say?—the lack of same."

"Oh."

I wriggled out of his grasp. "Why didn't you tell me it was really Robert Fusillo? You withheld material evidence from me."

"I can explain . . ."

"Like hell you can explain! Like you've explained everything else so far? What else are you holding back from me?"

"Nothing. Sandy, I swear."

I wanted to belt him again, to inflict more punishment before I listened to reason, or what masqueraded as reason these days.

"Look, you have to understand," he said, pulling me down to the sofa. He sat on the edge of the cushion and faced me. I was still steaming mad. "Bob Fusillo is a brilliant doctor, one of the best I've come across. He's got a brilliant future ahead of him. He's also got multiple sclerosis, focused in the right parietal lobe. It had been in remission, but the last several months it flared up again. It's a progressive disease, but I thought there was a good chance this transplant could arrest it, turn it back. And so far, at least, it's working.''

"Does he know what you did?"

"I didn't want to take a chance on him. He was the one who insisted on it. He wouldn't let me *not* try it if it could possibly cure him. So of course he knows.''

"What about other people? Anyone else at Halsted?"

"No. And that's just the point. No one else there knew about his condition, either. How many people do you think would let their brains be operated on by a surgeon with progressive MS? I was the only one he confided in. That's why we fudged the record and did him in the middle of the night.''

It would also account for why Fusillo was so fiercely loyal to his boss and idol, Dr. Ramsey. "And did you fudge the record on the patient who died because of his incompetence?" I challenged. Maybe Dr. Bob wasn't so brilliant after all.

Nick bristled. "Nothing was ever proven about that," he insisted. "Not to ruin a career over.''

I wondered if Nick knew more about that than he was telling. It was amazing to me how members of the medical community instinctively pulled the wagons close to protect each other—the very thing people are always getting on cops about.

"But still, you had to have other people working with you," I said. "What about nurses, the anesthesiologist?"

"I prepped him myself. By the time the scrub nurse and anesthesiologist arrived in the OR, he was fully draped. The only thing exposed was the shaved part of his scalp and the small section of skull I removed. He was transferred the next morning by private ambulance to Arlington Hospital, where he was registered under an assumed name. We covered his recuperation time by saying he was taking a visiting fellowship in California. Since I'm neurosurgery residency director at Halsted, all this needed was my signature.''

"Why didn't you tell me about him?"

"There was no reason to.''

"There was no reason to tell me about someone who would have instantly become a suspect? A suspect, by the by, who has the surgical ability necessary to remove internal organs, for instance, or locate a heart precisely in the chest. Or, for that matter, to casually walk in and lift a penlight off your desk or out of your lab coat pocket."

"I guess that's why I didn't tell you. I know you'd jump to conclusions, as you just have."

"So the dumb old police don't have to know this part. This part you can handle on your own."

"Up to a point, yes. That's what I was doing on the night of the last murder."

I stood up and placed my hand on my hip. "Maybe I'm dense, but I think I'm missing something here."

"That night, I knew you'd be following me. That's why I lent Bob my car."

"We figured out that part."

"Okay. I knew the car would be followed. If Bob was the killer and he tried to do it again, the police would be right there to stop him, and we'd know for sure. If he wasn't, then there was no harm done."

"Except we come off looking like assholes."

"You've got to understand I had as much motivation to figure out what was going on as you did."

Again, the explanation either made perfect sense or was a perfect alibi for why he actually wanted to evade us that night.

"Did Bob have any contact with Julie Fox?" I asked.

"Sure. He assisted me."

"And I know that he spoke with Jerry Ashburn on the phone."

"So what are you saying—you're going to put your bloodhounds on Bob?"

"No," I said on my way to the kitchen. I definitely needed a drink. "Since you withheld crucial information from me at a crucial time, I can't go back to my captain now and tell him, even if I want to. I've about used up all my credibility chits on your behalf already."

"So what are you saying?"

I poured straight vodka into a glass with ice. It was the only hard stuff I had in the house. "Here, you'd better have one, too." I pushed it across the pass-through to him and poured another for myself. "We'll have to work this on our own tomorrow."

"Follow him, you mean?"

"Only he won't know he's being followed. We'll be there with him at the hospital tomorrow night. Then, when he leaves, I'll hand him over to Vince. It's the best I can come up with on such short notice."

"How will I explain your presence at the hospital?"

"Explain it however you want," I said sardonically. "You're good at coming up with stories when you have to. Say that we're 'involved.'"

He took a step closer to me, set his drink down on the counter, and put both hands on my waist. "And would I be telling the truth if I said that?"

I didn't answer, but I didn't move away, either.

Slowly, and with his tiger's grace, he pulled me down onto the sofa with him. Then he began undoing my buttons. I could already feel my skin tingling and my nipples going firm as he slipped his hand inside my blouse.

"Do you trust me?" he said.

We were straining forward toward the edge of the sofa now. He had the top of my dress down off my shoulders and had freed me from my bra. His fingers had found their way under my skirt and between my legs. Mine had torn through the buttons of his shirt and were inside his open fly. I could no longer control myself.

Soon we were on the carpet, rolling around, climbing on top of each other, fighting for supremacy like two kids playing king of the hill. I could feel my pulse pounding in my temples. My dress was bunched above my waist, my panties twisted around one ankle. I drew my nails across his back and shoulders, drawing little beads of blood. He would have to fight for me.

He had his hands under me, digging his curled fingers sharply into my buttocks. I uttered a series of short gasps and kissed his neck roughly. I took in the sensuous, earthy scent of his sweat, tasting salt as I licked the wiry hairs on his chest, moving down to his stomach until I finally reached his erection and let him feel the sharp edge of my teeth. I didn't let up until I could feel him pulsating on the brink of climax, when the thrill of power made me bring him momentarily back down.

We continued scrabbling on the floor. I used my feet to force his trousers and briefs down over his legs and heard the loud rip of fabric as they met resistance at his ankles. But that didn't stop me.

Our tongues fought with each other for dominance and control. I tasted his spit and felt mine dribbling from the corner of my mouth. He held me down and climbed on top of me, pinning my arms hard against the floor, forcing my legs apart with his. I felt his teeth closing in around my rigid nipples and then traveling down to the sensitive insides of my thighs. Little jolts of sublime anguish rippled through me. I cried out with the pain and the release the pain offered, which urged him on even more vigorously.

He was inside me and seemed to be everywhere at once, filling all my dark corners and empty spaces. I wrapped my legs firmly around his hips as he kept grinding relentlessly into me with an ever-increasing rhythm. We were both huffing and grunting and growling like hungry lions on a kill.

"You're good. You're very, very good," he almost chanted.

My hands were clutching tightly around his shoulders, and I could feel myself about to explode, and him within me.

Nick! I kept thinking. *Nick . . . oh, Nick!*

And just as the inevitable moment approached, I arched upward, rolling us both over on our sides. It felt as if he shot right through me. And as we came together for what seemed in incredible and ecstatic eternity, he was flat on his back on the rug, and I was straddled commandingly on top of him.

"Are all cops like you?" he gasped.

"I wouldn't know," I responded honestly, just as out of breath. The point made, I rolled off him onto the floor. We lay next to each other, staring up at the dull gray ceiling, regrouping and getting our wind back.

When we'd conserved enough energy, he got up and called his answering machine—always the good and attentive physician. I watched him punch in his security code, marveling that he could shift mental and emotional gears so quickly. I hoped his compulsive doctor instincts weren't going to break the mood. But as soon as he had determined that no emergencies had come up and no one needed him urgently— no one other than me—we managed to make it into the bedroom, removing what was left of each other's clothing along the way.

And then we were at each other again.

I've known a number of men who threw themselves totally into whatever they did, but none more so than Nicholas Ramsey. His lovemaking was blazing and ecstatic and inspiring, demanding everything I had to give. He enveloped me in a way that transported my mind and stole my breath away. And when we were finished, glowing with perspiration, I clutched his shoulders and held him there, on top of me and still inside me, and I didn't ever want the moment to end.

He could do anything he wanted to me. Play infinite variations on my body and keep me breathlessly wondering what the next composition would be. The best thing that can happen and the worst thing that can happen are often so close to each other. Why did life have to be so complicated?

Afterward, he lay on his back and cuddled me against him protectively. The top of my head was tucked under his chin, and his chest hair scratched against my nipples. His hard thigh was pressed up between my legs.

"So what made you decide to become a cop?" he asked.

"Even in the sack, you can't resist getting into people's heads, can you?"

"It's in my nature." He ran his finger lightly along the length of my thigh, letting his hand stop and rest on my behind. "How'd a nice girl like you end up doing something like that?"

I rolled my eyes at the ceiling. "Please."

"No, I mean it. I want to know."

"I showed an aptitude at an early age."

"What do you mean?"

"In college, my roommate was raped and murdered."

"I'm sorry." He was quiet for a moment, then asked, "Were you very close?"

I nodded, swallowing to suppress a lump in my throat. "The police couldn't find out who'd done it. So I did."

"How?"

"By thinking about all the things I could hate about her. And then finding someone who felt the same way."

"That's it?"

"There was more to it than that. But that's the nutshell version. Physical evidence and victimology, though I didn't know enough to call them it at the time."

"Who was he?"

"His name was Shane Maddox. I told Vincent Robinson, the detective who was handling the case. He brought him in and got a confession. Vince's my partner now."

"What happened to Maddox?"

"He went to trial. His lawyer tried to mitigate by trashing Gabbie's reputation. I lost twenty pounds during the trial. Shane's doing twenty to life in Lorton. If they ever let him out, I'll hunt him down and slice his balls off with a rusty knife."

Nick winced. Not an uncommon reaction from a naked man, I suppose. "As a sworn police officer, you'd take the law into your own hands that way?"

"I'm not telling you it's right," I said. "I'm just telling you what I'd do."

We were quiet for a while. He shifted slightly and put one arm back behind his head. With the edge of my fingernail, I gently traced imaginary circles around his nipple. I could feel the muscles in his chest go tight to my touch.

"I guess you'd say both you and I are in partnership with the killers," he said.

I turned my head up at him and made a quizzical face.

"Whether it's in the operating room or out on the street, if it weren't for the threat of death, there'd be no call for either of us. We'd both be out of work."

"I'm not holding my breath."

"So what is it you like about police work?"

I thought a moment. I could feel his heart beating against my cheekbone. "It's the last place left where things are black and white, good and bad," I stated. We were both quiet for a moment. "What do you like about surgery?"

"Same thing," he replied.

36

IT was difficult getting out of bed in the morning. The only thing that finally motivated me was that Nick had to get up to go to the hospital.

We showered together, lathered each other until we were both covered with billowy foam, then did it standing up and wet, with the rockets exploding just as loud and brightly as they had the night before. I wanted him to possess me totally. And then as we dried off, close together by the side of the tub, I was still trying to process this new revelation about Bob Fusillo.

I was starting to reevaluate the relationship between him and Ashby—both being "patients," survivors, as it were. As I stood back just far enough to take in Nick's naked body, I wondered what else he was holding back from me.

That was what I wanted to find out when I called Patricia Ramsey and asked if I could see her. She squeezed me in between glowing expectant mothers at her office at Columbia Hospital.

I sat on the chair facing her desk. "Around the time Neville died, did you see a change in Nicholas?"

She nodded her head as if she'd read my mind. "There was something going on." She sighed. "I never could figure out what it was. But I'll tell you this: It scared me."

"In what way?" I asked.

"I wish I could put my finger on it. But he was even more intense, more driven, more obsessed with his work than ever before." She fumbled with her Virginia Slims pack and pulled out a cigarette. "How well do you know Nick? How well do you really think you know him?" On certain levels, pretty darn well, I thought to myself.

"I don't want this to go any further than it has to, but doctor to police officer, woman to woman, I'll tell you that Nick and I had had great sex together. There was always something intensely exciting about him, something dangerous. There was a kind of magic there. And yet around the time that Neville died, it was as if he abandoned all restraint, any inhibition he may have had. The things he did with me . . . the things he wanted to do . . . it was as if he had become . . . I don't know . . . predatory, maybe that's the word. It was as if he were trying to keep a little piece of Neville alive inside himself."

She took a long drag of her cigarette and looked straight into my eyes with a kind of understanding that made me want to squirm. "You've sensed that magic, too," she said calmly. "I can see it in your eyes." She reached out across the desk and touched my hand. "Sandy," she said, "please protect yourself."

When I got to work, the reporters and TV crews were already camped outside for the death watch. A couple of them recognized me as I ran the gauntlet, shoving microphones in my face and other vital and sensitive regions of my anatomy.

"Is it true you've made an arrest, Detective?"

Sometimes it's difficult to restrain yourself to a terse and enigmatic "No comment" when a forthright "Get the fuck out of my way, asshole" would be so much more satisfying and fulfilling.

Inside the office, the atmosphere was as tense as you might expect. Russell Morgan had finally cracked under Vince's interrogation and confessed to the Joyce Fabrizi murder. Then, as long as he was on a roll, he confessed to the Fox, Hazeltine, and Ashburn murders, too, giving him the glory he so desperately sought in his drab little life. But it had become pretty clear pretty quickly that Russell Morgan was merely a copycat. A gloom had now settled over the squad. The periodicity was back on, and today was D-Day.

Cops spend their entire working lives waiting for the other shoe to drop, and it's one thing they never get used to. We were either going to get it right this time around, or by tomorrow morning someone walking around this very minute was going to be painfully and very publicly dead, and the popular outcry for our mangy hides would be deafening. Such is the respect and admiration with which we are embraced by a grateful citizenry.

———————

I went over to the hospital right after lunch. Nick was still in the OR, so I went up to the gallery. There was something incredibly exhilarating and dramatic about watching him probe and cut into an exposed human brain. "Star Trek" tells you that space is "the final frontier," but they're wrong, folks. That three-pound gray glob between our ears is the real final frontier. And I'd be less than honest if I denied what a pure physical turn-on I still found it watching Nick work. It made me want him intensely all over again.

The viewing gallery was connected by a door to the gallery of the adjoining operating room. So I wandered over to see what was going on in there. It turned out to be an open-heart operation—a coronary bypass—and the contrast between the two rooms couldn't have been greater.

Everything in the heart operating room was bright and glaring, with activity that bordered on chaos. The patient was laid out practically naked on the table, his body painted with yellow Betadine solution so that he looked like a cooked chicken. His chest was splayed open like a high school lab specimen.

There were twelve or fourteen people around the table, all in constant kinetic motion, like ants in a colony or bees in a hive. There were monitor lights flashing and instruments gleaming everywhere you looked. And everywhere you looked was blood—on the patient's body, spurting from his open chest cavity, covering the gowns and gloved hands of the surgeon and his assistants. A group of younger-looking people was observing in the back of the room—interns or medical students, I supposed—and a couple of them seemed on the verge of losing it.

Contrast this with Nick's operation, which was dark and quiet, a single bright light trained on the small operating field—the only part of the patient you could actually see. There was only one assistant, one scrub nurse, and the anesthesiologist. It was like a chamber music recital compared to a rock concert.

I left as Nick finished up and met him outside the scrub room. He gave me a wink, but he looked tired and on edge. For the first time he seemed vulnerable, like the rest of the world. I kept thinking about last night and this morning. But another part of me couldn't forget that one way or another, whether he was lying or whether he was telling the truth, he was directly responsible for everything that had happened and everything that still could happen.

We went upstairs together, saying little. Nick went about the second half of his workday while I stayed in his office and got caught up with the doings of the rest of the squad.

Over the phone, Vince gave me the rundown on Chris Taylor. He'd left his house around eleven-thirty, met friends for brunch on Wisconsin Avenue in Georgetown, walked down to M Street and tooled around the shops, met another friend, and gone jogging with him on the Georgetown University track. That was it so far. No suspicious action or agitated behavior. No indication he'd picked up the tail or was even conscious that anyone might be following him. If he was planning a murder for tonight, he was remarkably cool about it.

I checked up on Fusillo, who'd posted at the hospital shortly before seven that morning. He and Nick had scrubbed together on one procedure, then he had another of his own and was supposed to be in the building all day.

I went downstairs to the hospital pharmacy. I flashed my badge and was quickly ushered into the chief pharmacist's cubicle. She was a young Oriental woman, Korean, I assumed, when I noticed her nameplate said "Park."

"This is routine," I assured her. "There's been a rash of drugs missing from hospitals around the city, and we need to know if you have the same problem here."

She leaned back and sighed. "We try to be secure. But 'incidents' do happen. When you're dealing with this many pharmaceuticals and this many people in and out, you do run into some 'inventory discrepancies.' "

I nodded sympathetically and told her the substances I was interested in. She promised to check and get back to me.

"And, Ms. Park, please believe me that we're as sensitive to this as you are. I won't be saying anything to anyone else at this point, and you don't have to, either." She thanked me for my discretion and assured me, therefore, she'd have the answer as soon as possible.

Around five-thirty Nick came back to the office, looking even worse for wear. "How about we grab something to eat?"

"Sure," I said. "Where?"

"I know this great little cafeteria on the second floor. The food's fairly greasy, but it is high in calories and substantially overpriced. How's that sound?"

"Best offer I'm likely to get."

We went down to the cafeteria and got in line. I surveyed the various hot selections: generic chicken . . . generic meat . . . generic fish . . . oh, and lasagna. Why do these places always have lasagna? It must all be cooked in the same giant kitchen. I'm amazed that hospitals, which you think of as places that promote health, seem to have the least appetizing, least nourishing, least healthy food in the world.

I opted for a big salad. Nick chose the generic fish.

Because of their early starts each morning, hospitals also tend to be somewhat ahead of the rest of society throughout the day. So at half-past five, the cafeteria was already crowded with diners. We were holding our trays and looking for an empty table when I spotted Dr. Bob in the far corner of the room.

We maneuvered our way through the crowd. "Mind if we join you?" I asked. Fusillo looked up with surprise, one eyebrow noticeably raised, but didn't say anything. Friendly, outgoing soul that I am, I took this as an open-arms welcome.

"Hello," I said, smiling pleasantly. "Nice to see you again."

Fusillo's eyes darted from me to Nick and back again. "Anything wrong?" I asked.

"No," he said too casually, "just a little surprised to see you here, to see you two together."

This guy really didn't like me. People tend to look at you differently when you've come upon them stretched out on an Oriental rug in their birthday suits. I know I would. But Ashby had gotten over it; he could, too.

"Anything interesting happen today?" Nick asked, trying to break the tension.

"The Georgetown first-years were in to watch cardiac surgery this afternoon. Some of them didn't deal too well with the blood," Bob reported with a kind of sadistic smirk. "I was in the scrub room when a couple of pukers came out."

"I'll bet they were both men," I commented.

He stopped for a second, surprised. "Yeah, they were."

"How did you know?" Nick asked.

"The same way I know female rookie cops handle seeing wounds better than rookie males," I replied, smiling somewhat patronizingly.

"Why do you think that is?" Nick asked, intrigued.

Men. "Long before she reaches medical school, every woman already knows what it's like to have blood on her hands."

This didn't do much to relieve the tension, which still hung heavy in the air. I didn't know if Bob knew what I knew or not. He coughed and cleared his throat—a deep, guttural sound. "Must be getting a summer cold," he said, shaking his head. "So, how's your investigation going? I hear you made an arrest."

"I wouldn't put too much stock in what you hear on television," I said, wondering how interested he actually was.

He balanced his fork precariously above what was left of his generic meat and leaned in on his elbow. "What about you, Detective? You ever kill anyone?"

"Once," I replied. "How about you?" Nick kicked me under the table. I kicked him back, harder.

It went on like that for a while until it was clear that Robert Fusillo had enjoyed about as much of my company as he could stand. He pushed his chair back, got up, and said, "Well, if you'll excuse me, I've got to get back to work."

Nick skillfully asked him, "Are you here for a while or are you knocking off early?"

"No, I've got to lead a support group in the family lounge at eight, so I think I'll try to get caught up on paperwork until then." He regarded me coldly, then turned and walked out.

"Was Neville like that?" I asked when he was out of earshot.

"No," said Nick, shaking his head. "Of all the things Neville was, he was never impolite."

"No, I don't suppose he was." At that level of mortal cruelty, common unpleasantness would seem a silly and superfluous affectation.

———————

We were walking back to the elevator when I said, "The surgical support meeting tonight—how large is that?"

Nick shrugged. "I'm not sure. Last one I went to had about fifteen or so."

"Who comes?"

"Each department has its own guidelines. We encourage patients to come for at least a couple of months, longer depending on what they've gone through or if they seem to be having problems coping.''

''And Fusillo's leading this one?''

''Believe it or not, he's very good at it. I've always said that doctors' bedside manner would improve enormously if they were forced to the other side of the bed once in a while. Even if it was just having to use a bedpan. Look, I know you don't respond very well to Bob. But he leads three or four of those groups he was talking about, and the patients respond to him. He brings a real empathy to it, having been there himself.''

''I'd have to see it to believe it. Can I sit in tonight?''

''That wouldn't be a good idea. No outsiders.''

''I'm supposed to be keeping track of him.''

''With an outsider there, they might not feel comfortable opening up. The postsurgical reaction can be a peculiar one, particularly in brain surgery. You might be surprised to find that the patient's reaction to the surgeon can be ambivalent, even to one who's saved his or her life.''

''I thought cops were the only ones who got dumped on for being good guys,'' I said.

''Guess again.''

But at least he could afford to drive a Mercedes for his trouble.

''I want to know where he is every minute,'' I insisted.

''He certainly won't do anything crazy in front of a bunch of witnesses,'' said Nick. ''Tell you what, I'll tell him to check in with me as soon as the meeting is over.''

———————————

About twenty minutes to eight I went down to the second floor and checked out the family lounge. It was a large room with comfortable, built-in oak seating upholstered in brightly colored fabrics. Framed children's finger paintings graced the walls in a touchingly self-conscious attempt to provide upbeat and cheerful surroundings. This was the room where friends and loved ones gathered to wait anxiously—often for many hours—until the surgeon came in to deliver the few sentences that they would remember for the rest of their lives.

I went back up to Nick's office to wait out the meeting and keep an eye on him. It was plain to me that no matter what I said, Captain Owen still considered Nick the prime suspect. Maybe he was punishing me for ''demoting'' Russell Morgan.

I read magazines and watched television in the Neurology Department waiting area while Nick worked on a paper he was presenting on clinical trials for the Ramsey neural modulator next month in Zurich. The last place I got to go for work was Rochester, New York, in the dead of winter. But never mind.

Fusillo stopped by around ten. As an excuse for calling him, Nick gave him what he'd written and asked him to take it home for review. Dr. Bob nodded to me formally—actually I'd say it was more of a glare—then left. I immediately picked up the phone and rang the dispatcher. I gave her Vince's radio code and had her patch me through.

"He's leaving the meeting now," I reported. "So start looking for him at the garage entrance in about three minutes."

"Right," the muffled, crackling approximation of Vince's voice came back. "Catch you later."

"Catch someone," I said hopefully. Now I could relax a little. Fusillo was off my watch.

"Where to now?" I asked Nick. I was worn out from tension and ready to go home. Maybe we could pick up where we left off.

"I've still got work to do," he said.

"What kind?" I said, somewhat crestfallen.

"In the OR."

"Another operation?"

"No. Preparing for one."

He picked up a videocassette from his desk, stood, and led me down to the surgical suite. It was still and empty and spooky in its quietness. We went into OR number four, popped the tape into the VCR, and began watching the monitor intently.

It wasn't exactly *Swedish Snow Bunnies Go Berserk*. Instead it was all details and extreme closeups—recorded through the optic of the impressive Zeiss microscope that hovered just over the surgical field.

So this was what Chris Taylor's brain looked like. It was still difficult for me to relate to this reddish gray mass—this thing I had seen casually splattered against pavements and walls and car windows—as the controller of the sum total of human behavior and experience.

I glanced around the room. "It looks a lot different from down here than it does from up there," I said, gazing up at the gallery, then back down to meet Nick's eyes. "It's like being one of the gladiators in the arena."

"Let me take you through this," he said, freezing the frame.

He put his arm across my back and positioned me in front of the screen. Then, holding me that way, remote control in hand, he led me on a step-by-step journey into the farthest realms of consciousness. At each juncture, he stopped the tape to explain.

It didn't take long to become totally engrossed . . . transfixed, actually. At the same time, I felt incredibly vulnerable, almost violated. It was like watching a real-life version of *Fantastic Voyage*—that movie I saw as a kid in which a team of scientists is miniaturized and injected into a blood vessel so they can dislodge a clot threatening another scientist's brain. How far would you have to be miniaturized, I wondered, before you could actually see a thought happening, or an intent, or a motive? How tiny would you have to get to positively ID a truth?

The journey was harrowing. But there was a naturalness and grace to Nick's authority, like the airplane pilot calmly flying you through a hurricane. This was his domain, and no one surpassed him here.

Deeper and deeper we probed, gradually peeling away all the protective layers. Finally we reached the critical point. The gleaming tips of tweezers came into frame, looming large, and they held the nondescript gray wad Nick identified as the piece of Neville's brain.

What was in there? I asked myself. What part of Neville Ramsey was inherent in that small chunk? How would it interact in its new environment? I could feel my heart pounding. I could see the tweezers move into place, then wedge their treasure into a precise fissure the scalpel had cut into the receiving tissue.

The next phase showed Nick making a small incision in Chris's shoulder and implanting the NeMo unit—beginning with the placement of the thumbnail-size generator pack between the trapezius and sterno-cleidomastoid muscles, Nick explained. ''From there, a narrow-diameter wire lead is laid subcutaneously along the soft tissues of the neck, up to the temporal area of the head, then through a tiny bore in the cranium.''

As the final stage, he placed a hand-held transmitter unit wired to a computer terminal next to Chris's shoulder and, while staring at the computer screen, began pressing buttons on the keyboard. ''Once it's in, the adjustment is completely noninvasive. It runs on a rechargeable lithium battery, and we use electromagnetic inductance to transmit 'instructions' to the unit.''

''Jerry was right,'' I said almost to myself. ''You are going to make a fucking fortune.''

I don't know how long we watched, how long I vicariously relived Chris Taylor's ordeal. I had lost all sense of time, just as surgeons themselves often report in the OR. It could have been hours. I felt rung out and almost limp, as if I'd been operating myself.

At one point I looked momentarily away from the screen. Nick was staring at me. Right away I could see something different in his eyes— something more akin to what I'd seen last night as we tore off each other's clothes and fought for dominion on my sofa and floor.

He saw me looking at him and said, "You are so beautiful, Sandy." He continued staring at me and said, "I dreamed about you last night."

"What was I doing?"

He smiled, and his eyes sparkled from the overhead light. "Same thing as when we were awake." He held me by the shoulders and began softly caressing my arms. "What would be the greatest luxury to you? Tell me your deepest, secret fantasy."

But a warning was going off inside my head. Was I ready to deal with this? Was I prepared to push the edge of the envelope again? Could we both handle this right now?

Sandy, please protect yourself.

"Let me share it with you," he implored gently, moving his hands down to my hips. "Let me make it happen."

"Here?" I said.

"What better place?"

Once, early in the Job, I did have a fleeting but overwhelming desire to make love in a morgue. I've seen it written that sex is the ultimate triumph over death. Just like medical science.

"What's your greatest fantasy, Sandy?"

"What's yours?"

"Some other time. Tonight is for you. What is it, Sandy? Tell me."

What's wrong with me that all of the things Patricia found so threatening and uncomfortable are what draw me like a moth to a flame?

So I took a deep breath and attempted a full gainer off the high board. My deepest secret fantasy?

"Letting go," I murmured. "Not having to make decisions . . . not having to be in control." Which also happens to be the thing that scares me most in all the world. The best and the worst are so close to each other, and the great is the enemy of the good.

Staring into my eyes, he held me around the waist and gracefully lifted me onto the operating table. My shoes slipped off my feet and dropped onto the floor. He set me down and guided me back until I was lying flat, staring up at the ceiling.

Briefly, he stepped away from the table and came back with a coil of rubber tourniquet tubing. I watched him with an excited edginess as he picked up a scalpel from the instrument tray on the cart next to the table. He held it up and seemed to study its short, rounded blade as it sparkled in the overhead light. He held it to the tubing, which he stretched to its maximum tension and then cut into three lengths. The scalpel sliced through the rubber tubing as easily as it sliced through human flesh.

He lifted my arms back beyond my head and crossed them at the wrists. Then he began wrapping one length of the rubber around them.

My body went suddenly tense. I parted my lips to speak, but he touched them with his finger.

"Will you finally trust me?" he whispered, still mesmerizing me with his eyes.

I didn't try to say anything.

With exquisite gentleness, he positioned my bound wrists in the center of the table above my head, then tied the other end of the tubing underneath the table. He pressed the floor pedal to raise the angle on the table, making my head and torso a little more upright and stretching the rubber rope tighter. I could feel the subtle throbbing pressure in my wrists. Then, with the other two lengths of tubing, he proceeded to bind my ankles to either side of the table's base.

"Just trust me, Sandy. You don't have to be in control anymore. There's nothing you can do. Just let yourself go. Just let it happen."

I was quivering with excitement, and I was trembling with fear. Was this what Julie Fox felt like? I wondered, then forced the thought from my mind.

He unbuttoned my blouse and let it fall away on either side of my chest. He delicately slid my skirt under my behind and up to my waist. He gripped the waistband of my panty hose and slowly peeled them down until they reached the bonds around my ankles. He turned, picked up a pair of angled surgical scissors from the instrument tray, then systematically cut the nylon away from my legs. He let the fabric drop to the floor.

His eyes came to rest on my blue string bikini panties. Almost the same shade as the ones Russell Morgan had taken. Nick played with the elastic band, then pulled them down to my thighs, turning the fabric inside-out and revealing a glistening, dewy patch. Our eyes met again, and I felt myself go hot. My heart was beating like a drum.

Ever so lightly, he kissed the soft down on my belly.

His fingers searched for the closure of my bra, circling around from the front. When he didn't find it there, his hands went under my back. He fumbled underneath me for a moment, but when it wouldn't come loose, he picked up the scalpel again and drew it near my chest. I held my breath.

"Just trust me," he said as he inserted the blade under my bra, right in the middle between my breasts. I could feel the back of the blade pressing lightly against my skin, then quickly he brought it up and sliced through.

In rapid succession he sliced through both shoulder straps, one and then the other.

Julie Fox's bra strap had been sliced through with a thin, sharp instrument.

He laid the scalpel back in the tray and picked up a little silver pinwheel with sharp points, the kind of instrument doctors roll along the skin to test feeling and sensitivity.

He started at my wrist and moved it slowly down along my arm. I felt tiny, delicate jabs of pain as it reached the tender area of my underarm. From there he moved down to the inner surface of my thighs, which made me twist and squirm against my bonds. I prayed this torture would never end and at the same time silently begged for him to take me right this very second.

But then he stepped away again. Was he going to leave me here—worked up into this state yet helpless to do anything about it? I strained to follow his movements and could see him bend down and open what I thought was another cabinet. What was next? I wondered. What was he going to do to me now? When he came back he was holding a large ice cube. Somewhere, there was a freezer in the OR.

For many long minutes he teased me with the ice cube, making me quiver as he came to every new part of my body—my lips and tongue . . . armpits . . . nipples . . . belly button and lightly down into my bush. My body tingled where the ice dripped.

He put what was left of the cube in my mouth, where it melted quickly, and began caressing my entire body with his insured and talented hands. I shuddered deeply as they went between my legs, then he bent his head down to take their place. Little jolts of electricity coursed through me as I felt his darting tongue find its target.

Do me now and do me hard, I prayed silently. I can't take any more of this.

He hoisted himself up on the table and straddled me. He moved his hand back toward my groin. Tenderly he spread my lips and dipped two fingers easily into me, then brought them up to my nose and mouth, holding them there for me to lick. Balancing himself above me with one arm, he nimbly worked his way out of his shirt, which fell back behind him on my legs. He unbuckled his belt, and at the same time, I saw him reach back into the instrument tray. He lowered himself onto me. I could feel his erection large and firm against me.

And yes I said yes I will Yes . . .

A loud commotion, then: "Police! Freeze!"

I froze.

I turned my head in horror and saw Patrick Owen, his gun drawn and held steady in his thick hand. Behind him were Marc Volmer and Rafe Cardenas, their weapons drawn, too. All three mouths were wide open. So was mine. So was Nick's. Whatever he'd been holding clattered back into the tray.

"What are you doing here!" I gasped.

"I could ask you the same question," Owen replied, "but the answer seems to be fairly self-evident."

He pointed the gun at Nick. "Move slowly back toward the wall, Doctor." He turned to the others, who were straining their necks to see around him. "Wait outside."

They complied reluctantly. Nick climbed over me and off the table. He managed to grab his shirt and cover my middle.

Still holding the gun, Owen moved closer to the table. He averted his eyes discreetly. He picked up the surgical scissors from the tray, focused on the tubing holding my wrists together, cut it, then held the scissors out to me. He walked over to Nick. Nick buckled his belt.

My heart was still racing. I bent forward and cut my ankles free. I hurriedly restored my panties back to their approximately proper position and lowered my skirt.

"Put your hands on the wall and spread your feet apart," I heard Owen say. He quickly patted Nick down and found him clean. I could have told him that.

"What are you doing?" I cried, skidding down from the table as I

MARK OLSHAKER ——————— 277

buttoned my blouse. I could feel my panties wedged uncomfortably between the cheeks of my behind.

"More important is what I've just done," Owen declared, "which is to keep you from becoming victim number four."

"What!"

Nick had recovered from his initial surprise. His face showed a combination of hurt and anger. "You set me up! I can't . . . I can't believe it!"

"No, I . . ." I realized how this all looked. I wanted to sink into the ground.

"This would have looked great in tomorrow's headlines," Owen ranted on. "Lead detective on the case found—"

"What are you talking about?" I pleaded. My head snapped over to Nick. "I had no idea . . . I'm not . . . Believe me."

His face softened into confusion.

Owen said, "Doctor, would you mind waiting outside with the two detectives?"

Nick looked to me for reaction. "Sandy, I'm so sorry," he said. His eyes shifted back and forth again, still not quite certain. "I think." Then he started for the scrub room doors.

Owen picked up his shirt and threw it to him.

"You had no right to do this!" I insisted as the doors swung closed behind Nick. I tucked my blouse into my skirt.

"Let me set you straight on that," Owen retorted. "I'm the captain. I had every right, not to mention responsibility."

"You were spying on me!"

"We were backing you up."

"Everything was under control."

"If that's how you define being tied up with your pants down and him with a tray full of sharp toys to use on you the same way he used them on Fox and Hazeltine, then your definition must be different from mine."

"You just don't understand."

"And if you're going to tell me you were setting him up to make his move, save your breath."

"You're supposed to trust me."

"And you're supposed to merit that trust."

"I don't understand what you're doing here," I stated feebly.

"What are we doing here? Fine, I'll tell you. I got to thinking, Okay,

Sandy's right about Morgan, which in my book means Ramsey is still our top suspect. So the more I thought about it, the less comfortable I felt having you going without backup. That's what we're doing here—backing you up. And I see we got here just in time.''

"That's one way of looking at it," I said sardonically. I wanted to fix my underpants but couldn't without being obvious.

"We just saved your life. A little gratitude wouldn't be out of order."

"Are you kidding?"

"Sandy, you're off the case. And you're suspended—as of now."

"What! For not showing gratitude?"

"No. For showing incredibly poor judgment, for compromising yourself and the investigation, not to mention the reputation of the MPD if any of this gets out. And if Volmer or Cardenas talk, by the way, I'll have their nuts."

"You can't suspend me," I protested, "I'm so close."

"That's a matter of opinion," he countered. "And I just did. Give me your gun and badge. Now."

"But . . ."

"And don't make me angry. At the moment, I'm still calm and rational."

Miserably, I went over to the counter and opened my bag. I took out my Glock 17 and my badge, brought them back, and handed them to Owen. He received them solemnly. I felt as if the life were draining out of me.

Owen was as furious as I was. "This is absolutely the most unprofessional behavior I've ever seen!" he continued ranting. "I've let you bend the rules in the past because you're good and you could get away with it. But this time, you've gone over the edge. You've lost all your perspective, all your critical faculties. I should have trusted my own judgment and yanked you the first time I thought about it."

"You don't have enough to charge him," I said.

"No, we don't, thanks to you," he agreed. "At least we'll slow him down till we can get the goods. And if he so much as twitches, I'll have his ass in jail on three counts of murder one."

"I'm telling you, boss, the real guy's still out there."

"And I say we've just interrupted the real guy. But we'll know that by morning, won't we? We'll be watching him and if there's no murder tonight . . ."

"Why don't you polygraph him? You'll see."

"If the guy's a psychopath who gets his kicks out of torturing women to death, you think it's going to raise his blood pressure to lie to a metal box?"

It was pointless, I realized. There was no talking to him.

"Sandy, what was going through your head?"

"You wouldn't understand," I said morosely.

"You hit that nail on the head. Put your shoes on," he said. "Pull yourself together, get a cab, and get yourself home."

There was nothing else to say, nothing else to do. As I trudged out of the room, I picked up the remnants of my panty hose and bra and dumped them in the scrub room trash barrel. At least my mother would have been pleased to know I was finally learning to clean up after myself.

37

I woke up with the sun beating down on my face. I was still in a daze, still in my clothes, with bare legs and no bra. My teeth and tongue felt as if they were covered with moss, and when I staggered into the bathroom and saw the way my makeup had run and dried, I realized I'd done a lot of crying.

Sitting dejectedly on the john, I mentally replayed all of last night's events on fast forward. Nick's reputation might have been killed by this, and my career was very likely over.

I flushed the toilet and stood up. As I lowered my dress I noticed a large dark bruise forming on my hip where I'd landed when we rolled off the sofa together: a souvenir of Monday night's adventure I'd carry for the next week or so. It seemed as if every encounter with Nick left me bruised or bleeding. Somehow I'd never found love to be pain-free.

What a fucking mess.

I wondered if he would call me. Or if he hated me now, the way everyone else seemed to.

I looked in the mirror and didn't like what I saw. Well, you've really done it this time, Cassandra.

I heard the doorbell ring. Who the hell wants to . . . ? I don't want to see anyone. But maybe it was Nick.

It was Vince. He gave me the once-over and immediately scowled. "You look like hell."

"Thanks," I said, "I've been hearing that a lot lately." I glanced down at myself and realized my blouse was fairly transparent. Never mind, it was only Vince.

He stepped inside and closed the door behind him. "What's doing?" I asked.

He maintained the scowl and added a head shake of disapproval. "You'd be the expert on that." There was a long, painful silence, then, "I knew something like this was going to happen, the way you were going."

"If you came over to beat me up, can we do it later?" I pleaded. "I'm just not up for being whipped this early in the morning."

"No, you seem to prefer it later at night, the way I understand it."

"Come on, Vince, I need at least one friend." I sighed and rubbed my eyes. "You want some coffee?"

"No thanks."

"Well, I need some." I walked over to the kitchen and put a pot of water on. Vince followed me. "So I guess the captain is really pissed."

"Let's say he's severely disappointed."

"What happened with Chris Taylor?" I didn't know what I wanted to hear.

"He went to the theater. Then he and two other actors went to Pied de Couchon for something to eat. They dropped him at his apartment—alone—where he remains to this minute."

"What about Bob Fusillo?"

"Clean as a whistle. He went directly home with the girl. They were in for the night. I'm sure they had more fun than I did."

Or me. No murders last night. The city was a little cooler, and my ass was in the fire. I abandoned whatever slight hope I had of convincing Owen he hadn't arrived just in time to foil the crime of the century.

"Have you talked to your friend, Dr. Ramsey?" Vince asked.

I shook my head.

"If you do, you'd better tell him that Owen's out for his hide. If he did it, we'll make the case."

"I'm telling you, Vince, he didn't do it."

"You may be just a little too close to the situation to make that judgment," he suggested.

I wanted to protest, but I realized it was pointless. There was a long, awkward pause. It felt very weird. Most of the time, Vince and I could complete each other's thoughts. Finally I said, "How's Dee?"

"Okay. She's concerned for you."

"Tell her thanks. How about Lucy?" He managed a nod. "Give them my love?" He nodded again. "Nothing got in the papers, did it?"

"No, and you'd better hope it doesn't."

There was another long moment of silence. I said, "I'm in trouble this time, Vince, aren't I? Owen's really got it in for me now."

His eyes agreed with me. "I'm afraid so."

"Do you think I ought to call him?" Maybe that's why Vince was here—as Owen's emissary.

Vince shook his head. "I'd wait for the dust to settle. You stick yourself in his face right now, you're just going to stir things up even more." He watched as I poured steaming coffee into a Fraternal Order of Police mug.

"You know, I really feel naked without my badge and gun."

He glanced down at the sheer fabric of my blouse. "I can imagine." My hand went automatically to my chest.

"So what are you going to do with yourself?"

I shrugged morosely. I hadn't really faced that yet. "Sleep, I guess, get caught up on the papers, exercise, go to the movies, all the things I don't have time for when I'm working. Maybe try to catch the killer."

"Sandy, please don't do anything stupid . . . anything else stupid."

I could feel my eyes growing moist again. "I've got to do something, Vince. I can't just sit here and . . ." The tears were rolling down my cheeks now, tears of frustration more than anything. Why don't things work out the way they're supposed to?

I put down my mug and moved closer to Vince, hoping for a hug. "Please don't hate me," I implored him.

"I don't hate you. I could never hate you. I'm angry as hell at you," he said as sternly as he could. "But unfortunately, I've never been able to stay angry at you long." He took the handkerchief from his breast pocket and handed it to me. "Dry your face."

"By the way," I said softly, "why did you come over?"

Men like Vince aren't much good at expressing sentimentality. "To see if you were okay," he said simply. He paused. "Are you?"

I nodded.

"I'll do whatever I can."

I walked him the short distance to the door. As he opened it, he leaned toward me. I hoped he wasn't going to kiss me on the forehead or anything I wouldn't be able to handle. But instead he patted me on the shoulder as he would any colleague.

"Take care," he said as he left.

I walked back to the kitchen, picked up my coffee mug, and started to cry again.

———————

I caught a TV interview with Chief Price, assuring the public that they were close to a suspect in this series of crimes that had shocked and terrified a city and a nation. The discreet and judicious chief was unwilling to entertain speculation or give a time frame. But I knew it wouldn't be long before they thought they had the elements on Nick, then every pseudopsychologist who'd ever gotten a rise out of having a camera pointed in his face would be holding forth as to what would make a world-renowned healer imitate the heinous acts of his infamous brother.

Fortunately, there was no mention of me, though as soon as it got out that I'd been suspended, that was guaranteed to make the news. Nothing like public humiliation to make you feel completely worthless.

I turned on my answering machine and tried to turn off my mind and my emotions. I would lick my wounds and let them bleed out and let my brain lie fallow for a while. I took a long shower and then lay on my bed watching Sally Jessy Raphäel discussing "gay couples who adopt outside their race." I'm not kidding.

The phone rang, and I listened to my recorded voice kick in.

"It's me. Call me." It was Nick. I scrambled across the bed to the nightstand and picked up the receiver.

"Hi. Where are you?"

"At the hospital. I called your office, but they said you were home."

I brought him up-to-date.

"I'm sorry," he said. "And there was no murder last night? They asked me thousands of questions before they let me go home last night, but they didn't tell me anything."

"There was no murder," I confirmed.

"Do you have any idea why?"

"No," I said. "Do you?"

"What's that supposed to mean?"

"Nothing. Sorry."

"I guess this makes it all the more critical I get to Chris Taylor as soon as possible."

"What it makes all the more critical," I snapped, "is to let me tell my captain what really happened with Neville's brain . . . assuming he'll even listen to me."

"No, you can't do that!" Nick insisted. "It'll ruin those lives, and even we don't know for sure. It could be disastrous for future research."

"I can't worry about that now."

"You have to. Promise me you won't say anything."

"I'm not sure what I can promise anymore."

"It's bad enough what I have to do about Chris, but at least I can say it would be worse if I did nothing."

"Nick, my bosses think it's you."

There was silence on the other end. Then, "What about you? What do you think?"

All the time I'd spent with him—all the conversations, all the arguments and confrontations and deceits, the dangerous, sensational love-making, and then last night in the operating room—all of it came swirling together in my head.

"Just tell me, Nick," I said, "and tell me for real this time. Did you or did you not kill Julie Fox and Sarah Hazeltine and Jerry Ashburn, and were you going to kill me last night?"

"I don't see how you can even ask me that question. Is this conversation being taped or something?"

"Just answer the fucking question, Nick."

"Of course not. Of course I didn't kill anyone." Dead silence. "Now . . . do you believe me?"

I took a deep breath. "Yes, I believe you," I said wearily, and at the same time asked myself what was the basis of this belief. It may be a cliché to say that I couldn't be that wrong about anyone who made me feel the way Nick did, but if I'd developed any instincts at all in my ten years on the Job, I had to be willing to lay them on the line.

The next question, in these new and difficult circumstances I found myself in, would be what to do about it.

38

"**S**O will you help me, Vince?"
     I sat cross-legged on my bed and pleaded into the phone
receiver. I'd been wrestling with this all night and called
him as soon as I woke up.

"You trying to get me suspended, too?" he said. "Now tell me
exactly what it is you want from me."

"Get the surveillance detail on Chris Taylor reinstated, and arrange
threat response protection for Bonnie Sharpless, the dancer at the Touch
of Class. You're the only one I've got left."

"Why does she need protection?"

"The less I tell you, the more deniability you have if there's a
problem," I said.

"A problem?" he repeated.

"Just say that since she was a co-worker and close friend of Julie
Fox, you have strong concerns the killer might threaten her."

"And is that the case?"

"It may be," I said as elliptically as I could. I'd already checked
to make sure she was listed in the phone book—a critical component
of my plan.

"Sandy, I don't like the sound of that."

"Please, Vince, just trust me on this." There was that word again.

"Can't you leave something alone for once?"

"No! Because no matter what Pat Owen thinks, the case isn't
closed."

"I hate to belabor the obvious, but it isn't your case anymore."

"Vince, who was it who told me that to get to the truth, you pursue it to the ends of the earth if you have to—that that's what carrying the badge is all about? So will you do this for me?''

Vince took a long deep breath, and I could sense he still hadn't made up his mind yet. At last he muttered, ''Sometimes I'm sorry I ever brought you onto the Job.''

———————————

By early afternoon, Vince called to say the protection detail was in place. ''I did this on my own authority,'' he grumbled. ''Owen doesn't even know about it. You'd better not make me sorry.''

''I'd better not,'' I agreed.

I called Chris Taylor and asked if he would see me. He said he'd be at the theater rehearsing an understudy so he'd see me there.

We sat across in his modest dressing room. ''How's the run going?'' I asked pleasantly.

''Going good,'' he said. ''Good reviews, and the audiences have been terrific. But Richard's a tough role, mentally and physically. Everything in the play turns on his choices and actions, and it's a strain to have to be that evil eight times a week.''

''I'll bet it is,'' I said, ''though I know some drug dealers who could do it with very little strain.''

Could he be this unflappable sitting across from a cop if he really was the killer? I asked myself. Well, Neville Ramsey had been, and if that was where he got it from, then I supposed it was possible.

''Christ, I don't want to alarm you,'' I said solicitously, beginning my setup, ''but something new's come up, something I thought you should know.''

''Oh?''

''Someone has picked your picture out of a set of photographs as being seen with Julie Fox just before the time we think she was murdered.''

''Why would they pick me out?'' he asked, suddenly becoming appropriately agitated. He cleared his throat in that most unpleasant way of his.

''I don't know,'' I said. ''Maybe it has something to do with Dr. Ramsey. I would say it's probably a mistake, except for the fact that you did contact us in the first place, which does seem to connect you somehow to the case. Is it possible Dr. Ramsey might want to use you as the fall guy?'' I wondered if he would mention this new procedure Nick had asked him to submit to.

But all he said was, "Why? He saved my life. Why should he want to destroy it now? And I've never even met Ms. Fox. Who is it who said this about me?''

I leaned in toward him. "I shouldn't be telling you this, but you've been so cooperative, I feel I owe you something. Her name is Bonnie Sharpless. She's a dancer who worked with Julie Fox at the Touch of Class. Do you know her?''

"Bonnie Sharpless." He repeated it as if committing the name to memory. "No, I don't know her."

"She's prepared to testify. But I really don't want you to worry.'' Right. "If you say she's wrong, we'll get it cleared up."

The trap was baited. If Nick was mistaken about Chris being the one, he wouldn't do anything other than fret, and Bonnie was in no danger. If, on the other hand, it was Chris, he'd have to make some kind of move. And we'd be ready for him.

———

My next appointment was with my old pal, Dr. Bob Fusillo. With no great enthusiasm, he agreed to meet me for coffee in the cafeteria before he started making rounds. Among other things, I wanted to know if Nick had told him anything about Tuesday night.

Dressed in surgical greens, Fusillo was waiting for me at a table in the back. We got coffee from the machines and went back to sit down.

"I understand your masters don't approve of unauthorized diddling with the enemy,'' he commented, the sides of his mouth forming a neat little sneer. Well, that answered my question. Was there anything Nick didn't share with Bob?

"They're trying to destroy Nick, aren't they?''

"It's possible," I said.

"Do they have enough?''

"If it's there, they'll find it."

And is that good news or bad news for you, Dr. Bob?

I decided to turn things on him. "Do you think it's possible he's the killer?'' I asked.

"You'd be in a better position to know that than me,'' he said. "But

I'll tell you: If you think Nick is just going to sit by and let this happen to him, you've got another think coming.''

Okay, fella, we're both concerned about what's going to happen to Nick, and we've both been nailed by the cops with our pants down. That should give us at least a little common ground. So why don't you try lightening up just a smidge?

"You're aware, of course, that the murders they're associating Nick with mirror his late brother's crimes pretty closely."

Bob nodded noncommittally.

"If you had to guess, what type of person do you think did commit them?"

"Why are you asking me? You're the detective."

"I'm asking you." He was starting to piss me off again.

"Someone who's trying to destroy Nicholas."

Interesting. "Is he nervous? How's he taking it?"

He glanced down as he poured artificial creamer into his Styrofoam cup and swirled it into the instant coffee with a plastic stirrer. Then he raised an eye in my direction and with false concern asked, "How are you taking it?"

I decided to let the question pass, but he pressed on. "So as I see it, the only way you can save yourself and your job is to prove Nick is innocent, isn't that right?"

Whatever else he was, no one said Bob wasn't smart and perceptive. "How are you going to do that?" he inquired.

Pay attention—I'm trying to do it right now.

"Bob, you may not like me, and you may not like my relationship with Nick . . ."

"That's none of my business," he said plainly, but doctors aren't as good as actors in covering subtext.

"Whatever. But you have to know I'm pretty ticked off about what's happened and what they've done to me. So regardless of how you feel about me, I'm going to give you some information that I probably shouldn't."

He looked at me with surprise, which quickly turned to a kind of anxious expectation.

"One of the women who worked with Julie Fox—Bonnie Sharpless is her name—picked out your photograph and said she'd seen you with Julie just before she was killed."

Strictly speaking, of course, this wasn't true. Or even loosely speaking, for that matter. But we did have eyewitnesses who placed a dark-haired white male in his late twenties to early thirties, of medium height and build, in the vicinity at approximately the right time. And since that general description fit both Chris and Dr. Bob (not to mention about two hundred–odd thousand others in the metro area), I figured I'd use it as the basis of my game plan.

"Now why would she ID you?" I asked innocently.

"I . . . I don't know," he said nervously. It's just amazing the way ordinary people tend to suddenly stop being snide and arrogant when you implicate them in a series of murders.

"Did you know Julie?" I asked.

"I examined her when she came in for her sciatica. There was another woman with her. Maybe it was this Bonnie. Maybe she noticed me then and got confused. That's the most logical thing I can come up with."

I'll bet. Though if I give you a little more time, maybe you can come up with something even more logical.

"Frankly, I don't think there's anything to it," I went on blithely, "but it was something I thought you ought to know so you could protect yourself."

"I appreciate your telling me," he said, and I could already see the wheels turning.

———————

Before I left the hospital, I stopped at a pay phone and called Ted. I couldn't just leave things hanging after the other night. And I did feel bad about it about using him and then blowing him off. I told him about the suspension. After all, whatever had gone down between us, he'd still been my husband. And right now I was feeling like I needed all the friends I could get.

"That's a tough break," he said sincerely. "What can I do?"

I'd been thinking about that.

"When can I see you?"

I'd been thinking about that, too. "I don't know if you remember, but every year there's a picnic after the league softball game closest to the Fourth of July—which is today. West Potomac Park, near the Lincoln Memorial."

"I remember."

"I was wondering if maybe you'd like to meet me there after the game."

"Sure. Sure," he said again with building self-possession. "If that's what you want."

"I'd like that, Ted. Thanks." I hung up the phone and stood there for a moment, reflecting on what I'd just done. But I was so low and my life had spun so far out of control, what was one more complication?

39

"I'M surprised to see you here," Vince said as I walked onto the field in my shorts and team T-shirt, glove tucked under my arm and my hair tucked under my blue cap. "The fact that you showed up either means you have a profound and insatiable love of the game or . . ."

Or it was a way to hold my obstinate head high and keep my nose in things at the same time. Just as we both knew Vince was here to prove to the assembled multitudes that contrary to vicious rumor, he was not yet an old man.

"I'll keep your secret if you'll keep mine," I whispered. He didn't smile.

Our team was made up of personnel from Homicide and Sex Crimes, the office right across the hall from ours. We played at something of a disadvantage since we had a smaller pool to draw from than most teams, the average age of detectives being greater than of uniforms and the Sex Crimes Unit having a high percentage of women. And let's face it, no matter how we'd like the world to be, on average men are stronger and more coordinated and have been playing ball with their fathers since they were two.

On the other hand, a lot of the teams in the league are composed of lawyers, who tend to be high-strung and competitive and not nearly in as good shape or as athletically talented as they think they are. In fact, I've found they tend not to be as . . . as *anything* as they think they are.

Today we were playing the public defender's office—the lowly paid bleeding hearts who attempt to spring from jail the very people we've just busted our buns to put there. So each year this was always among our scrappiest grudge matches. Their shirts read "The Great Defenders." Clever, huh? Ours just had the MPD badge and our team numbers. The suggestion our team might sport the catchy legend "Sex and Violence" was summarily vetoed by Chief Claudel Price himself.

The Defenders were taking fielding practice in the outfield, and our side was loosening up at the bat. I walked over to our team bench and nodded to a couple of the people from the Sex Crimes Unit. They nodded back discreetly, not quite sure whether they should treat me as a normal person or pariah. I'd known the whole thing was going to be awkward, but you either suit up for life or you don't.

I tossed my glove on the bench, picked up a bat, and began limbering up. As I said, it'd been several weeks since I'd played, and my arms and shoulders felt stiff. And I wanted to make a good showing here.

Marc Volmer was pitching batting practice. I was just stepping up to the plate when Joe LaRocca raced up and insinuated himself in front of me.

"What's she doing here?" he demanded.

"What's the problem, Joe?" said Marc, coming in from the mound.

LaRocca was emphatically pounding his fist into the pocket of his glove. "League rules specifically state that all players have to be *active* members of their employing organizations."

"So?" said Marc.

"Someone on suspension is *not* active."

"Okay, forget it!" I said. I whipped off my cap and began storming off the field in disgust.

But Rafe Cardenas stopped me. He moved past me and, pragmatic soul that he is, said to LaRocca, "So what are we supposed to do for a shortstop? We've lost the last three games."

Marvella Harris from Sex Crimes came up and joined the fray. "If Sandy can't play, I'm not playing, either," she declared.

"That'll be a loss," LaRocca supportively remarked.

I was so angry, I was blinking tears from my eyes. I turned away because I didn't want them to be misinterpreted. I'd rather die than let LaRocca think he'd made me cry.

"I don't see anything wrong with it," said Volmer. "After all she's still one of us and this is a social thing and—"

"Rules are rules!" LaRocca insisted.

"And if you got nailed every time you broke a rule, you'd be wearing a gray uniform and sweeping Chief Price's office after hours,'' said Cardenas.

It was Vince, as usual, who took charge. He walked up to the plate and waved over Rich Carstairs, captain of the Defenders. ''Mansfield's on administrative leave,'' he explained.

''Suspension,'' LaRocca interjected.

''You have any objection to her playing?''

''Not as long as you don't mind Goldberg's wife, who helped beat the crap out of you last year,'' Carstairs replied. ''I mean, come on. It's just a game.''

''Fine. It's settled, then. Sandy, take your batting practice.'' And as he walked away, I saw Vince grab LaRocca by the arm and in a low voice suggest, ''Joe, for once in your life, do yourself a favor and stop being such a complete and unadulterated asshole.''

When I finished taking my swings, I walked back over to where Vince was standing. ''Thanks,'' I said. ''It never ceases to amaze me what a jerk LaRocca can be.''

''LaRocca is a jerk,'' said Vince. ''No question about it. But you've got to understand the situation, too, Sandy.''

''What do you mean?'' I asked defensively.

''You're like the chickens I remember back in South Carolina, running around the barnyard after their heads'd been cut off. They were still operating under the old rules, not yet realizing that the situation was now drastically different.''

———————

In the bottom of the first inning, we were already down two–zip. We had no one on base and two outs. Just before my at-bat, Joe LaRocca leaned over to me on the bench and said, ''You know, Mansfield, there's a biological, historical reason why men make better cops than women.''

I looked straight ahead and tried to ignore him.

''Since the beginning of time, men have been the hunters and gatherers and warriors. Women have been the food preparers and the child tenders and the keepers of the hearth. It's always been that way. It's supposed to be that way. So don't fight it, Mansfield. History's against you.''

I said nothing.

"By the way, I understand that Ramsey's a real operator!"

You can only take so much. "Why don't you try sucking your own dick, LaRocca," I suggested. "Maybe you'll break your neck."

I walked up to the plate and on the first pitch smacked the ball past the right fielder for a stand-up double. LaRocca pulled a short single, then got tagged out grandstanding, trying to steal second, leaving me stranded at third.

"Who taught him how to play?" Marvella muttered as we took the field.

"Same one who taught him everything else," I replied under my breath.

———————

We lost the game 7–5. I was three for four. LaRocca was one for four with a critical fielding error. Maybe there is a God after all.

When we left the field and went over to the picnic area, Ted was already there. He was wearing his preppie khakis and tennis shoes, which looked too new and white.

"Thanks for coming," I said as I walked over to him. "I'm glad you're here." He nodded and took the remaining step toward me. I let him kiss me.

Then I spotted Captain Owen. I wasn't sure if he'd show up, but when I saw him, I made a beeline through the crowd before anyone else could get to him.

He seemed a little awkward at having to see me, which I hoped I could use to my advantage. "Hi, boss."

"Hi, Sandy. How are you getting along?"

No sense mincing words. "Please take me back," I said. I was willing to humble myself, kiss his prominent butt, prostrate myself on the ground, if that's what it would take.

"I can't do that."

"Why not?"

"Well, for one thing, I've lost confidence in you."

"What can I do to restore that confidence?"

"I don't know, and right now I don't have time to think about it."

Maybe a tougher tack would be better. "I'm due an administrative hearing."

"True. But detective isn't a protected grade. The best you'd do is end up back in uniform. And you'd make me say things neither of us might feel comfortable with."

Owen looked at me with eyes that were at once penetrating and sad. "You've always thought you could do everything your way, Sandy. You can't."

I trudged back over to where I'd left Ted standing alone. "Any luck?" he asked.

I shook my head.

"What'd he say to you?"

"The same kinds of things you always did."

I saw Dee Robinson. We hugged, and I asked her about Lucy.

Dee shook her head with a "you know how these kids are" look. "Too big to be seen in public with her momma and poppa."

"Too big for her own britches, if you ask me," Vince offered.

"I knew this day would come. I just didn't think it would come so fast. I guess you never do." She gave me a concerned smile. "How are you getting along, Sandy?"

"I'll be okay," I said.

"Why don't you come over for the day on Saturday?"

"Thanks, Dee. I'll have to let you know."

She took my hand. "Sure, honey. You just call me."

Lieutenant Newcomb's wife, Marianne, came over with their five-year-old daughter, Megan—ash blond and even more adorable than last time I'd seen her, around Christmas. I picked her up and asked, "How are you, cutie?"

She gave me a funny look, wrinkled her little button nose, and said, "Daddy says you were bad and now you're in trouble."

"Megan!" Marianne called out.

"Did you get punished?" the little girl persisted.

"I sure did," I replied.

Flustered in the awkward, parental way, Marianne said, "I'm sorry, Sandy."

"It's okay. Why shouldn't she know? Everyone else does."

Hold your head up high, I said to myself, and never let them see you sweat.

And I had to admit, it did help having Ted here. Seeing me with him, LaRocca left me alone, and I didn't feel so detached and family-starved as I would have if I'd been here by myself.

I watched Ted, slightly ahead of me, heaping chicken and cornbread onto his plate. He really wasn't such a bad guy, I reflected. A lot of it was my fault for the way I reacted. I really was having a good time here. I kept trying to catalog all the reasons I had for not being able to live with him.

But as we sat next to each other, leaning against the trunk of a large oak tree, eating barbecued chicken and baked beans, the vehemence of my need to move my life away from his was evaporating into the air. In his own way, he loved me and cared for me. If he hated my life on the Job, it was as much because he was worried for me as because he felt threatened by it. We'd had fun times together, and pretty good sex, and unlike most of the men I worked with, I could always have a satisfying, intelligent conversation with Ted. We'd had a lot going between us—more than most couples. What had been so terrible? Maybe I was in a particularly exposed and vulnerable position right now, but maybe this whole business had to be rethought. Maybe he was good for me after all.

After we ate we got up to rejoin the others, but we were never far apart. We pitched horseshoes together. We played badminton. Being there with someone took some of the sting out of my disgrace.

There was a picnic table set up with a giant aluminum tub of beer. As always, it was the centerpiece of our picnics. Norman Sidecki, by the look of him, had been tending it most of the afternoon. He was also known to carry his own flask and was not much of a sharer.

"Hey, Mansfield, how's it cooking?" he called out as we came over. Yep, I thought, looking into his eyes, he was definitely past the point of no return.

"Pretty raw," I responded.

"I guess that's a metaphor, huh? You always were the intellectual of the place." He eyed Ted and held up his bottle in a mock salute. "You back with this asshole?"

Ted made a move toward him. I pulled him back. "Ted, please . . ."

"He called me an asshole, Cassie."

"He's drunk. Forget it."

"Who's Cassie?" Sidecki wanted to know.

Ted was insistent. "He called me an asshole."

"It's slang," I tried to cajole him. "Kind of like a technical term."

"For what?"

"For anyone not on the Job."

"Yeah, well, maybe you think it's technical, but no one's going to talk to me that way."

"Ted . . . don't . . ." By this time we had a small audience, which only made things worse.

"What's your problem, Professor?" Sidecki slurred.

"Maybe you're my problem," Ted ventured forth boldly, "and all the reverse evolution cases like you."

Sidecki grinned and took another swig. "Maybe your problem, sonny, is that your old lady packs a bigger rod than you do!"

That was it. Negotiations had broken off. Time for the SWAT team. I tried to restrain Ted, but he broke free angrily. And then he took a swing.

But in the heat of the moment, Ted seemed to have forgotten the one material fact that was self-evident to the rest of us. To wit: He was a slightly built, sober academic, and Norman Sidecki was a large drunken cop. With one quick and efficient movement of his arm, Sidecki broke Ted's hold.

Then, with one quick jab, he broke his jaw.

It was a single punch—clean, simple, and direct. I heard bone crunch, and then Ted was on the grass on the green-stained seat of his nicely pressed khakis, moaning and dripping blood.

"Oh, shit," was all I could think of to say.

We didn't have to wait long in the G. W. Hospital emergency room. Ted was still bleeding and made enough of a fuss that I think they took him back for treatment just so he wouldn't bother the other patients. In his defense, his jaw had turned a rich shade of purple.

When they finished working on him and the intern came out to say I could go in to see him, I found him sitting stiffly on the examination table, his face swollen and mouth wired shut. I winced when I saw him, as much for his humiliation as his pain. I was no stranger to pain, but I knew I was tougher than Ted.

"How are you feeling?" I asked apprehensively. "That looks very uncomfortable."

He wouldn't say anything.

"Talk to me, Ted. Please."

"Maybe it's my fault," he said finally through his forced clench. "I kept thinking it could be the way it was."

"In some ways, it can."

"But for some reason I've never been able to fathom, you're determined to screw up everything in your life, including us." It sounded all the more hostile and accusing coming through his wired mouth.

"Ted, I'm so sorry . . ."

"It's not a question of sorry, Cassie. I've lost you, and I know I'm not getting you back. We're finished. It's just not going to work out."

"Ted . . ."

"Please get out. It's difficult to talk this way, and you're just agitating me."

"But how will you get home?"

"I'll manage. Please leave me alone, Cassie. Now."

"I . . . I'll call you," I said. I turned and walked slowly down the emergency room corridor. For a little while this afternoon I'd felt so good, so positive about things . . . and now this.

What the hell is wrong with everything I do in my life? I flogged myself. But he was right. It just wasn't going to work out. We were like the story of the octopus who fell in love with a bagpipe. It might have seemed interesting for a while, but no matter how passionate the octopus was, ultimately the relationship was doomed to failure. I was desperate, and I'd turned to him to relieve some of that desperation. But it was no good. We have to stand on our own and figure out who we are. And I was Detective Sandy Mansfield. I just wasn't any good at being Mrs. Cassie Monahan.

I was feeling very shaky. I felt tears coming on and didn't want to be alone. I went over to a pay phone on the wall, put in a quarter, and dialed Vince's number. He and Dee should have been home from the picnic by now.

I let it ring once; then, without consciously thinking about it, I put the receiver down.

I swallowed dryly and waited for the coin to drop, then picked up the receiver and dialed again.

"This is Dr. Ramsey," announced the voice at the other end. But then I hung up that one, too. I had to work this out on my own.

40

I spent another miserable night beating myself up over how I'd gotten into this mess. I felt as if I wanted someone to hypnotize me. I wanted to decipher what it was in my distant and sordid past that made me need to understand what cannot be understood and control what cannot be controlled; that made me rush toward whatever was most dangerous and fall for men who defined the very notion of bigtime trouble. And I admitted to myself that for whatever reason, what I'd been doing since I joined the squad was what I really wanted to be doing, and nothing else. Now I'd blown it all.

I woke up early and tried to keep myself busy cleaning up the apartment. When that proved predictably unsatisfying, I went out for a long run to turn my mind off, but I kept thinking about what would happen now. There'd be a hearing on my suspension. There'd be a trial that would require my testimony. My name and deeds would be hauled through the tabloids and TV shows. I'd finally make it into *Playboy* after all. They'd never take me back. Who was I kidding? I'd be so dragged through the mud, I'd never be able to get another job anywhere in the country.

I came back dripping with sweat and feeling thoroughly miserable. I changed and was about to go to the laundromat and lose some more socks when Nick called.

"I've missed you," he said.

"I've missed you, too," I admitted.

"What are you doing with yourself?"

I told him how fulfilling my morning had been. I thought I detected a barely suppressed chuckle.

"What?" I demanded.

"Nothing," he replied, "just that you're very cute."

"Great." I grimaced. "I've lost my badge, my gun, probably my job. No one's afraid of me anymore. And now I'm cute."

"I'm afraid of you, if that's any consolation."

"You don't show it."

"I don't show a lot of things."

True enough. "They're looking to charge you with three counts of murder one. How can you be so calm?"

"Couple of reasons," he said brightly. "First—you got me into this, so I'm confident you're going to get me out of it."

"Your faith is reassuring." Was this the same kind of blind, optimistic confidence patients routinely placed in their surgeons? If so, it was a chilling prospect.

"And I'm going to help you."

Great again. His help had certainly paid off so far. "What's the second reason?" I asked.

"I have some good role models."

"What do you mean by that?"

"Most of my patients have problems a lot more serious than I have."

"Mine too," I realized.

———————

Around the middle of the morning I showered and got dressed in my normal work clothes and took the Metro over to the Touch of Class. I no longer had my badge to do the talking for me, but fortunately the missing link at the front of the place remembered me from last time and grunted me toward the backstage door.

Bonnie Sharpless was already there, half-naked and seated at her dressing table. She seemed distressed to see me. Very seldom are people happy to see homicide detectives. You get used to it and don't take it personally.

"Is anything wrong?" she asked with alarm, highlighting her wide, fawn-in-the-headlights eyes.

"Just a precaution," I assured her. That's what we always say, and if there's ever a civilian who fully believes us, I have a couple of bridges I'd like to sell him.

"Have you heard any more?"

"I just want to make sure no one's following you or anything like that. You haven't noticed anything, have you?"

"No. No," she was quick to respond, as though her sureness could convince both of us that everything was under control. I hated having to torture the poor kid this way, but then anyone who gets herself a job dancing at a strip joint isn't exactly looking for a career teaching Sunday school.

Veronique, the statuesque black woman who had the dressing table next to Bonnie, came in and noticed me.

She flashed me a broad grin. "You back here again, girl? What is it now? You looking for a little moonlighting action—or should I say 'daylighting action'?—in your spare time?" This struck her as extremely funny. Bonnie cracked the barest of smiles.

"I don't know," I replied, eyeing Veronique's bountiful chest. "I'm not sure I've got the qualifications."

She let out a crude laugh. "Sure you do, honey. All's you got to do is smile for the customers and shake that cute little booty of yours with the music, and you got it made."

"I'll keep that in mind," I promised.

"Here, check it out!" She tossed me one of her silver sequined thongs. "We can always use another girl at lunch."

Tempting as it was, I handed her back the G-string, knowing I could end up doing worse.

"Okay, girls: two minutes!" a woman called from the other end of the room.

"God, look at me, I—I'm so nervous," Bonnie stammered, "I'm already sweating through my makeup." I looked. Tiny beads of perspiration were seeping through the heavy rouge on her breasts.

"I'm not going to let anything happen to you, Bonnie," I promised.

"I wonder if anyone said that to Julie," she said. Then she slipped through the cheap velvet curtain and out to meet her public. I found a vantage point over on the side where I could peek through the curtain without being too obvious.

I must admit I didn't find the show—if you want to dignify it by calling it that—quite as stimulating as some of my male colleagues might have. Joe LaRocca would have been in hog heaven. But I will say that if Bonnie was nervous out there, you sure couldn't tell it by the way she shook her booty, as well as every other shakable aspect of her anatomy. I don't think I could ever look that natural.

The first set came and went uneventfully. Nothing happening in the audience roused my interest. Bonnie came back to her dressing table, sat down and caught her breath, reapplied her makeup, and then stared blankly ahead until it was time to go on again. There wasn't much breathing room between the two lunchtime shows. I made a few half-hearted attempts to engage her in conversation, but there wasn't much I could do to take away her anxiety or remove her from the complicated grownup world in which she now found herself.

It was a couple of minutes into the second set that I hit pay dirt. Bob Fusillo came in alone and stood self-consciously near the entrance.

Bingo bongo! I said to myself.

He was wearing a tan linen sports jacket and an open-neck white shirt and had on dark racing sunglasses. He pulled them down his nose and looked around the room as if he were casing the joint. He seemed concerned someone would recognize him. But he also seemed to know what he was looking for and where to look, so my guess was this wasn't his first visit.

Once he got his bearings, he moved over to the bar and sidled into the crowd. I could see him order a drink. There were four girls dancing now, including one on a platform at the end of the bar. Every so often she would go down nimbly on her knees, leaning back so that gentlemen admirers could take their time stuffing bills into her thong.

Bob studied her a moment, then cast his eyes on the ensemble that included Bonnie and Veronique. I squinted to watch his eyes as for several minutes he seemed to follow their every movement. Then I could see him begin concentrating on Bonnie.

From then on, he never took his eyes off her. He stayed through the set, and as soon as the music stopped and the girls disappeared, so did he.

And this time, when I saw Bonnie backstage, she had an ashen paleness that no amount of cheap heavy makeup could hide.

"I saw him," she whispered to me, her whole naked body trembling subtly. "He was looking at me the entire time. The kind of look that gives you the creeps. They warn us about looks like that. Now I know why you're here."

"Who was it, Bonnie?" I asked, making sure we were on the same wavelength.

"That doctor. The one who worked at the hospital where Julie went—you know, about her leg."

"The one who was in charge or the assistant?"

"The assistant. What does he want with me?"

"Probably nothing," I said, "but we're going to make sure."

"Don't leave me alone," she whimpered, putting her hand tightly on top of mine. "Please stay here with me."

They don't want to see you, then they don't want to see you leave.

41

I stayed with Bonnie throughout the day and sat with her as she got ready for the dinner sets. I was surprised to learn there was actually a difference from what they did at lunch. Among the subtle but telling touches, the makeup wasn't quite so bold and the costume paraphernalia not quite so glittery.

"It's a more sedate crowd at dinner," Bonnie enlightened me as she wriggled into a correspondingly more sedate, but equally revealing, black sequined thong. "Some guys bring their wives and girlfriends. You don't see that much at lunch."

So then if I was going to take Veronique's advice and get into this business, dinner would be the slot for me to start.

I assumed my place to the side of the stage, waited, and watched. As I expected, the shows went uneventfully. Nothing and no one aroused my attention. Bonnie came back after the final set, peeled the thong down her wet and glistening legs, and got dressed, then I went home with her.

Bonnie lived in a small one-bedroom apartment on Belmont Road, between Columbia and 18th Street. It wasn't all that different from Julie Fox's apartment on Capitol Hill or Sarah Hazeltine's place. Or mine, for that matter. That gave me a chill. Her apartment faced the front of the building, and when we got inside and I looked out the window, I noticed the scout car a little ways down the block.

I surveyed the place quickly, looking for somewhere I could hide myself. I found a storage-type closet between the living room and the bedroom that seemed to fit the bill. I could keep the door open just a crack, hear anything that happened between Bonnie and her visitor, and get to her quickly if I had to.

I didn't like not having the gun. It was a creepy feeling after all those years, and I didn't feel safe. I had even briefly considered "obtaining" a temporary replacement on my own. It should come as no surprise to learn that this sort of thing is not a difficult undertaking in the District of Columbia: certainly a lot easier than, say, getting your cable TV fixed on a weekend. But with the new possession laws they've got now, if someone in my position had been caught with an unregistered firearm, it would have been the end of whatever career I had left.

So I went into the kitchen, opened all the drawers, and mentally inventoried the knives, noting the ones I'd go for if the situation called for it.

Bonnie had followed me in. "What are you doing?"

"Just being prepared. Isn't that what the Girl Scouts say? Or is it the Boy Scouts? I had some gender identity problems at that age." I don't think Bonnie got it, but I saw her try to suppress a cold shudder.

Once we got settled, I took Bonnie out for a late dinner around the corner at Omega. With the prospect of being without a paycheck soon, it would probably be one of my last splurges, but what the heck.

I ordered us a pitcher of sangría, then I had seviche and Omega's excellent paella. Bonnie had a shrimp cocktail and then a chicken enchilada. Adams-Morgan is unquestionably the best restaurant neighborhood between Richmond and Baltimore, but I think she would have been happier at Bob's Big Boy.

Unfortunately, that was pretty much the way it was going. I liked Bonnie, but we had nothing to say to each other. There's a certain amount of female bonding when two women, both under severe stress, get to spend some time alone together. But that was about the extent of it. We came back to her place, sat around, and watched television.

And I had to admit that this was probably the most worthwhile function anyone in my job could fill—keeping someone from getting killed instead of just trying to figure out who did it, after the fact. It seemed somewhat ironic that I had to be on suspension before I could take the time to do something like this. Bonnie was so sweet and innocent and trusting, there was no way I was going to let anyone hurt her.

She offered me a long T-shirt, and then we sat around her living room sharing a bottle of cheap sherry. It was hard to believe I was waiting for a killer to strike.

All of which brought me back to thinking of Gabbie and the great times we had together. I felt a lump forming in my throat and blinked away the beginning of a tear. It had been a long time since I'd had any kind of real relationship with another woman; maybe even since Gabbie. After she died, I think I probably closed myself off to new people, and by the time I was ready to open up again, my life was filled by a new set of folks, mostly men on the Job like Vince. It was also about this time that the cracks in the relationship with Ted started widening into canyons.

"So you have a boyfriend, a pretty girl like you?" I asked, trying to make conversation.

"No one special."

"Haven't found the right guy yet?" Woe is us when we start sounding like our mothers.

"I thought I did. I even married him."

"When was this? Where?"

"Back in high school, out in Hyattsville. That's where I grew up. He was an auto mechanic, liked to hunt and stuff like that. Spent almost every weekend out with his buddies. Then he lost his job, started drinking more, beat me up a couple of times. I decided he didn't have the right to split my lip and bloody my nose just 'cause he was drunk and frustrated, so I took off and moved into town rather than going home to my mom and having her say 'I told you so.' "

My heart went out to her. Her story was so basic, so cliché in its simplicity, and so maddeningly common. I could just about predict all the other details of her life from that brief synopsis.

"How long were you married?" I asked.

"Only about ten months," she said sheepishly, as if that were the ultimate measure of her failure. "You married?"

"I was. Didn't work out, either."

"How long?"

"Longer than yours. My sense wasn't as good."

"You got anybody at the moment?"

The question caught me by surprise. I took a sip of my sherry and thought about it, rolling the thick, heavy liquor over my tongue. "I'm really not sure," I said awkwardly.

I was surprised by how uncomfortable I was talking about myself. And it made me realize I hadn't gotten through to Nick. "Bonnie, can I make a call?" I asked.

"Help yourself."

I went into the bedroom, closed the door, and called Nick at home, but I got his answering machine. Instead of leaving a message, I called mine to see if he'd tried to get in touch with me.

The voice was unmistakable from the first syllable. "Cassandra, this is your mother." Cassandra already—not a good sign. "You promised you'd call. How am I supposed to know if you're all right? Listen, dear, I heard about that awful murder—the burning. Was that what you were working on? My neighbor, Marge, was asking me, and I wasn't sure. It's all over the television out here. So let me know how you're getting along. I'm very angry that you haven't called. Love you, sweetie."

If I played my cards right, I could soon have the entire world pissed at me.

There were a couple of hangups, then, "This is Nick. Where've you been? Chris Taylor just gave me two tickets to his play tonight; thought you'd like to come along. Maybe we could work on my defense afterward . . . or yours!"

I'd been wanting to see the play, and I definitely wanted to see him. So why'd he wait so long to ask me? But even if he hadn't, this was more important. God, I felt like I was back in high school thinking like that.

There was another hangup, then I heard a deep, raspy throat clearing. "Detective Mansfield, this is Chris Taylor. Hi. I called you at your office, but a Detective Sidecki said you weren't there. I explained the situation, and he was kind enough to give me your home number. I wonder if you could meet me at the theater tonight after the performance. I've been thinking about it some more, and I may be able to resolve things for you."

His tone was picking up urgency as he talked. "It's . . . it's . . . *achemmm* . . . very important that you come, and make sure you come alone. I'll wait to see if you get this message."

"Resolve things." What did that mean? But I wasn't going to waste any time finding out. And Nick was there. God, don't let me be too late! I glanced at my watch. It was almost midnight. The play would have been over a little past eleven.

I hung up the phone and pulled off Bonnie's T-shirt as I hurried over to the chair where I'd left my clothes.

"Bonnie," I called out.

"What is it?" she came in as I was putting on my bra. She reacted with some alarm as I buttoned my blouse. "Is everything okay?"

"Yeah, but I'm going to have to leave for a while."

"No. Please!"

"Something's come up. But it's okay. There'll be a police car outside all night." I took a business card from my purse and scribbled on it. "And if you have any problem, or think you do, you call Detective Vincent Robinson. This is his home number, and this is his beeper. You know how to call a beeper?"

"I . . . I think so," she said, still stunned.

"Good. Everything's going to be okay."

By this time I was fully dressed. I stepped into my shoes, kissed Bonnie on the cheek, and then I was out the door.

42

I ran up to Columbia Road and flagged down a cab. I piled in and was about to flash my badge to get the driver to haul ass when I remembered I no longer had a badge to flash. So I told him instead I was in a god-awful hurry, and the insinuation of a big tip was enough to make him step on it.

Fortunately, it was a driver who happened to speak English. Unfortunately, he liked speaking it a lot.

"Everybody's in a hurry these days," he said, dividing his attention about equally between the road ahead and the rearview mirror. "Not that there's anything wrong with that, mind you. It's just that I been driving a cab in this city since Eisenhower was in office, you know what I'm saying?"

"I know what you're saying," I said idly.

He was balding, with a rim of white hair, and his paunch grazed the lower end of the steering wheel. "You know how they talk about Washington being a sleepy southern town in those days?" He devoted an unequal portion of his attention to studying me in the mirror. " 'Course you wouldn't. You weren't even born then."

And if one more person from Vince's generation reminds me that they remember exactly what they were doing when they heard President Kennedy had been shot while I was just lying in a crib, cooing and messing my Pampers, I'll shoot them.

"Everybody my age remembers exactly where they were when they heard President Kennedy had been assassinated. I was in the cab, stopped at the light at Connecticut and Calvert . . ."

Fortunately for him, Captain Owen had taken away my gun. "I am in a hurry," I reiterated.

" 'Course you are, and I'm gonna get you there just as fast as I can, young lady."

We sped down Columbia Road till it hit Connecticut Avenue, careened around Dupont Circle onto Mass, and cut down 14th Street to Constitution, then down 7th Street and into Southwest.

I didn't know what to expect, what I was going to find, but my heart was pounding up into my throat.

It's very important that you come, and make sure you come alone.

"I don't want you to think I'm intruding, but I hope someone's meeting you down there. Take it from me, I see all parts of this city, and a lot of them just aren't safe for a pretty young woman like you, especially after dark."

"I think I can take care of myself," I said distractedly.

"You have to be careful. Southwest isn't what it used to be, you know."

"I will be careful," I promised. "Thanks."

We reached the corner of 7th and Maine Avenue. "This'll be fine," I said.

"You sure you don't want me to leave you off in front? Same zone, it won't cost you any more."

"No, that's okay."

"Want me to wait for you?"

"No, I have an appointment." I reached into my purse, pulled out a scrunched-up twenty, and tossed it into the front seat. "Thanks," I said.

There wasn't a soul on the street. I had to admit, it was creepy. The Arena itself looked dark and deserted. The performance was long since over, and there was nothing to hang around for in this neighborhood. It almost looked like an abandoned movie set.

I circled the building and came around to the entrance on the 6th Street side. I tried each of the glass doors. They were all locked tight. I kept moving around the building until I reached the parking lot, which was where the entrance to the smaller, Kreeger Theater was. It was locked, too. I made one more circuit, climbing up each of the four metal staircases that serve as exits after the performance. Each one was locked. He must not have waited for me.

Have I missed anything? I asked myself. There was just one other possibility. I doubled back past the Kreeger entrance and into the parking lot. Under the raised metal terrace off the main lobby upstairs, there was a set of large metal doors. It probably led to the scene shop, since the doors were unusually wide. It was too dark to see much detail, other than that they were flat on the outside, without bars or handles. I ran my fingers along the cool metal surface, but when I reached the center, something stopped them.

I lifted my hand and felt around. It was a ridge about an inch deep. That meant one door was slightly ajar. He must have left it for me this way.

Okay, now! I tried to pry it open, but I couldn't get any kind of grip. Quickly I felt along the inner edge of the open door until I found the bolt slot. I wedged the tips of two fingers into it and leaned backward for leverage. I took a deep breath. The heavy door began to creak open.

I found myself in a narrow corridor. "Chris!" I called out, "Christopher Taylor. It's Sandy Mansfield, Chris."

I didn't hear anything. I felt something nudge the back of my calf and practically jumped through my skin. Then I realized it was the door, swinging closed again. Christ, I did not want to get locked in here.

Holding the heavy door with the flat of my hand, I used my outstretched foot to rummage around the floor nearby for something to prop the door open.

Just to the side my toe hit something hard. Stretching to keep the door cracked with the heel of my opposite foot, I bent down and put my hands on it. It was a cinder block, obviously there for just such a purpose. I dragged it over between the two doors. It left a good eight inches of space between the doors, letting in a dull shaft of moonlight. At least I'd be able to get out now.

Carefully I moved forward, stopping every two or three steps to listen. It was really creepy. My mouth was dry. I wished I had my gun.

"Chris!" I called out again. "Chris Taylor, can you hear me?" But still nothing.

I thought of Bonnie and the look on her face when I announced I was leaving her so abruptly. God, I've left this poor girl unprotected, I thought to myself. If anything happened to her because I'd left her unprotected after I was the one who'd put her in danger, I couldn't live with myself. Maybe Owen was right. Maybe my judgment had gone to hell.

I felt my way down the corridor. It was pitch black, but I sensed from the change in room tone that I was coming into a larger space. This must be a scene or prop shop or a rehearsal hall of some sort, I thought. There are all kinds of rooms in the basements of theaters.

There had to be a light switch somewhere. It would be on the wall close to the corridor. Then I could get my bearings and look around. Maybe Chris left me a note.

There was a funny smell in the air, too. Having spent a lot of time in theaters when I was in college, I'm used to that old, musty-dusty smell most of them have. You feel as if you always have to wash your hands. But this was different. Sweeter, more pungent. Like someone had left a half-eaten sandwich out since lunchtime, which was certainly a possibility.

I put my hands out in front of me, turned to my left, and groped forward, looking for the wall. I found it before long, but even though I traced all around its rough concrete surface, I couldn't find a light switch. I had to reverse myself and do the same thing in the other direction, which wasn't easy in the dark.

But I did finally reach the wall, skinning two of my knuckles in the process. I let out a quick yelp of pain and surprise, put my fingers up to my mouth to suck the sting away. Then I started patting the wall down inch by inch, searching again for a light switch.

Come on, damn it. You've got to be here somewhere.

Finally. Thank God! Four, right in a row. I flipped them in rapid succession, and the blessed lights came on.

I was right, it was a scene shop. Fairly large, with a high ceiling. Painted, canvas-covered flats were stacked up against one of the walls. Prop chairs, bookcases, and end tables were bunched together in one corner, probably being prepared for the next play. There were several workbenches covered with power tools and carpentry equipment. I could see a doorway leading to the costume shop and its pipe racks jammed full of hanging outfits.

And in the middle of the room was Norman Sidecki.

He was slumped over on a folding wooden campaign chair, obviously a Shakespearean prop. A long blond, braided wig from the costume shop was plopped on his head, and his bulky body was stuffed into an ancient Roman-style woman's toga, or whatever they call it. His eyes stared out at me blankly, his face was ghastly white, and his mouth, which still bore some trace of the shock at what had been done to him, trailed streams of blood down from the corners. There was a bloody stab wound on the left side of his chest, near his heart. And when my eyes traveled down his torso, I saw that his arms ended in two bloody stumps with a pool of blood congealed in the white fabric of his lap.

I gagged, trying to keep from throwing up.

His two hands with their hacked, ragged wrists lay discarded at his feet. Hands that could pick any lock and steal into any building in Washington. Hands that just yesterday had broken Ted's jaw with a single punch.

Bloody latex surgical gloves lay on the floor next to the hands, almost like a joke.

My gut convulsed into a violent retch. I thought I was going to heave right on the floor in front of me. I opened my mouth and took a deep breath, trying to stave it off. A silent howl welled up in my chest. My head was exploding. Oh, God in heaven, Norman! . . . I thrust my fist into my mouth and gnawed down on it to keep from screaming.

Chris Taylor calls me at the office, but I'm not there. Sidecki answers the call. He must recognize the name. So he decides to follow up himself. I find him dressed as a woman in a wig and ancient women's dress. Hands have been cut off.

God help me, I think I know what this means.

With my fingers trembling, I opened my shoulder bag and clawed in it for my handkerchief. I finally found it. I put the bag down on the floor and stepped up to the bloody figure. Taking pains not to touch the flesh except through the cloth of the handkerchief, I strained with my thumb and forefinger to pry open the clenched mouth.

Inside was another bloody mess. Sidecki's tongue had been cut out. I didn't have the stomach to look for it.

Yes, I know what this is. I studied drama, too, and Chris knows that.

In *Titus Andronicus,* Shakespeare's bloodiest, most gruesome play, Titus's daughter, Lavinia, is savagely raped by Demetrius and Chiron, sons of Tamora, queen of the Goths, in revenge for the slaughter of their brother. They then cut off Lavinia's hands and cut out her tongue so she cannot identify them. And as I gawked at the hideous scene and took in its surroundings, two things were transparently, brutally clear:

It would take someone deeply involved in the theater to come up with a scenario like this one. Most people have read some Shakespeare, but not *Titus*. The way Norman had been dressed, it had been meant for me. And Chris Taylor was a far greater actor than even I'd given him credit for.

He must have surprised Sidecki and stabbed him first. Otherwise, how could he have neutralized him? Sidecki was a big guy. He wasn't tied down. Chris couldn't have done this to him while Norman was still alive. Why had he struck again tonight? A thousand questions raced through my mind.

I had to do something. I had to call the squad. But first I had to find Chris.

I scrambled back to my bag and rifled through it until I found my address book. I picked it up and staggered around the room, looking for a phone. I spotted one on the rear wall, behind the carpentry bench. With my hands still trembling, I dialed Chris's phone number.

There were four rings, then, "Hi, this is Chris Taylor. I can't take your call, but you can leave a message at the beep. If you're offering work, *please, please* leave a message!"

Shit. Where the fuck is he?

God, I hoped he hadn't gone to find Bonnie. I dialed my own number, hoping there'd be another message, but there was nothing.

What was next? Where was Nick? He would have been here at the theater tonight. Was Chris on to him and what he wanted to do? Jesus, if Chris did anything to him . . .

Shakily, I punched the buttons again. With my heart jumping out of my chest, I waited through two rings. Then his machine came on.

Fuck and a half! Answering machines have taken over the world.

But wait a sec! Maybe he'd gotten a message. How could I find out? His machine had the same beep tone as mine. It was probably the same brand. I had five seconds to punch in his code before it would hang up on me. But what the hell was his code?

Hold on! I'd watched him call his machine after we'de made love. What numbers did he punch in? Come on, Sandy—you're supposed to be an observant witness. Think!

2-2-9. That was it! It must be his birthday—February 29! As odd as everything else about this case. But that was it. Yes.

Quickly, I punched in 2-2-9. I waited a breathless second, then heard the reassuring mechanical voice: "Hello. You . . . have . . . one . . . message."

That was all I needed if it happened to be the right one. I waited another moment in absolute agony.

"Nicholas, it's Bob . . ." His voice was urgent.

"Hang on, Bob, I'm here. Just walked in the door." The machine must have clicked on before he reached the phone.

"You ducked out early from the play. Ashby wanted to say hello."

So while I'd been waiting for him at Bonnie's, Fusillo had been with his main squeeze right here! One big party.

"Yeah, sorry about that. I thought Christopher Taylor was—"

"Listen, Nicholas, let me get to the point. I got a call from Taylor. I'm at the hospital. Get here right away."

"What is it?"

"Just get to the OR and scrub. I'll explain then. We'll be waiting for you. You've got to hurry."

"I'm on my way."

The mechanical voice came back on. "Saturday . . . Twelve-forty-one-A.M. That-was-your-last-message. You-may-hang-up-and-I-will-save . . . your . . ."

I hung up the phone. Chris must have been injured. Struggling with Norman Sidecki. Twelve forty-one. I looked at my watch. Less than ten minutes ago.

But there was something strange here. Why did Chris think to call Fusillo?

Because he and Ashby were at the theater tonight and . . .

Wait one minute!

Because he and Ashby were at the theater tonight! With Chris. Who was not at the surgical support group Tuesday because of the play. Unlike the previous three meetings, when he was. And that's when the first three murders took place—on alternate Tuesdays after the meeting—when all three patients were together. But there was no murder this past Tuesday night after the meeting because Chris wasn't there.

But there was a murder tonight! Of course! Because he and Bob and Ashby were here, too. Together. Nick's lecture at Georgetown. What did he call that phenomenon? That's what was happening.

Morph . . . morphic resonance. Could that be it?

Like the rats running his maze. When the three of them come together, something clicks! They aren't fully aware until they come together. Then they must reach some sort of critical mass. That's when Neville takes over. Like the myth of Osiris—putting together the pieces of a dead man.

I had to send help to the hospital, but would anyone listen to me at this point? And a cop on suspension still doing cop stuff would be in big trouble.

I had to get there myself. I had to get to Halsted. But I had to deal with this mess here.

Because if the cops burst in on them all and I wasn't there to explain it, they'd all panic and be killed, and I couldn't let that happen. No one else understood or would understand in time. And I'd be stuck here explaining how I found Norman and what I was doing here and what he was doing, and meanwhile Halsted would become a slaughterhouse.

But how was I going to get there? I wasn't going to find a cab around here at this hour.

Have to push the edge of the envelope again.

I picked up the phone again and dialed Vince's number. I can't call the cavalry, but he can. Come on, Vince. Pick up the damn phone! Don't give me your answering machine, too.

He came on after the third ring, slowly rousing himself from sleep.

"Vince, it's me."

Where . . . where are you?''

"Arena Stage." There was a pause in which I could tell he was trying to focus on his clock. "Is anything wrong?''

"Very. Sidecki's dead.''

"What!''

"I don't have time to explain. Just get down here.''

"Are you alone?''

"Yes.''

"I'll phone in backup.''

"No, Vince. Don't do that! Wait till you're here. You get here first.''

"But that's—''

"Please don't argue. Just get here right away. Alone.'' I hung up and cut off his options.

———————

I was waiting for him at the double doors when he pulled up less than ten minutes later in his silver Ford Thunderbird—Vince's idea of a sporty car. He must have come from his house in Northeast at ninety miles an hour. He bolted out of the car.

"Now tell me what happened.''

"I don't have time,'' I stated tensely. "Give me your keys.''

"What?''

"I need your car. There's a phone on the wall inside. Call for backup, tell them you're here on an anonymous tip. Leave me out of it for now. I didn't touch anything except the door, which I wiped down, and the phone receiver, which you'll cover with your own prints. Then meet me at the hospital."

"Sandy, this is—"

"Please, Vince. You have to trust me. Now give me your keys! And get ready for what you're going to see in there."

Reluctantly he forked over the keys. "If this turns out to be—"

"Right, I know. You can do whatever you want to me. But you'll have to stand in line." I snatched the keys from him, hopped in his car, and left him standing in confusion on the parking lot sidewalk.

43

I tore around the block and gunned the Thunderbird up 7th Street, over the Southwest Freeway, and across the Mall with the looming, floodlit Capitol Building to my right. All the while I was scanning for cops, knowing I had no ID and that any explanation I could give would just slow me down. I had to get to the hospital. I wished Vince kept a Kojak light in his car. Please, don't anybody stop me.

So many footprints on the carpet at Hazeltine's apartment. So many footprints on the grass and the dirt at the Ashburn murder scene. Fusillo had developed a relationship with Fox after she came in for her sciatica. He'd procured the drugs used on her and Hazeltine. He'd done the anatomically correct cutting and taken the penlight. Chris had used the sword and come up with the *Titus* scenario. Ashby had befriended Sarah and done the scouting. The three of them together had probably moved the bodies into position. They'd meant to kill me tonight, and now they'd lured Nick into their trap.

I knew it sounded like a long shot, but I'd seen that long shots were Nick's stock in trade. Whether anyone would believe me was another question.

At Mount Vernon Square I turned right onto K Street, drove several more blocks, and then into the Halsted compound.

I pulled into the parking strip off the emergency room and raced through the door. Fortunately, I knew my way around well enough by now that I didn't have to pass through any public areas where I might have been stopped.

I didn't see anyone. I raced down the corridor and turned the corner at the elevator lobby toward the surgical suite. I barreled through the double doors in the direction of the central nursing desk. I didn't know if it was manned this time of night, but if it was, I'd have the nurse call security and seal off the area. Assuming they were still here.

But the desk was empty, and there was no time to waste. Keeping up my pace, I made a box around the three hallways that ringed the block of operating rooms and hustled down toward room number four. I pushed the scrub room doors open in front of me.

Nick was standing at the washbasin, drying his hands. He looked tense. "What are you doing here?" he asked in surprise. Through the glass panel of the swinging doors I could see the backs of the gowned surgical team.

He was threading his fingers into a pair of surgical gloves.

"Nick, don't go in there!" I shouted.

"Chris has an epidural hematoma. If I don't operate immediately, he'll die."

That's what he said, but I knew what else was going through his mind. This was his golden opportunity, his chance to scientifically undo what his scientific brilliance had created.

"It's not just Chris!" I declared.

He stopped. "What are you talking about?"

"It's all of them. All of them together."

"What?"

"Morphic resonance. All generating the same brain waves, I guess. Just like your rats. Like bees in a hive, fireflies flashing on and off together, girls in a college dorm synchronizing their periods. Vince is calling in the police, but I'm afraid of what they might do when they get here, so we've got to—"

"What are you telling me—not to operate?"

"I don't know," I stammered, "but I just . . .."

"This is crazy," he cut me off. "I don't have time to stand around here and—"

He pushed his way through the swinging doors into the OR. I followed right behind him.

Chris Taylor was lying on the table, covered by a sheet up to his neck. The left side of his head had been shaved. Bob Fusillo stood over him, and to Fusillo's side was a scrub nurse.

Fusillo saw me. "What's she doing here?" he challenged.

"Just tell me what's happening," Nick instructed.

Fusillo related tersely: "Presented with progressive mental decompensation after a classic lucid interval, drooping right eye, dilation of right pupil, and climbing pressure. CT confirmed a left temporal-parietal epidural with herniation and left-to-right shift. From the look of the CT, I thought a local would be safer than general.''

Nick went over to the wall to study the Cat-scan films mounted on the light box. I was totally conflicted and confused. I wanted to do something. I wanted to stop this. But what if I was wrong? I didn't trust my instincts any longer. Could I stop an emergency medical procedure based on a theory? I'd be killing Chris. Of course, wasn't that effectively what Nick would do anyway with this equivalent of a lobotomy he planned?

When Nick came back to the table, Fusillo stepped to the side.

"Hand me a scalpel," Nick ordered the scrub nurse. "I'll want suction and saline irrigation ready." Then to Fusillo: "Get the cranitom." Fusillo reached for a particularly evil-looking device with a round blade on the end.

The nurse slapped the scalpel's handle into Nick's gloved palm. He shifted his grip, then shifted his demeanor as he looked down at Chris. "How are you doing?" he asked soothingly.

Chris's eyes fluttered open. "I'm doing okay, Dr. Ramsey. How are you doing?"

With that, Chris's hand came out from under the sheet. He was holding a revolver—a Smith & Wesson .38 Chiefs Special. Norman Sidecki's gun. He was pointing it at Nick.

Nick's eyes bulged with incredulity. My heart skipped a beat. I felt as if I'd just been kicked in the gut.

Nick lifted the scalpel.

Chris sat up on the table. "Put it down, Dr. Ramsey . . . Nicholas."

Nick turned to Fusillo.

"You heard me," the chief resident said.

My head whipped around. I felt a hand on my arm. It was the nurse. She was holding another scalpel, its point pressing against my neck. "You don't want me to have to hurt the girl, do you, Nick?" She pulled down her mask and smiled. It was Ashby Collier.

The breath left my body. Nick's eyes grew wide. He looked almost paralyzed. His hands started to tremble.

"Give me the gun, Chris," I said, trying to keep the tension out of my voice. "We can deal with this." I tried to reach out, but Ashby was holding the blade rigidly.

"Come one step closer and I'll blow your fucking tits off!" the actor screamed. Then he cleared his throat.

Fusillo said, "You just couldn't let me rest in peace, could you, Nick?"

"Neville," Nick said flatly.

"What's left of him," Fusillo replied. He snatched the scalpel from Nick. Then he grabbed him by the front of his shirt and smiled. "You gave me immortality, Nicky. You played God. Didn't you think there'd be consequences? Didn't you think there'd be hell to pay?"

"Chris," I said, "why did you kill Detective Sidecki?"

"Oh, that," Fusillo replied matter-of-factly. "A little wrinkle in the plan. We knew Nicky was coming to the theater, which was why we thought you'd be there, too. But when he came alone and you were unreachable and Detective Sidecki showed up instead of you, well, what were we supposed to do?"

"Art creates its own necessity," said Chris.

"Pity he had to die for your sins," Ashby observed. "Life is short, but art is long."

I was right. They must have surprised Sidecki. I knew Chris couldn't have overcome him all by himself.

"All right," said Fusillo, grabbing Nick firmly by the arm. As if thinking the same thought, Chris simultaneously grabbed his other arm. Then he climbed off the table. I had to make a move, but Ashby held the scalpel precariously tight.

Bob and Chris pulled Nick away from the table. He struggled to free himself, but the two of them were able to hold him firmly. "You just stand over here out of the way," Bob directed. Then he commented, "What luck we're finally having, after the disappointment of not being able to get you two together at the theater."

"Bob, how could you do this?" Nick pleaded.

"Why don't you just call me Neville?" he replied. "It would be so much more intimate that way. Anyway, down to business. Here's the scenario: Whoever comes upon this scene will discover your two bodies. The lovely lady will appear to have been your next victim, just as the police suspected of you. After all, she was the one who fingered you in the first place. The motive is perfect. Then, when they see your body, it will appear that you have killed yourself directly afterward."

"You would have known there was no other way out," Ashby added, "and decided to go out in a blaze of glory."

"Of course," said Fusillo, "I had the foresight to leave some of your surgical gloves and a set of your car keys at the Arena, just as I'd left the penlight in the park. And many people saw you in the theater tonight, so that should establish your presence rather nicely.''

Chris positioned the gun barrel up under Nick's chin.

''Now, Ms. Mansfield,'' Bob instructed, ''if you wouldn't mind, lie down on the table. On your back, if you please.''

''You've got to be out of your fucking mind!'' I blurted out.

''A number of detailed and distinguished monographs have been addressed to that very point,'' Ashby said, and giggled.

''Now! Move!'' Bob ordered. ''Assume the position. Unless you want to see your boyfriend's celebrated brain splattered across the ceiling.''

My eyes darted around the room, evaluating my options.

''Don't do it, Sandy!'' Nick called out.

While Chris kept the revolver barrel jammed up under Nick's chin, Bob grabbed me. Ashby kept up the pressure of the scalpel, and together they dragged me toward the table. There was nothing I could do before Chris could have killed Nick. We were outnumbered, and they had the gun.

They got me to the edge of the table and manhandled me until they had me up there on my back. Ashby pressed down on my shoulders.

Fusillo grinned sadistically. ''Ready? Good.'' He had picked up what looked like a pair of leather wrist cuffs. ''We use these to restrain patients who might go into convulsion,'' he explained solicitously. He fastened one around each of my wrists, buckled them both closed, then attached the connecting straps to the rails of the table. ''Human sacrifice will be an affecting way to end this current religious cycle, don't you think?''

My heart was pounding furiously; I thought it would burst through my chest. I was helpless now. Ashby took the blade away from my neck but went to help cover Nick. Fusillo came over, grabbed the two sides of my blouse with both hands, and ferociously ripped them apart.

''Of course, in medicine, we always look for other options to the knife,'' Fusillo said, picking up the Bovi electrocauterizer. ''That's the wonderful thing about art—so many possibilities.'' He held the glowing tip of the instrument a millimeter from my chest. I went rigid with terror. It was so close.

With an evil glow in his eye, he tormented me for several moments. Holy Christ, where in fuck were the cops?

Then he pulled the Bovi away abruptly. I took my first breath since

I could remember. But in his hand now was the silver scalpel Ashby had just handed him.

I was wearing a demi bra that left part of my breasts exposed. Fusillo stared at my chest for a moment, then looked straight into my eyes. With that same sadistic smile on his face, he drew the precision-honed point ever so lightly across my right breast, maybe an inch or two above the nipple. A thin line of blood instantly appeared, followed a moment later by a sharp, focused pain.

"What is it Hitchcock always said: 'In the third act, torture the heroine'?" I was terrified what he would do next.

"Don't!" Nick pleaded. "Leave her alone!"

"But I get ahead of myself," Fusillo commented, oblivious. "After all, this is your show, too, Nick."

There were tears streaming down Nick's face. "Why, Nev? Why? How can you even think about it?"

Chris had Nick positioned right in front of the table now. He removed the gun from Nick's chin and pressed it hard against his back, where he had better control.

"When we were growing up," Nick pleaded, "you were always the one I turned to, the one I relied on. You weren't like Dad, you always had such . . . such empathy."

"There are many kinds of empathy," Fusillo replied calmly. He handed Nick the scalpel. "Do it, Nicky! Rip her chest and belly open. It's what you want to do. Empathize with her as you do it! Feel her exquisite agony in the very core of your own soul. Plunge your talented hands into her and luxuriate in the delectable sensation of her entrails between your fingers. Sacrifice her to the forces of nature and the gods of your own genius."

There was a glazed expression on Nick's face. His eyes were dilated, as if he couldn't process what was happening. He held the scalpel out in front of him and studied it, as if he'd never seen anything quite like it before.

He rolled its handle around in his hand, trying to get comfortable with the feel of the slender instrument. His gaze traveled downward and our eyes locked, but I had no idea what was behind them now. Certainly nothing I'd ever seen before.

My mouth was as dry as cardboard. It was as if, somehow, his brain had locked in phase with the others.

Like a robot, Nicholas took a step closer to me. He raised the scalpel above his head as I stared up at him in horrified amazement. I felt my bowels go soft. He started bringing the gleaming blade down, and I squeezed my eyes shut on the last image I would ever see.

I braced myself for the moment of agony. I heard a dull thunk. But then, nothing.

I was still alive. I opened my eyes again. Nick had sliced through the strap binding my right wrist to the table rail. Before he could turn around, Ashby stabbed him in the arm with an open hemostat she'd picked up from the instrument tray. He staggered backward and fell.

In the confusion I rolled over on my side to try to get my other hand free. Frantically I fumbled with the wrist buckle, but I couldn't get it undone.

His face frozen in fury, Fusillo came at me, raising an open pair of surgical scissors over my head and chest. I tried to fend him off with my free right hand, but I didn't have enough movement or leverage. I could keep him away from either my face or my chest, but not both, and that wasn't good enough.

The point of the scissors was coming right for my eyes. I tried to move to the side. His reach was too long; I couldn't get far enough away. Another second and I'd be blinded.

Just then, the blade swerved. From the floor, Nick had grabbed him by the ankle and thrown him off.

I grabbed for his weapon. I had it. My hand shaking, I cut through the remaining wrist strap, then hurled myself off the table and quickly looked around.

Nick, his arm bloody, had recovered his senses and was coming at Chris. But Chris had the pistol aimed at his head. He was starting to squeeze the trigger . . .

There was no time to think, only react. Holding the scissors out in front of me, I threw myself at him, landing on top of him and knocking him toward the floor. We hit the deck hard, and as we did, the point imbedded cleanly in his neck.

The gun dropped from his hand. His face betrayed the sudden shock. His carotid artery fountained blood. He arched up from the floor for a frozen instant, then collapsed, his neck wound still pumping blood.

I scrambled to an upright position and barreled into Fusillo, knocking him off his feet. I prepared myself for his counterattack, but he just sat there with an odd expression. He looked confused.

"What are you doing here?" he asked. He looked at my chest. "What happened to you?"

Ashby dropped the bloody hemostat. Nick came over to us.

Fusillo turned in his direction. "Nicholas," he said. "God, look at your arm!"

I ran over to Chris. The floor around him was covered with blood. I clamped my hand over his wound and at the same time put my ear against his chest. Bob rushed over and pushed me out of the way, feeling both wrist and neck for a pulse. Nothing. Oh, God.

"I guess if one piece of the brain stops functioning," said Nick, still dazed, "the circuit is broken."

"Neville's dead," I said.

"Who's Neville?" Ashby asked shakily, as if just waking up from a long sleep. She noticed Chris lying in the pool of blood and screamed. Then she collapsed on the floor.

"Ashby!" Bob rushed over to her and grabbed her wrist. "She's fainted," he reported. Then, after a moment, "She'll be okay. But . . . what are we doing here?"

Nick glanced around the room. "They don't remember anything."

I pulled the remnants of my blouse together and held them closed with my hand. "Let me get you something," said Nick. He went into the scrub room and came back with a greens top. I took it from him, then turned away and put it on over my head.

I glanced down at Chris's body, and a great pain welled up inside me. I felt as if I were still living in a nightmare.

"I'd better give Ashby something," said Nick, reasserting his dominion over the operating room. He walked over to the refrigeration cabinet, took out a vial, and prepared a syringe. He came back over to where Bob still held Ashby.

"Three milligrams of lorazepam," Nick told him, one doctor talking to another. Bob held Ashby's arm while Nick jabbed in the needle.

"Let's get her up," Nick said. He put his hand behind Ashby's back to lift her.

Bob stood to help. Then I saw something pick up the light just beyond his thumb. He was holding a scalpel.

Suddenly his arm went up in the air and he lunged forward.

"Nick!" I screamed, racing toward them.

Nick looked up and turned his head just as Bob plunged the blade down. He managed to swerve his head and chest away, but the scalpel sliced into his thigh. He let out a howl of pain and surprise as Fusillo lost his balance and Ashby fell back to the floor. But Bob quickly scrambled to his feet and ran out through the scrub room doors.

I took off after him, through the scrub room and into the main corridor of the surgical suite. He stopped momentarily, his head darting in both directions, trying to decide on his best option.

Where was he going? It wouldn't be to any areas of the hospital populated at this time of night—the emergency room, the ICU, the wards. He raced down the corridor and out the main entrance to the suite, with me right behind him. He darted across the hall to the staircase, flinging the doors violently outward behind him to slow me down.

Where were my fucking colleagues?

I heard him scrambling down the metal steps at least a flight ahead of me. I grabbed the rail for balance and hurled myself around to the next flight, as fast as I could move. My heart was pounding. Why had he done this? Why was this happening? Chris Taylor was dead, yet Bob had still tried to kill Nick.

"I feel as if someone's controlling me, telling me what to do," Chris had said. So maybe it wasn't Neville Ramsey. Maybe it was Robert Fusillo. If you could even separate the two at this point.

He reached the subbasement level. I emerged from the stairwell just in time to see him disappear around the corner of the darkened hallway. Where was he going? There must be some entrance to the parking garage down here. That had to be it. He had the advantage. I'd been down here when I snooped through the laundry, but he knew the building better than I did.

I raced down the hallway and turned the same corner, but I'd lost him. He couldn't have made it down this whole corridor yet, but he wasn't here. He must have ducked into one of the doors along either side.

Cautiously, tentatively, I moved down the quiet corridor. God, I wished I'd picked up Sidecki's gun, but there hadn't been time. He was armed and I wasn't. Still, I couldn't take the chance on letting him get away. Who knew how many more dead bodies there'd be before morning if he did? He was desperate now.

I passed the laundry and the central supply office. Everything was deserted down here now. I hadn't seen anything that could have led to the garage yet.

Then I saw a door slightly ajar. I looked up. It was the hospital morgue.

I went in and faced a second door. I opened it.

Everything was cold and dark. I couldn't keep myself from shivering. Stealthily, I moved around the room. I was holding my breath, my hands feeling in front of me, listening for another presence. I backed up and hit something hard. I put my hand behind me and felt cold, rubbery flesh. It must have been a body on the dissecting table. A shudder rippled through me.

Suddenly the lights flashed on. I was momentarily blinded. Then I saw Bob Fusillo standing in front of the door I'd just come through. The light switch was just to the side. He was still holding the scalpel, now stained with Nick's blood.

"Well, you certainly have a way of fucking things up at the worst moment," he sneered.

"Bob," I said, "Neville . . . whoever you are."

"You've ruined everything!" he ranted, taking a menacing step toward me. I edged myself to the side of the table.

"Tonight would have been my triumph—both of you gloriously dead and Nicholas with the credit!"

"But I don't understand," I said breathlessly, desperately trying to buy time. "Didn't all three of you have to come together to commit the . . . to do what you did?"

"You're a smart girl. You should have become a doctor. Yes, we had to come together, and I made that possible. With my dear brother Nicky's help, of course." He had either become Neville or thought he had. At this point, it hardly mattered which. I had to stay out of his range and still find an opening.

"You mean through the surgical support group?" I said.

"That was convenient. So was NeMo," he replied. "The Ramsey neural modulator. Do you think he named it for me? It was all right there. Once I had the other two together, I could adjust their beta and theta waves to match mine. You've heard, no doubt, of the so-called fourteen and six spike?"

Right. That was the EEG reading that was supposed to be associated with severe psychopathic personality disorder.

He eyed me like a tiger stalking its prey.

"You changed their electrical rhythms from outside," I said, trying to keep him talking while I figured my options.

"Haven't you ever noticed the signs in hospital cafeterias warning patients with pacemakers to stay away from the microwave oven?"

"And then after you'd committed the crime, you'd restore them to 'normal.' "

"Precisely," said Fusillo. He made a subtle move in my direction.

"And they didn't remember?"

"A little hypnosis goes a long way, particularly with people in a highly vulnerable and suggestive state to begin with. And as a detective, you should know there is also substantial evidence that people tend to block out memories that are just too traumatic to deal with."

It was why Chris couldn't tell us anything other than his vague, dreamlike memories. But he knew someone was controlling him.

There was something wild and mad in Fusillo's eyes. "Bob, we can still work this out," I insisted.

He looked at me as if I were the crazy one. "That's ridiculous," he said calmly. "I'm not stupid. I know I have to kill you."

He started moving in on me, and I started circling behind the dissecting table. He moved one direction, I moved the other. I tried to rush him on one side to get to the door, but he was ready for me, and I hastily retreated behind the prone body. It was a white male in his fifties, fairly heavyset.

I knew what that blade could do to me and tried not to think about it.

I glanced at the counter behind me. Why couldn't they have left any dissecting tools out? The scalpel was the only weapon in the room.

Somehow I had to get it away from him. I'd have to take a chance.

I inched up to the edge of the table, a "come and get me" posture. Bob took the bait. He thrust forward over the other edge, jabbing the scalpel forward in a wide cutting arc.

Just in time, I pulled myself back a fraction of an inch from the tip, making him thrust out farther, which threw him slightly off balance. I used this momentary advantage to duck down away from him. Then I used my shoulder and concentrated all my leverage to push the body off the table and down onto him.

He was momentarily stunned. But that was enough. I bolted over the table and down onto him on the floor, grasping for the scalpel he was still clutching. I landed on the dead body. Desperately I climbed over it and reached for Bob's wrist before he could recover. I dug my thumbnail into the nerve. The scalpel's blade sliced into the fleshy base of my thumb. A bolt of pain ripped through my hand and arm, blood flowed out freely but I held on. I elbowed him in the jaw, and he finally let go.

The scalpel clattered to the floor. Both of us dove for it. He got there first and lunged back at me. I came around from the side and locked both my hands around his, trying to deflect the blade from my chest. The bleeding weakened my grip. For several eternal seconds we held like that, but I could feel myself faltering. The scalpel was coming down at me.

With whatever I had left, I arched my back and brought my knee up into his groin. He doubled over, and as he did, I used all my might to force his hands over and down toward his own chest.

I heard him scream as the blade pierced his skin. It plunged in all the way to the handle. It had to have gone cleanly between the ribs, probably the fourth and fifth—the same blow he had used to kill Julie Fox.

I heard a gasping, sucking sound. I saw blood bubble up through Fusillo's lips. Then I saw him die. I collapsed on the floor next to him.

I heard the door open. I looked up. It was Vince, his gun drawn, six or seven armed uniforms behind him.

"Where were you when I needed you?" I said.

He gave me his hand and helped me to my feet, regarding me with that look of parents whose child has just run into the street and narrowly missed being hit by a car: not knowing whether to belt the kid or hug 'em. He wrapped his handkerchief around my bleeding hand.

"You could have gotten yourself killed," he castigated me, his voice flooded with exasperation and relief.

"I know," I replied shakily, still leaning on him for support. "Isn't that what we get paid for?"

44

I T was nearly dawn. We were in the family lounge, the same room where the surgical support group met. Nick and me, Vince and Captain Owen and Chief Price. Officers guarded the door and were positioned throughout the floor.

Nick's arm and leg and my hand had been treated and bandaged. The cut across my breast wasn't deep. I just hoped it wouldn't leave a scar. The hand had needed several stitches, and it had hurt a lot while they were sewing it up. I knew it would hurt more in the days ahead, especially when I picked up a gun.

Nick had a metal cane. He wouldn't be doing surgery or playing racquetball for a while. Ashby Collier was still under sedation, and Nick had used the NeMo master controller unit to restore her sensor to its proper values. Chris Taylor had been taken down to join Bob Fusillo in the hospital morgue. Nick had asked to be present when Jack Beauregard conducted the two postmortems.

This case was over for me. For him, I knew, it was only beginning. Vince had sent the uniforms up to Bonnie's apartment to assure her she was out of danger. I'd have to go see her, after I got some sleep. It was the right thing to do.

Nick and I had gone over the entire story from beginning to end. He'd explained what he'd done and what he thought had happened. I felt empty inside. Drained. Too weary to cry anymore.

A young uniformed officer knocked on the door. He came over to Owen, bent down, and whispered in his ear. He handed him something in a folded manila envelope, then left.

Owen came over and gave it to me. He was smiling. I opened it. It was my badge.

"I had someone stop by my office and pick it up," he explained. "I wanted you to have it back tonight. You'll get your gun after you've recovered and you're cleared by the U.S. Attorney's Office." Any officer involved in a fatal incident automatically goes on administrative leave with pay.

"With that hand wound, you'll have to go down to the range and requalify. But even after you're cleared, I'm ordering you to take some time off. It'll still be admin; won't count against vacation days."

"I don't need any more time off," I said wearily.

"If you don't cooperate, Vince has threatened to call your mother."

"You got it," Vince confirmed. "So just do what you're told for once."

"I give up," I said. "Whatever you say." For only the second time in my career, I'd killed in the line of duty. Two people this time. I'd taken two lives tonight. And someone I cared about deeply had died tonight in my place.

"So let me see if I can get this straight," Chief Price said. "Was it actually these three pieces of your brother's brain coming together that made them commit these crimes, or was it Dr. Fusillo hypnotizing the two others and messing with their brain waves with that device of yours?"

"I don't think we can say for sure," Nick answered him. I could tell he was still struggling to make meaning of everything that had happened, not only what had happened tonight, but over the last ten months. Or maybe over his entire life with Neville.

He shook his head in grim wonderment, as if still trying to comprehend it all. "There's so much we just don't understand yet. I wish I could tell you. Did Bob become a murderer when I implanted Neville's brain tissue, or was he thinking that way already? Did Bob just get the 'bad piece,' the physical reason Neville was the way he was? Or even possibly, did Neville's brain tissue affect Bob the way it did *because* he was already prone to this type of thinking and action?"

I wondered again about that patient of Fusillo's who'd died mysteriously. We'd have to look into that one.

"I can't even tell you with any confidence whether it was the resonance from the compatible pieces of brain," Nick continued, "or the neural modulator that coerced the other two into going along with him, or whether it was pure psychological influence over vulnerable and suggestible patients still recovering from major trauma."

Fusillo's influence over Ashby could have been enormous, I thought to myself. Essentially, she had become his hostage. And twenty years' experience in hostage situations has shown that captives often begin thinking like their captors.

"It may have been a combination of all three," Nick conceded.

"You're the brain surgeon," Price challenged. "You must know what you did in there."

"I thought I did," Nick replied, humble for once. He was struggling to explain himself to Chief Price, to somehow justify himself. "The brain is an incredibly elastic organ. Physiological changes can cause mental and emotional changes, which in turn can cause physiological changes. It's still a black box in there, and there's a universe of research yet to do."

There are more things in heaven and earth, Horatio, than are dreamt of in your philosophy.

"About that, Dr. Ramsey . . ." The chief leaned forward. "I don't know if you're a genius or a monster, and I'm not qualified to decide. If your work really is as important and revolutionary as Detective Mansfield says it is, I'm not going to be the one to destroy it. And I don't want to destroy Ms. Collier's life, either. She won't be charged, but it seems to me she's going to have a lot to work out to get over what she's been through. I leave it to you how much to tell her."

A woman who simply posed for Neville is still institutionalized, I recalled. I could hardly imagine the grief and turmoil Ashby faced. Just like freed hostages. Or worse.

Price slapped his hands onto his knees, hoisted himself off the sofa, and stood facing Nick. "But I can't ignore what you've done and what's happened because of you, and you'd better know I'm going to be watching you like a hawk. You understand what I'm saying, Doctor?"

"I understand," Nick said.

"All right. What we've talked about here tonight doesn't go beyond this room. I guess that's about it. Pat, Vince, I'll see you in my office tomorrow morning and we'll figure out how we're going to close this case."

He started for the door. Owen followed him, then turned back to me once more and said, "Remember, Sandy, I don't want to see your bod in the office until I say so."

I nodded obediently. He and Chief Price went out the door, leaving just Nick and Vince and me.

Vince gave me his hand. I took it and pulled myself to my feet. "Why don't you come with me?" he said. "Spend a couple of days with us and relax."

"No, I'm okay," I assured him.

"Then I'll take you home."

"No, really, Vince. Just leave me be. That's what I need right now."

He saw my tears but he'd already used his handkerchief on me. Instead, he touched my face lightly with his fingertips and wiped the tears away. "After all these years, you're still looking for perfect justice, aren't you, kid?" He gave me a hug and a kiss, then just as he got to the door he turned and said, "I'll call you tomorrow."

I nodded.

When we were alone, Nick looked up at me. "So do you trust me now?"

"I don't know what I trust now," I replied, almost collapsing with fatigue onto the sofa. I let the back of my head rest against the wall and closed my eyes. "Maybe I'm just too tired to think."

I realized Captain Owen was right. I did need some time off. I almost looked forward to it. I'd catch up on my sleep, recharge my batteries, let my brain go numb. Then I'd get myself back in fighting shape for the ongoing and endless war. That was all I really wanted to do, I'd also realized.

I would put on one of my black dresses and go to Chris Taylor's funeral and Norman Sidecki's funeral and even Bob Fusillo's funeral. In the next couple of days I'd make the trip down to Quantico, talk to Douglas and Wright, and try to sort out as much as we could. I wanted to look deeply into Fusillo's past and see how many skeletons we found there before he came in contact with Nicholas and Neville Ramsey. I would formally interview Nick, find out exactly how much he'd confided in his chief resident, how much opportunity he'd given Bob to absorb Neville and his personality. Then maybe we could figure out where this new monster had come from.

We keep asking ourselves the precise nature of evil. We may never know, but that doesn't mean we ever stop looking.

I wondered if Nick was already thinking about his next step, the next frontier, or whether he'd even stay at Halsted now to pursue it. He had to be thinking about Bob and the love-hate feelings Bob must have had for him—the type that often leads stalkers to kill their heroes; the same type that Neville must always have had for his younger brother. Nick would have a lot of emotional sorting out to do himself.

He maneuvered himself into position next to me. He grasped my hand in his and moved them both down to my lap. "Come home with me, Sandy," he said quietly.

A warm and inviting feeling came over me. Yes, I thought. Then I struggled with myself before I said, "I don't think so, Nick."

There. I was in control. I had called the shots. But it didn't feel very satisfying. In fact, it hurt like hell.

He seemed to wince. Whether it was from his wounds, or my response, or his own burden of confusion and guilt, I couldn't be sure. "Why not?" he said.

"Because I need some time to figure this out, to put the pieces back for myself. We both do."

"We can put the pieces back together," he pleaded. "Right now, you're all I've got left."

I felt the tears coming again and turned my head away. "Nick, I don't want to lose what we've had. But I can't forget what it was that brought us together, either, and everything that's happened because of it. Innocent people are dead, and another innocent person has been given a second chance at life. It's going to take me some time to balance that. Life and death," I mused, "that's what it's all about."

"Other people always have to suffer for us to do our work," he said. "It's basic to what we both do, to what we both are. It's why we need each other." He touched the side of my face and forced me to look at him. "Sandy, whenever a patient dies, we try to figure out why, to learn as much as we can so that the next one has a better chance, so that the death won't have been without meaning. I don't know if I'll ever be able to find out the meaning I have to in what's happened here, but I've got to try if my own life is ever to have meaning again. I've got to go back to square one, to tear everything up and start again. And I need you there with me. On every level, I need you."

I was fighting for control. "But I've got to sift through it all and sort it all out. And you need time to grieve for Bob and time to bury your brother, once and for all."

"Start sorting it out tomorrow," he implored me. "Come home with me tonight. And as for burying my brother, I need your help to do that. Just like you, I thought I could do it all alone. I realize now there's a lot I need help with."

I didn't say anything for several moments, letting it all spin around in my head. Why was I always so convinced that everything I truly wanted was bad for me? Well, maybe it was and maybe it wasn't. But Nick was right—I didn't have to figure it all out tonight. We both needed to heal, and maybe we could heal together. At least, there was a chance.

When he put his hand up to my face, I realized I must still have been crying.

"Give me the keys to your car," I said. "You're in no condition to drive." Obediently he turned them over to me. "Do you want a wheelchair?" I asked him.

"No," he said, clenching his teeth and using his good arm to hoist himself painfully to his feet. "I'll walk." Rivulets of perspiration streamed down his forehead.

"You're sure you're up to this?" I said. He nodded with determination.

So, as he steadied himself with his hand on my shoulder, we walked out of the building together, past the officers still on duty, the night shift leaving, and the first of the morning people just arriving. I took the wheel of his Mercedes, and as the summer sun rose over the nation's capital, we drove home.